NEW

WHITLEY STRIEBER

WALKER & COLLIER, INC.

NEW

A Novel
by
Whitley Strieber

Walker & Collier, Inc. 20742 Stone Oak Parkway Suite 107

San Antonio, Texas, 78258

www.unknowncountry.com

www.strieber.com

First Walker & Collier printing, first edition, 2018

Cover design by Lisa Amowitz

Library of Congress Cataloging-in-Publication Data

Strieber, Whitley

New/by Whitley Strieber

ISBN (Paperback) 978-0-9858131-8-5

ISBN (Electronic Book) 978-0-9858131-9-2

A child said, What is the grass? fetching it to me with full
hands;
How could I answer the child?. . . .I do not know what it
is any more than he.

"A Child Said, What is the Grass"
Walt Whitman

This book is dedicated to Anne Strieber, whose faith in it and editorial support were essential to its creation.

1

SECRET OF THE AGES

For the third time, Beth Cooke drove past Barrett Scientific's campus. Once again, she saw nothing but a silent black glass rectangle of a building. Silent and, frankly, a little sinister. More than a little. It was an office but nobody came and nobody went. Since she'd first gotten their letter of offer and commenced doing her off-campus interviews with Dr. Greg Keller, she'd come past here many times. During the day, it was like this—nothing moving. At night, it was lit up like a football field.

For all the world it looked like some sort of classified lab, but there were no signs and no indication that Barrett was involved in defense work.

There was also no sign of any animal enclosure, nothing that would explain why a drug company would want to interview an expert on primates. They had no registered animal testing facility here or anywhere. That was the first thing she's researched, even before she responded to the letter. And the job on offer was definitely here, not in their New York office and not abroad. They specialized in the development of pharmaceuticals. There was no animal testing going on, and so no primates...or should be none.

It worried her husband Charlie. A lot. It also worried her. But the salary was a hundred and fifty grand—enough to save their primate center that was the love of both of their lives.

From that first letter, it had been a strange business—very strange —but she was desperate for money and the offer was fabulous.

She'd met Dr. Keller off campus two times. He was a rather tight-lipped but affable man with an outstanding record of achievement. He had distinguished himself searching for plants in the jungles of Indonesia and Latin America, and had more than thirty papers to his credit either as single author or participant.

Her cellphone alarmed. Her first on-campus interview was ten minutes away. She turned around, drove back to the campus and turned in, then drove up to the tall iron gate that protected the featureless black glass block. There was no way to signal, but after a moment it opened for her. Obviously, somebody was watching. It felt exactly like entering a classified facility, which she'd had to do once or twice in her career. But Barrett didn't do classified work.

She didn't want to apply for a security clearance. In fact, didn't dare. An official background check would uncover things that didn't need to be uncovered. The Texas Primate Center could get closed down, and Charlie lose his freedom. The company's check had been unnerving enough.

She found the cold, unwelcoming lobby enveloped in silence. The empty expanse of black marble floors, punctuated by a few gray stone benches certainly fit the impression of a fortress that was communicated by the exterior. Across the center of the lobby and blocking any access to the deeper building stood a stark marble counter. Behind it sat a security guard who was ostentatiously armed with a big chrome pistol. He was perched on a stool, there, she thought, so that you would be sure to see the weapon.

He sat behind his monolithic stone desk like a judge. He didn't appear bored, either, not like most security guards planted in empty lobbies. His eyes moved methodically around the room. Each time they landed on her, they rested for just a bit longer than they did on the walls. There had already been detectives coming out to her facility, questioning her, looking everything over. Normal companies looked up your Twitter feed and your Facebook page. They didn't send detectives to paw through your life.

"I'm here to see Doctor Keller. I am Doctor Cooke."

"Yes." He didn't move. Finally, she took a seat on one of the benches.

Even the background checks that they had done had been nerve wracking. Last week, her father had called her, furious that an FBI team had visited him and interviewed him about her. At first she'd been nailed to the spot with shock, her heart dancing with the fear that Charlie had come under investigation. But then she'd realized that the vetting agreement she'd signed allowed Barrett to send its own investigators to anyone she had listed among friends and family.

She'd asked him if they'd showed him FBI identification. No, he'd said. He'd just assumed it. 'Don't,' she'd said. 'I've applied for a primatologist position at Barrett Scientific. They're just doing due diligence. Those were private detectives, not FBI.'

He'd calmed down, but his tone had remained cold. Beth and her mother were not friendly, and he loved his wife. Beth loved them both, deeply and dearly. But only if she gave up her facility—surrendered and returned home abject —only then would she be received back into the graces of wealth and comfort that were being denied her, and only then would either of them drop their guard.

They thought the primate center a mistake. Not that they objected to Beth helping animals, but they felt she'd put too much family money into the project. Her trust funds. Almost everything, in fact. And as far as mother was concerned, the primate center wasn't her only mistake. It was a costly affectation, yes, but there was worse. She characterized Charlie as 'a vague sort of a man,' meaning that he had no social connections, and thus was the wrong husband for the daughter of an old and prestigious family.

They had been a close family and Beth kind of an innocent. Then a summer working as a zoo attendant had changed her. The animals had captured her heart, especially the monkeys and apes, with their close families, towering emotions and helplessness. Her love of them had taken her to Texas A&M for a degree in primatology, not to the

University of Texas for something more traditional like English Literature. And she hadn't joined mom's sorority and her mother just had not understood.

So here she was sitting in the lobby of an unaccountably mysterious drug company, hoping to use the salary she'd make here to save her primate center, which what she loved in the world.

She glanced at her watch. Where was Dr. Keller? This lobby was like a mausoleum overseen by an ominous, pistol packing creep.

The guard gazed at her. She gazed back. He turned his eyes toward the entryway. Just as well. She'd been tempted to give him some tongue—just the tip. But it wouldn't have been a good idea. Greg Keller would have been told, she felt sure, and she doubted that he would have understood.

She had been astonished when she'd gotten an email from Barrett via her Linked-In profile. It looked damn well like mana from heaven, but Charlie had said immediately, "They've got a lab and they're doing testing and they've got problems. You don't want to touch it."

That was not true, though. There are registries and Barrett wasn't on any of them. If there was animal testing going on here, it was illegal and they would be fools to reveal this to a PhD primatologist who would risk her career if she didn't turn them in.

A black door opened at the far end of the lobby and Dr. Keller—compact, careful— emerged.

"Beth, good to see you again!"

"Good morning, Doctor Keller."

He stood over her, his smile, as always, carefully constructed. From his own Facebook and LinkedIn pages, she had discovered that he was forty-six and unmarried. Barrett has been his only employer. He had spent most of his time in jungles searching for plants and had found a number of important ones. He had been well on his way to becoming a major scientific player, but the last paper had been now ten years ago.

"Come to the conference room, we can talk there."

"I was hoping to see the operation."

"Shortly."

He led her across the broad lobby to a glassed-in conference area. On the far wall was a door that led into the facility itself. She noted that it had to be opened by a keycard.

As they sat down, he pressed a button on a small console on the long, gleaming table. "Water, tea, coffee?"

"Coffee, thanks."

He opened a file. She could see pages of notes, probably produced by the detectives who had been exploring her life.

"How's the Center doing, Beth?"

"Knocking along. Funding's always a problem."

He laughed a little, then opened a folder full of newspaper clippings and printed web pages. "I can imagine." He looked up at her. "Now, what have you learned about us?"

"That you have sixty drugs in your active portfolio, and a first-class collection operation, of which you have been a major part. But no longer. Instead, you're here."

"What do you think we do here?"

"Something concerning primates, I'm assuming."

He nodded. "In a sense."

What in the world could that mean?

A tall young woman—not exactly furtive, but very carefully enclosed in herself—came in and put down a tray with a silver coffee service. Beth saw that it was Regency silver. Priceless. She was astonished, frankly. This was an office. Coffee came in mugs, not fabulous antiques.

Keller glanced at the young woman. "Thanks, Rebecca." As she left, he went about pouring. He was precise, his movements oddly calculated. She could have believed that he had rehearsed this. But why? They weren't on a stage—which, she realized, was exactly where they were.

There was a gleaming fisheye camera embedded in the ceiling. So how many people were watching, she wondered, and who? The reclusive Robert Barrett himself, perhaps? Could she be so important? She'd had no indication of that.

Keller said, "People don't look up, but you did."

She tried to make light of it, and looked up again. "Hi, all."

Her own face stared back, distorted to caricature by the lens.

Keller sat down and leaned back in his chair. "I should tell you that this is a final interview."

"Other candidates?"

"Will your price go up if I say no?"

She laughed easily. "Could be." She was trying to project warmth. If you worked in a corporate environment, you needed to be a team player. In reality, she was pretty reclusive herself. Feeding and caring for needy apes, struggling for money, putting off the landlord and the suppliers—that was her life. The apes were her life, and the only person who could really reach her was Charlie, who could cut through her obsessive concentration by enveloping her in his arms and holding her, and he always seemed to know just when to do that.

"I—we—" Keller glanced up. "We want to know if you have any objection to some confidentiality clauses."

So here it came. Something hidden in this glass sepulcher was indeed secret. Not good, not good at all.

"If I'm being asked to respect the confidentiality of corporate research, of course."

"And the legality issue?"

Oh, boy. "I'm not a lawyer, but if I saw something that required me to engage in activities that I thought might be illegal, I would want to consult one."

"A company lawyer?" He looked at her steadily.

"My lawyer."

He sipped his coffee, continuing to stare at her. It was just starting to get weird when she noticed the gleam of an earbud in his ear, and realized that he was listening to somebody. He said, "Good. You passed the test. We go on."

"Excuse me, may I know what the test was?"

"If you had said that you would seek the advice of internal counsel, that would have meant that you were probably also willing to keep an illegal matter secret. That's not how Barrett operates. We want only personnel with the strongest ethics."

She felt a rush of blood heat her face.

His smile returned. "You blush."

"With relief!"

"Good. I'm not going to conceal what must be obvious to you by now. We have animals here that are in need of support from an expert primatologist."

"There's no lab registered."

"They're not in a lab."

She was stunned. What in the world could he mean?

"If they're not in a laboratory, where are they kept?"

"In humane surroundings. It's all quite legal, if that's what you're worried about."

"I'm not worried, I'm confused."

"You want to back out?"

"I don't know. I don't know what you're doing. Tell me that and I'll tell you what I want to do."

"We need somebody who doesn't just understand primates, but who loves them, and you love them. But what about Charlie? We're still a little fuzzy on Charlie."

"We met in Africa. I was studying mountain gorillas and he was on a vet program treating them in the wild."

"That's challenging work. I wouldn't want to give a gorilla a shot."

"They trank them." But it was indeed hard and extremely dangerous. Gorillas live in societies. If they see one of their family members go down and get surrounded by strange creatures, they often get violent.

"Has he ever visited any labs—you know the kind of places I mean."

The most dangerous question. "I don't know everywhere he's been. When we got married—"

"You were just out of grad school. He was just back from Iraq."

"Not exactly. By the time he got to Africa, he was eight years back from Iraq and was a fully qualified veterinarian."

"What did he do in Iraq?"

"I don't know. It was secret."

"Nothing you can tell me at all?"

What was he driving at? Did he know about the labs Charlie had popped, as he called it? How could he? Nobody knew.

"I know that he jumped out of airplanes. He penetrated fortified positions. He has nightmares. That I know."

"And he manages the Center's plant."

"And treats the animals. He's an excellent vet and manager both."

"But not good enough to keep Moreland at home."

Oh thank you, God! It was Moreland and his escapes that Keller was driving at, not Charlie's illegal activities. "We have new locks," she said tartly. Moreland's escapes were a notorious local story, but nothing that might cost her this job. Still, she needed to bring this probing to an end. "Can I see the animals?"

"Will you accept our offer?"

"Now? Right now?"

"Right now."

"Can you let me see the facility?"

"I go to two hundred thousand dollars. Final offer."

That was major. Huge. She wanted desperately to say yes. But she said, "I need to see the facility."

He hesitated, listening again to the earbud. Then he spoke. "At that dollar figure, I feel that I deserve an immediate answer."

She understood that she was talking to Barrett. Keller was only a surrogate. She was impressed. Whatever was going on here, it must be extremely important to the company.

So, should she try for two fifty and take the job sight unseen?

"You're hesitating."

"I'm thinking."

He listened to the earbud. He said, "Answer."

If the offer was withdrawn, she lost the primate center. That was the stark reality.

Barrett's reputation was not only that of a recluse. He was intense and uncompromising. Dedicated. He had inherited a struggling company from his father and turned it into one of the leading profit centers in a very profitable industry. You don't do that by being hesitant. Unless she jumped on this, it could go. He could easily pull somebody out of a local university system for a hundred and fifty.

She said, "OK, yes. I'm on board." And she felt instantly very, very bad. She would have thought that Keller would at least smile, but he did not smile. He said, "There will be a contract delivered to you tomorrow. Also various agreements, all quite standard confidentiality stuff." He turned a few pages in the folder before him. "This is something that needs your signature now."

He slid it across to her. She read that she was agreeing to the salary and would sign the contract and the security agreement pending her review. But it added, "agrees not to seek other employment for three months from the date of this letter."

"I've never seen anything like this. What if the contract differs from the details here?"

"It won't."

"But if it does?"

He shrugged. "You should feel free to amend it to conform to this letter. But it won't."

"Doctor Keller—"

"Greg, please."

"Greg, I need to see the facility."

"The secrecy agreement can't go into effect until the contract is signed. Once it does, we're in business."

"I can't sign anything until I see what I'm getting into."

"Beth, let me show you something." He reached down and brought a book out of the briefcase he'd brought in with him. It was a dog eared copy of *Primate Politics.* "I've read your book carefully, as you can see. And let me assure you, we run a very ethical operation here. Ethical even by your standards."

"I don't see any outdoor space for apes." One of the things she argued in her book was that captive animals needed replicated environments and enough space so that they wouldn't feel trapped.

"I don't see it at your Center, either."

"You've been to Texas Primates?"

"At your open house a few weeks ago."

That failed money raising attempt. "It's been very frustrating." She had hoped some angel would appear, but that hadn't happened.

"I'm sure. But your animals are in superb condition. They look very low stress. I was impressed."

She'd bought a chimpanzee from a bankrupt carnival rather than see him sold into testing, gotten a pair of bonobos from a defunct roadside attraction in Oklahoma, and bought some capuchins who were slated to be destroyed from labs. Others had been donated, a few even with stipends, but not many. And then there were Charlie's Angels, the stolen ones.

Once the facility was saved, her great dream was to expand it. More space was essential. Texas Primates could not afford to offer the kind of facilities she argued for in her own book. It was a major irritant.

Keller had been listening once again. Now he stood up. "When you've signed, bring the papers in. You can see what we're doing here."

"That's final?"

"Final."

The letter lay before her. She took her pen in her hand.

She could practically see her apes and monkeys gathered at the fronts of their cages, whooping and grabbing at her as she walked past, tumbling, crying out, the capuchins shrieking with excitement just to see her again. She could definitely feel them in her heart here, now. What would it be like to watch them disappearing down the road in trucks? What would it be like for Charlie if he had to certify the destruction of those that could not be placed?

She signed and stood up. "I'll be waiting for the paperwork."

Keller came around the table and extended his hand. "Welcome to Barrett Scientific. Let me tell you, you're going to have the experience of a lifetime in this place." He walked her to the big main doors, all glass and black steel. "Very frankly, Beth, you're going to be elated. Beyond elated. At first, a lot of secrecy and it will be tiresome. You'll be aching to talk about what you see here. Later, after the need for secrecy is past, I promise you that you're going to publish extraordinary papers. Nobel-level papers."

She was quietly stunned. *Nobel*? What in the world could he be talking about?

They reached the door. "I have to admit that I'm more than curious at this point."

He gestured vaguely. "Secret of the ages, Beth. Literally."

She turned, then, and left the conference room and went across the lobby, then out to the parking lot and her car. When she got in, she hesitated. Secret of the *ages*? He sounded like a pretentious fool. Deluded, even. And this sounded more and more like the mistake of a lifetime.

Should she call him on her cell and tell him to forget it? Or was it too late for that? It might be. He had her signature. And it was two hundred grand and no apes being hauled away in trucks

She started her car and drove down the winding driveway to the gate, which opened for her as she approached.

As she drove along White Road in the glaring late-morning sun, she looked back from time to time. The building remained as it had been, a dark box in the middle of a treeless green campus. Nothing moved. Nobody entered. Nobody left.

She turned onto the highway, and it was gone. Not from her life, though. Not at all.

2

BUT WE'RE MARRIED!

When Joe's call tone chimed, he raised his hands to signal he was pulling out of the line, then hurried along the white tile hall to Keller's room. He did not knock. Only the others had to do that. He and Keller ran this thing. He entered and sat down.

Keller laughed. "I need to get a high chair."

Looking up over the edge of the desk Joe signed, 'Haha.'

"Look, we want to try a new genetic mix. I want you and Crunch to change girls. See what happens."

He heard the words but did not understand them. He and Betty were married. Flutter and Crunch were married. It was all just like TV and that was how it was supposed to be. Didn't Keller know that love means you belong to each other?

He signed, 'Betty is my wife.'

Keller chuckled. "Your *wife*? Where did you pick up an idea like that?"

Joe didn't want to tell him. It was people business, not for the shatterfaces to know about. 'Don't want to change wives,' he signed. He thought of Betty in his arms, the precious woman of his heart, and of how Flutter and Crunch sat in front of TV, hand in hand, head leaning against head.

"We have wives. Not you."

He signed hard: 'Betty is my *wife*!'

"Now listen to me, if you don't do this—" He showed the top edge of the snickersnee, drawing it up from behind his desk. "You disobey me and the others all get a nice hot taste. Everybody except you. And if you still disobey, they get more. Until you obey, they get more and more and more, and it's all your fault, Joe. Your fault!"

He did not want to cry. But Betty, her heart would ache. And his and Crunch's and Flutter's. He signed, 'Please don't make us sad.'

The snickersnee crackled.

Angrily flicking the tears from the edges of his eyes, he nodded agreement.

"Atta boy, Joe!" Keller reached across the desk and ruffled his hair.

'It's not right,' he signed.

"Whatever I say is right, Joe."

'Betty be sad. Flutter and Crunch, too.' He raised his eyes, but only for an almost unendurable instant, to Keller's shatterface with its dark raging holes where people had eyes. If you looked too deep into shatterface holes, the shadows came out of them and chased you down in your dreams.

"I'll be watching and listening. You do as you're told."

Joe got up to leave.

"And Joe?"

He waited, once again looking down.

"I know you're teaching the others speech. That's not what I want."

A rush of surprised terror almost made Joe turn and run. How could he know this? They did it deep in Z-time when all was quiet and dark. "Ah daon! Liffen to me, ah cannn-*tuh*."

"I agree. So stop trying."

Forcing himself, Joe lifted a smile.

Keller did not smile. "There's talking late at night. I hear you."

Joe backed toward the door.

Keller came around the desk, advancing toward him. "Okay, Joe, just stay away from the talking. You're not equipped for it and you're only going to frustrate yourself and the others if you try."

Joe rushed back to the familiar comfort of the factory with its humming assembly line. The room was white and filled with light so bright that if you looked straight up, your eyes would hurt. So you kept your head down as the assemblies, silver and full of wires, went past. You did your movement, screwing a screw, then another, then another, on and on, as assembly after assembly flowed along the belt.

Joe's throat was choked, he wanted to crawl down under the floor with Crunch and stay there in the oil-stinking bottomside watching the gears and collecting the drops from above. He wanted to tell Crunch how sorry he was. But instead he looked at Betty and he looked at Flutter, and the tears that were stinging his eyes made him miss a move, then another. If he wasn't careful, the belt would alarm and stop, and then he'd be in even bigger trouble.

He continued on, his heart hurting inside him. 'I am a husband. That is what I am.'

He worked in silence with the others until the day ended, the bell rang and the Big Voice announced suppertime.

Betty had watched him go and come back, but when she raised an eyebrow at him, he only bent closer to his assembly position. She signed to him but he pretended he didn't see.

Betty wondered what had happened with Keller. That was one nasty shatterface, that one. She gave up asking Joe about it. If he wouldn't say, he wouldn't.

After dinner, the TV turned on, which meant it was time to relax. They watched 2 Broke Girls, then Bob's Burgers, then Stephen Colbert and Betty loved Stephen Colbert. Soon it would be time for her and Joe to be together alone and she just *loved* Joe. He said he liked the factory but she didn't believe him. He had to say that to be boss, which he did like.

Bang bang, click click, put it in, push it down, snap, *wham* here comes another one till the Big Voice says "Morning break." Then you go back and snap, *whap*, bang and clang, *wham* here comes another one till the Big Voice says "Lunch break." Then back on the line for a real long time, until the Big Voice says "Suppertime."

When she and Flutter had tried to quit the assembly line, Keller said, 'Dance while you work, it'll make the time go faster. But you can't slow down, that you cannot do.' Keller had a watch. It beeped and told him things. Betty wanted one, too, but she wanted hers to be green like her dreams. She loved the green. They all did. They should be called the green people, they loved it so much.

Now when the line clattered and clanged, they danced. Throw this, catch that, up in the air, down to the floor, in and over and out the door. Which was better. A little. Maybe.

Betty liked to play cards. Play Clue. They had a rule: Somebody didn't win Clue in five turns, everybody lost.

Betty also knew that Flutter wanted Joe. Of course she did, she wanted a man who wasn't in the hole like Crunch was, 'cause that made him bottomsider and her low woman. Flutter wanted to be just as good as Jill and Betty. She wanted to be with a topsider, too. That meant you gotta have Jack or Joe. They were the topsider men, and Joe was *boss*. He even had glasses, just like Keller. Boss glasses. He was Keller's special friend.

But Crunch loved Flutter so bad that Flutter would sign, 'He is my man'. The wives signed together about the husbands. They worked on how to make their husbands smile.

When your husband hugged you, your insides smiled.

Betty was wanting Joe, to sit together during TV like always, especially Colbert. So where was he? She went into the hall behind the TV room, but there was nobody there. Finally, she went down it and into their own room.

Are you hidey under the *bed*? Are you hidey in the *john*?

No and no.

She made the whistle that they used to call to each other, their special music.

He didn't answer.

The world wasn't big, so—she sucked in a breath. Could he have finally done it, gotten out into TV? No, not without her. He'd never go into TV and leave her behind, not the only one he loved!

She made their song again, this time louder, her voice echoing up and down Room Street where they had their bedrooms, one for each couple.

Still no reply. Rooms were private. If you had your curtain down, nobody could come in. Her and Joe's curtain was up. Jill and Jack's curtain was up. Flutter and Crunch's curtain was down.

She went close and touched the rough gray cloth. There was movement in the room. Fear tickled at the back of her neck, making her feel cold under her long pale hair. *Where was Joe*?

Then she was sad, and tears rushed into her eyes. 'He *did* get out into TV and didn't take me!' Every night, they signed under their covers, 'I belong to you, you belong to me, we go in TV.'

A sigh came from the other side of the curtain, then another.

But...what was that, now?

Never mind being polite, she threw back the curtain and stepped in.

Joe was hugging Flutter and there was Crunch huddled in a corner with his face in his hands.

That was—*no!* She launched herself across the length of Flutter's stinkin' stinkpot room and then there was a big *whammo* and Joe was off Flutter and Betty was *screeeeaaaming*. Betty got Flutter down and stared straight into her eyes. She lifted a hand and signed, 'How could you? How could you?'

They were friends, all of them. So what was happening here?

Joe jumped on her back then but she didn't care, she was going to thrash him too when she got him home. She signed to Crunch, 'Hey stupid, she's *your* wife, why you let her hug *my* husband?' They knew where hugging went. Where it always went.

Then Joe was off her back and signing so fast was hard to read. 'I got told do it by Keller. I gotta, Betty. I gotta!'

Keller? What would Keller be doing interfering with her? Did Keller hate her?

'Not Keller,' she signed back.

'Yes,' Joe signed. He nodded hard, eager to convince.

Betty had never been mad like this. She hadn't known how it made your face hot and made your lips turn down and made you hit like she'd hit. But if Keller—really—well...

She got off Flutter and Joe instantly went back to her and hugged her again, which made Betty's throat hurt and tears come.

This time, she threw the chair at them. It hit Joe in the back and he howled and Flutter shrieked and in the corner Crunch crouched with his face behind his hands and screamed as well.

"Quiet!"

Instantly, they all stopped.

It was Keller, and Betty saw what dangled carelessly from his hand, a familiar gray rod with an ugly black snout. He raised it, and raised his eyebrows. "You're always welcome to some." His black pits of eyes shattered them all. "Anybody?"

Nobody moved. Nobody made a sound. Betty felt her heart turning over fast. She felt a shivering in her that almost made her sick.

"OK, we understand each other. I'm glad. Flutter and Joe, congratulations. You've earned yourselves Mounds."

What, a reward for hurting her? Keller *did* hate her! She ran at him, she wanted to rip him, she would rip him!

The snickersnee crackled.

She stopped, then edged closer.

It popped a little more and she drew back.

Joe came to her and put his arms around her. He pointed at Keller, then signed again, 'He made me, Betty'

She pulled away and signed back, 'You are still mean.'

"What are you two signing? Go slower."

Joe signed slowly 'Tell her.'

Keller laughed. "Go up to the rec room, you three. Jim's there with candy. Betty, we need to have a little talk."

Joe shook his head and signed miserably, 'not hurt Betty.'

"That's my business."

Fast, he signed to Betty 'He made us hug. He wants me and Crunch to change wives.' She saw the tears washing his eyes.

Alone with Keller, Betty waited to be hurt with the snickersnee. Keller said, "Joe hasn't made a baby with you. Maybe he will with Flutter. You girls want babies, don't you?"

She dared not answer. What the shatterfaces called babies, the people called spiders.

"Of course you do," Keller said.

She forced the ends of her lips to turn up.

"Atta girl! Now go on up to rec. This'll be fun. You'll see."

Betty went. Out of Keller's sight, she could not help her head going down and her lips going down, and the tears going down.

As soon as she entered the white light of rec, Joe came to her. He held out a piece of Peter Paul Mounds. His head was also down. Tears were hitting the floor, one by one.

'I am not your woman now.'

'You have to be. I love you. But we have to obey Keller.'

Betty did shatterface words: "Nawt seep raon!" *Why can't we talk?* Exasperated, she signed, 'I say no sleep around.'

He continued to hold out the half Mounds.

Betty was so mad at him, she was just burning and she did not even want to look at anybody cause she just felt like curling up under the covers forever. She took the Peter Paul Mounds, though. Joe watched her, smiling that 'oh yeah' smile of his.

'Marriage doesn't matter to Keller,' she said as she ate.

'Come on,' he signed. He ran toward their room. She went running and squealing and swept him right off his feet and they were in their bed. He signed, 'I like our own place. No Crunch smell.'

But there was Crunch smell, because Crunch came in, and Crunch's eyes said he was mad. He signed, 'I want to hug Betty now.'

Nasty taste came up in Betty's throat. Crunch had no business with any woman except Flutter. Marriage was marriage and Keller was wrong.

From rec, the sound of the TV got louder. The Big Voice said, "Return to rec. Nobody on Room Street until after Colbert."

Everybody ran out except Joe, who went more slowly. What Keller had made him do had hurt Betty in her heart. He had been forced to turn his back on his own wife! It had hurt Crunch, too. He had seen his wife taken away from him. And it had scared Flutter.

Keller was mean. He was. But why had he done it? Did he want to hurt Betty's feelings? Did he not like her?

No, it was because of spiders. Keller offered the women Snickers if they would make spiders. The shatterfaces wanted the people to have them, but why? Nobody would ever let a spider out, not ever. There was room in the world for six people, no more.

Joe slouched toward rec, but he didn't want to watch TV. When he did, he wanted so badly to be out in it that his head hurt. Why couldn't people go in TV, was something wrong with us? He wanted a two piece suit. He wanted shiny shoes. Betty and Flutter and Jill wanted Revlon lipstick and curl-your-hair and J-Lo clothes and high heel shoes.

He wondered how it would be in TV, surrounded by shatterfaces. Shatterface eyes sent cuts down into you so deep you didn't even know you could hurt there. Still, though, he wanted to be in TV, not just in the world.

This was just a bad day because not only had their marriages been ruined, tomorrow the factory was going to speed up again. He had figured out how to count and kept a count of days and every thirty days, the line went a little faster.

Keller had said last week, 'Soon you'll be making electronics.' Joe did not know what those were, and he would never, ever ask Keller a single question. That would be showing weakness, and his rule was never show weakness to the shatterfaces. They already thought they were better than people. Don't give them more reasons. Down in himself where not even shatterfaces could see, he could hate Keller. Hate was when you wanted them not to be alive anymore. Hate was that.

The line had been oh my fast. You were stamping and jumping and pull the lever and let out the steam and *go go go*.

Tomorrow would be faster.

Keller said, 'it's training.'

The TV went off and the lights went down. So it was time. His time. He was boss of the people, and now he had to tell them.

He stood up on a chair.

He signed, 'Change tomorrow. Time for a new line. And faster.'

Silence. Then Jill grabbed her hair in her fists. Her face went terrible, her lips curling, her eyes looking from wall to wall. Crunch raced off down the hall, doing his stations. He skidded into station one—rec room wall behind the food counter, then hit that wall hard as he could. Station two, skip the black squares going past chairs till you get to Jill's chair that has a tear and pound that tear. Then a long run all the way down the hall and a huge jump, smack the wall there, station three, then the door to Room Street, kick it hard, that was station four.

Gasping, glaring he signed, 'I can run ninety-eight stations! I can count to four hundred and sixty three!' He threw out his chest and slammed it with his hand. 'And I can count *beyond*."

Jack held Jill, who was crying wicked tears. Betty came to Joe, and took his hand.

The Big Voice said, "OK, we get it. You want a little more time."

They were silent. TV went back on.

Jack leaped up, signing frantically, 'Setup! Setup!'

Joe looked and yeah, there was a setup coming in an old Three's Company. A setup was when there were exactly as many shatterfaces in TV as there were people in the world, which was six. They had to act out all setups. That was their rule.

TV said, "Hi. Jack home?"

"No Larry, but you can sit down and wait."

Everybody sat down to wait.

Jack came in and said, "Could you excuse us? This is man talk. I got into an argument with this guy down at the Regal Beagle and now I've gotta fight him."

'I've gotta fight *you*' Crunch signed, sticking his lips out at Joe. Joe gave him a sort of mean grin—just enough to say, 'I dare you to try.'

"Bite your tongue, woman," Larry said in TV and Betty and

Flutter and Jill all had to bite their tongues. Jill did it too hard, so she rolled all around and yelled.

Jack signed, 'Dummy!' He picked her up and in a second they were hugging and laughing.

Mr. Curly said, "I never had anybody stand up for me before."

Everybody stood up.

TV Jack said, "I wanna tell you how much I'm lookin' forward to the fight."

Now it was Crunch's turn to grin. The setup had told him and Joe to do just what he wanted.

Everybody got ready. Joe got in the front and Crunch got in the middle. The girls started clapping in six-rhythm quick, four-two-four. Up, down, in your nose. Red hot peppers! Go go go!

TV laughed and everybody laughed real, real hard. They had to laugh louder than TV or they wouldn't feel funny inside and they liked to feel funny inside because the world was hard and it was a hard night, worrying about tomorrow.

TV said, "Doncha *see*, he'll chicken outa the fight, you'll be off the hook!"

Crunch wanted to be off the hook. He was tired, he needed to go to bed with his Flutter, she was warm. They called him the bottom-sider because they didn't understand engineer work and he couldn't make them.

Joe didn't want to hit him and he didn't want to get hit. Nobody was really mad anymore. Then they all started hugging. They liked each other again, the fight was over before it started.

"Jack, what're you doing out?"

"Oh, I was just...shadowboxing."

"At three o'clock in the morning?"

"That's when you get your best shadow."

Everybody made shadows with their hands. And then TV went off and the Big Voice said, "Bedtime, folks. This time for sure. Count-down to lights. Ten. Nine." Joe and Betty ran to their room and hopped under the covers. "Eight. Seven." Jack and Jill slipped between their mattress and their springs, just like they would if they were really going to sleep. "Six. Five." Crunch held onto Flutter, Flutter looked out the door.

Lights out.

Okaaaay!

But wait. Wait, one, two, three. Gotta be careful of the shatterface eyes in the walls. Make sure the lights were not going to come back on, which sometimes happened. Shatterfaces could see anywhere in the world when the lights were on. Maybe off, too, you never knew.

So they waited a little longer, 'till all was quiet and the Big Voice hadn't said anything for a while, and it was real dark, night dark.

Z-time: They all came out and got in line: Joe first and in his glasses, then Betty, Jack then Jill, Flutter and Crunch. Crunch wanted glasses. Joe guessed he thought they'd help him move up from bottomsider. But that would be a 'no.'

If Keller was watching, let him. This time, it was going to work. Joe was sure he had finally figured out just exactly how to open the barrier and go in TV.

Toes touching heels, noses to heads, arms and legs moving together, they went along the hall, through the rec room, past the video games and the exercise machines and the ping pong tables, to the long corridor behind. The barrier was at the end, a silver steel blankness that you could not open.

Joe knew—*knew*—that TV was back there. Had to be, because it was where the shatterfaces came in and went out. Keller's room was in the world, but he had to have another one outside in TV. Joe had asked Keller why shatterfaces like Stephen Colbert never came in the world. He'd laughed. Joe had added that laugh to reasons why people should hate shatterfaces. But he was careful to keep his hate to himself. Stephen Colbert wouldn't come into the world because he thought people were no good, Joe was sure of it.

People were good!

Keller talked the door open, so his idea was to approach it making sounds like Keller talking. He'd been practicing and practicing, talking into his pillow. That was what Keller had heard.

This time, he had it right. He did. He was certain.

Step. Step. Step. Move your right hand up beside your ear, then take it down again, just like Keller. They had to make every single move that Keller made, step, raise the left shoulder a little, step, swing the arms, all together, the line packed tight, one after another, step, step.

They got to the barrier, all of them moving in unison, copying Keller's every single action.

Now was the moment. Joe clenched his teeth and closed his eyes. This had to come out perfectly. All the people were behind him. The idea of lockstep was that the barrier would think they were just one person, and not close until they all got through.

Joe had heard Keller mutter "stupid system" more than once. He had concluded that this meant that the system that controlled the barrier was stupid. Therefore, he thought, it could be deceived.

Jill said, "Do we get flat?"

He ignored her. She whined about that every night. You got flat in TV. Obviously. But it didn't bother the shatterfaces so it didn't matter. Also obviously.

He cleared his throat. He opened his mouth. He spoke in a loud, clear tone. "Jimmy can you buzz me through?" It sounded good to him, just like Keller.

The others wanted to be in specific places in TV, like in Friends or Seinfeldrerun, Modern Family or one of those places, but Joe just wanted to be in whatever was *in there*.

"Jimmy can you buzz me through?"

It stayed closed.

Jack signed, 'I don't want to be flat either, Joe.'

Joe didn't bother to sign back. Jack and Jill said the same dumb thing every night.

He felt along the crack with his fingers. He'd thought this time surely it would work. They had been *so perfect*, they did just what Keller did! And he'd talked, *he had talked*. But no, the barrier was just as hard as ever.

He signed, 'Did I sound OK?'

Jack signed 'You sound like this' He said, "Jigee kanna beezm tru?"

Crunch signed, 'Jack's right. You sounded stupid again.'

He pressed himself against the barrier, wishing himself through it. His lips just got all tangled up in words, any words. The truth was that, as much as he'd practiced, he'd sounded just as stupid tonight as he did every night.

He slapped the barrier, slapped it again and again, harder and harder, until his hands stung so badly he had to stop. He bent down and smelled the crack. He loved the smell from under there, like the best MacDonald's and the best Pepsi and the best Peter Paul Mounds ever. And Snickers all the time.

He had made each of them tell him what they wanted. Betty had chosen clothes. He had agreed. Why did people have to be naked and only shatterfaces could wear clothes?

Crunch wanted to meet Elaine Benes. He sort of liked the way shatterface women looked. They were ugly and pretty at the same time, not smooth and beautiful like real women, but still interesting. He was curious.

Flutter wanted to go up stairs like in TV, because there was always somewhere else up there. Joe agreed. If only there were stairs in the world, maybe they could walk up and finally be somewhere else instead of sniffing under the barrier every night.

Jill wanted to get a pen like Keller had. They didn't get things like that and she liked black and gold shiny pens.

Joe felt along the floor crack, then bent way down with his head on its side and saw under the door the dark green floor that was the start of TV. There was maybe a shadow there, somebody walking. He smelled Mamma Mia Whatta Pizza.

Everybody started smelling then, suck that air, smell at those smells! So much was in there!

The Big Voice started going, singing the song at the close of day.

"Lullaby and goodnight,
lay thee down now and rest.
May thy slumbers be blessed.

Lay thee down now and rest."

Joe signed 'We are not going to obey anymore, the shatterfaces are not the bosses of us,' but nobody saw in the dark, as he knew they wouldn't. It was too scary to say so it could be seen, but it was in him, deep in there.

They went to their rooms. The lullaby meant that inspection was coming soon.

Joe was mad. He was sick of the line, sick of the world. He didn't want Keller to throw his marriage out. He wanted to go in TV. He wanted everybody to go in TV!

3

MIRACLES

From the moment that Beth had conceived the Texas Primate Center, she had known that it would demand all of her mind, her labor and her heart. When she'd floated the idea with her grizzled wild man of a husband, he had said, "Well, hell, girl, I never met an ape I didn't like."

Mom had cried, and that had hurt. Dad's silence has been his tears. They wanted her to love the ranch, to cherish its tradition and to eventually inherit it and pass it down in some Texas family they knew and respected, not to the children of a hippie stranger like Charlie.

Beth sat in her cluttered office that had been a pantry before she'd pulled out the shelves and dragged in a desk bought from Goodwill. Charlie was pacing in and out, reading her paperwork.

Outside, Murders' Row was roaring, shrieking, laughing, screaming and just generally cutting up. Mr. Ramos was feeding them, which was always a noisy proposition. They had all suffered, these beings, but they were happy now. Right now. That's what their world was, right now. They lived in right now, and there was something sacred in that, a trust to those of us who know the future and remember the past. People see. Animals are.

She would far rather be out there doing her share of the feed than in here with this monster of an agreement to contend with.

It said to sign in black ink. Beth surveyed the desk. She had only blue pens. "Charlie, do we have a black pen?"

He came rumbling back in.

"I'm begging," he said. "I am reading this and I am now officially begging."

For the third time today, she gulped back what was supposed to be her last cup of coffee. She went through the motions of lighting a cigarette, unwrapping the gum that was her substitute, stuffing it in her mouth, chewing. She'd started smoking at age seventeen, in the mountains of Rwanda. Stopping had been a challenge for a few months, but her craving, she had thought, was in the past. And then they'd started to go broke.

"Black ink," she said.

"Excuse me?"

"It says here, 'black ink.' We only have blue pens."

"Give me that."

"You'll tear it up."

"I will."

"Two hundred thousand dollars a year. A guarantee that the work is ethical—"

"It's testing, Beth. Gotta be."

"Ethical by *my* standards, that's what Greg Keller promised. And he knows my standards. He's read *Primate Politics*, and carefully. He has a dog-eared, underlined copy."

"Dog-eared and underlined by a flunky an hour before you showed up for the interview."

"Then he was well briefed. I think that I'm going to be doing something very much like this with a whole lot more generous budget, frankly. And Barrett Scientific—it's like signing with Prestige, Incorporated."

"You're sitting here getting ready to sign the most stringent secrecy agreement I've ever seen. The *worst*. I say no. I am telling you."

Charlie's time in Iraq had given him a demanding edge. Initially, he had been an enthusiastic warrior there. That had lasted until he got a live, in-the-flesh glimpse of Dick Cheney at Baghdad International Airport during one of his inspection tours. The man had seemed so cheerful that from that moment to this, Charlie had seen the world of authority differently and more darkly.

Sometimes in the night, he moaned. Once, deeply drunk, he had wept. He had whispered that he had killed with his hands.

From the deserts of ancient Sumeria to the fleshpots of Houston and San Antonio had been a kind of a long hop, skip and jump, but you could count on one thing about Charlie: he would do what he set out to do. There was darkness within him, but it was also true there had never been a more affable man. He was as stubborn as a tree stump, as smart as God, as sly as a snake and as sweet as a puppy. She thought she'd also managed to raise his consciousness—finally—about the fact that marriage was an equal opportunity workhouse.

"You're not telling me, Charlie," she said. "That's not gonna fly, as we have discussed." As she spoke, she heard a whine tremble in her voice. Clearing her throat, trying for a more controlled, professional tone, she added, "You oughta be glad. You oughta be proud!" But then another whine burst out of her mouth, "Charlie, it's *two hundred thousand dollars a year*!"

Charlie went over to the window and turned off the air conditioner. He threw open the free sash. She could hear the apes much more clearly now: Tofu was calling to her, for he was in love; she could hear Mizzi and Farouk arguing in the chimp enclosure, Mizzi who wore electrodes in her head left there after a seizure experiment, Farouk who'd had a finger eaten off by rats when he was dying of the cold. He'd been abandoned on a roadside in the dead of winter by an unknown party. As hypothermia immobilized him, the rats had eaten the finger and part of his upper lip, which made him always appear to be smiling, but not like a chimpanzee. His permanent grin, twisted up to the right, extended his mouth in a clownishly ironic line. But chimps do not do irony, and seeing it in one of their faces was disturbing, because it made you wonder if maybe they did.

"I'm doing this because I have to, and that's the bottom line and we both know it."

"We'll find the money somewhere."

"Where? The Ford Foundation? The Liebermann? We're burned down, as you well know."

That was because of Moreland. The newspaper clipping that had so amused Greg Keller had been about his exploits. The enormous old gorilla had escaped into the nearby neighborhood—twice, unfortunately. This exclusive enclave, called the Gardens, was a local millionaire's row, a wonderland of tract-home palaces. This manicured, coiffed and Beamered paradise was very definitely no place at all for a gorilla, especially not one who liked people and had a sense of humor.

The Center had become a cause célèbre, written about by local columnists who seemed pleased that a gorilla was walking the Gardens' golden streets. But the ever-vigilant animal testing industry had picked up on the story, and had lost no time in sending complaints about mismanagement to the Center's granting foundations, complaints that had been taken seriously.

Moreland was a silverback with a lock picker's brain. He also loved kids, having spent many years being admired by them up close at a small Midwestern zoo. But he'd gotten too old for the zoo. They wanted a younger gorilla, one who didn't require so much medical attention. Moreland had congestive heart failure and bad eyes. To the credit of the zoo, they retired him to the Center with a stipend.

Blind or not, he could still hear, and the distant voices of children drew him to genius-level escape attempts. When he finally succeeded, he rumbled off in the direction of the young voices. Next thing anybody knew, the VIP children of one of the VIPs the Gardens contained had a ton of gorilla join them in their swimming pool. The kids had been terrified at first, but Moreland had soon proved to be a keen, if clumsy, playmate. By the time momma happened to glance out the window, there was nothing visible of her twin four-year olds. Instead, she saw the brown back of a huge animal crouched in the shallow end. She rushed outside to find her toddlers playing in the gorilla's lap while he smacked his toothless smack, rolled his head and simpered.

To say that this lady had become fantastically upset would be to seriously understate her reaction. Screaming, white-hot terror was still a rather benign description of the thunderous, eyes-rolled-back-into-the-head denunciation she had issued on the evening news, a tantrum so spectacular that it had ended up on CNN along with a beauty shot of Moreland and the backyard with the splayed swing set, the collapsed slide, and, of course, the now empty pool, in which men in coveralls were using sanders.

It had been extremely dangerous, of course. Moreland's fading heart was in the right place, but his mind was in no way up to backyard babysitting. He could not understand the effect his bulk could have on a child. Thankfully, no harm had come to the children, but the incident still woke Beth up in the night.

They had reworked Moreland's security, but then, only eleven days later, it happened again. This time, he appeared in the parking lot of a K-Mart half a mile away, and in a very different world from the Gardens. Here were big crowds of shoppers, a cross-section of mid-middle Texas, all watching him. As he loved an audience, he capered around sitting through convertible tops and leaving dents in hoods.

He knew how to play a crowd, so when he heard what got the best reaction he did more of that. Unfortunately, he could not distinguish between screams of laughter and screams of terror. Despite the panic around him, he rolled with delight.

Amid a massive police presence, Charlie and Beth tried to tempt him with apples, hoping to God none of the cops would shoot. As far as tranquilizing him went, with his heart, Moreland might or might not have survived that.

He had ended his show by pushing a string of fifty grocery baskets into a display of garden gnomes, store personnel and an elderly nun who had, for whatever reason, been shopping for a gnome. The press had dubbed Moreland 'the K-Mart Kong.'

The insurance company had cancelled their policy. The foundations had howled: are our funds being correctly applied, are you people smoking our money or what? Investigators had been sent by no fewer than three of them. Biomed Natural, a large local testing facility that had often been on the Texas Primate Center Newsletter's Cruelest of the Month list, organized a write-in campaign and agitated in the Gardens to get a zoning change that would force the Center to close.

The zoning board, weary though it was of complaints and demands from the Gardens' powerful residents, let Texas Primates stay, but on probation. One more escape, even of the tiniest critter, and the Center was done. But there was another result that almost amounted to the same thing as being zoned out of existence. This was that their granting foundations had put them on hold, and some had cancelled grants. Worse, no new grants were moving ahead.

Nowadays, Moreland stayed at the far end of his enclosure, leaning against the fence, as close to the sound of the Gardens' children as he could get, a sad old guy with longing in his eyes. A gorilla is too large and too simple to live in the world, but smart enough to understand the meaning of a cage.

Charlie, she knew, was seeing saw all these thoughts passing through her mind. They were why he'd opened the window to the sounds of their apes. If she signed the contract, Barrett would all but own her. But if she didn't, then the apes would be gone. Why didn't he get that?

"Thing is," he said, "if they're legit, then why all the secrecy?"

"They have apes that need attention. That's all I care about."

"If it's illegal?"

"Barrett's got a big rep. They're not going to be breaking the law."

"You know, when you choke on your words, you're hard as hell to understand. Could you run that by me again?"

"Oh, God, Charlie, I just don't know. We didn't pay on the lease last month, which you know."

"Mr. Berry will—"

"Terminate us if we don't pay up in thirty days. Which you also know."

He lowered his head, digging into himself. After meeting Beth and coming to this place, he'd formed a profound commitment to the idea that animals are conscious beings and understand things like captivity, and have rights that we do not acknowledge. It is illegal to torture an ape, but it is not illegal to fit electrodes into his brain or inject him with drugs to see if they kill him or cause him agony or ruin his mind or his health, and it is not illegal to condemn him to prison for life simply because he exists. He didn't believe that zoos should be closed or their captives freed. Most of them would die in the wild in any case. Like Beth, he believed that zoos should replicate natural habitat, and keep only animals who would not feel trapped in whatever simulation could be provided.

Moreland could not be repatriated to Rwanda, and no zoo was going to offer him a home in an appropriate habitat. So he had to watch from the other side of his bars until he died, never understanding why he could not go where he wanted to go, or how to stop the hurt. When you look into the eyes of a captive chimp or gorilla or Orang, what looks back at you is a lost world.

Charlie came to her and put a hand on her shoulder.

"No," she said.

She did not want to cry, but she felt the same flood of woe she'd experienced on the day he'd brought the capuchins in. They'd been burned during a testing accident and were slated for destruction. She and Charlie and Mr. Ramos had worked around the clock twenty-four hours a day for a month, and saved every single monkey.

The capuchins were still furious, though, a year later. They would always be furious. She could hear them now, and could tell each monkey by its cry. Outraged or not, they were enjoying the sunny day with all the wonderful emotional intensity that had been granted their species.

"Don't leave us," Charlie said.

How he had obtained the capuchins, she did not know. She did not ask questions like that. He'd driven up at three one morning, his face covered with dirt, the bed of his pickup stacked with cages. End of story.

"The way I see it, we can probably take five thousand dollars a month out of what I make and put it on the Center's bottom line."

"We'll find the money!"

"Charlie, this stops right now. If we were gonna find the money we'd have already done that. Right now we feed the critters or we pay the rent, but not both. Do you understand that?"

He would not reply.

"And when we do close, what if we can't find space for our critters? Everybody's underfunded, nobody has room."

"We will not close."

"And if we end up having to destroy them?"

"That's a bullshit question! If you're not around here holding up your end, we're screwed anyway, sooner or later."

"It's *the* question, my love. *The* question."

He did not answer, could not. Bluster though he might, he knew the truth just as well as she did. For throwaway animals, there is no net.

She pressed her point. "If you and I have to sacrifice a little, okay. So I work eight hours at Barrett and eight here. I can do that. You accept it, too, Charlie. That money is gonna keep us rolling until we get back on some grant lists." With that she signed—in blue ink. Let the bureaucrats fix it.

Charlie shut the window with a loud bang. Then he came and sat on the edge of her cluttered desk. He looked down on her with those fabulous brown eyes of his. That was the first thing she'd seen of him—his eyes boring into her in a high jungle in Burundi. She'd been on a college field trip.

They had both been in love with the people of the forest. It was their mutual passion that caused them to discover each other. The explorations of mind and body that lead from passion to love began for them on a jungle trail, sitting on a little bench put there for the altitude-challenged. She had never met a man who so enjoyed kissing. She said to him, as their two weeks together sped to an end, 'you've kissed me more than anybody else I ever knew.' His response had been to kiss her again. She had been twenty; he was forty-four then. There remained something about their age difference that made the relationship seem very special and tender. He had history. The journey of his life, from enthusiastic killer to smoked-out hippie to dedicated veterinarian, had been a complex one, and had made him a haunted, guilt-ridden, dedicated, loving and just plain fascinating man.

Her trip home from Africa, not knowing if she would ever see him again, had been the hardest journey of her life. He was in love, she could tell that easily enough. But she was *really* in love, and she could not be sure that his feelings were strong enough to survive separation, not to mention the slow and unreliable mails of Africa. He was far beyond the reach of the internet, up in the blue mountains of Burundi.

She had come home to Texas and spent the last month of summer resting up in her old room in her old house in an exclusive old neighborhood where the Gardens *noveaux* feared to tread. In the ancient nights of home, with the moonlight flooding her tall windows, she had wept for a lost man in a lost world.

Then, one afternoon about six weeks later when she was back at school, her dorm room door had edged open and there he was. When she threw herself into his arms, this big, rope-faced tough guy had been trembled like a boy.

They'd married too early, with too little planning and forethought. They'd done it all wrong—gone to Reno instead to Christ Episcopal where her family had worshiped for four generations. They'd had a small civil ceremony with two paid witnesses instead of stiff rows of aunts and uncles and cousins filling the pews. Then had come her own personal struggle to graduate while simultaneously living with a maniac who thrashed in his sleep and dreamed of creating an ape farm.

She'd gotten an internship at the Maynard Primate Research Facility in Ogden, Utah, and it was there she had seen what they did to apes in the name of science. She had spent her days and nights with the oppressors of the animals, and found them to be perfectly decent people. It was just that everybody seemed to have a switch turned off inside themselves, the switch that extended compassion to the creatures in their possession.

After she had realized what Charlie did in his secret nights, she had told him, seemingly casually, about the horrors of Maynard.

It hadn't taken long for Maynard's apes to end up in the back of a truck. But, typically, Charlie and his friends hadn't foreseen what they might do with eleven chimpanzees, some injured, some carrying exotic diseases, some crippled—and all contraband.

The Texas Primate Center had been born of the experience of trying to find homes for them. When she'd ended up funding it with her trust money, her parents had apoplexy. Although daddy had sent the Center a check for a thousand dollars last year, mother still wouldn't talk to her. As for Charlie, he had no family, no money, nothing but his veterinary sheepskin, his passion to save suffering animals, and a kind of blind trust in what he called karma, which was anything good that came his way. The concept of bad karma, let alone bad luck, was not part of Charlie's reality.

Four of his original rescues were still here at the Center, old geezers by this time. Old, but still with hurt in their eyes. They had felt so much, not only physical pain, but the anguish of not understanding why. Most of the apes here had that kind of intricate hurt in their eyes. The thing that is so hard for people to see is that a creature can have rich, powerful emotions without being human.

The contract signed, she had to admit that its secrecy clauses set her teeth as much on edge as they did Charlie's. Fortunately, none of Charlie's lab popping had been discovered by the detectives, so they both looked perfectly clean. His radicalism was well concealed, largely because he was so damn good at what he did. But lab popping was in the past. The Center couldn't afford the slightest risk of a criminal complaint. The State of Texas would not hesitate to sell the animals right back into the labs.

"Charlie, I'm gonna drive over there."

He nodded. He was silent. So he'd accepted the defeat. This was his usual pattern. Tonight, he'd drink a little, then probably try to make love and maybe succeed and maybe not. If he did, he'd sleep all curled up against her. If not, then he'd say "well, hell," and lie there with his hands behind his head and stare at the ceiling.

She went out, crossing to the parking lot via the storage sheds in order to avoid the riot that always ensued when she passed the cages. One thing about apes, they have strong feelings. Most of the male chimps were partial to Beth, and showed it. The females were ready, correspondingly, with spitwads and bits of dung if she got too close to them. They, on the other hand, started displaying the second they heard Charlie or Luis or Henry coming their way. Then the males would be waiting with the spitwads and the dung.

And if a staffer got zapped? Laughter all around. Whoever said that only humans had laughter was dead wrong. Apes laughed. They joked. And they could pine for whom they loved, most assuredly.

She got in her old Volvo and headed out. She called Keller cellphone to cellphone.

"Beth!"

"I'm on my way."

Short silence. Then, "Great!"

It was an hour's drive from the Center to the campus, and Beth spent it listening to music rather than thinking about the future. When she stopped showing up at expected times back at the Center, she knew that the apes would pine. They would pine until she returned, even if it was years, or forever. They were totally loyal and in their universe there was no time.

She was tempted, as she arrived at the campus, to stop her car in the winding driveway and walk across the grounds...just to see if there were security devices around the place. The driveway was cut through the limestone of the Texas hill country, and flanked by live oaks, cedars and stands of wildflowers. Until recently, this had probably been part of a wealthy oilman's show ranch. Oil was not doing so well, though, and he'd probably had to sell off some acreage. As you got closer to the building itself, the scrub had been cut away, and a halfhearted attempt made to start grass in the barren, rocky land that remained.

There was a small brick plaza in front of the forbidding black building, and a chunky limestone pillar beside the entry doors with a black steel plate on it that read in deeply etched gold letters, 'Barrett Scientific.' The word communicated by this entrance was very clear. That would be "No."

She got out of her car to the trill of a mockingbird, who stood on a corner of the roofline flicking his tail and singing his heart out.

As usual, Greg Keller was waiting for her in the foyer. As he came forward, his gleaming shoes snapped against the black marble floor. For a building so quickly constructed, Main, as they called it, was full of luxurious touches like the marble and the tall, tinted windows that looked out on a view across the dreaming Texas hill country.

"Beth, I can't tell you how pleased I am."

He took the contract from her. He examined the signature so long that it began to see a little odd. Pompous, even.

"It's mine," she said finally. "I really signed."

"Okay," he said. "Let's get you badged up and then we can take a little tour. I'll bet you're curious as hell."

"That's accurate."

She followed him into the facility, deeper than she had ever been. Walking along behind him, watching his narrow shoulders, she felt a sense of being trapped that was almost strong enough to stop her. She didn't know any secrets yet. She could still take back the contract. She could still go home.

But then she heard, very faintly, a cry. It was long and strange—strangely musical, even. What might it be? Which species? Some kind of rare howler monkey? Keller walked faster.

"What was that?"

"From the enclosure."

"Because I've been assuming that this is about apes, not monkeys. My primary expertise is in apes."

"It's right for you, Beth. I've told you that."

Up until this moment, Keller had been a friendly, informal kind of man, very democratic in his approach. But not now. Now his voice had terse crackle in it. She was no longer a candidate being wooed. She worked here.

They were moving down a corridor floored with gray tile and lined with black numbered doors. Each door, she noticed, had a security lock on it. She was amazed by this. A secrecy agreement was one thing, but this—well, it smacked of the paranoid.

Keller stopped before one of the doors. They entered. "Dr. Cooke is ready," he said.

A man came to his feet behind the desk, a stocky man with plastic-framed glasses and a huge Montblanc pen in the pocket of his rather dirty white shirt. "I'm Martin Horsman," he said. "I'm glad you're here, I don't want to miss my flight."

A click made Beth turn around. It was the sound of the door closing. Keller had left.

"Barrett's the best place to work in the world," Horsman said. "They treat you like a god. But first I've got to identify you, so we can slot you into the security system."

He took her into an inner room where she was fingerprinted and photographed. She was made to sign on a pad that recorded her handwriting, then asked to stare into a flickering screen until a facial recognition program satisfied itself. They already had her DNA from her interviewing process. Finally, she was given an actual, physical security manual and told that it had to be read and each page initialed as it was completed, and that it could not leave the building. In fact, no records of any kind could leave the building, and all paper used in the facility, she was warned, was treated so that an alarm would sound if it was taken out. Ditto computers, thumb drives, any form of electronic media.

Her personal computer at home would be monitored, and she should be aware that anything she did on it, from typing notes to herself to sending e-mail to surfing the web, would be recorded via the keylogger she had agreed to allow to be installed. He knew that she wasn't a cyberabuser, but she had to understand clearly that her private use of the internet was, well, not private anymore. Similarly, she should not expect privacy on telephones within the facility. All of her online activity, phone calls, etc., would be encrypted, but not by her, and the use of encryption software not approved and controlled by the company was strictly forbidden.

"Here's a list of apps," he said mildly. "Any of them on your iPad or your phone have to go."

She looked at the list. Many familiar apps, including a couple of games she had. "May I know why?"

“They’re all backdoored by intelligence agencies. Mostly Chinese."

She took out her iPhone and stared at it and wondered, ‘are you staring back?’

By the time he had issued her keycard and combination code, she was in a state that might as well have been called shock. No matter how stringent the contract, this setup was spectacularly invasive. Frankly, she was revolted by it. Barrett didn’t treat you like a god at all. It treated you like an enemy.

“I don’t think—”

Horsman held up a hand. “You hate it.”

“Yeah.”

“We all hate it. But when you find out the reasons, you’ll be glad. I want to be frank with you. We’re all vulnerable here. This whole project is vulnerable. It’s extremely sensitive and publicity would be devastating. Believe me, the security protects you, too.”

Next, she was shown her office, which turned out to be lavish. It was on the second story overlooking the back of the campus. A lawn, in which the patchwork in the recently laid grass was still faintly visible, stretched off to a gleaming new cyclone fence.

Keller reappeared. With him was a young man much more appropriately dressed than Mr. Horsman in his business suit. These days, jeans and t-shirts fit scientific facilities much more than coats and ties.

“Let me introduce you,” Keller said. “This is our logistics manager, Jim Thomas.”

Thomas extended his hand. “Welcome,” he said in a nervous, somewhat too-loud voice. He proceeded to instruct her on office procedures, including things like minimizing the use of electricity. It was utterly fantastic, and, as she was learning, utterly Barrett. The company was careful about money—very careful. And yet the facility was astonishingly lavish—marble, expensive wood, lovely office furnishings. Primatologists didn't have offices like this. Theirs was a world of steel desks and obsolete computers. There was two thousand dollars worth of furniture in this office, and a bank of monitors and other high end equipment. The laptop she'd been assigned was a Mac so high end that that she didn't know how high end it was. Hers was nine or ten years old. At least.

She turned her mind to her first check, and how much money would be there for her critters, just to keep things in perspective.

Keller said, "All set." He looked from Horsman to Thomas. Both nodded. Keller nodded to her. "Let's go, then. Curiosity killed the cat." He took her down a long corridor that led to a control room and a big, silver door without a handle on it. Keller opened it with a keycard.

She entered, then, into the world of the new.

4

SHATTERFACES

Shimmering sparks went sailing lazily to the floor from Flutter's station. If they touched you, it was a hard bite, and the shatterfaces would have to come and make it stop.

Joe watched the sparks bouncing along the floor, listened to them hissing, then spitting themselves out as they rolled into pools of oil under the line. Up on the catwalk, shatterfaces gave voice to each other, 'writing' on paper with pens. These marks annoyed Joe. They meant some kind of shatterface stuff he wanted to know. He wanted to know what the Big Voice knew and what Keller knew. Especially Keller, because he went in and out of TV most often and as he was the one with glasses, he was the head.

He smelled Betty, who was just across from him on the press. There was sweat under her hair. He wanted to get all cuddled up under their sheet with her.

"Pepsi-Cola time," the Big Voice called, echoing up and down the line. Joe pulled his release valve and watched as the pressure dropped on the vacuum mold. It filled him with joy that the work was over now. He ran down the line laughing, and was the first to swing up and head for the break room. Behind him, he could hear Betty yelling, and Jack and Jill coming more slowly, probably holding hands like always. Crunch came up from underneath. Ever since Joe had done Flutter, Crunch had been giving him long stares. There was still a fight brewing, yah.

Joe got a cup of coffee with cream and a box of Krispy Kremes. He liked that word, cream. It made his stomach feel good when he signed it. Cream this, cream that. Cream for my coffee, cream over my pie, cream doughnuts.

Then something new—a real good smell. Keller came in. Everybody was pretty happy to see him. He was the one who brought doughnuts and enchiladas and burgers and all that primo stuff out of TV. He had an awful bad shatterface, though, with super-black eyeholes that Joe would sometimes dream had roaches living in them. Keller stood way up to the ceiling in his dreams. In his dreams, he knelt down and his whisper-voice inside him said, 'I am smiling at you Keller, help me Keller, get me Peter Paul Mounds all the time and make it so I win Clue.'

One time Keller said, 'Prayer is when you ask your god for what you need. So when you pray, you pray to me, Joe. But also tell me. Always tell me, too.'

Betty's theory was if you looked too hard at a shatterface, you'd fall into its eyes forever.

Joe felt something brush his neck. He turned around to find Crunch staring at him. His first impulse was to haul off and slap Crunch stupid. But he contented himself with a long, careful stare back, right across the two tables between them.

The Big Voice got in it. "There will be no fighting, Joe." He did not want to listen. "Break that stare, Joe." The hell with the Big Voice. "Joe!"

Uh-oh. He told himself it wasn't because he was scared, but because he wanted doughnuts and coffee a lot more than he wanted a piece of Crunch. But now the guy was practically sucking Betty's face from halfway across the room.

The smell got stronger. Joe was the first to realize what it was, which was the most amazing thing that ever, ever happened. Because that smell, you see, that was a new shatterface.

One second later, everybody else realized it too, and they all started yelling and whooping and clapping and jumping up on their tables because here was this new shatterface coming right into the world through the barrier with Keller. Would it be Elaine, would it be Jerry, would it be Stephen Colbert?

Nope, this one wasn't from TV, this one was—*in green*! Shatterface clothes, but all green!

Joe wanted to kneel down and jump up and yell like crazy all at the same time.

Then everybody was looking down. Jack was kneeling, Flutter was kneeling. Couldn't look up, not and risk the new eyes, which were really awful.

Joe sucked in air. Yeah, there was goop smell and quim smell—a woman. Woman shatterface. What the hell, you only saw *those* in TV. A *shakeya* blast went through him now so hard he *did* yell —*Oaaayyyyyy*! And Betty, she yelled even louder *OAAAAAYYYY*! Then everybody was yelling all kinds of yells and Jill was jumping on the tables going *yakkityakkityakakak*! and pushing doughnuts in her mouth real fast so they'd go down around her yell.

He jumped up and danced, going down hard and fast, step and jump, hump and hop, jumpjumpjump!

A new shatterface and a womany woman okayyyyyy! And in green!

Crunch threw back his head and yelled the loudest loud yell of all, *BAAAAAYYHHOOOOAAAY*! Then he spread his lips back all the way and went across the room on his knees hitting his forehead because he was so surprised and signing furiously with his one free hand—green green green green!

Then Crunch, he got up, he stood right in front of the new shatterface...and he looked. *He LOOKED*! Then he turned back and closed up his lips in a line and tossed his hair back and forth over his head and he went off strutting and swaying his bottom like he owned the place.

Except he hadn't *really* looked, Joe didn't think. You didn't look at shatterface eyes and not get the inside of your head burned so bad you couldn't even walk, let alone act like that.

Flutter dove across their table and threw her arms around Crunch. Then she glared at Betty and Joe, and tossed her hair back and forth, too. Her man had done this brave thing. *Her* man.

'He didn't do a thing,' Joe signed. 'His eyes were closed.' He closed his eyes and wobbled his head from side to side, mocking Crunch.

Betty was hanging onto Joe and Flutter onto Crunch. Jack and Jill came over and joined Joe and Betty, winding up in a knot of people. Everybody started snorting out the smell of the new shatterface. They were tormented with worry about getting shattered by the new eyes.

Crunch strutted and danced and went *"hup-hup-ooo!"* Just showing off as usual. He was scared, too.

Flutter started making the smoking sign with her fingers. She remembered how cigarettes made you feel good and she wanted to feel good, because having a new shatterface made you feel all funny, bad and good at the same time. They all felt very upset and Joe knew Crunch did to. That butt-swaying strut was a damn lie.

Roberts had taught them to smoke. They hadn't seen him in a long time. Roberts was good. He brought bacon, too. He had made pictures of them in a thing and you could look which was eerie but fun, too. Roberts was gone, you never smelled Roberts anymore.

"No cigarettes, Flutter," Keller said.

Joe thought he sounded pretty nice right now. He was going to be nice. Oh, very nice, he even had Peter Paul Mounds, Joe smelled it definitely. Eager to take the lead back from Crunch, he jumped up on the table and signed everybody, 'Peter Paul Mounds, Peter Paul Mounds.' He struck his left hip with the flat of his hand and rolled his eyes. He was the boss. He straightened his glasses.

"They've smelled the candy," Keller said to the new shatterface who now stank of sour sweat and leaking piss. It was a spindly shatterface with a really narrow nose and long, thin hands. And it was *looking right at him*! Oh...

Keller grabbed it and turned its head and it went, "Hey!"

"Don't do that!"

Now it was hiding its shatterface, looking down. *O-kaay*! Joe stood up up up! He stood allllll the way! Now he was tall, now he was up to their shoulders. Shatterfaces were real tall. They were made out of sticks under their clothes. That's why they hid themselves, because sticks were not strong. You found sticks in packing for the assembly line supplies sometimes, and they busted all apart.

He went to her. Behind him, the people began making noises, pretending to talk. He signed back to them to shut up. He didn't want the shatterfaces to hear their dumb gabble.

The new shatterface was taller than Keller but he was thicker. Her woman scent was all mixed up with some kind of goop odor. They all wore goop on themselves, goop under their arms, goop on their faces. Shatterface goop.

Now everybody was getting courage. They were following him up to the new shatterface. Crunch had come and run. He stayed. He was braver than Crunch or Jack or anybody in the world. Yah, he was Joe! He went up to her and slapped himself on the chest. *Yah, Joe*!

Betty's opinion was that the shatterfaces came out of TV at night. Stephen Colbert came out of TV and put his hand on her twat, she said. Joe did not hold with this theory. He had watched at night and nothing happened. Next morning, Betty would smile all the way across her whole face and sign, Stephen came out of TV last night. It was Crunch doing it, of course.

Now he was standing right in front of the green shatterface.

Now he was raising his head. Forcing himself. Higher. Higher yet.

He could feel her eyes, they were knives in his face.

His head hurt, his temples thudding. His stomach got sick. Fire came up out of his gut and made him choke.

He looked into her eyes, bright as Crayola green and ringed by shatterface shadow.

"Emerald," she said, "his eyes are emerald!"

He finally noticed that Keller was yelling at him. "Back off, Joe," he shouted, "Back off, Joe!" Then, to the shatterface: "I repeat, do *not* meet their eyes!"

But the new shatterface was still looking at him anyway, and right in his eyes, and her eyes were a hole in the world. Joe couldn't turn away, it was too hard, he felt himself falling, dropping into the hole.

"Turn away," Keller yelled. "Turn away!"

Then he was just seeing Keller and he had Peter Paul Mounds and just like that it was all okay again.

The new shatterface started barking. It barked and gobbled and water came on its cheeks. It went 'uh goo, ah ah, uh goo' which Betty decided was funny. She started laughing, 'yak yak yakkidy kak!' and so did everybody else. Then she ran around, hopping tables and waving her arms and yelling *'kakakayakakakakkity'* like she liked to do and wobbling her head and grinning 'cause she was happy and scared both at the same ding-dong *time*!

All the people burst out yelling and running. Crunch went roaring through his stations slamming the walls and chair backs so hard the whole place shook. Flutter followed behind him, hitting them twice as hard and yelling twice as loud. Betty got up on the cafeteria counter and ran it, then came back sliding on the tray bars and howling. Jack and Jill jumped up and down together in the middle of the room, slapping their hips in time to the jumps.

Joe stood proud, he stood silent. Inside, he was running and laughing and scared and happy and all wild just like them. But he was not like them. He felt it hard in him, but would not let it out.

Look at that Jack, pissing right out here instead of in the toilet! Keller oughta give him a good long *yowtch* with the snickersnee. Well, fine. Look at that Jill going *whoop whoop* and sticking out her teeth at the shatterface.

He held his head up high. He did *not* let the shatterface know that her eyes had hurt him. Just like Stephen Colbert, he extended his hand. He smiled. She took his hand in her hand, which felt like a mouse, all slippery slidey.

So that was done, so then he gave her one, two, three, four *high five*!

"You have just been accepted by the leader," Keller said.

Joe knew that his standing up and everything would calm the

people down, and it did. They went quiet now. Now everybody wanted to shake and do high five with the new shatterface. Only Crunch did not do high five. He thought it was stupid. He shook and she said, "This one is so courtly."

Keller said, "That's Crunch. He's a very adroit engineer."

Betty rushed up and grabbed her face and gave her a big smack, then ran off kackiaking again. Joe looked down all the way at his feet. Couldn't she *ever* calm down?

Betty kissed TV when shatterface women wore green. So maybe it was okay. Shatterfaces only wore color in TV. In the world, they always wore white. So maybe it was okay she was now doing backflips and shuddering her boobies at the shatterface and sticking her teeth *way* out. You could understand her excitement...sort of.

"Okay, people," Keller yelled. "I want you to *get in line*!"

They did the line fast and straight—nose to head, body to body.

Keller put one Peter Paul Mounds into each hand.

Oh, was that good. That was soft, that was sweet, that had big ole heart in the waaaaaay it tasted! And then it was gone, down the hatch!

The shatterface was gone, too, right out through the barrier as easy as anything.

Joe went up and slid his hand along the familiar hard coldness of it and hung his head.

5

COUNTRY ROADS

Beth drove. She drove blindly, roaring down back roads without regard to where she was going.

Dear God in heaven, they were not apes. Apes did not have human feet, they did not walk upright, they did not have flowing hair, they did not have those...faces.

They weren't a genetic cross of some kind, were they? Human genes engineered into gibbon or chimp genes? No, that was impossible, nothing but internet rubbish. Even if somebody did manage it, the result wouldn't look anything like this. Because the fact was, these creatures didn't look like apes *or* like us.

They had seemed at once innocent and terrible. The way they'd looked at her—those were the eyes of another mind, but not like an ape mind or a dog mind. This mind was acute and watchful. It was frightening, there was no other way to put it. New and therefore frightening. Because they needed her, though, she must not fear them. They were fearful of her, too, despite their powerful bodies.

Their bright eye colors—especially the emerald green of the one with the glasses, and the rose red—made them seem very strange. Of course the intense coloring was for the same reason that jungle birds were so colorful—so they could be seen more easily by others of their kind.

She realized that every turn she made was taking her closer to the Lucky KT Ranch, and that was just fine with her. She needed home now, and the Katy was the home of her heart and her soul. She'd spent her childhood summers on the Katy, riding her beloved quarter horse Running Red, swimming along the treacherous Guadalupe Bend where her great uncle Harrison had drowned in a canoeing accident in 1966, and just enjoying the quiet of place and when she grew bored, the endless succession of grinning, eager boys who had made her young life the joy that it had been.

She got out and punched the gate code, then drove the mile and a half to the house, automatically tooting three times long and one short to let Timothy Green the caretaker know who it was.

She drove another quarter mile through the back pasture behind the house, known as the goat pasture for reasons that were lost in the past, listening to the long summer-yellow grass hiss against the sides of the car.

When she was deep enough in the ranch, she stopped. Silence absolute. A jay called on the distance. Bluebirds flitted around the bluebird houses she had set along the fence that separated this pasture from the river strip down below.

She had to think—try to think—because one thing was certain: this was totally beyond anything she had expected.

She had been afraid of them and she had to get past that. It was the primitive fear of the unknown that horror movies were designed to evoke. Fear of the alien, the 'not like me,' the demon in the dark.

They were so *helpless*!

For a long time she sat behind the wheel, staring blankly, remembering what she'd seen. They had high cheekbones, that wonderful, hair, russet and brown and tan. Their mouths were wide and sensitive and the hair flowed about their heads like uneasy halos. Their skin was so vivid that it almost seemed to glow. Two of them, Joe and Flutter, were light gray. The rest were more of a charcoal hue. Their skin color was a nod to camouflage strategy. Pressed against many sorts of jungle tree, they would be almost the color of the bark. If they closed their eyes, they'd be camouflaged. Open them, and others of their kind could spot them easily.

Their arms weren't designed for brachiation. They couldn't swing through trees. No, they lived on the forest floor. But their big shoulders and hands suggested that they could most assuredly climb.

What in the world *were they*?

She thought of Joe, self importantly wearing glasses frames, apparently as a status symbol. She had seen a ferocity in his eyes, but it was not like the fixed stare of an angry gorilla. It was subtle, concealed behind a simpering smile. She thought that he had the capacity to be a killer, but not like an ape. No, this one would be stealthy and deceptive.

Or no, perhaps that was just her own fear. This had been another intelligence, with none of the dullness of the animal. She'd felt completely out of control, and now the feeling came back and she began to shiver and sweat. Instinct caused her to lock the car.

She stopped herself. She was being an idiot. She must not allow primitive feelings to overtake her reason and her training. She needed to think about them clearly and calmly, and focus on their needs.

She got out of the car, slamming her door so hard it sounded like an explosion. Moving fast, she went down to the river. She felt a need to run, to scream—anything to get the fire out of her head.

She had come to her place of peace to find a way to suppress the panic, because Charlie must not see her like this, no way. He would try to rescue those creatures, and never mind the guards and their guns.

Pacing up and down the bank of the lovely, deceptive old river, she listened to the chuckling murmur of the small rapids that were just the other side of the swimming hole. Made herself listen. She forced her mind back to slow summer afternoons, the voices of the friends of her childhood and their gentle laughter, ghostly now in the late breeze. The sun was sliding toward the west, and the long shadows of the great cypress trees that lined the banks were swaying in the water where she had so often played as a child.

She sat down on the cypress stump they'd been using as a bench all of her life.

Those faces—the eyes. Oh, no...

She covered her own face with her hands. She could not control the sound that came out of her, nor had she ever heard it before. It was a howl of woe that came from somewhere so deep and so dark that she had never been there before, not in any of the tragedies her life had presented to her.

Were they monsters—cute little Frankensteins—or some sport of nature or—good God, *what were they*?

Here, she had also dreamed the dreams upon which her soul was founded, that genuine rights would be extended to the animal world, that we would wake up to the fact that everything—every flitting bird, every bored tiger in its rusty old cage, every outraged monkey—was conscious. Not as smart as we are, but brimming with self awareness and the hope that goes with it, a fellow traveler in the majesty of being alive.

They had been naked but not ashamed. They'd touched her blouse, the females' fingers trembling with some kind of...she didn't know. She wanted to say excitement, but how could she know their minds?

Science was just beginning to understand that everything, even insects, had some level of consciousness. Pigeons can tell the difference between a Monet and a Picasso. Dogs laugh. Cats lie. She'd branded calves, gone on roundups, seen the steers off in the black, rattling trucks, their curious eyes peering out between the slats. 'Where am I going? Why?'

And yet, compared to being devoured by a lion, dying in a slaughterhouse was merciful. So she would not be sentimental. She refused. Nature is brutal. That's reality.

What in the world was being done to these creatures? No, beings. Or people. Yes, that was right. *People*. She stopped and she crouched down beside the slow water and looked in at her face staring back and she said, "People. Those were people."

Sobs burned her throat and contorted her gut. She drew back from the mirror of the water and slumped down onto the bank. She rolled over and looked up into the soaring crowns of the majestic cypresses. Some of these trees had been here when Indians drank at this stream. She felt them as sacred in their silence, in the slow waving of their crowns, green washed with the pale light of the late sun.

She walked a little more, to the grassy clearing just down from the low-water crossing. When she was a girl, she'd imagined that she could feel the turning of the earth in this place. Just now, a lazy white cloud drifted past, beneath it buzzards using its thermals to gain altitude.

Another wave of tears came, and again that hollow mourning, a sound she had not known she could make.

Here she had spent the eternal hours of summer, explored the bodies of trembling boys and trembling herself under their uneasy hands. Coming here in the late night when she was fifteen and sixteen, she had first laid eyes on the male in his nakedness, swimming here with boys like pale immortals.

"Now," she said to the sky, "where are my ghosts when I need you?"

Grandfather Saunders, six foot four, genial and wise, had been easily powerful enough to get the Texas Rangers to raid that unholy lab to which she had just indentured herself. Dead, though, these ten years. Dad was powerful, too, but lost to her.

How beautiful the creatures—beings—were. They wanted more, she knew that. The way the female fingers had ghosted along the edges of her blouse had said 'I want to look pretty, too.'

They had suffered visibly when she had looked into their eyes. They hadn't been able to bear it. Lock eyes with an ape, and he will not be able to handle it for long, either.

They were *so beautiful*. They did not speak, but their vocalizations were *very* complex, and their flying hands—they were signing at a proficiency level that seemed almost inconceivable.

Unless their vocal chords were undeveloped, and the sounds she had already heard suggested that this was not the case, they could be taught to speak. She didn't know what their throat and mouth structures were like, so they might have trouble pronouncing human words. That remained to be seen.

They were animals, Keller insisted. He'd said straight out: there is no human DNA involved. She believed him. The appearance of the creatures—their stature, their facial structure, their skin coloring and their irises colors—supported the claim. You simply did not find eye color like that in the human genome, and she was pretty sure that their skeletal morphology was novel, too.

There was no precedent for this, certainly not for putting them to a task like running an assembly line. 'Training,' he said.

They were to be factory workers? That would be grotesque.

What he had was a group of intelligent beings who were easily smart enough to do complex repetitive work, but not human beings, and so not covered by human rights laws. No, these creatures had the rights of pigs and horses and apes. For them, slavery would be a step up.

Keller and Barrett and all their kind were greedy bastards with their black glass fortress and their cages and their guns. Move over third world, here comes the *real cheap* labor.

Of course it was all a deep secret. Publicity was not going to be helpful here. Far from it.

But the money would be extraordinary. Slavery was returning, but without the headache of slaves. These were just animals. They could be carried off in trucks like the steers, kept in sheds, exposed to all sorts of privation and danger, left naked before the world.

There could be breeding colonies developed, teams of the poor things leased like packs of cattle dogs, and as for safety and comfort: animal rights laws, insofar as they existed at all, were hardly meant to protect sensitive beings like these.

But the plan would work. If they could be made to breed, the offspring would certainly sell. It was one thing to spend a million dollars on a robot, only to have to refit or replace it every time the task structure changes, another to spend the same amount on one of these creatures, with no rights, that has only to be fed, and can be retrained again and again for a few bucks.

These little beings were going to be far cheaper than artificial intelligence, much less costly to manage, and completely legal to own.

She pitched forward and was sick into the water.

She found herself wanting to go upstream and swing on the old rope. Swing back to her teenage years and never return. Sweet sixteen. Except, of course, she'd been a hellion. When she was seventeen, she'd waked up one afternoon scrunched up on a loveseat in a friend's apartment, wearing only panties and her left shoe. She'd been both hung over and still drunk. She'd remembered lights below, noise and being in the air. She was chugging aspirin when the memories had come into focus: she and Rupert Dix had gone flying. They'd flown in his dad's Cessna, wildly in the night.

Rupert had landed it, she remembered that, but not at an airport. She smiled to herself, remembering the long driveway and the house. She'd gone up to it, rung the doorbell and asked to use the toilet, the plane still buzzing away behind her, its landing lights flooding the front yard.

Had she passed out in the bathroom? Yes, and been driven home by the kindly old lady who owned the house.

Since then, she had never been drunk again. That had been it for Rupert, too. He'd taken off again, still failed to find the airport and set the plane down in a beet field. The rough landing had busted the wheels. His dad, as she recalled, had not been amused.

Her mind returned to the present. She was still wild and married to a man who was even wilder, but she wasn't crazy-wild, not like she had been when she was rich and young and did not yet realize that the world is full of need.

The idea of lab popping drifted into her consciousness.

No, don't even think about it. *Do not.* There was no unsecured way in, and even if they did manage to penetrate the place, there was damn well no way out, either. Barrett would see them in jail for sure... assuming they survived.

In fact, the problem Keller had presented her with was as complex as it was infuriating. His issue was that the "animals" were not breeding. They were perfectly healthy, so it was a behavioral problem, as he saw it. Yeah, even if they didn't understand it, their instincts were telling them that they were enslaved. That would be the behavioral problem, you bastard.

It was as if nature was saying no babies, not here...or maybe, she thought, it was God. Maybe God was saying no. Except, was there one?

She pulled off her shoes and scrunched her toes in the sandy crack just below the rock she was on. Here, on this rock, she had first been kissed. That boy, Maynard Crouch—what had become of him? His dad had been a general, commanding this or that at Fort Sam Houston. Maynard Crouch had been shaking like a Chihuahua, but he had also been strong, and the sensation of lying back in his arms and feeling the trembling insistence of his kiss had seemed to her then to be the most wonderful thing she had known. She remembered Maynard's profoundly cute freckles, and the wonderful way his halting innocence contrasted with his clumsy strength.

Even after all the cruelty and pain she'd seen in her work with animals, she still considered the world to be what this place had taught her that it was: a vast, exquisitely balanced act of grace. Somewhere in its balance was Maynard Crouch, somewhere her beloved Charlie, somewhere even the repugnant Keller. Somewhere also, these six beautiful strangers.

She considered that they might be *homo floresiensis,* hobbit-like proto-humans who were supposed to have gone extinct fifty thousand years ago. God, that would be a wonder.

But she wasn't a paleobiologist. Her expertise was centered in Earth's living primate population. As for Charlie, veterinary medicine was not likely to be helpful, either. But what would be? Doctors were going to be starting from scratch, too.

She recalled how they'd looked standing in their rod-straight line, each in turn stepping forward, fishing in Keller's pocket for a segment of candy bar, then stepping politely aside. They wanted to please. They worshiped or feared Keller, or both. And why shouldn't they? You worship and fear your god, and he was the only one they knew.

A line from an old poem drifted into her mind, 'There was a child went forth every day, and the first object he looked upon, that object he became.' She drew a ragged breath, gobbling back the sob that had come with it.

"Welcome," she shouted, "welcome to the world!" Then she got up and strode off, heading back to the car. She walked fast—too fast for this rough ground—and the next thing she knew, there was a knife of pain in her left foot.

Shit, snake! Damn, damn, damn!

Or no. No, it was a scorpion. She'd stepped on a scorpion in her fool bare feet. She saw it, ruined on the rock, its legs still scrabbling. Dropping down, she looked at her right foot. It was red along the edge of the arch. There was a welt in the arch, too. You needed to use a Sawyer extractor to draw out the venom, then soak the foot in ice water to help neutralize what was left. But she didn't have an extractor pump, let alone any ice water. The river was cool, not cold.

Cursing her own inattention, she hobbled back to her car and began the long voyage across the darkening hills to home. The scorpion's sting burned and throbbed, almost to the point where she became too dizzy to stay on the road.

Pain or no pain, she could not stop thinking about her situation. By signing that contract, she'd committed herself to the unknown, and the unknown turned out to be evil—far worse than anything she had imagined. She had been shown her own book and assured that the situation was ethical as well as legal. Maybe it was legal and maybe it wasn't, but it surely was not ethical, and she had signed her name to it.

Driving along the old ranch road, she could see the bats of evening fluttering. Gone were the graceful, narrow-winged birds of old called bull bats. Their softly haunting cries had left the evening forever.

Ultimately, this was the question: does intelligence alone confer what we call human rights, or does it have to be human intelligence, and what does 'human' even mean?

The judicial system had uniformly refused to address the issue of high level rights for animals. No dolphin, no chimp, was going to be included in the rights of man, largely because they could not manage themselves in the human world. Again and again, that had been the decision handed down by the courts, and, unlike her firebrand husband, she wasn't sure that the courts were wrong.

Animal rights were protections, not freedoms. How could you give a chimp the freedom to walk the street? It was absurd.

But for these creatures? They were at or near human intelligence. What if they could learn to manage their own lives, what then?

She rolled down the windows to drive away the dizziness, jammed the gas pedal to the floor and shot off down the road howling because her foot hurt like the devil and she was as mad as hell.

By the time she arrived at the Center, the foot felt like it was the size of a watermelon, which it probably was. She pulled into the parking lot, to her place under the tin car port. Charlie's ancient and beloved junk truck was there, and she could see lights in the windows of the well-shaded old farmhouse that served as both their home and their headquarters.

And now came another level of fear. She had to face Charlie. He would know instantly that something was wrong and she would not be able to tell him what it was.

Her marriage was the most precious thing in her life. What about the trust that was its foundation? What about the sharing of their troubles? No secrets, but what did that mean now?

She was glad that she knew about those poor creatures but she wished to hell that there was some road to go down that was not this road, because down this road their lay only lies, distrust and broken hearts.

She knew that a lot of folks who couldn't go looking would be missing her, so she struggled out to Murderer's Row. She not only wanted to make them happy, she wanted to be near her apes and monkeys, to feel their spirits, to commune with them. After what she had seen today, the simplicity of her apes would be like a long, healing soak in spring water.

Moreland left his listening post and ambled over to his love-me station, waiting there for her hand. She went to him, and they touched, and he tasted her fingers. "Oh, baby," she whispered to the huge creature. He sensed her unease and reached up and touched her cheek. He was so sensitive, this big, glowering creature. His kind was going, some roasted over the campfires of Africa, others sold in illegal backstreet butcheries from Jo'berg to London. Bushmeat was a sentimental delicacy for many Africans.

And then something happened. Something happened to Moreland. It came in stages. First, his nostrils dilated. Then he sucked air, sucked it hard. Then he challenged her, something he had never done before, not In all the time he had been here. He would challenge Charlie, of course, and the other male staff. All the males did, even the little capuchins, screeching away and courageously baring their teeth to men five times their size. It didn't matter how much food and care they'd been given. Males challenged males. Rule of the primate.

Moreland did his 'tour,' running down to the end of his enclosure, climbing to the top of the cage, brachiating halfway back, then running at her waving his arms and bellowing. Primate behavior, same as she'd seen among Keller's creatures. And then she understood—he was picking up the scent they'd left on her.

His cries instantly woke everybody up, and the whole place was at once in an uproar. Beth felt her heart speed, felt sweat breaking out all over her. She turned round and round, her arms out, palms raised, eyes to the ground. Usually, most of the males would accept this gesture, but not tonight. Tonight, the uproar only increased.

She had brought the strangers with her, their scent clinging to her clothes like some volatile oil. Their mystery now filled the air. She recalled the line of Blake, 'what hand or eye framed thy fearful symmetry?'

She saw lights go on in the house, then saw Charlie's flashlight on the walkway.

"Beth," he yelled as the beam found her. He came running up. "What is it?"

Snakes coming around could cause a ruckus, but nothing like this.

What could she say? She had to lie. "I don't know."

"Hey! Moreland!" His approach to the apes was different from hers. She mustn't submit, but he had to go farther, he had to actually dominate. If he didn't, it would only make for problems later.

He shone his light on his own face for added emphasis and glared at Moreland, who grudgingly threw aside the branch he'd been wielding and moved off into the shadows.

As Charlie continued to glare, the others settled. Then he kissed Beth, and that felt good. "Glad you're back," he said. "I missed you like crazy." He laughed. "What're they, pissed off at you?"

Beth kissed him back, a tentative, uneasy peck.

They started over to the house.

"You're limping."

"I stepped on a scorpion."

He gave her a shoulder to lean on, waiting, as was his long-established habit, to see if she was going to explain how that had happened. If she stayed silent, he wouldn't press it. That was not his way.

She wanted to talk about a hell of a lot more than the scorpion, but her agreement contained some very specific and very clear language: 'no activity carried out upon Company's property, or on behalf of Company, shall be disclosed to any person whatsoever without specific permission of Company's representatives.' The penalty was draconian: a fine of a hundred grand, to be imposed after a hearing before the company's internal review board, whose decision would be binding. Among the papers she had signed was a right of unrestricted garnishment. If they decided she'd broken her secrecy agreement, they could simply strip her accounts of every penny in them. If that wasn't enough, they could take her property, whatever they fancied, up to the value of the fine.

They would take the animals, of course. Zoos wouldn't buy them, but labs and carnivals would. Collectively, they were worth in the low sixes.

So all she said was, "I went to the Katy after work. Stupid me."

"And took your shoes off?"

"Like I said, stupid me."

He fell silent.

When they got to the kitchen, she dropped into a chair. "I'm so damn tired," she said.

He took some bean salad and a bottle of Lone Star out of the fridge. "Beer?"

"Yep."

He came around the table and took her up in his arms. She enjoyed male strength as much today as she had that first time down by the swimming hole, in that lost boy's arms. She lay against him, smelling the sour damp of his t-shirt and feeling the scrunch of his beard against her temple. Finally, she pulled away and sat back down. "It hurts more than I thought," she said by way of explanation. She meant the day. He assumed, as she had intended, that she was talking about the scorpion.

"How could it hurt more than you thought?"

"I was ignoring it. Stupid me."

"Stupid me, stupid me," he said mildly. "As we have agreed, you're one of the least stupid people I've ever known."

"Sorry."

"And as we have also agreed, you do not say you're sorry when there's no reason to be." He got a wide pan and put in ice cubes and water. "Too little too late, but maybe it'll help some," he said as she laid her foot in it.

Then he got up and very deliberately sat down across from her. He looked straight into her eyes. "The job's a disaster," he said. It wasn't a question.

She wanted to deny the truth of it, but she could not. What could she say, thoiugh? She heard herself laugh a little, heard the screech of anguish in it, knew that he was hearing it, too. "It's—I don't know how much I can say."

"Beth, this is me."

"I signed an agreement."

"I repeat, this is me and you've got a problem and I know it."

His eyes were as brown as mahogany, his lips straight and firm. He played the guitar and the Jew's harp and he could burn a fiddle to the ground. He could also be trusted and they had always shared everything—except, of course, his Iraq experiences and his criminal activities.

"So okay," she said, "now we both have our little secrets."

Except hers was not exactly little, was it? No, hers was the damn secret of the ages, for real.

Through her tears and almost angrily, she attacked the salad with a fork, then took a long pull on her beer. He got up and moved off into the house. In a moment, she heard a bath running. Oh, thank him, thank him for knowing her better than she did. Hearing the splashing water, she realized that she was literally desperate to sink down into their wonderful old clawfooted tub and close her eyes and make believe that she was returning to the sea and becoming part of the sea.

He reappeared. "Is it cruel?" he asked. There was a directness about Charlie that reminded her of the animals. Animals had plain minds, too.

But not all animals. She considered Joe, his bright eyes flitting up at her, as that cunning, and, she thought, bitter smile of his played across his wide lips.

"Is it cruel?" he asked again.

She wanted to look at him but that was almost as hard as it was for Keller's slaves to look at her.

"I'm here," he said.

She raised her eyes. How very familiar that face was, that long nose, the lips arranged as if by a sculptor, at once inviting and somehow hard. It was the face of a Puritan who was good in bed.

"Beth, is it cruel?"

"I don't know!"

His hand came to her cheek and expertly gathered a tear that she had not realized was there.

"One of the things I love most about you is you can't lie worth a damn. What you got, you got on your sleeve, and you are one miserable madonna right now."

"No sexism, please."

"OK, grrrl. Point taken."

She closed her eyes and put her hands over her face. In memory, Joe's broad forehead gleamed, his emerald eyes flickering here and there, his essentially human nose dilating slightly as she came close. His plump lower lip gave him a genial expression that was probably as deceptive as hell.

She shook away her tears, then got up and hobbled to the kitchen sink. She wiped her face with the threadbare hand towel and drank a glass of their faintly sulfurous water. It was cold, though, an antidote to the thick air of the night.

"Bath's ready," he said.

She went into the bathroom. He followed.

He knelt and helped her with her pants, carefully drawing them past the swollen foot. She stood naked. Still kneeling, he embraced her around the waist, and laid his big head against her belly. A thought appeared, unbidden and out of place of her womb, full—what that would be like. Then it was gone. With the burden of the primate center, they couldn't begin to afford a baby.

She gazed down at him, touching his peppered hair. "Happy times," she said, her voice shaking a little.

Groaning and laughing, he went to his feet. Now her supplicant was tall and full of unconscious mastery. Plain gorgeous, the way he could use his body to express so many different aspects of his complicated inner self, and all of it with hardly a word spoken.

She stepped into the tub. "Oh, God, God, thank you," she said as she sank down into the promise of steeping oblivion.

They were silent. Even if the secret the contract enforced hadn't amounted to much, it would have been between them now.

Finally, she spoke. Whispered. "I love you, Charlie."

He reached down and laid his hand on her forehead. She closed her eyes.

It will not be forever, she thought, this little couple called Charlie and Beth. One of us will slip away from the grasp of life some day, and the other will be stranded in the haunted half of the marriage. But not now. Now, the crack that this secrecy has caused must be carefully tended. It must not be allowed to grow into other parts of their relationship.

He took her face in his hands and kissed her seriously.

She drew back.

"Hey, now," he said, "hey, now."

She gave up all resistance and just sank into his arms.

Off in the night, a chimp cried out, and soon everybody was whooping and shrieking and cackling and roaring.

He pulled away. "The possums are in there again."

They waited, listening. As the upset slowly died away, she said, "The possums have withdrawn."

Late in the night when neither of them was sleeping, he said into the dark, "You're scared."

"No I'm not. I'm not."

"Sure you are."

6

THE DREAM ANGEL

Joe had been dreaming the green dream which he did not like because it made him think of that scary new shatterface and its green clothes.

Everything was all green in the green dream, and it smelled the best. He'd been going in the fluffy green things, and they had felt so good against his skin. When he touched them, it felt like he was really and truly there. For a little while, he kept his eyes closed, but his head was hollering and he knew it would not stop until he did every single thing that it said.

Beside him and halfway draped over him, Betty slept.

Would Keller force him to go back to Flutter? It was wrong but Keller did lots of wrong things. Why? Because he was better. He lived in TV with the other shatterfaces. People were only people. Shatterfaces ruled them. Shatterfaces could use the snickersnee.

He listened to the sleepy sound of Betty snoring, then gently traced the line of her nose with his main finger of his main hand.

Trying hard not to wake her up, he slipped out of their bed. He crossed the room and got the chair and took it to under where the wind was. He set the chair against the wall and climbed on it. By standing on total tiptoe balanced on the arms, he could just manage to stick his nose into the wind.

With his eyes closed until they scrunched, he inhaled long and deep.

Yes! Oh, there it was, that oh so great...what *was* it that smelled like that? What was in TV? Again he sucked air, again, again, again.

He did this every night, inhaling again and yet again, smelling *it* and wondering, and asking himself the question, if the world is out here and TV is in there, and that's everything, then where is the smell from? Maybe TV, but it doesn't smell like TV looks. It doesn't smell like shatterfaces or Mama Mia Whatta Pizza or McDonalds or Oreos or Peter Paul Mounds.

Again he smelled, and there it was, a little stronger this time, the magical, mysterious sweet and open smell that seemed to put its arms around you and whisper to you in song.

He was going to get in TV. And not only that, he was going to go all the way to the end of it and find out everything. He wanted to know everything. How deep was TV? Did it go in all the way, and where was that? Where was Stephen Colbert? Where was basketball, where was Elaine Benes?

Would he get flat if he got into TV? If he didn't, how would he walk around? He'd tried to ask Keller what it was like to get flat when he went back in TV, but Keller said his sign made no sense.

Yeah, right. Keller wasn't about to tell him the secrets of TV.

Joe listened to them in TV, to the words. They talked of many things that Betty and Crunch and the others didn't notice. Like, this guy had once said to Colbert, "What we loved was the river."

What was 'river'?

He wanted a piano. He wanted to play 100 Piano Masterpieces! Not listen, *play*! He came down from smelling and flickered his fingers in the air. 100 Piano Masterpieces was so pretty it made his dick crinkle.

Here was his top ten list: Go in Seinfeld and lick Elaine. Wear glasses with real glass in them, just like a shatterface. Be in the place behind Stephen Colbert with the lights. Have a piano. He also wanted clothes and a gun.

He had to get in TV!

He went out into the hall, across to Jack and Jill's place. He went in and sat on their chair and watched them sleep. He reached down and stroked Jill's hair. In whisper, he talked to them: "Ah wuuuve yew." Then he said, "Ah mm Cho. Cho. Ah mm Cho an I wuve yew." He went close to them and he put his cheek on Jack's cheek. "Cho wuve yew."

He got up and went into Crunch and Flutter's place. He stood beside them and watched them sleep. They had done a pump and fallen asleep still together. He reached down and felt Crunch's balls and made him smile in his sleep. Then he went to the top of the bed and leaned over and first he kissed Flutter on her hair, and then he kissed Crunch on his hair. He smelled Flutter's hair. "Ah smeww yew. Ah wuve yew."

Then he went out into the rec room, which was locked but he had got *that* figured out, sure, so he rattled the door up and down just right and went on in. He could still smell the new shatterface. His dick went wood from her smell. He could still smell Peter Paul Mounds.

Ahead was the barrier, waiting for him, taunting him.

He took a deep breath, smelling the cold metal of it. It had its own special smell, the barrier. On his knees, he approached the door, sliding slowly along, his head down. Mother Angelica on Catholic Channel used to say pray the rosary to get what you want from God. The Holy Version will help you. 'Okay, I got no black rattle beads,' he said in his imaginary perfect talk in his head, 'but Holy Version, please get me in there. I want this. Joe wants to be in there.'

Shatterfaces talked so good. "Opann a dawrr. *Daaawerr.*" He bowed down before the hard, cold metal of it and covered his face with his hands. Holy Version, come on! Hey, hey, somebody is here and wants to be there! Hey, Holy Version!

His heart went to bouncing like a dropped screw on a fast line and his face got all wet and his lips went so far down he grabbed them and pulled at them till it hurt, till it made him gag. He hated his voice, hated it so much, because it would not just say, "Would you please open the door for me, Jim?"

Sometimes they did it with a card that they pointed at it. That was how Jim did it almost always. He would make one. They were silver. He would make one out of a silver can somehow. Only he didn't know how, not yet.

He knelt in front of the barrier and he said, "Ah'm guuud fer teee*veeee*! Let Cho in!"

He hit it and hit it and hit it, and then he clawed at his own throat till it hurt and there was skin under his nails. "Tak *tak* yew durn stoopit stoopit *stoopit*! *TAK!*"

He held his face and gobbled his weeps. Talk was just for shatterfaces, because they were better. Just better, that's all.

He rocked back and forth crying and tearing at his hair, making it hurt really, really bad and doing that on purpose. He wanted to hurt. He wanted Keller to roast his ass with the snickersnee. He grabbed his own balls and crushed them so hard his hands trembled and vomit came up in his throat all hot and sour. He was no good, *no damn good*. He thrust his face against the bottom crack where you could just see into TV. He looked for feet walking. He loved to watch that.

Finally, he drew back and turned around. He stood to his tallest. He listened toward the people. All of them were sleeping quiet.

And then there was a click.

He jumped back. The barrier—it was—oh! Oh, he was scared. He was really scared, he'd—but...how?

The light coming up the crack transfixed him, fascinated him, rooted him where he stood. He wanted to run, but he fought that. No, it was opening and he was *not* gonna run, he was going in TV. He thought, 'thank you Holy Version.'

But can I come back? What happens when I leave the world? Maybe you don't never get to see the people again. He wanted to see Betty right now.

A figure appeared, dark against the blast of light from behind him.

Keller said, "Joe, why aren't you asleep?"

The barrier closed behind Keller. It had just been him coming in, that was all. The Holy Version hadn't listened to Joe at all, but Keller had. Damn that ding-dong dumb Holy Version!

Keller came down to him and put his arm around his shoulder. "Hey, buddy, what's this? You have a fight with Betty over the change? I was afraid you might."

He shook his head no. He'd never tell Keller anything like that, not private business like that.

"Then what is it, buddy? What's the trouble?"

There was no way to sign it. Anyway, Keller would never let him in TV. People did not get in TV, that was the rule.

Keller went into rec and sat on a chair. He patted his lap and Joe went in it. Keller said, "You want special candy?"

Joe signed yes.

"No, Joe. No. Unless you talk. I know you can talk. I was looking in the eye and I saw you and I heard you. You know I can do that."

Joe shook his head.

"Say it, Joe. Say, 'give me the candy.'"

He signed, 'You told me not to talk.'

"You can't, except with me. With me, you can talk and you must talk."

He could smell it, the candy of great reward, Snickers. Beyond too-too good. But he talked like a stupid dumb lump.

"Say it."

"Kwimmecnnn..."

"No, you can say it better than that. I know you can. Now you say it. You talk."

His mouth went down, he looked at his tummy. Keller stroked his hair and that felt pretty good. He leaned his cheek against Keller's front and he said, "gim ee cannee. Cangy Can-*gnee*!"

"That's right!"

"Cangee! Dee. Dee. Can-*dee*."

"Say it!"

"Candy!"

"Say it!"

"Candy! Candy! Dandy candy!"

"That is amazing. That is simply amazing."

Then Joe was eating Snickers and he was very happy and ate almost all of it but then no, he was going to save part for Betty, wake her up.

Keller held him for a long time, so long that he slept. He had a dream, the face dream. The most sweetest face. She had long hair and everything is all green all around her. She is not a shatterface, she is a person and she is like a song singing. Her eyes are green just like his. She takes Joe in her lap, and grooms him and all around them are other people and waaaay tall sticks go all the way up. Great big sticks in the green. And their rooms where they lived, green as green, and inside them, the winking of their fires.

"Rise and shine! Ten minutes before you get on the line!"

Joe blinked his eyes. He was confused. One second ago, he'd been with Keller out in rec. So how'd he end up here in his bed? He sat up...and the angel face dream hit him. It always made him real sad, and he leaned against the wall and didn't want to look at Betty.

She knew, of course. They all had angel face dreams and they made everybody sad.

Then he heard the clink of breakfast bowls and that was the end of that. He raced up with the rest and got his Cheerios and as many bananas and apples as he could carry all at once and his juicy-juice in a box and went to their table. He ate his cereal with his spoon. Betty shoved hers in just like the others did. But you had a spoon and you should use it. He went and asked for the Cheerios box. It was a new box. He sat on the floor with it eating fruit and looking at the shatterface code all over it. Now, he knew the shatterfaces made the code turn into talk. Keller could do it.

Joe signed, "We got us that new line today for sure."

Then he noticed that the others were all clumped up together signing like crazy. What was this? Eyes were going his way, then more signing. Then Betty came out of the clump, and she was not a happy camper. But Flutter was strutting and shaking her hair. Betty was looking down.

Crunch glared at him.

The hell. Dumb bottomsider'd gone nuts. "Line up," the Big Voice said, and they went in a loose line. Joe hurried to the head of it, but Crunch was there already, Flutter behind him.

What was this?

Betty was standing in the very rear, head down. Then Keller said, "Joe, we have a very challenging job in the hole on this line, and I need you down there. You'll learn the ropes a lot quicker than Crunch."

The shock made him stick out his teeth like a dumb-bunny. Go down in the bottom? *Him*? Keller couldn't do that! The shatterfaces didn't get to choose who was bottomsider. That was up to the people.

Keller had to understand this. Joe was boss. He was boss of all the people, he had the glasses. He was number one on the line. If he worked in the hole, then it was all ruined. He went up to him. "Candy," he said, "*candy*!" Not because he wanted any, but to remind him that should be boss because only he could say words right. A word, anyway.

Keller laughed and fluffed his hair. "Not now, buddy. You folks are gonna be late for the line."

There was no way to sign his problem, so all he could do was just shake his head from side to side as big and wide as he could.

Keller laughed harder. Joe felt the inner tightness that meant he was going to cry. The others were all watching him. Crunch's grin was all teeth.

But then Crunch broke out of line and came to him and put his hand on his cheek. Was he going to be nice? Him? He came closer. His eyes looked all soft. Joe lifted his own hand to cover Crunch's. But then that grin came back, Crunch's lips curling and twisting, making him look meaner than ever.

Crunch signed to the others, 'follow me to the line.'

Joe signed, 'follow me, me!' He pointed to himself for emphasis and stepped out.

Alone. Everybody else lined up on Crunch, and Joe ended up running along behind them.

They went down the hall...and Crunch, the dummie, decided to show off his new power by leading them all over the place. Why do this? It made them look like dumb fools and they were *not* dumb, they were okay.

Joe followed along, walking on beds and all kind of dopey stuff, then everybody had to sit on Crunch and Flutter's pot one after the other, *then* they went through the open door to the line.

They stopped. They stared. Joe had never seen so many wires. There were sheets of black stuff, rolls of wire, boxes of colored beads and other supplies unlike any they'd ever had before. There was a smell of heat so strong it made them want to get right out of here. Nobody liked to be burned, no way, and it smelled like it was going to happen more than ever on this line. The new tools were real complicated, too.

Jim Thomas and Harry Lerner and Sam Beach put white caps on everybody, but nobody put a white cap on Joe. He was going to be bottomsider *and* no white cap! Might as well toss his glasses. Now they made him look stupid.

"Come on Joe," Keller said. He went down the damn steps to the dopey bottom. Joe followed, and with every step he took, felt a little worse about himself. He was ruined. He was the dope now.

What if this meant that Crunch also got to take over his room as well as his wife? Crunch couldn't take his room where he had his pictures put up! Nobody else wanted pictures, nobody but him and he wanted them very bad. He had a picture of a piano and a picture of a car and a picture of an animal called Donald Duck that he liked because he talked almost as bad as people, and a picture of Jimmy Dean Sausage.

"Okay, Joe, now that it's just you and me, I want to tell you, this is the ultimate line. After this line, we are going to start demonstrating the team to potential customers, so we need to look really sharp. Do you understand?"

Sharp? What was to sharpen? He nodded eagerly. He would not let a shatterface know he didn't understand something, not unless he had absolutely no choice.

"What you're making are printed circuit boards and down here is the test station. They are extremely complex, for use in artificial intelligence applications. Too intricate for human assembly, so you guys have to learn to be as efficient as robots. And you can be. More so. And to be able to change assembly patterns quickly and easily. That's where your value lies, and you want to be valuable, don't you?"

Peter Paul Mounds were valuable. Snickers were more valuable. What was he talking about? Joe filed this new mystery away, to be puzzled out later.

"Vaubuh!" he shouted.

Keller grinned at him. "That's the spirit, Joe!" He held up a square thing that wasn't a cracker but looked like one that had gotten tangled up in wires. "These will drop into this rack here. You take them and plug them in, and they'll come up on this scream. Do you understand?" He pushed the board into the end of a socket, and a whole bunch of green lines showed up on the scream. "You see that?"

Joe nodded.

"Now look—see how that one glows red? That's a non-testing circuit. You take the mouse. You know what a mouse is?" He had a plastic egg. Joe looked around but saw no mice. So okay, Keller called a plastic egg a mouse. That was okay for just a shatterface, he supposed.

"You roll this around on the pad. You see the arrow on the screen?"

Joe nodded.

"You put the arrow on the red line, and then you make it go click. Here, touch it, make it go click. See what happens?"

The red line on the scream started blinking. Then it turned green.

"It's re-etching the bad connection." He pulled the board out.

"Then you just put it back on the tester. When all the lights are green, you stick it in the exit trough and it goes out the door."

He rubbed his hand in Joe's hair. "This is special. You're the only one I can trust with this."

Then he went up out of the hole and upstairs all the gibble-gabble of Jim and Mark showing the topsiders how everything worked soon stopped.

There was a loud buzz and a clank of machinery and the new line began to speed along. About a second later a board came down. The new bottomsider, mouth down, eyes stung with tears, took it and did just exactly what he had been told to do.

7

DEAR SUMATRA

In the deep, late hours, screaming burst out. Beth flailed. The apes—there was something wrong.

No, it wasn't screaming, it was buzzing. Just the alarm clock buzzing. Damn. It felt like she'd only been asleep for a few minutes. Probably true, too.

She clicked the alarm off, then rolled over and pulled the pillow down on her head. Dark. Warm. Stay here forever.

Nope.

She sat up, hit the floor with her feet."Ow!"

That scorpion had definitely left some of its poison behind. Refusing to acknowledge the fact that she appeared in the bathroom mirror to be a corpse, she spread toothpaste on her brush and started in. Then she hobbled to the shower. Maybe the steam would melt the bags under her eyes....or just melt her altogether. Nice thought, melting. Problem is, though, then you go down the drain.

Hell, as an employee of Barrett Scientific, she was already there. First steady job she'd ever had, poor little rich girl. Formerly rich. As mommy said, "You fed your money to the apes."

Yesmommy!

Since melting was obviously out, she let her mind drift a little bit more toward reality. All night, she'd been trying to understand what the hell she was facing with these creatures. Four and a half to five feet tall, soft faces that contained more of a shadow of the human than ape, but were neither. Scared of her but using their sweet smiles to try to charm her. They were good at being charming. Or, put another way, they were good at concealing themselves.

Fear. For them? Yes. Of them? Yes again.

She had gone through the ridiculously cluttered closets of her mind to inventory every known hominid species going back three million years and had come up only with *Homo floresiensis*. That had to be it...somehow. But what in the world were they doing here, and in a containment like that? It was all very odd, and no wonder Greg Keller and Robert Barrett were so obsessed with secrecy.

By the time she was drying herself, she'd pretty well returned to life. As she dressed, she heard Charlie in the kitchen. Toward dawn, he had made love to her, sweet, slow love.

My man. Mine.

He was not lovely just now, though, the guy in pajama pants who was standing over the stove scrambling eggs.

"Why, thank you," she said as he slid a plate under her nose and poured a piping hot mug of coffee for her. Their usual pattern was that he made breakfast on weekends, she did it during the week...or they just ate cereal. Or nothing. That was on the menu about half the time.

She ate mechanically. What were the creatures doing now? What would it be like to see them again?

"Hello?"

She looked up at him in surprise. "I'm sorry, did you say something?"

"You were on Planet Barrett Scientific. I've been doing due diligence on them. Too squeaky clean.

"Charlie, please."

"Sorry."

She returned to her food and her thoughts...the burning, awful thoughts that had made her night a sweating, miserable hell.

Apparently they were confined all the time. But they needed the outdoors, the sky and grass and trees. She thought that they also needed knowledge. Although she hadn't evaluated their intelligence yet—and she wasn't even too sure how to go about that—she had the sense that they were hungry for both experience and information.

"Hello!"

He was staring straight at her from two feet away. "Don't startle me!"

"Boy, are you off in never-never land."

"No. No, I'm sorry."

He laughed a little. "More coffee?"

She shook her head, got up. "I gotta move." Barrett started at eight thirty. They had been very clear about that. Pointed, even. Judging from the way they did things, she'd probably be docked for every minute she was late. Two hundred thousand dollars was—what—a buck and a quarter a minute.

She was limping to her car when Charlie suddenly burst out of the kitchen, letting the door slam behind him. He came up to her and whirled her around. "Beth, tell me what the hell's going on!"

"Charlie, you know—"

"I know you came home really strung. And you're even more strung now. Something's making you crazy and I wanna know what it is, goddamn it!"

"Not crazy. Crazyish."

He grabbed her arm, hard. "What is it?"

She looked down at his hand. He snatched it away, a little boy caught shaking a kitten.

She left him standing there. Could this thing be eating at him more even than it was eating at her? Well, yeah. He had sensed that something was very wrong and he knew it had to do with primates or she wouldn't be involved.

Would he be trouble?

Yes.

Would that put him in danger?

Barrett was doing something very ugly so yeah, they could be assumed to be dangerous.

This was a commercial enterprise, and it was about enslaving these very smart creatures. Three breeding pairs. How long was their gestation? From the size, probably about six months, and they would reach sexual maturity in around eleven years. So, do the math. In fifty years, mankind could possess a race of slaves. They'd still be pretty rare, of course, so, although they might be in a few exotic, ultra-high tech industrial settings, most of them were going to belong to the very wealthy, spending their lives as servants and, frankly, living toys.

The west had shed blood to purge itself of the parasitic, corrupting practice of slavery. But it could come back, and many, many people would welcome it—especially this new, guilt-free version. 'They're just animals, right?'

Make it happen, woman!

The Stewart Elementary school bus turned into the spreading dawn ahead, behind it a line of cars. Along here there were condos where people lived who, like all their neighbors, were uneasy about the Center. Not as bad as the Gardens, where they hated it. But still, the area was all so lovely in its way, the spire of the Methodist Church that stood on the corner just touched with morning light, cars driving through the Starbucks, a squadron of teens on hoverboards gliding toward the nearby high school, two women pushing strollers, all of them part of the great peace of place that is one of the core achievements of modern civilization—as long as nobody pulls a gun, of course.

She turned onto the rural road that led to the campus. In half an hour she was passing the Katy. Going to be hard to do this every day, being reminded of so much happiness on those hallowed acres. There was little traffic to negotiate, and she proceeded to arrive at the campus an hour early.

When she'd last come here, full of innocent curiosity, there had been a sort of ominous romance connected with the featureless, gleaming darkness of the structure. No more. Now it looked to her like what it was, a prison.

There was space in the parking lot for fifty cars, but yesterday afternoon there had been only six. Now there were three, and a Sysco food service truck pulled up to the building's cargo bay. As she crossed the tarmac, she heard the scrape of machinery. Supplies were being offloaded, which reminded her that she needed to take a careful look at the diet. She needed to do blood workups, but what comparatives would be appropriate? She'd have no idea if their cholesterol levels were high or low, if their nutrient profile was optimal, if their blood counts were normal—none of it. She needed a doctor on staff, but he'd have the same problem. There was no baseline.

A doctor or maybe a vet. A vet would know many different adaptations, many different sorts of dietary and health needs. A vet might be ahead of a doctor on this one.

Charlie was a vet, but he must never, ever be allowed to know what was happening here. Charlie would die for these creatures. No question. If giving up his own life would free them, he wouldn't hesitate.

As she entered the building and crossed the lobby, the security guard watched her with his wary, impassive eyes.

"I belong here," she said. How very lame it sounded.

"You do," he responded. "Go on through."

She dodged around the desk and went down the long hallway toward her office. She was off to the right, but straight ahead was the control room, within it the metal door that led to the enclosure.

Should she go in? On her own?

No, not yet. She didn't want to end up in there alone with…them.

She went into the control room. Nobody sat in any of the chairs before the various monitors. There was no sound save the hissing of the air conditioning vents. She began to fool around with the camera joysticks, looking for the creatures.

"Good morning, Beth."

She almost screamed, Keller had come up to her so quietly and was standing so close.

"I'm sorry," he said, stepping forward and extending a hand. "I didn't mean to startle you." When this dour, intent man smiled, there was a transformation so intense that it shocked. The smile was that of a little boy with the best toy of his life, which, given what she knew of what he actually possessed, made it all the more disturbing.

"We need to discuss your duties," he said. He spoke as softly as he might to a scared child. Then he smiled again, the pinched face once again transforming into a study in contrived warmth. "I'm very excited about this, you know," he said. Then the smile dropped away and his face resumed its former peering intensity.

During the moment of that smile, something else had appeared behind his eyes—a hint, she thought, of fear. She realized with surprise, that Keller was scared. But of what? Surely not her.

"Well, I am, too. Very excited about this. Follow me."

They entered a large office, lavishly furnished with a broad mahogany desk and an array of monitors. To their right, a fireplace awaited only the need for a fire. Somewhere down the halls of time, maybe. South Texas winters did not generally require fires.

"Like your office?" he asked.

"It's fine."

"Fireplaces in the offices, no less," he said. Now emptied of their artificial warmth, Keller's eyes had taken on the appearance of frosted glass. He burst out laughing so suddenly that he startled her again, which made him laugh all the more. "In *Texas*," he chortled.

"Excuse me?"

"A fireplace! As a perk! My God, they curse us even with their blessings." Lightning flickered in the eyes, then, and she had the hopeful thought that he might hate his employers and what they were doing. Maybe he, also, had been trapped by a secrecy agreement.

He leaned forward, his little hands grappling with the air. "We're losing touch with them. We don't know what they're thinking. We can't read their sign."

She was stunned.

"They've added to it, slanged it up—and you see how fast they run it. You slo-mo it on video, you can understand maybe every tenth word. The fact is, we've lost it."

This was absurd. You couldn't 'lose' something like a system of sign language. "Well," she said, "we have to find it if I'm gonna get anywhere with them."

"You find it, lady." He reddened and his voice rose to a hoarse, barely contained shout. "Job one!"

Coming from a quiet, formal household, she had never become comfortable with all the yelling and shouting that seemed to go on nowadays.

He seemed to realize his mistake. "You find me unpleasant."

"No, just noisy."

"You cannot imagine the corporate pressure. The company needs a revenue stream from us."

"How will that work?"

"The revenue stream?"

She nodded. She wanted to hear it from him. Make it official.

"There are all kinds of ways to make money with a brilliant animal, my dear. High-technology factories, such as the lines they're been training on for the past year. Outer space—they're light, thus economical to put into orbit. Mechanical repairs in confined spaces like airplane wings, because they are small and dexterous. Applications beyond our present imagination."

"Servants? Toys, perhaps?"

He shrugged. "Expensive toys."

She struggled to communicate an enthusiasm she certainly did not feel. "Hey, no unions to worry about, no salaries."

"Low upkeep is a factor, of course. They reproduce themselves, providing their own replacements. Potentially. These are all significant factors."

It was hard for her to believe that he was being so open about this monstrosity of a plan, much less that he didn't see how revolting it would be to anybody with the slightest sense of ethics.

"What if they don't want to?"

"Want to what?"

"If they don't want to comply. What then?"

He did not respond.

"Do we really have a definition of what a human being is? The spark?"

"They are not legally human."

"What makes us human is intelligence. Theirs needs to be measured."

"I take your point. But there's a more subtle thing, Beth. It's a matter of personality, even of inner being, if you will. I refer to the way they simply *are*. And they are not people."

"Do they pass the mirror test?"

"I don't know what you're talking about."

"The mirror test of self-awareness. Do they recognize themselves in a mirror?"

"Like chimps do, but they aren't considered human."

"Only because their information is too limited. Did you know, at the St. Louis World's Fair in 1904, they kept African pygmies in the same cage with baboons, on the theory that small, black men who smelled strange couldn't possibly be people. Because, you see, the physical and cultural differences were so great that the idea that they might be human simply never occurred to anybody. They must have suffered terribly."

"We've already got a standards and practices manual. No sales without a legal guarantee of a certain level of humane treatment."

"So you do regard them as human?"

"Of course not. As I said."

"Then the use of the word 'humane' was figurative?"

He slid open the mahogany cabinet that covered the wall opposite the window. "Your observation post." As in the control room, there was an array of screens, each one showing a different area of the facility. "These joysticks move the cameras. You can't talk to them. They only hear what we've named the Big Voice. So if you've got anything to say to them let me know what it is, and I'll take care of it." He took the joystick of one of the cameras and focused it on the assembly line. "Look at them," he said.

She was so surprised that she gasped loudly enough to make him chuckle. "Amazing, right?"

"Yes!"

The line was going so fast you could hardly see the components flashing past under their flying hands. Heavy metal rock thundered and the creatures danced while they worked on complex circuit boards. They looked like a dwarf dance troupe bebopping in unison on a stage-set assembly line, and doing it at blinding speed. These creatures would put any robot to shame. Given that they were brilliant at assembly, what else might they be capable of? Engineering? Design? Art? Philosophy? Becoming a companion species on the long, long journey toward truth?

"They understand symbols very well," he said. "We use something we call the Tanda keyboard."

"Tanda?"

"As in Orang Tanda. Means shadow people in the local dialect. That's what we've been calling them."

The keyboard was full of intricate symbols. It would take her hours to learn it.

"How bright are they, did you say?"

"Under evaluation."

"When using the board, you'll have to watch carefully. They can be very subtle. They can lie."

"Are they as bright as we are?"

"I don't know of any form of measurement that would be reliably comparative."

"Because of their confinement and lack of information? Or because you just would prefer they not be that bright?"

"Follow me, please." He led her out of the control room and down the hallway to another office, a bleak inner chamber. It was unused, except for a stack of large, square objects that she recognized as the most intricate primate communication keyboards she had ever seen. A normal board might contain 200 symbols. But there were hundreds here, and the symbols were smaller, too, reflecting a fact that had become very apparent: these creatures could use their long, thin fingers with the greatest skill. He should add sewing and tailoring to the list of potential occupations. But they seemed destined for higher-end sweatshops than that.

"These are very complex."

"Our animals have a lot more to say than apes."

Keyboard communication had started with a chimpanzee named Lana, who had been taught to use a computer keyboard with symbols on it. Some studies suggested that this proved that apes were capable of abstract thought, but that was not at all clear as far as Beth was concerned.

"It's time for your first session."

"Session? What sort of session?"

"*Mano a mano*, with one of the animals. Come on."

He left the room.

Good God. No way was she ready for this. She hurried along behind him, her mind casting about like a ferret in a cage.

"You'll meet Joe. He's the one who attempted to vocalize in English last night."

"Wait a minute."

He half-turned, an eyebrow raised, then continued walking.

"Dr. Keller!"

He stopped, his body hunched. He did not turn to face her.

"Jesus Christ, Doctor, you don't do science like this. Give me some time to get into this."

"Time is something I don't have, Doctor."

"Yesterday afternoon I saw the strangest creatures I have ever seen in my life. Strange beyond my imagining. You must realize the impact of that."

"It was a shock, I'm sure."

"I'm certainly not going one-on-one with one of them, or even continuing to work here for that matter, without knowing precisely what I'm dealing with."

For a moment, he stared at her. Still evaluating, still unsure. There followed a brief shake of the head, but one that communicated eloquently that she was disappointing him. "Come to my office, then."

She hadn't seen it before. Her interviews had been conducted on the other side of the security barrier. Her office was lovely, but this room was sumptuous. The desk was an a fine antique. In fact, everything was antique. There was what appeared to be a Cezanne over the huge fireplace. Was it real? Almost as if posing, he stood before the fireplace, under the Cezanne.

"How can I help?"

"I want to know the science behind these creatures. I want to know their species, their origin, everything."

"They are refugees."

She tried to think what that might mean. "From where?"

"The island of Sumatra."

She waited. Obviously, they were not gibbons or Orangs.

"We were going to do this later, but I can show you now if you prefer."

He went to his desk, threw open a small door cut into the side of it and pressed a button. Silently, a big screen TV slid down out of the ceiling. He turned off the lights, then went loping from window to window dropping the blinds. "Sit," he said. "Enjoy. Learn."

First, a snazzy logo. Barrett Scientific. Very blue, very slick. Then a shot of a jungle taken from a plane. Immense sea of treetops. Twenty or so miles away, a volcano rose into the sky.

"*Kerenici seblat*," he said. "Do you know it?"

She shook her head.

"A park in Sumatra. Enormous...but terribly endangered."

The video image changed, abruptly losing its professional gloss. Now the footage was blurred and full of flashes. Somebody was carrying the camera through the deep jungle, moving fast.

"Have you ever heard, then, of the Orang Tanda?"

"Of course. The shadow dweller. It's a cryptid. Who's that woman who tracked it back in the nineties? Wasn't her name Maya Belen?"

"You're well informed."

"That's why you hired me. But the Orang Tanda isn't—" She

stopped. An awful thought crossed her mind. But no, that was cryptozoology. In other words, nonsense.

"You didn't finish your sentence. You were going to say, 'isn't real.'"

"Maya Belen made her best case. No hard evidence."

"You have no idea what really happened. Few do."

Then they were watching an enormous tree being felled. Her heart screamed with the screaming of the huge saws. "Do we have to watch this?"

"Prepare yourself."

A shadow moved past the camera, so close that it seemed more like a defect in the lens or a whipping mass of leaves. But then the image froze.

"We have done computer enhancement."

A shimmering wave crossed the screen and the image became more clear. Another wave, and it was in fairly good focus, visible now as the head of a speeding animal of some sort. The face was a concentrated blur of intensity. The hair flying out behind the head gave it a curiously human—and very familiar—appearance.

She knew. She knew it all, instantly. The Orang Tanda were quite real, but not an ape, not at all. She was looking at the same thing that was down on that assembly line right now—a hominid, but not us, not *homo sapiens sapiens*.

"Flores man?" she asked.

He chuckled a little. "You needn't whisper. This isn't a church."

"It feels like one right now."

"Possibly a variant of *homo floresienesis*, but their bone structures are different from the fossils we have. I have named them *ultima apis*."

"The final ape. Clever PR. What if they're the first man instead?"

He sighed. "They are animals."

"Maybe the only real difference is that we lost our forest before they did and had to farm and therefore we're more experienced. For all we know, they've been intelligent longer than we have. Maybe lots longer. They could even have had civilization in the deep past, then returned to the jungle."

"There's no sign of that."

"There are all sorts of odd ruins in the Pacific. There are pyramids in Indonesia."

"Pyramids are human constructions."

"What about *Nan Madol* in the Carolinas? Nobody knows what sort of construction that is."

"How is that relevant?"

"Seven hundred and fifty thousand tons of two and three ton basalt logs laid across twenty-three artificial islands. Structures so strange that they may well be the product of nonhuman thinking."

"It wasn't them."

"You don't know that."

"There's an innocence to them—I don't know how to put it in words."

"Yeah, it's always hard to concretize fantasies. You should free these creatures."

"It'd kill them."

"Not if it was properly handled. As I'm sure you know."

He flushed but did not raise his voice. "The company has spent millions. I have an obligation to meet. And I have to tell you that what's wrong here is your approach. Not that I didn't expect it, at least initially. But you're going to realize that you're wrong. They are not human, as you will discover when you screw up your courage enough to really get to know them."

"If you're so sure they can't handle freedom in our civilization, put them back in the jungle."

As if cued by her words, the tree fell in the video, crashing toward the camera, causing whoever was using it to go racing madly back and out of danger. Limbs thrashed, the camera shuddered.

"What jungle?" Keller asked dryly.

There came then another image, this of an Orang Tanda on the ground. It was a mature animal, old. It's gray hair was matted with black blood that was still flowing. It's rich, complex face was not quite still. One eye was destroyed, the other open and staring. The lips—wider than ours, just as sensitive—were moving slightly.

"She had three children, all babies," Keller said. "We found them that afternoon. Crunch, Jill, Betty. In her womb was Flutter. Joe and Jack were found abandoned a few days later. Apparently their family had been shot by loggers who feared that the forest would be protected if the Tanda were discovered."

"She didn't look pregnant," Beth said faintly.

"Their anatomy conceals a pregnancy until the last two months or so. Look at Betty. You wouldn't know she was pregnant."

"She is?"

"She hasn't menstruated for eight weeks, so yes."

Beth's mind started speeding so fast it felt as if she was losing control. She kept her mouth firmly shut because if she opened it, she thought she would have hysterics. Real, garden-variety screaming hysterics. Not because of the horror, not only that. It was the oil and water mixture of great evil and great wonder that was making her crazy.

"They're human beings," she insisted, trying not to allow her voice to quake with her thundering heart.

"You must accept that this is not true, my dear."

"Don't you patronize me!"

"Then don't patronize me, either, with your holier-than-thou pontificating—from pure ignorance, I might add. I have studied this matter thoroughly. These creatures come from the Island of Sumatra, where there is a long tradition about them. The Orang Tanda is farther from us than the chimpanzee, genetically." He paused. "It was the challenge of being forced onto the *veldt* when our jungle dried up that forced us to become intelligent. But in Sumatra the jungle did not die, not until logging started. In Sumatra, the Orang Tanda have continued to live as we lived in the jungle, and have not developed our level of intelligence."

"Tanda," she said, tasting the word. "Tanda..."

"Orang Tanda. What they're called back in the jungle."

He came close to her. She wanted to back away, but his presence was hypnotic.

"I have given them a home, a chance to find their place in our world, if they possibly can. Their jungle is now tables and office paneling and automobile dashboards."

"There are other jungles."

"Stop that. It's not a path for you, and certainly not for them. My creatures have been raised in a controlled environment, which is the only place they know. Put them in a jungle and they wouldn't last any longer than you would. And these—these six—it is my firm belief that they are the only ones left."

"But you don't know."

"It's an educated guess."

"Why couldn't you have raised them in a jungle habitat, eventually freed them."

"Are you so doctrinaire that you'd rather be right even if they die? If so, I'm a fool for choosing you and I chastise myself." He flushed and his voice rose. "Or is it just stupidity?"

"I am not stupid, and I've told you not to yell at me."

"Then I repeat, very calmly and quietly, they have no natural habitat left. Get that through your head."

"Then educate them!"

"I'm doing that!"

"I'm not going to work with somebody who screams."

"My heart has been screaming since the day I gathered up those Tanda babies and carried them out of the woods. I was shot at! Did I tell you? Shot at, my possessions stolen, even the bush plane fired upon!"

"I'm sure it was very hard."

"Very hard indeed. You speak of educating them. What do you propose? Perhaps American culture? Or is that too oxymoronic?"

"Thank you."

"Oh, no, thank you. But please do think. Try to. I am educating them now. I am creating a situation in which they will have economic value and therefore their population will grow into thousands, then tens of thousands, then more. And then—*then,* my dear—they will demand whatever level of freedom they can handle. They will find their way."

"How noble of you."

He shrugged. "Indeed. I am trying to save them from extinction. If you will let me."

"I'm just an employee with zip seniority."

"And a great deal of nerve. Listen to me. Mankind is an extinction event, a force of nature. Do you know that the species of the earth are dying out right now even more quickly than the dinosaurs did after the comet that struck Yucatan sixty-five million years ago?"

"I do know that."

"The Tanda are victims—our victims, in fact. If we do not want this truly remarkable creature to perish and be lost forever, then we must do it this way. Trust me, I am quite correct in every detail." He went to his desk and sat down. "I have to work. You see Joe. See what you think. You can help them, Beth. You can and you must."

"I will not see Joe today."

"You know already that I don't have time for delays, which means that the Tanda don't either."

"I need to go about this in a careful, methodical manner. As a primatologist, you want me to learn their social structures, assess their intelligence, finally to intervene in their culture in such a way that they'll become comfortable enough to breed. Wearing my biology hat, I assume you want me to learn enough about their bodies to make determinations about their health. We will need a vet who will need a biological baseline, and I've got to develop that, obviously."

"Yes, all of that."

"That's quite a lot on my plate, and I can't be urgent about it or I won't get it done right."

"Then please look at another tape. It's short." He pushed the remote control.

The screen turned blue and a long list of titles appeared. Video clips, dozens of them. He scrolled down to a particular clip. "November the twentieth of last year. Flutter and Jill. Prepare yourself."

The two females were lounging around watching TV, the old HBO program "Oz," a series set entirely inside a prison.

"Why Oz?"

"We like intense drama. Good versus evil. We also like lots of talk in our shows. Love to listen to talk."

"But we're not allowed to see outdoor scenes, are we?"

"Very astute of you. We have never seen the outdoors, not since we were picked up. We don't know that it exists."

"You never take them on excursions? Have they ever been in nature at all?"

"When we enter them into the world, it will be very slowly and carefully. No shocks. We don't have any idea how their minds work. We need to be very conservative there."

In the video, Flutter and Jill were now playing with one another in a rundown room with plain gray walls and a narrow bed with no coverlet. There was a stuffed toy gorilla on the floor. Games and other toys were strewn around.

"Where is this?"

"Jack and Jill's bedroom. Jack is off with Joe and the other two. They are playing cards."

"Oh, come on."

"We play Go Fish, Crazy Eights, Old Maid, even Hearts. We love Old Maid. And we enjoy board games, too. Perquacky, Checkers, Clue."

"Chess?"

"We like to laugh. Chess is not a laughing game."

Her attention was taken by what she was seeing on the screen—this was most certainly not part of any kind of primate or human behavior that she'd ever observed before.

Flutter had Jill laid face-up across her lap, and she was slamming into her belly with her closed fists. The blows made Jill screech, and Beth jumped with every tortured cry. She wanted to throw her arms around both of the creatures.

Though she screamed, Jill remained completely passive, allowing the beating. Soon the pain was making her vomit bile.

"Stop it," Beth whispered.

Keller did not move.

"Stop it!"

"This is three months into a pregnancy."

"Gestation?"

"Unclear. We've never had one come to term."

Beth's muscles tightened, her gut heaved—she could almost feel the blows, which went on and on, as the anguished, squalling voices of the two beings filled the luxurious office.

Then Jill went limp, her arms flung back over her head. Flutter changed her approach, spreading Jill's legs, then reaching into her vagina. That brought Jill back to consciousness, and she uttered a throat-ripping howl that Beth thought was more filled with agony than any sound she had ever heard, even than the wail of a chimpanzee mama whose baby has been stolen by raiders.

Flutter had a bloody mass in her hands, which she took into the bathroom. The toilet flushed. She returned, her hands and forearms still bloody, and took Jill's head in her hands and began stroking her cheeks.

"That, my friend, was an abortion."

"I know what it was! But you didn't intervene! You just—"

"We missed it! I've told you it's hard to detect their pregnancies. We've been suffering cutbacks for two years. We're understaffed and we missed it."

"What about Betty?"

He smiled thinly. "It could happen any day. It's up to you."

She had to go to animal rights organizations, she had to go to the state, the feds, anybody who would listen. She had to get these poor creatures some surcease from the horror that was life under Keller.

"I don't know if I can help them," she said carefully. "I may need to consult other specialties."

"What specialties?"

"Well, veterinary medicine, to start, as I've said."

Her plan as of right now was to get out of this hellhole, get in her car, go home and start a campaign to rescue the Tanda.

"I have tried to communicate my problem to you. There isn't time for all these tests. We have a contract to meet. A deadline, if you will."

"I—"

"Don't you give me that holy damn look! They are my love, the love of my life, and I will tell you, I took every blow that struck Jill. I felt her agony, screamed her screams in my heart."

Angry at herself for even feeling it, she rejected the impulse to comfort him. "What treatment did she receive?"

"There was severe hemorrhage, but we believe we saved the womb."

Not the woman, the womb. "Good," she replied. "We wouldn't want to lose a valuable womb."

"No, we would not. If we fulfill an order we have from General System Services, we will keep the whole program going. It calls for a breeding couple in good condition. That we can provide. But the female must be pregnant, and we do not receive full payment until the baby comes to term."

"So," she said, "let's see if I understand your problem."

"*Our* problem. Remember that you work here."

"Our problem is for me to make them content enough in the hell you have created for them to make them want to bring babies into it."

He picked up a small porcelain figure from a table beside his chair. "My father was an air force *attache* in Germany. The day before the bombing, he mailed this to us."

"The bombing?"

"Dresden. He was killed at Dresden."

"Your father?"

"A pilot. Hungarian Air Force. I never really knew him. I was two when he died. But what do you think of a man whose sensibilities were such that he would choose to mail this particular object from Dresden during the worst, most monstrous year of the war?"

It was a gentleman in a tricorn hat and powdered wig. He was bowing, the hat gallantly raised.

"Your father had some human sensitivity."

He stared away from her. "My mother was hanged during the

Hungarian uprising. Hanged by Russian tankmen from telephone pole in 1957. I was six. Before they hauled her up, she pleaded with them to hide my eyes. They forced me to watch."

He put the statue down. "Will you do this?"

"I signed a contract."

"They are the most extraordinary thing that exists. My Tanda are the wonder of the world." He made a small sound in his throat. "Is it not so?"

"I'm very methodical. It's my nature. I want to see everything I can, read all the records. Then I'll start. I will go as fast as I reasonably can."

"Barrett Scientific is not the enormous company that it appears. We have—oh, God—I don't want to think how much money is at stake."

"I have to do my best for the Tanda, not for the money men. That's my final position."

"Give me your best guess. Should I worry that they will never breed?"

She spoke as gently as she could. "Instinct is telling them that something is wrong with the way they live, even if you've prevented them from understanding what it is. They sense their confinement and are living in a state of tremendous stress, just as people do when they are crowded into negative, artificial environments like concentration camps."

There was a silence, then. It extended. She watched him. She saw defeat, she saw the inner fire of the fanatic, and the love of an arrogant man for his possessions.

"Help us," he said.

8

THE LAND OF OZ

Joe's mouth was down real far and he couldn't get it up because he just plain felt so sad. His head was hanging too, because he didn't want to look at anybody. Plus he kept getting tears all over the ding-dong circuit boards and when he did the red light wouldn't go out.

Then the big voice goes "Pepsi Cola time!" The dumb stupid shatterface sounded so happy. Joe went up out of the hole right away but they were already marching off toward rec without him. He had to run to catch up...just like he used to make Crunch do. Maybe he should have been nicer to Crunch.

He went to his and Betty's table. But Betty was at Crunch's table. So he signed to her, 'hey, come on over.'

She did not sign back.

A whole lot of fire blasted up from inside him. This fire made him mad in his head. They were each other's. Keller hadn't been able to change that, but him getting put in the hole sure had.

Crunch's lips were curled up his face. He was about to start whooping. Joe leaped all the way across his table and across Crunch's table and *right in his face*. He bunched up his fingers and hit and hit and hit and Crunch took the blows one, two, three, his head flipping side to side, his lips flopping, spit coming out. Harder Joe hit, harder and harder. Crunch squealed, then screamed.

Then somebody was pulling his hair and hauling his head back and making huge hurts go through him because they were yanking real hard, *real* hard oh that *HURTS*! He twisted back and it was Jack and Betty and Flutter and Jill, all of them were on him. Their eyes were shiny like ball bearings. That must mean that they had hated him all along. They had followed him because they were scared not to, that was all, but inside of them there was nothing but this mean against him.

He squalled out his sorrow and his anger and his surprise, squalled and struggled as they all got him down together and then Crunch was sitting on him and smashing his face with his closed fists and where were his glasses now? He couldn't move his arms or his legs, so he just had to take the smashes even though they made flashes in his eyes and hurt his nose and his lips and kept coming, hard, hard—and then he knew they were killing him. They were killing Joe just like they killed guys on Oz. Then the dead guys got dragged away, it was over for them.

This was Oz, they were playing Oz but it was real, they were killing him and did that mean like in TV when you are dragged away and not in the show anymore? Then somebody was kicking him, and Crunch was still hitting and hitting and he was twisting and squirming and now he was on his side, he was getting his arm free—and he had hair in his hand. With all his strength, he pulled. He heard Betty shriek and he knew it was his *wife* and that made him—

Hurt her! Hurt her hard as you can! He *yanked* and *yanked*, then Crunch had his shoulders and was slamming his head against the ground—pow, pow, *cr-rr-ack*—and he was seeing things dopey and the rec got far away and then real far away.

There was this woman with these eyes, the woman who lived in the green. She held him and cuddled him like Keller, and it was scary. Scary good.

She said, "Joe, why did you fight?"

He realized that he was in the shot room. He was on the hard bed where shatterfaces stuck you. One thing shot room meant—when it was all over there was a Snickers for you, a great big one all for you! That was pretty good. You had to hurt for it, though. Jill said she hurt in here a whole lot before they gave it to her. She was in shot room for a whole lot of shifts, just a *whole* lot. That was after Flutter took the spider out of her.

Then he remembered that he hurt and a great woe overcame him. Slow tears squeezed from his eyes.

"Joe," she said, "tell me why."

Now what the heck did *that* mean. Why anything? What was was. It was stupid shatterface don't make no sense talk. Slowly and carefully so she would understand, he signed, 'I want to go in TV forever.'

"On television, did you say?"

He nodded.

"How do you think you would go about doing that?"

This dumbhead shatterface couldn't even talk *their* ding-dong talk. One of these days he was gonna just plain hit one of these things and knock its big, fat head off like in Oz where they *hit* and they *cut* and they *shot*. But he couldn't shoot 'cause no gun. He could cut. He could make a knife outa something. He could make a knife and cut 'em all. He could cut them all!

"Any particular program you like, Joe?"

She smelled like shatterface goop. She had lips that looked like apple skin. Her hair was fluffy. Her eyes were even darker than Keller's.

'Take me in TV. I want to go to—' There was no sign for 'Oz,' not that a shatterface would understand.

"Go to?"

No sign. No way to tell her.

"Can you tell me what happened?"

He just wanted in TV. He had to leave the world. The people didn't want Joe anymore. Somebody else would have to be the bottomsider, somebody they liked at least a little bit.

She got up and went to the desk. She went behind it. That was shatterface country, back there. Go back there, you got popped with the snickersnee.

"We're not understanding each other, Joe."

She brought out the old signboard from when they were kids. Okay, he would go with that. Slow way to talk, though, slower even than shatterface sign.

She pointed to a symbol for tree. Okay. "Tree," she said, "what is that?"

Stupid shatterface, it's a symbol on the dongdiddy *board*! He tapped it twice. It's itself. What was she asking? This shatterface gotta be a real dope.

She pointed, pointed again. "What is this thing?"

Oh, okay, here was one who signed like a baby, which they all did, but this one could not even talk the board. He tapped the symbol three times sharply and gave her a 'back off' look, hard stare, right on her black shatterface holes.

He expected to suffer for that. Take a real burn inside his head. But no, he...sort of saw. He sort of saw! He SORT OF SAW! A shatter-face without forever holes for eyes. A shatterface that did not shatter you!

And also, under all that goop she smelled like a woman. He wanted to have a looksee at her, but not while she was behind that desk, no. You get with Keller when he's back there, you are going to get the snickersnee send a spark on you *eeee-YOWTCH*! This one, she might do it even harder, all he knew.

She was signing again—How—you—feel?

What a dumb question. He pointed to 'bad'

Why bad?

'People. No. Me.'

"The people are not you? You don't consider yourself a person?"

Oh boy. He tried again. 'People no sugar me.'

"Candy? You don't like candy?"

He went to pure American Sign, putting his thumb and forefinger together, then drawing them out of his chest, as if from his heart.

"The others don't like you?"

Finally! He nodded hard. He used the symbols: 'go' and 'TV' Then he pointed to himself as hard as he could, grinning and nodding.

She laughed. "You can't be a TV star. Anyway, that'll just make them jealous. Do you know what 'jealous' is?"

"Oooooo boiiii! Boiii, tupid! Toooo*pid*!"

"You're talking, Joe. Dr. Keller said you could."

"Esssss. Aah tak. Aah wan enn tee-ee! Enn tee-*eeee*!" He sounded so bad he just threw back his head and screamed.

"Hey, slow down, I understood you! You want your own TV. OK, not a big deal. I'll make it happen. A nice big TV just for you!"

He went down in front of her and he bowed his head and he begged. "Mee *enn* tee-vee. Preeze preeze o preeze!"

She came down and held his face, drawing it up. "You had a fight, Joe and you're mad and you feel just awful. But being a TV star won't help. It's just going to make the others more mad at you."

She did not make sense and he wanted her to make sense, he needed her to! What was this "star" word? And "big TV" when TV was little. Did she expect him to believe there was big TV somewhere? He sure hadn't ever seen it.

"You can't be a TV star. We need to find another solution."

Pitching away from her, he hid his face in his hands and let out a scream he hoped would shake the whole place down forever. Again he screamed, and fire got in his heart, and again, louder, and fire got in his face and hands and arms—and he wanted to *tear* her and *hit* her hard as he could and just break her dinggity dongity shatterface off her fat bone head!

"Joe!"

He came at her snarling.

'Use the cattle prod,' Keller had said, 'do not hesitate.'

She had been disgusted with the very idea. But she needed it now, because this furious little creature was just about to tear into her. The thing was, what did he want? It seemed as if wanted to be a TV star and he was ready to kill her if she didn't make him one. But how could that be true? She was misunderstanding him and making him furious was what was happening here. She went to the locker where the cattle prod was kept.

"Back off, Joe!"

He came closer. His hands were tight fists. The intensity of the sorrow and the rage twisting through his face was incredible.

She opened the locker. "Joe, I don't want to use this." She took it out.

He launched himself—and she thrust the prod at him. It snapped as he struck it full with his chest. The blow threw her against the wall behind the desk. He ended up sprawled on the floor, writhing and holding his chest, gobbling back his agonized groans.

The stench of singed hair mingled with the stink of sweaty fear. His eyes were fixed on the end of the prod. "Cho soee soee so—rrr—ee," he gabbled.

"Calm now?"

He sat up on the floor and nodded.

She came down to him, stopped him from cringing away from her, then took his shoulder and lifted him to his feet. She put her arms around him.

His arms came up, and came around her also, and they held each other, bridging with deceptive ease the gulf between their different natures and different hearts.

"Joe," she said. "Joe, Joey." His head was against her chest now, and she laid her hand against it. "Joey. I'll call you that, just between us. It's a special, friendly version of your name. Joey."

Once again he met her eyes, then immediately looked away.

"I'm sorry, Joey, I had no choice. You must know that."

Slowly and carefully, he signed, 'OK." He raised his eyebrows and nodded hopefully. He pointed behind the desk.

"OK, sure. Come. But slowly. No jumping."

She watched as he sidled along, head nodding, waiting after each step, once again trying to come behind the desk. His eyes flickered toward the cattle prod.

"I won't use it unless I'm attacked. I promise." She held it behind her back.

He reached the narrow space behind the desk and instantly his fingers danced toward the desk drawers. He slid the top drawer open. Then he stared toward the cattle prod.

"It's okay," she said. She took it out from behind her back. "I won't use it."

The moment she touched it he raced back to the middle of the room, then knelt and bowed.

She was embarrassed. "Joey, come on back. You can look through the drawers. It's ok."

He shook his head.

"Here, I'll put it away." She went to the locker and put it in, then closed it with an exaggerated crash of metal. "See. It's gone. Come back and get what you want."

Slowly, he returned. His fingers scrabbled quickly through the drawer, pushing aside pencils, a calendar with a picture of a car on it, a box of paperclips.

He was looking for something quite specific, that was very clear. She let him open the other drawers, go through the stacks of papers, the various office supplies. He was extremely fast and extremely thorough, his long fingers dancing.

When she tried to stop him, he made a sound—"*nuuuunnnhh!*" that cause d her to move away from him. His search grew furious—and as suddenly ended. Last drawer.

His face, when it was again raised to hers, shocked her so much that she must have gasped, because he recoiled, instantly looking away. The eyes—they had been terrible, glaring with menace. He was absolutely furious about something. But what? What did he want? It wasn't candy. He had pushed aside the Snickers bars that were kept as a special treat for patients.

She was struggling in the quicksand of incomprehension. What had happened among them this morning, for example? The explosive fight had taken her and Keller and Jim Thomas and Sam Beach to quell. They'd used the cattle prod and it had been awful to see the poor creatures cringe away from it. But it had seemed clear that they were killing Joe, who had been their leader up until then. Keller himself was in a state of shock. He'd been in here hovering while Sam diagnosed Joe's wounds. Another few minutes, and Joe would have been dead.

Gently, she steered the insistent fingers away from her purse. He flared at her, trying to push past her. But why? What did he want? She decided to give him a little more leeway. She dropped her hand away.

Immediately, the fingers came back. He was aggressive now, whining in his throat and trembling. He was clearly still on the edge of violence. He plunged a hand deep into the purse, the quick fingers rustling.

"Joe, stop!" She put a lot of command in her voice, which rang out. She was good at this, she'd learned it working with apes.

He went still, his head down. His arm muscles were tight, his fingers clutching the purse.

"What do you want, Joey?"

"Tee nee! Peeze!"

"There's no TV in there, Joey."

"Go in tee nee!"

Actually, it was kind of a clever solution, when she thought about it. He gets humiliated, so he wants to attain a position of unassailable prominence by appearing on television. Probably more than a few politicians and movie stars operated from the same motive.

"Nothing in my purse can help you do that."

In response, he plunged his hand deep. He came out with her keycard and at once she understood.

This poor creature—this man—knew that he was a prisoner. "Joey," she said gently, "that's mine."

He held it away from her, his lips pulled back, his eyes bulging.

And then she knew. Joe didn't want to become a TV star at all. To him, their television set was a window into the outside world. The poor guy wanted to run away.

"Oh, Joe," she said. She held out her open hand. He glared at it, his whole body trembling. His fingers clutched the keycard so tightly that his hand shook like a leaf.

Her heart went out to him. He was too uninformed about reality to know how alone he and his kind really were, and how hopeless was his quest—and that was probably just as well.

"Give it back, Joe."

He took another step away from her.

As much as she agreed in principle that they should be allowed their freedom, she definitely did not want one of them getting out of the enclosure on his own. No, they had to be introduced to the outside world in careful stages. Keller had been a fool to isolate them like this, but as matters stood, they would certainly be unable to cope if they were introduced to the real world too quickly.

She took a step toward him and he took one back.

"Joe, that is not yours. Give it to me now."

Tears welled up in the poor guy's eyes. But he only held it more tightly.

"Oh, Joe..."

He shook his head hard, his hair flying. He held the key behind his back. He snorted and gasped, trying to fight his tears. Watching him suffer like this was excruciating, but she could not stop it and she dared not let him get out of this room with that keycard. She had no doubt that he knew how to use it.

They had to have richer lives, more room, above all more food for their starving minds. No matter how hard the company might try, it could not create what it wanted: smart workers who were ignorant, imprisoned, compliant and contented enough to breed. The Tanda didn't know how to express it, but they were like prisoners everywhere—they wanted out.

She stood before him with an open hand. As much as she hated to, she said, "You have to give it to me and you have to do it now."

He stared defiantly back at her from the mystery of his mind, and his *otherness* struck her once again. Reluctantly, she went to the locker. "Now, I don't want to have to take that thing out."

He didn't move.

She withdrew the cattle prod. Inside herself, she felt only disgust. But what else would work? This was all he knew.

He began shaking, his lips crinkling away from his neat, square teeth. The human face was wonderfully complex, but if anything, the Tanda's was more so. In terms of expressiveness, these creatures were alone on earth.

She pulled the prod's trigger and it snapped loudly. "Put the card in my hand."

His mouth drooped. But he did it. Clearly, he was giving up the most precious thing he had ever possessed. She put it in her purse, put the purse in a drawer, and locked the drawer. In fact, she locked them all.

He threw himself down on the floor, and the poor guy bawled. She waited a moment, then went to him. He waved her away. She put her hand out. He slapped it away—did it hard. If she persisted, she knew that his grief would turn once again to rage. As much as she hated the cattle prod, she picked it up again.

Finally, he came to his feet. His hands reached out...and she put the prod on the desk and took them both. They stood like that, the jailer and the prisoner. He was pulling himself together, his mind visibly striving to master his tortured heart. Joe would try again to make the life he had work for him.

"Do you know the word 'fight?'

He nodded, signed, 'I fight.'

"You fought Crunch."

Big nod.

"Why?"

He thrust his face at her and inhaled, his nostrils dilating, his almost-human lips pursing. In his eyes there was an eager sort of a gleam. Again the nostrils dilated, and the head came closer. Then his hand rose. It came up slowly, moving with oddly feminine grace. The elegantly tapered fingers extended.

What was he doing now? She watched, waited.

To her astonishment, the hand glided over and touched her cheek, caressing the line of her jaw with the sensual expertise of a practiced lover. His movement was so fluid and swift that she had no time even to blink, let alone turn away. She felt the cool of his skin, the delicate dryness of his pale fingertips as they slid along her throat.

He released his breath slowly, a warm breeze.

There was an immediate tightening deep in her belly, the same tightening that came to her when Charlie's hand slid along her thigh. She shifted, and Joe's eyes grew slow and careful. His lips, moving subtly, seemed to suggest that they might like to follow his fingers with a kiss.

It should not have surprised her as much as it did. But he had moved from being a sinister, violent little clown to this new state so quickly that she was caught entirely off guard. His presence did not feel like that of any animal any more. This was a man, and he had changed tactics. He was now trying to seduce her.

She spoke in what sounded to her like the awkwardly prim tone of an uneasy girl. "Was it a fight about love?"

He signed quickly, obviously irritated. She did not understand the flutter of fingers.

"Answer on the keyboard."

He jabbed at the symbols me and man. Then 'you' and a question mark. Meaning, "I'm a man, what are you?"

She said, "I think you know perfectly well that I'm a woman."

His lips now spread back from his teeth and his smile became huge. She smiled back, laughing a little, still not quite believing that he had decided to attempt to win her compliance this way. As she watched, amazed and fascinated, his smile subsided into a smoldering, sidelong stare.

She found herself moved and deeply so. This guy, with so little on his side, was trying everything he could think of.

"Do you want me to be your woman?"

He went to his full height, hands on hips. Then his eyes shifted... and he took his work apron from the peg where she had hung it. He held it, but did not put it on.

The way he was looking at her—it was sexual, inviting and frank. But those eyes—they were so gentle. Joe was obviously a volcano of emotion, but he was as certainly a sweet, warm guy.

He strode to the table and jammed his fingers at symbols. You. Pretty. I. Alone. He touched the last symbol again: Alone.

She asked a question on the board: You. Sad.

Yes. Sad. Alone.

Now he gave her a soft, big eyed glance that just begged for a cuddle. But if she did that—if she were to hug him now—it would be an unmistakable message of assent. The fact that he would still fail to obtain the keycard would leave him humiliated and full of self-doubt.

He pointed to symbols, using a flowery kind of gesture, as if there was some kind of poetry intended: You. Rose. Me. Stick. Dance. Us.

Dear God, he meant 'You're the rose, I'm the thorn. Shall we dance?'

Laughing a little, she shook her head.

He put his hand to his face, hiding one eye, and looked at her. The communication was utterly clear: I've embarrassed myself.

"Oh, no," she said, "Joey, you're charming."

He cocked his head. 'Charming' had lost him. Not surprising, in the cheerless and sterile environment of the enclosure. She looked down at the keyboard. How to communicate this? Not really an available option. Like Yerkish, the symbol language was object oriented.

She decided to try again with American Sign. She signed 'you', then lifted her hand up her chest in the sign for 'happy,' and put a question into her smile. "You happy again?"

Everything changed. He seemed to sink into himself. Obviously, he was far from happy. "Peeze," he said in his low, whispery voice. He held out his hand, thumb to fingers. "Peeze me go."

"You want to get out?"

He frowned, obviously confused. Why hadn't he understood that? There was a deep confusion here between television and the outside world?

He pleaded with his eyes, scrabbled his hands at her.

"Joey, not now. One day, yes. But not today."

"*PEEZE*!"

She could see his muscles tightening again. The air still stank of burned hair from the last time she'd used the prod. She said, "We're finished for today, Joey."

He pitched back and slammed himself against the wall. He shook his head wildly.

"Joe, you have to go back. Go back to your people. We won't let them hurt you." She went to him, took his hand, and guided him firmly to the door. He ran out and threw himself against the exit to the enclosure, which was just at the end of this hall. He smashed into it, kicking it and slapping it so hard that the walls trembled.

Then he turned around. His eyes were blazing. They glared at her with such venom that she backed away a step, ready to close the door if he charged. But the darling little man with the great big eyes and the mile-wide smile went right past her, striding off down the hall in a state of helpless, white-hot rage.

9

TUNNEL OF LOVE

This time on the commute home Beth wasn't troubled by tears. Driving beneath the endless streetlights that lined the expressway, she was struggling to contain fury. Joe's was a voice raised from the mystery of a really complex nonhuman mind, the first such ever encountered by man. But it was also a voice crying out in the universal language of the oppressed. Joe had only poetry to pit against prison. His only route to escape was charm. "You're the rose, I'm the thorn. Shall we dance?" The poor man's abnegation—his abject state—embarrassed her. It also hurt her to the point of being an actual, choking pain.

She pounded the steering wheel, she threw her head back and howled. At once she stifled it, afraid she'd have a wreck from not watching the road. Nothing must go wrong now, no, absolutely not. Never in her life had she been more needed.

The Tandas' vision of reality was a cruel distortion, brought about by Keller's ugly, self-justified act of concealing the truth. Without access to the richness of life, this wonderful mind was an absurd mockery of itself.

Of course they aborted their fetuses. Although they couldn't articulate it, they were just plain miserable. They had no choice but to make the best of what they had, but their spirit was crying out.

She arrived home in such a confusion of anguish and fury that she could hardly remember the drive. She parked and went up the gravel walk to the kitchen door. She paused and collected herself. Charlie mustn't see her like this, no.

She opened the door and walked into the warm light and the pungent deliciousness of his spaghetti sauce. She burst into tears.

He came to her, a wooden stirring spoon in his hand, his apron smeared with tomato paste, and took her in his arms. For a few moments, she tried to choke back her anguish. But he was just so comfortable and so familiar and she needed him so bad.

Off in the living room, a droning voice on the History Channel recounted a story about a man who had tried to escape from the Lubyanka Prison in Moscow. She did not want to hear a story about a prison, but she also didn't want to go in the living room and turn it off or ask Charlie to or move or talk. The spot where she was right now was like a bomb shelter, the bomb shelter of her husband's arms. If she moved, if she so much as uttered a word, she knew that she was going to tell him everything, which she absolutely must not do. He'd go after the Tanda and those bastards over there would shoot him dead.

"You want some spaghetti?"

She nodded. He brought it with a side salad covered in store-bought croutons, not the wonderful, crisp ones she had learned how to make from her family cook, Mrs. Bettner. Beth and Charlie cooked together. Tonight, her part of the meal would be missing...and that started her crying again.

Oh, dear God, he was going to have to know. Because she had to do a thing that was going to get her into a whole world of trouble, but was the most important thing she had ever done.

"Charlie?"

He put his hands out across the red and white check of the oilcloth that covered the table. His face was gentled by concern, his eyes wide, his expression serious. Her pain mattered greatly to him, a fact which only made it hurt more.

"They're brilliant," she said. The two words hung in the silence. Charlie waited for more. She dropped the bomb: "They're a species of hominid. I think they're probably as intelligent as we are. Or more."

And there it was on the table between them, the bomb.

He made a small sound, as if somebody had struck him a mean little blow in the gut.

"You don't believe me?"

"You know the simian brain better than I do. You can't make an ape as intelligent as a man. You haven't got enough cerebral cortex, for one thing."

"Charlie, they aren't apes. They're from Sumatra. A species of hominid."

"As in Java Man?"

"As in Orang Tanda. Possibly *homo floresienesis.* Related, certainly. The tallest of them is five feet. They have humanoid feet and hands. They have different eye colors from us, emerald green, pink. Their teeth are essentially like ours. Their bodies are hairless, pigmented toward gray, probably a camouflage adaptation. They have long hair hanging down from the backs of their heads. It's soft and flowing, and ranges in color from Joe's dark brown to Jill's russet."

"Russet hair?"

"Red brown with rose-pink eyes. She's amazing looking. They all are. There are six of them."

"I'm getting a picture."

"Which is about one tenth of the reality."

"I wouldn't be surprised."

"Until you've seen somebody like Joe with glowing emerald-green eyes and that incredible, complicated, sweet face—"

"Like some sort of advanced ape?"

"Get past the whole ape assumption. This is in no way an ape. Imagine a person with real broad cheeks and lips that are amazingly expressive, and skin that crinkles around their eyes when they smile.

Oh, Charlie, when they smile it's like light coming down from heaven! But when they get sad, the mouth turns down and they hang their heads and that hair falls down around their faces and I swear to God, you've just gotta cry. You have to. Because their faces—their faces are more powerful than ours. And that *hair*—they're bald until about midway on the scalp, then it just sweeps back in a long, flowing mane."

Silence from him. His eyes were far away. "My God," he said softly.

"I'm told that they're not breeding-capable with us. They're farther away than chimpanzees. I suspect a lot farther."

He took the bottle of wine and drank out of it. "Shit," he said.

She didn't quite understand. "They threaten you?"

He nodded. "Sure they do."

"Why?"

"You need to ask that?"

"Yeah, I do."

"An alien creature among us. A different mind." He laughed a little. "A competitor." His smile was rigid and there had been a high, hard edge in his voice when he spoke. A little panic back in there. Scared. She did not want Charlie to be scared, she wanted him to be wise. Needed it.

"Charlie, do you want to know why I'm so upset?"

"Because you just got displaced by a better critter?"

"Stop it! Just stop it!"

At once, the old softness returned to his face. "I'm sorry. It's just... it's a shock."

Beth decided that she had to shock him more. She had to engage that compassion of his, to challenge what was best in him so he would give her the help she needed.

"Charlie, the reason that I have been hired is to solve a behavioral problem. Rather than carrying their babies to term, instinct causes them to abort themselves. Of course it does, because it's telling them that they're prisoners. But unless they breed, they cannot be sold. So that's what I'm supposed to do—get them making babies so breeding pairs can be sold to industry to form the nucleus of a race of slaves. That is why I have been hired."

He came around the table and drew her up into his arms and held her again, this time with a surging strength, and she let herself melt into it and was glad.

"We gotta get 'em outa there," he said.

She pulled back from him. "No! Oh, no. I need you as a sounding board, to let off steam, Charlie. You cannot pop that lab. Absolutely not. Don't even think about it. Nobody could get in there. It's beyond penetrating."

"No it's not."

"You haven't seen it."

"You don't know anything about security systems. There'll be a way in and a way out. Trust me."

"It's alarmed, there are guards with guns, every door in the place has a lock and the guy that runs it is a complete fanatic. So no, don't even think about it."

"We have to get them out."

"That's not why I told you! You'll go to jail or get shot"

"Murder? I don't think so."

"This is Texas and you'd be on their property. They will kill you and get away with it."

"We have to try."

"I told you because I need your strength."

"You told me because you want them out of there."

"I told you because you're my husband and this is obviously illegal so the confidentiality agreement is null and void, and I need your moral support. Moral!"

"We've got to bring the community in and get shit rolling."

He meant the activist community, people who would do anything, take any chance, who will give their lives if they had to, for a suffering animal. Their commitment was magnificent, but they were not careful and they were not skilled.

"This is not about your crazies! Leave them out of it. I need to take legal steps and what I need from you is emotional support."

"I read your contract. You agreed to forfeit all your possessions as surety if you take legal action against the company. Your possessions include our apes. First legal step you take, Barrett comes in and hauls them away."

"Barrett is violating the law, so the contract is not binding."

"What law are they violating?"

"False imprisonment! Slavery!"

"Now you sound like me and my crazies. The facility is clean, isn't it? Safe?"

She was silent.

"There's no law being violated, Beth."

"These creatures are intelligent. They cannot be enslaved."

"I think 'creatures' is the operative word here. They are creatures being kept in clean surroundings, well fed and treated with care."

"The Endangered Species Act protects them."

"Does it?"

As they were unknown, she realized that they wouldn't be on any endangered list. "Shit!"

He sat down across from her. "Eat your spaghetti. I worked hard boiling that."

"I'm not hungry."

"Beth, I got the skills to do this."

"You have the skills to try and fail."

I went in a lotta hard places, as you know."

"I have no idea what you did in Iraq. You haven't ever said a word about it. As you know. So I do not know what sort of skills you have. But I do know that Barrett Scientific is a heavily defended fortress."

"I can penetrate anything. Fort Knox, piece of cake."

"You were eighteen in Iraq, old man."

"You go the legal route, they will move the Tanda offshore. They're gonna chew you up and spit *us* out. They'll take the shelter and sell our animals back into the lab system. And the ones they can't sell will get the needle."

"The courts—"

"The courts don't give a damn about animals! Jesus Christ, woman, read the decisions! Nuke the whales is where they're at. So get your head out of your ass. And don't sign any more contracts. Jesus H." He shook his head. "I knew I was right." He thought for a moment, then shook it again. "Ah, shit!"

"If I hadn't signed it we wouldn't know the Tanda existed."

"You can be remarkably stubborn. Maybe I'll go in armed."

"Who's calling who stubborn? You need to get past the soldier in you and help me *think*."

He gazed away. "I know what I am and what I'm capable of, and I hate it. But I can also use it for good."

"They have guns, lots of guns. They have alarms. Lots of alarms."

"Did you know you can kill a man with your thumb inside of five seconds?"

"Oh, God, Charlie, we gotta save them!"

He hugged her again. She let him again. She lifted her face and he kissed her.

She thought to herself, 'he's a little bit like Joe, sweet and violent both.' "You're amazing," she whispered.

"Nah. Just screwed up."

From outside, she heard a soft *hoo-hoo*. Moreland was aware of the fight, and he wanted some reassurance. "We upset him," she said.

"Yeah, mean old me."

"Charlie, you're a wonderful human being."

"There's some hungry ghosts think different."

His nightmare companions, she knew them well. "I'm mistress of your ghosts." She pecked him on the nose. "I tell them what they may do and what they may not. Hurting you and making you suffer for doing something you could not help is a 'may not.'"

"Baby, thank you for hooking up with me."

Hand in hand, they went down to the cages. She leaned up against Moreland's bars. He snorted, but got close anyway. This time, he was more accepting of the scent of the Tanda. Animals are good at getting used to what they can't change.

In the late night, she knew, she and Charlie would make love. In the late night, the miracle of their love would wipe away all the discord, and carry them forth on the swelling tide of life, forward into whatever awaited them.

She was absolutely terrified.

10

IN TV

Joe lay with his face pressed against the barrier, sucking in the mysterious and wonderful air of TV, smelling and wondering and smelling more. He also looked at shadows along the floor outside, something he loved to do, especially when somebody was out there, which was true now. A shatterface was right there, just a little ways away and they were *in TV*. It smelled like Harry Lerner. But he'd smelled Harry lots. Harry was like Keller, part of TV that came in and watched the people every so often. Why TV would want to watch the ding dong people when it could watch itself he could not imagine. But that was probably why nobody like Colbert or Elaine Benes ever came in. People didn't matter to them. They were in TV!

Joe closed his eyes and sucked air as hard as he could, and *yes*—he smelled the other smell, the wonderful one, the mystery smell, which was the smell of TV itself. Down the hall behind him, he could hear Stephen Colbert, so he knew that the smell, so fresh and free, was Stephen Colbert himself.

He ran down the hall to see Harry Lerner and Stephen in TV together since their smells were together, but Stephen was talking to a woman shatterface who gleamed like floor polish. They talked and moved their heads around like always. They smiled the strange, faded smiles of the shatterface at each other.

The people in the TV window could not be smelled, only the ones on the other side of the barrier. Why this would be was a mystery, but it was a true thing and so he had to accept it. Last night the only smell under the door had been Harry as usual, but there was a rumble on Oz, so there were obviously a lot of shatterfaces out there who you couldn't smell. Joe had run back and forth between the TV window and the barrier door. He had figured out that the warden's office in Oz was the first place you got to on the other side of the barrier. But then they had showed the warden's office and Harry wasn't in it.

TV was a mystery, that was for sure.

Not wanting to be with the others, he finally quit running back and forth and stayed at the barrier. He lay down and resumed sniffing under the crack and watching shadows on the gleaming floor.

The others didn't want him, then fine, he would stay away from them. He had stayed down in the hole for lunch, quietly practicing his talking. He had stayed down there for the other breaks, too. All he could think of now was learning to talk as good as a shatterface and going out into TV. Then the Big Voice said suppertime. As always, it sounded happy. The Big Voice was always happy. It didn't care how people felt. Why should it, it was in TV, so of course the ding dong thing was happy!

At supper he had moved his table so he could eat looking at the wall instead of at the people. He had thrown Betty's chair all the way over there so hard it went *whaammmm* and the whole damnit thing split all up. She had showed him her teeth and gotten another chair. Joe had put apple brown betty and hamburger on his plate. He liked hamburger a lot.

Once again, he stood up from the crack. He went over the whole situation. If only that new shatterface had given him her key card. He knew just where it went, you slid it right through there. He licked the spot, sticking his tongue into the crack as far down as he could. Not a ding-dong thing happened, of course.

Why could shatterfaces go in and out of TV anytime and people couldn't? That was just so hard to figure out. Was it because people couldn't talk? Or was it because shatterfaces were ugly and seeing how good people looked made them sad? Maybe TV was even smaller than the world. Maybe it just looked big. Maybe there was no room in it for people.

He slouched along the hall, past the shot room where that stupid dumb kinda okay shatterface gobble-gobble talker had hit him with the snickersnee. What a stinkin' stupid shatterface punish meanie it was. And look at it, it *smiles* and says, "You saaaaad, Joe?" Oh no, you damn ding dong dip, my mouth is down 'cause I'm sooo happy!

He had tried hard to get her to let him in. He had really, really tried but she just played mean games with her key card and she *would not* let him in. The shatterface thinks you are not as good as it is. Why would it ever think that, though? The dumb stupid pieces of junk aren't even ding-dong *people*.

Then it wants to call him 'Joey 'cause he can't talk no good and that's how he says it if he wants to or not. Joey. He spat. *Joey*! He spat again, spat as hard as he could, spat right at the barrier and the green dress shatterface and the whole of TV that he could *not be in*!

Like always when it got late, his eyes grew heavy. He wasn't like Betty who could stay up playing cards or whatever. Once supper was over, he had to fight to stay awake.

He went down the hall and slipped into his room where he had his pretty pictures up.

He would look at his pictures but he would take down the one Sam took of all of them in the Olaroid and he would chew it and chew it and then spit it on the floor. He would *spit* that damn thing. He was going to look at his picture of the piano. Some day, he was gonna play 100 Piano Masterpieces just like those hands in TV did. Those were shatterface hands, they were dick-colored. People were beautiful colored, soft and deep. Betty was so pretty, her skin like pale light. Shatterfaces looked like they had been painted.

Thinking about her made his dick stir. He wanted ask her to be nice again. To *pleeze*. So he went in their room, but it wasn't just her there. Crunch and Flutter were there, too. Then he saw that his pictures were not there. He pointed at the wall and signed "Where?"

Crunch shrugged like that didn't matter. Then Joe saw some white bits on the floor near the bed. Bits of a picture, looked like.

He lifted the mattress and there they all were, torn to bits.

"AAAAOOOOooooeeeee" and again like that and again like that, and Betty was scared but Crunch, he was *smiiiling*. He danced on Joe's bed, a-one, a-two, a-hump an jump an hop that big lump bump! Big lump stupid head!

Joe wanted bad to give Crunch an all forever Oz hit that would make him lie down always. Except Betty and Flutter would hit him and Jack and Jill would come in and they would all hit him. Then he would be the one to lie down always.

He signed to Betty, 'why?'

She signed back, 'fun.'

It was fun to tear up his pictures? 'I liked them.'

Crunch signed, 'You're a Costanza No Hair!'

Joe got so mad he heard crazy things in his head, things like, 'tear his face off,' 'break him up.' But there was more in his head this time. They were all people together, all in this world they did not like, all together. He did not throw himself at Crunch. Instead, he looked to Betty. He forced himself to sign, 'I am sad.'

She signed, 'Good, then I am happy.'

He went toward Flutter, but she backed away from him. 'Not me,' she signed, 'don't look at me!' She stomped her foot and went behind Crunch.

So Crunch would have two and he would have none. They would stay in his room. He went off to Crunch's room where there were no pictures. But then Crunch hollered real loud and Jack and Jill came and they all bunched around Joe, and they would not let him in any room. He didn't get *any* room!

Betty seemed a little sad for him, when she saw how he looked with his mouth down and slumped like he was. She signed 'Go up to rec.'

He shook his head. He had been good to them. He had held them tight when they had green dreams and were sad. He had made them laugh. You see, he had this shatterface face he made where his lips got crinkly and narrow so it looked like they were shatterface lips, then he got his eyes real big and scary so they were like shatterface eyes, and he goes, 'Peer Paaawww Maaaoonz! Peer Pawwww M*aaaaaa*oounz!'

So he makes his lips crinkly and his eyes great big and he goes 'Peer Paaawww Maaounz!' Except Jack does not hold his chest and rock back and forth laughing, and Flutter does not hit herself in the top of the head and laugh, and Betty stays still, and Crunch glares right into his eyes. 'Peer Paaaawww Maaounz,' he repeats with his tight lips and wild shatterface eyes.

Silence. Why if something was funny yesterday was it not funny today?

Then Crunch, he gets *his* mouth all crinkly and little and makes his eyes sort of big but it does not look very funny. Then he goes, 'Paawmzz. Pawmzz.'

Betty throws herself back and throws her arms up and falls back on the bed going *eeee eeee* with her eyes scrunched closed. Flutter does it just the same on the little corner of the bed she can have, *eeeee eeee*. The others all do it, falling down, grabbing their chests, laughing and laughing.

Joe did the only thing he could think of to do. He ran. He just ran all the way down the hall and into rec and around and around in rec, and he got Crunch's chair this time and he held it over his head and he ran up and down yelling, *rraaahhhh, rrrraaaaaahhh*, trying to make the most terrible sound he could ever make and then he threw that chair all the way up and across the room, and it hit the top of the wall and *bang* it came down—and so did this other thing.

Joe looked at the thing, lying there on the floor. What might it be? When he looked to see where it had come from, he saw that it was the air hole. Air was kept in cages all over the world. Every room had one in it, maybe two. Rec had three of the little air windows with bars in them.

Joe was so amazed that he completely and immediately stopped being upset. He was amazed because he had never realized there was a tunnel back where air sneaked out between its bars. He jumped up on the counter where they passed across food and went tiptoe so he could see in there. It was way away long and dark. Kind of made his hair crawl along his neck. Made him look real hard all around. Made him not want to look in there. Except...what if it went to TV?

He got his chair and Jack's chair and put them up on top of each other. It was easy to climb, he didn't even think about it, it was slickity easy. With his head just at the bottom edge of the tunnel, he stopped. He took a deep breath.

Oh! Oh! TV! But so dark and making that *aoooooo* noise that never ended, like it was sad somehow.

Real quick, he looked. *Realquick* he came down.

That tunnel went *waaay* away. He stared up at it. If he could turn his head to the side and push himself along, he could go in there. He could find out what was in there. If the smell of TV was in there, maybe—but no, TV was behind the barrier and in the TV window, not in some tunnel.

It smelled awful much like TV, though.

Again, he went up on the chairs. Closing his eyes so tight that he saw spish-spash sparks, he raised his head. With the air going *aaaoooo* all around his ears and blowing his face and even his hair behind him, he opened his eyes wide.

Dark! Wow! But he could go in, yes he could. Oh, yes...

He put his head in. The air added a *ssseeee* to its *aaaooooo*. Was it hissing at him? Was it mad at him?

Air lived at the end of the tunnel. That had to be true. He knew that air started in TV because of the way it came in under the barrier, so if he could get to the end of the tunnel, he would be at the beginning of air, and therefore also at TV.

He drew himself up and pushed his head and shoulders inside. He was in the smells of TV entirely now. His breathing was TV air only. It had never been like this in his life. He could *not smell the people*! The inside of his chest went uppa puppa uppa puppa and he wanted to wet. He wanted to wet real bad but you gotta do that in the pot, you're gonna get the snickersnee on your bottom yowtch! He pushed and pushed and went farther and farther along. Then in front of his face there was light.

He gasped and drew back. Then he peeked ahead. The light was coming in through some of the bars. He slid closer and looked down. And there was Harry Lerner down there. That place he was sitting in, it was *not*, no way no SIR, it was *not in the world*. There were a whole bunch of TVs in front of him, and on them Joe could see the world. He could see—the *people*! Sleeping, except Jack, who was in his room...trying to unscrunch Joe's torn up pictures. And there was Betty trying, too. He couldn't see rec. Harry Lerner was staring at a screen with some weird stuff on it, stuff like dreams, green dreams.

He was looking in at some show with blue in it and green in it and things kind of smoothing along in the blue. *That* had never been in TV, not back in the world. Joe would never have forgotten TV that looked like that.

So, where was this place if it was not in the world and not in TV... and the world was part of its TV? Answer, ding-dong dummy: there is bigger TV that you don't know nothing about, and Harry Lerner is looking in it right now.

So this was TV for the other side of the barrier, big TV, secret TV, shatterfaces only TV.

His discovery excited him but also made him sadder even than he already was. There was a whole huge TV that people weren't allowed to see! His insides were wanting to cry so bad that he couldn't stand it almost.

But also, there was this TV that Harry was in. This TV he could see, it was right down there. He peered through the bars. Touched them. Pushed a little.

They seemed strong, except the ones in the world had fallen off, hadn't they?

These were tight. What had made the others fall off was hitting them with a chair and you couldn't get a chair in here, right, dummy?

He looked down with hungry eyes, devouring every part of it, striving to see more of the mystery TV that Harry was looking at.

Blue, green, everything so pretty! So maybe it was farther along the tunnel. He squirmed ahead.

The tunnel didn't end, though. It went on off in another direction, so far that you couldn't see an end. The thing was, should he go? Would he go in Colbert or Seinfeld, or would he go somewhere like the green of the green dream? And if he went, would he ever be able to come back?

He stopped. He thought, 'do I want to go back?' No!

Except...how do you eat in TV? What if only shatterfaces can eat there. Do you ever see people or is it all shatterfaces?

If it was all shatterfaces, then he would be sad. He had never once seen a person in TV. There were dogs and cats in TV, but not people.

He wanted to go in TV. 'Course he did. But—

He bared his teeth and groaned. His throat twisted until it felt like he'd swallowed wire. He was scared, he was ding-dong *very scared*!

He sobbed. He wanted go but—

Shatterface food that maybe nobody would give him. No people. Dogs and cats. And what else, who knew *what else*?

It would have been maybe OK if he had the people with him. That would be OK. But this was not OK, not just him alone, no.

Damn them for making him feel so bad! They didn't want him and he was scared to go in TV alone and that was the truth of Joe, the little nobody who didn't deserve topside and sure didn't deserve glasses or pictures or anything special at all.

Moving his body, twisting, he began to turn around. It was tight. Real tight. He raised his arms, lowered his head, pulled, pushed—and he couldn't. He couldn't turn around! A knife went through him, cold and terrible, a knife of fear that he was stuck. He wriggled, he twisted, he tried to bring his knees up, tried to put his arms down. A shudder passed through him, and with it a burst of need. He had to get out of here.

Sweat came all over him. His breathing got fast. Where was he, in some awful part of TV or between the world and TV? Why couldn't he move anymore? Was it a trap? There were such things. There were traps in Oz.

Yes, he must be in Oz, or on his way there. You couldn't leave Oz. Except if he could just back up, maybe it would be OK. Another surge of panic made him want to yell, but if he did, he thought sure they would take him out of TV and close up the tunnel forever, and he would be nothing but bottomsider forever again. Because if this tunnel led to Oz, the others had to lead to places like Seinfeld, Colbert, Piano Masterpieces. And maybe if he was nice and stopped fighting, he would get the people to come with him. Yes, that was it, tomorrow maybe the people would come. That idea made him feel a little better.

He definitely couldn't turn around, so he went forward again. He pushed hard, then *really* hard! It hurt his sides, it hurt his arms, but his body went *shusss* and *shuss* and every time it did, he went a little farther along the narrow tunnel.

So okay, he was curious. What if it was Stephen Colbert up there? If he could tell the people that they could go in Stephen Colbert, they would follow him for sure. He pushed forward again until he hit his head.

Now there was wind in his hair on the back of his head, and when he turned that way he was looking down an even longer tunnel, only this one had lots of windows in it, all with the little bars on them. He squiggled and wiggled along, racing to the first one. Who would it be, Seinfeld, Oz, Jimmy Kimmel, at last Colbert?

He turned his head, forcing it hard against top of the tunnel, and now he was looking down through bars into...a room. Yeah, it was like the shot room except no table. A Kellerdesk. So this wasn't TV, either. It was...what was it? If it wasn't in the world and it wasn't in TV, then where was it?

He slid along to the next one opening. Same thing. The next one, same again. He went past one and then another—and then the tunnel turned again and it was bigger. He could rise to his hands and knees. Low along the edge of the floor there were more windows, and when he looked through them he got the shock of his life and all time.

At first, all he saw was shiny. Huge shapes, all shiny. Then, down there, *way* down there, a shatterface in front of a little tiny TV watching some show that was farther away than anything he'd ever seen. This was the strangest looking shatterface ever made. It was dark brown. Nobody ever said they painted them different colors. It was a little better looking than Keller and the other white painted ones.

It had a gun.

So this *was* part of TV, 'cause they only have guns in TV, Keller says so. He looked at the little narrow bars. No way to get out. 'Course not. People *never* got in ding-dong TV! He got mad and he hit it. He hit hard!

The shatterface went to his feet. He looked right up here. Joe was so tired and so scared and so disappointed that he forgot his fear and just started crying, *aaahhheeeeoooo*, loud as he could, screaming and crying and hitting on the bars.

The light got brighter. Another shatterface showed up. It was Lerner. Not good, he was heavy on the snickersnee.

Joe could turn around here, so he did that and went *shuupp shuupp* all the way back to the world. He came down out of the tunnel and went onto the chairs and down. He put the bars that had come off back just exactly the way they'd been, then he returned the chairs to their places. He went to the barrier and cuddled down against it because there was no way he was gonna go down and have to sleep alone in front of them all. Betty had always liked Crunch more anyway, looking at him the way she did, being mean to Flutter. Okay, so he was only the boss of them because Keller had given him his glasses. Wear them anyway, he decided, bottomsider or not. Inside himself where he kept his secrets, he would still be boss.

He had his face pushed against the barrier when all of a sudden *ka-schoop* it opened and there was Harry Lerner.

"Joe," he said. And there was the shatterface with the gun! Boy, was he dark colored. What in heck had happened to that shatterface?

Harry came in. "We're gonna do a count," he said. He took Joe by the hand and they went down into the world. First, they went to Joe, which was, of course, empty. So then they crossed over to Flutter and

Crunch, and there were Crunch and Flutter all tangled up together and Betty on top of them. Joe moaned, and Harry Lerner squeezed his hand. They went in Jack and Jill, and they were both sound asleep in there.

Harry Lerner came down to him, held him by the shoulders. "Why were you out by the door, Joe?"

Joe signed, 'Sleeping.'

"Why not with Betty?"

He did not want Harry to see him when his face got hot. Keller laughed when that happened. Harry said, 'Joe, you're blushing.'

Harry went in Crunch and came out with Betty, carrying her. She was pretty big but he was way ho big. She was sleepy in her face. He took her into Joe and Betty and Joe went in, too. Betty lay down on their bed and went to sleep again.

Joe got in with her and Harry Lerner put their blanket over them and it was warm now. Joe didn't make another move until he left.

He held Betty tight. Maybe they all hated him and she hated him, but he could not hate her. He knew what this was. It was like when Keller rocked him and whispered "I love you," that was what it was. He whispered in Betty's ear, "Ah wuve oo." Then again, trying harder with his throat and tongue, "I rrrove yuw."

She opened her eyes and looked at him in surprise. She sat up, threw off the blanket. There was faint light coming in the door, and he saw her sign: 'You can talk good.'

He signed, 'You talk. You say it.'

She pursed her lips. Her mouth worked, her throat gobbled and gabbled. The she said, "Aoorrew." She clapped both hands over her mouth and threw back her head and laughed, a sound beautiful to hear.

"Say, *ah*."

"Ah!"

He tightened his throat. "*lllll*"

"Uuuh!"

He stuck his tongue out along his bottom teeth and showed her. "*Llll!*"

"Llaaggh!"

They both rolled around, their laughter rattling the walls. Flutter came in. She signed, 'What?'

Joe ached to tell them about the tunnels. But he wasn't ready to do that, not until he had figured things out. TV was bigger than he had thought. In fact, this wasn't the world, TV was the world. This was a little shut up corner.

Just thinking about it, prickles went up his arms and neck. What if they were in a program, that the secret was that their world was actually itself in TV? They might be in some part of Oz or something, that never showed up on their screen.

But also, there had been that other program that Harry had been watching, with all that big, wide blue and those green waving things. *What was that blue, what was that lovely green*?

He had to see more of the blue and green. He was going to see *everywhere*! But not right now. Right now, he had to try to get his place back, which he would do by showing everybody how to talk.

Crunch came in. He was moving slow, looking all around. He locked eyes with Joe. Joe got ready. But he sure didn't want it to be like this. The people mustn't fight, the people needed to be friends if they were ever going to get out of whatever this place was. He should've been nicer to Crunch and anyway, this whole bottomsider-topsider thing was dumb. All it did was cause fights.

Crunch jumped at Joe and glared right in his face. An idea went through Joe's mind like a rush of cool fan air during the heat of the line. He said, "Ah lluve you."

Crunch's mouth dropped open, he was so surprised. But not as much as Joe. That had sounded just like a shatterface. That had been really good! No reason to be embarrassed about that.

Betty said, "Cho gawk."

"Tak," Joe said. "Taaak!"

"Aaak!" Crunch, said. "Oh *whoaaaa*! Daaak! Daaak!"

Joe taught them. He talked pieces of words, and soon everybody was saying "Ah rrrove yew" and "Cho," and they knew what it meant, too. Except he was saying, "I rrove yu, I am Cho. I am Cho!" And he ran, then, up to the end of the hall and back down again, "Cho," he shouted, slapping his chest, "Cho, *Cho*! I am! I AM!"

Betty ran behind him yelling "Ah rrruve yew, Cho, Ah rrruve yew." Then Jack and Jill were saying it and kissing each other, and Flutter started crying, so they all gathered around her and they all said it, "Ah rruve yew, Fudder, ah rruve yew, Cho, ah rruve yew awl!"

And it was good.

11

INQUISITION

Harry watched Tom Morton examine the air conditioning grates.

"You find anything?"

"Dunno. Maybe the one in rec is a little loose."

"Could it have been pulled off?"

"Sure."

"So one of them is trying to escape."

"The one that was sleeping at the barrier, be my guess."

"Joe. He sleeps there a lot."

"So he wants to get out." Tom came down. "You know, Harry, that's the first time I've ever seen one. I have to tell you, that's the goddamndest thing I ever saw."

Harry said nothing.

"'Cause it looked like—sort of like a person. Was it an animal?"

Harry didn't want to go down this road, not with a security guard or anybody else. "It was an animal." If he slipped, here, he could end up getting the old shafteroo, and he needed this job in the worst way. A veterinarian who's lost his license is lucky not to be a security guard himself. Officially, he was staff biologist. What it meant was, night caretaker to the Tanda. The job had two qualifications: the ability to call Greg Keller if anything seemed amiss, and a high level skill at keeping his mouth shut.

"I want to say that was an alien. Or is that nutso?"

Harry laughed. "It's a lot simpler than that, Tom."

"'Cause, that's what they say. The rumor."

"I can't help what they say. It's a very ordinary situation."

"That howl—I never heard the like of it."

"The thing is, I can't see how you heard it at all. From way up in the duct work."

"Oh, I heard it all right. It was loud. Right on top of me. Woulda froze your blood."

He said, "Well, if the Tanda didn't get into the ductwork, it must've been the compressor. It's a humid night, maybe it's screwing up somehow."

"The thermostats are normal. I can't pull in off-site maintenance on a funny noise."

"Well, if you don't notice anything more..." He glanced toward the sleeping quarters. "I'll just have to ask them."

"They can talk?"

Harry laughed, "Not so's you know what the shit they're saying. They're primitive little animals is all. We use sign language with them."

"Well, they couldn't be too dumb if they can do that."

"About the smartest animals, but nowhere close to us."

Tom went on back to his station. Lucky man, Harry thought, thirty dollars a hour, not a worry in the world. Harry had a mortgage and Sarah and Fisher in Mt. Morris School and two car payments and a whole passel of crap to deal with in his life, so his hundred grand a year was essential. It was also deficit financing. He needed a raise in the worst way.

No time to worry about that now, though. Now, there was a more pressing question: to wake Keller or not to wake Keller? He did not doubt that Tom had heard one of the creatures. The sound he described was the wail of a Tanda in misery. Nothing else howled like that. Nothing. But waking Keller without being able to tell him exactly what had happened was a wrong move.

With Tom gone, he went into the infirmary and got the cattle prod, then moved quietly into the hallway that led to the bedrooms. All was quiet, but with the Tanda you soon learned that things might not be as they seemed. They were so uninformed that they at first seemed almost retarded, but they were actually as smart as whips. He'd played Clue with them once. Never again. They had excellent logical minds. Usually, somebody won on the third move, maybe the fourth. They were going to make the best damn scientific personnel in history, and companies were going to actually own them. Amazing.

As he walked down from rec, shadows darted out of Joe's room and into the others. So they were up, communicating in that fast sign they had evolved, that you couldn't follow. Damn things.

When he entered Joe's room, he and Betty flew into their bed. Their nervous haste told him that he would get his confession...and get a little of his own back in the process. This was going to be an enjoyable task. He crouched down beside the low mattress and positioned the prod so that Joe would see its tip as soon as he opened his eyes. He whispered low, "*Snickersneeeeee.*" It was named after the executioner's axe in the Mikado. Harry had named it himself.

There was a gasping intake of breath. Joe's eyes popped open and riveted on the tip of the prod.

"You got out. You're the one."

The horrible bright green eyes blinked.

Harry grabbed his arm. "Come on." He marched him off toward the infirmary where punishments were administered.

The little creature came willingly enough. They tended to be extremely compliant when they saw the prod.

There was a spattering sound. The little bastard was pissing himself as he ran along. Harry stifled the impulse to kick hell out of him. He'd get his chance to do plenty of damage in just a couple of minutes.

"Okay," he said, locking the infirmary door and turning on the lights. "I want the whole story."

Joe stood there, his head hanging down, his fists clenched.

They hated to look at you, so that's where Harry would start. He took Joe's cheeks and forced the Tanda to look him straight in the eyes. "You tell me! TELL ME!"

Joe shut his eyes tight.

"You got out, you fucking little prick! You tell me how! Sign!"

Shaking, lips twisted in terror, eyes shut tight, Joe stood his ground. Harry flipped him onto the examining table on his belly and hit him in the butt with the business end of the prod. It sparked and Joe shrieked. He scuttled up against the wall.

Harry had lost his vet license for killing a very vicious horse. No way would he kill an animal this valuable, but he was going to make it understand who was boss. He went for the creature's scrotum, and blasted it so hard and long it crackled like bacon.

"Sign, you bastard! Tell me!"

Here it came, frantic sign. The little pieces of shit couldn't take a whole lot of pain, that was for sure. The signing continued, fast and furious.

"Slow down!"

Joe recoiled, his bright green eyes bulging, tears pouring down his cheeks. He signed slowly, first the name of one of them—

"Crunch? You're saying Crunch?"

Joe nodded. He signed, 'He did it.'

"Crunch did it? Crunch was the one who got out?"

Joe nodded furiously.

One thing about the shits, they couldn't lie. They were smart, but not that smart. "Go back to your hootch, prickface," he snapped. Joe scuttled away.

He went down the corridor behind him, moving slow, planning his mode of attack. He'd come down on that sonofabitch Crunch like a ton of bricks. But you had to be careful with Joe, he was the boss's favorite. Brilliant, Keller would say. Yeah, fine.

Joe ran into his room. Harry strode across to Crunch's hootch.

Behind him, he heard Joe utter a complex noise in his raspy little voice. "Yew stoopip." Well, who the fuck knew what it meant? The scumbags couldn't talk, so the answer was probably, 'not much.' He grabbed the cowering Crunch by the hair, dragging him out as his mate shrieked and spat.

"We're gonna have us a little chat, Mr. Crunch," he said to the struggling Tanda, "just you and me, you fucking bastard, man to man."

12

THE ASIA CARD

Greg Keller opened his eyes. Beneath the wing of the plane, dawn light flooded the hard streets of Manhattan. Compulsively, he tried to pick out the small but elegant building on Fifth Avenue that housed Barrett Scientific. As the plane banked on its approach to LaGuardia, he lost his chance. He looked away.

As far as anybody had been told, Dr. Barrett had called this emergency board meeting because of the escape attempt. But Greg sensed that there was another reason, something that perhaps couldn't be put on paper. Maybe they had a second offer for the Tanda. Maybe there would be a bidding war.

He was pleased that, at this meeting, he would at last be able to demonstrate some progress with the breeding program, which had been *the* problem ever since the Tanda reached puberty. If there was no second offer, then at least he could state with confidence that there would be a baby in time to fulfill the provisions of the General System Services contract, which would get the board off his back for a while longer.

He wanted only to work with his Tanda, his little shadows. They were all he cared about, all that mattered to him. There was no question in his mind but that they were the greatest of all discoveries in the history of biology. He had found another intelligent species. If he could ever break free of corporate secrecy, he felt sure that he would be a candidate for a Nobel Prize.

He hardly noticed the landing, the walk through the airport, the always welcome discovery of his driver with the word "Keller" scrawled in black on a sheet of paper.

On the way in, he found himself scraping his feet on the floor of the limo, wishing that it would hurry the hell up. They'd sent a director-level car, a good sign. Maybe he was going to get that seat on the board he'd deserved for years. When they went public with the Tanda, the stock might triple, quadruple, more. He needed his seat before then, and the stock and options that would come with it. When the money flowed in, as it certainly would, he had more of a right to be under the spigot than any of the others. He'd struggled in that miserable Sumatran jungle for years, seeking bioactive plants while huge companies illegally pulled out hardwoods and built massive palm-oil plantations, ravaging the local biome in the process. It was ugly, but he couldn't really fault them. The profits were fantastic, and in any case, if it hadn't happened, he would never have gotten the Tanda.

He'd captured three of them from the hootch of their dead mother, then harvested her for a fourth, cutting into her womb. He'd taken Betty, Crunch, Flutter and Jack with him and nursed them for three months in the horrible little city of Bangko.

Incredibly, a party of Tanda had actually come into the city, apparently following the children by scent for a good twenty miles. He'd driven them off, harvesting Joe and Jill from another female in the process. He'd fed the carcass to wild dogs and sent word home to Barrett Scientific that he had a treasure worth millions, and he needed secure transport immediately.

It was not the story he told, of course, not even to Bob Barrett and certainly not to the board or that prissy new hire, the primatologist. He was a hero and the savior of a species, and nobody needed to be exposed to the ugly necessities that had been involved.

Barrett had whisked him and the Tanda infants out of Indonesia on a private jet. They had been listed on the cargo manifest as baby gibbons destined for the Houston Zoo, all paperwork in order. All forged.

They never got anywhere near any zoo. Fortunately, the customs officials did not notice that they were all playing with stuffed animals in their cages, or cuddling their blankies. Because of their appearance, they did not see them as what even then he sensed that they were—caged children.

His six were alone now. Of that he was fairly sure. Their forest had been completely leveled, and the companies involved took pains to kill any Tanda they found and incinerate the corpses. As far as the world was aware, *homo floresiensis* had gone extinct thousands of years ago. Companies knew that if a living population was discovered, the forests they inhabited would be seriously protected and that would be the end of the hardwood bonanza.

In the early days, Keller had assumed that their intelligence was somewhere north of the chimp, but well south of human. But as they matured, the quickness of their minds had become more and more apparent. They were goggle-eyed curious about everything. He could have taught them to read, to speak. In fact, as he knew, he could have brought them into the human world.

Too bad that wasn't part of the business plan. They'd find their place, though, he had no doubt of it. It would happen just as he'd predicted to Beth.

He was going to do what he was obligated to do for the company—sell them at a profit, as brilliant animals. Legally, he was in the clear. Once, perhaps, there might have been questions, but the law as to who was and wasn't human was now very clear. The animal freedom cases had made DNA the determining factor.

The car pulled up and the driver got out and opened his door for him. Nice. He usually was left to his own devices at the airport and had to take a cab. He arrived on the top floor and crossed the coldly elegant lobby, all gray and white marble just like the Texas facility. Dr. Barrett's taste was at least consistent. Outside, Manhattan shone in the morning sun. In here, there was a delicate aroma of coffee and the faint clink of dishes. Behind those tall, black doors across the lobby, the directors were breakfasting together.

He opened the doors—and Robert Barrett himself came over swung them wide. "The resident genius! Good flight, Greg? Sorry about the red-eye!"

"Great flight, Bob."

Bob had never greeted him like this. This was a good sign, a *good* sign. He was rarely up to eating at these meetings, but now he began to actually feel a bit hungry. There was a decent enough spread, as always, coffee and eggs and bacon, various types of sweet roll and muffin.

As Greg filled his plate, there were more greetings. Cynthia Delancy came over and asked him, "Can an ape ever be a poet? Have you got that one answered, yet, Greg?"

"I don't have that one answered, Cynthia." She'd been asking this question in her wheedling, querulous tone of voice for years. Maybe it was best that she saw the Tanda as apes.

"I suggest that you make a concerted effort. Because it looks like they won't be around very long."

"Yeah, I can see the end of the tunnel on the breeding at last. I've got a new specialist on board, who is going to solve that problem."

"We have a lot to talk about."

Her tone was...odd. "How so?"

"Eat, eat."

"No, tell me."

"There's another offer on the table."

"Ah, another bidder. Excellent."

"That isn't precisely the situation."

The room moved a little, as if somewhere a giant had stomped his great foot. Greg put his plate on the table and sat down. "What sort of an offer is it, then?"

"Hold your horses," Barrett said. "This is—let's eat, first. Have a nice breakfast! You play golf, don't you, Greg?"

Greg didn't want to talk about golf. He wanted to find out what was going on here.

"What sort of an offer?" he asked again.

"I can answer that, I think," Raymond Lipps said. He was the treasurer of the company. "We have a negative cash flow on this project approaching fifty million dollars, and—"

"And no prospects of recoupment," Cynthia said. "See if you think this is a good plan. We sell the facility in Texas, just for the value of the real estate and structure. The market's good, we'll get well in excess of ten million dollars for it."

"That's it? We sell? What about the Tanda?"

"We have an offer of five million dollars per animal."

This did not have a good sound. Not a bit of it. "GSS's offer is far better!"

"That's a money 'if' offer," Ray Lipps said. "This is money 'when.'"

"When what?"

"When we sign. They take the animals on an 'as is' basis, right now."

"Who is it?"

Barrett said, "World Biological. An all or nothing offer. Breeding or not breeding, they don't care. They just want the animals."

Greg was momentarily too shocked to breathe, as if he was in a jet that had suddenly begun to crash.

Barrett said, "Now, don't go—"

"I'm not going ballistic!"

"—ballistic."

"Jesus Christ!"

Lipps said, "This isn't a bad deal for us, Greg. We stop the cash hemorrhage at least."

He'd been totally blindsided. Nobody had mentioned anything about this at the last meeting. They'd seemed happy. Reasonably happy. But then again, the GSS contract was supposed to have been finalized months ago.

"I'm close to meeting the GSS criteria," he heard himself say.

Considering that he felt as if he'd just been pushed off a cliff, he thought that he sounded quite calm.

"Now, Greg," Cynthia said, "we want you to know that we've discussed this carefully. All of us. We have not voted yet. Because we are talking about a big step. For you, a very big step. But we have all known, always, that this had an eventual end. Either the program succeeded and we got this extraordinary and unique product on the market, or it failed and we quietly wound it down and took a fifty million dollar haircut."

"But they're healthy. They—" He stopped. He had better hear her out.

"The reason we have kept this whole matter so very secret is so that we would not end up hamstrung by regulatory bodies and public opinion."

"We all agree on that, Cynthia. So where are you going?"

"Where I'm going is that we're at the end of the road with this project. We need to pull out, Greg."

"But you can't—they're—" He didn't know what to say, how to deal with this. "They're fine!"

"The escape attempt is the problem."

"That's what sparked this?"

Barrett said, "They're more intelligent than we thought."

"Which is a plus. A huge plus!"

"It can be, Greg. I agree. A brilliant plus. But you've—you know those revisions you asked for? The 'humane treatment' clauses?"

"But that—that was for liability—and for them! Because they *are* smart. They're sensitive."

Barrett cleared his throat. "I think you know Michael Helmond."

Greg looked toward the small man who sat at the far end of the table. He was Barrett Scientific's legal counsel. "Of course," he said.

The man half-rose, extending his hand as he did. "It's a privilege to meet you, Doctor Keller."

Greg managed to smile. Just.

"What we have here is probably the most difficult liability issue this company—maybe any company—has ever faced."

"You say that now?"

"We started out assuming an I.Q. of 40 to 60," he continued, his voice soft with menace. "Which you led us to believe. Now that isn't a problem. A very smart animal. The situation is clear—decent treatment mandated, reasonably safe working conditions, no cruelty. Animal rights. And as far as ownership is concerned—well, an animal cannot even be a slave, so ownership is not slaveholding. Not legally, anyway."

"So we're okay."

Helmond raised a hand. "We were okay at 60. On the outside of the envelope, but basically okay. At 70, we're in court. Above that—well, this organization has a major legal problem. And where we are now—from what we're reading, you've got essentially human intelligence."

"Intelligence isn't the issue. They can't interbreed with us. They've got only a 97% DNA match with us."

"That's a lot of DNA—"

"It's not a lot! Chimps are closer. Gorillas are closer, for God's sake."

"But the Tanda are intelligent, Doctor. I have to tell you, I've read your reports. The way they play card games and board games—I think they're not only *as* intelligent as we are, I think they're conceivably more intelligent than many of us."

"It is not relevant. They could be transcendent geniuses and they would still not be human under the law."

"Don't tell me the law, please. They are highly intelligent. Just uninformed. Is that not so?"

The lawyer sat tapping his pen on the tabletop. Far below, the Fifth Avenue traffic hummed. Cynthia took a careful sip of her coffee.

In that moment, Greg Keller faced something that he had not been willing to face before, that he had been pushing out of his mind and denying and refusing to address for years. "Yes," he said in a whisper that filled the room, "they are."

"You understand that this extends into criminal liability—if this becomes known."

"In what sense?"

"The Tanda are incarcerated. Why? By whose authority? They have been in this country for years without any proper citizenship filing, without any alien registration, without even due notice of their presence here. They were smuggled in. Remember that. In an Immigration Service or Customs hearing—and we will face such hearings, I assure you—that will be important. The Justice Department lawyers will have the port of entry forms signed by you, Doctor Keller. Forms that contain false statements."

"I didn't know at the time. It was an innocent mistake."

"I'm not saying that we are without defense. But remember that we flew them on a private jet all the way from Indonesia to Texas. Now, that is hardly what you would do if you really believed you were carrying ordinary apes. No, the evidence for the prosecution is quite strong, I'm afraid. Against you, and against everybody in this room, as accomplices."

"Assuming intelligence is a valid test under the law."

"Perhaps you don't know the case law regarding slaves."

He did not.

"In 1858, Massachusetts was offering harbor to escaped slaves. It was argued in a Massachusetts court by the state of South Carolina that one Charles Farmer, a slave who had come into Massachusetts from that state, was not human because he was of the Negro race, and therefore must be returned to his owner as lost animal property, not as an escaped slave."

"They must've laughed an argument like that out of court."

"They wanted to, but no physician could be found who could state with certainty that blacks and whites came from the same basic stock."

"What possible relevance could a hundred and fifty year old slave case have now?"

"Doctor Keller, you have failed to do your due diligence here. Obviously, the old slavery decisions will have primary relevance in regard to the fate of the Tanda. In this case, Mr. Farmer was deemed by the court to be human because he displayed human intelligence.

He could neither read nor write, but he could speak intelligibly and make his mark. The judge's opinion reads that 'he is no less capable in any wise regarding intelligence than many white men walking the streets of this city.' I submit that the Tanda can do a good deal more than make marks."

"Had DNA been available then, intelligence would not have been the test."

"You do understand that the legal system works on precedent, do you not? Given their intelligence, you can make an argument that the Tanda are enslaved. Slavery is a very serious crime, Doctor. You will be facing many years in prison." He looked around the room. "As I warned the board earlier, both the animal and human rights communities are going to be against us." He fell silent. The others were rigid in their seats, also silent.

Keller knew that he needed to speak, that he must speak. But his mind was buzzing uncontrollably. They were talking about jail, here. It sounded insane. But this grim young man was entirely serious.

Beyond the wide window that opened one wall of the conference room to a broad view, he could see long white clouds racing past. Lovely clouds of freedom. He fixated on them, yearning toward the freedom of the sky. Then he thought of the Tanda in their containment, and was ashamed.

"Greg," Dr. Barrett said.

He opened his cracking dry mouth. "The DNA," he muttered, "will not be human."

"It's not an impossible argument, I grant you that. But look at the social problem. The press will pick the story up the moment it enters the courts. It'll become one of the sensations of the age. As brilliant animals, it was a fascinating story. Highly spinnable, though. We're not hurting them, we're giving them shelter, food and a new life, now that their old forest is cut down. There would have been animal rights protests, sure, but the public might well have come with us, I would think, as long as they were clearly animals. But this—we've got these brilliant, cute, appealing creatures imprisoned and working on an assembly line, and we're not even paying them—no, the public will not be with us, and neither will the judiciary. We won't be climbing a hill with this case, we'll be scaling a cliff. And we will fall."

"If that escape had succeeded," Ray Lipps said, "we'd be in the middle of a meltdown right now."

"That's too close for us, Greg," Barrett added. "This company has a hundred years of scientific innovation behind it and a magnificent reputation for honesty and fair practice. I cannot risk that."

"Why World? You know as well as I do that they're not going to care about the Tandas' welfare."

"With respect," Barrett said, "that isn't our issue."

"They'll kill some, experiment on some, try to clone them. God knows what they'll do."

Ray Lipps smiled softly. "We have written assurances."

"Which are damned lies, and you know it!"

"Oh, Greg. Greg. Please know that this is as much of a tragedy for us as it is for you. We have followed your work with awe, Greg. Awe for you and love for the Tanda. We all feel the same way. We love Betty and Joe and all of them. But we also have a responsibility to our shareholders, and that is our first responsibility."

Greg's mind sought for some alternative, some card worth playing. "Listen to me. It isn't time for this—to kiss this whole investment goodbye. All of that money!"

"Greg, money isn't the primary issue," Lipps said. "We'll get enough money to get past this and thank God for that. The larger issue here is damage control. Not letting this thing get out of hand."

"When we transfer them, what'll be on the manifest? Answer me that? 'Unknown animal'? That'll raise questions. Customs will want a looksee. There's no way around that."

He sat back, satisfied that he'd scored a point. Finally.

"The animals will be flown on a Thai Airlines flight, in a specially designed hold. Diplomatic immunity the whole way. Customs won't even be able to look at them. Meanwhile, back at the ranch, we do a little document shredding—your memos crowing about their intelligence, that sort of thing. Just as easily as that, we're home free."

"May I know who approached World Bio? Just for my own peace of mind."

There was uneasy movement around the table.

"Cynthia, it was you, wasn't it? What did you do—go to some UN party and whisper a few words in an ambassador's ear? Was it that simple? You've always hated my Tanda."

"I most certainly have not."

"No, I take that back."

"Well, thank you."

"You've been made uneasy by them. They threaten you in the same way that a smart black man threatens a poor southern white."

"Oh, come on!"

"You come on! You know it's true. So you saw an opportunity to get rid of an irritant, and you took it. You're sending them to ruined lives and death, and you know it. All of you."

"Greg," Barrett said, "now wait. Wait. We're all in this. All in agreement here."

"You listen! Listen to me! I have a new hire. One of the world's leading primatologists. She's going to solve the breeding problem. We'll be in business."

"When," Lipps asked.

"We have a pregnancy going right now and it will come to term in four months."

"Pardon me, Greg, but you've played that same card before. And we've ended up with nothing."

Barrett folded his arms. "This conversation isn't relevant, I'm sorry."

"Of course it is! I'm looking at thirty million dollars per breeding pair! That's a hell of a lot more than you're getting from those damned butchers."

"I resent that," Cynthia said. "Nobody talked about killing them or experimenting on them or anything remotely like that. Only you, Greg."

"You give them the Tanda, you sentence them to death, probably a slow and agonizing death."

Cynthia leaned toward him from across the table, her darkly liquid eyes glittering in the sunlight. "We've committed ourselves to you, Greg. Heart and soul. You promised us an incredible product, and you tried your best. I can't fault you. A superb job. But now you can't deliver and we're in danger."

"Then give me a few more months to meet the GSS criteria!"

"Greg," Barrett said, "GSS has pulled out."

"That can't be true."

"I can assure you that it is. Our options are pretty stark. It's either World and shut the thing down, or deal with you and your charges as a growing financial problem and a terrifying liability issue. I'm sorry, Greg. We all feel the same way about the Tanda, and we admire you enormously for saving them, for caring for them—for all you've done. But, in the end, our backs are up against a wall, here."

"What would happen if you had no buyer?"

"We haven't gone that far."

"Sure you have. What's the contingency? I want to know, I have a right to know."

Nobody spoke. Finally Barrett said in a quiet voice, "Shutdown would necessarily involve termination of the experimental animals."

"So my choices are to give them to World to be killed or keep them here at home and kill them myself?" He went to his feet. "Over my dead body. And I mean that literally. *Over my dead body*!"

"Oh, God," Cynthia said. "Save me from Mr. Keller and his *Gotterdammerung*. You're so Germanic, Greg. *Sturm und drang*. This company does not have a hit man on retainer, you'll be surprised to know."

"I'm Hungarian, damnit," he muttered. He did not want to threaten. He dared not. But he had to make them see reality. "No matter how you cut it, this is going to result in a monstrous press problem." He spoke softly, diffidently, but the message was clear: if they sold the Tanda to World, he would talk.

Barrett replied carefully. "It'd be sad to see your career end like that, in a media storm."

"And facing criminal liability," Helmond added. "The smuggling problem. The enslavement and incarceration of six people."

"You know why I've never liked this project, Greg?" Cynthia said. "Nothing to do with xenophobia. I couldn't care less about whether or not the Tanda are human beings or animals or whatever they may be. I'm here to make money, and the truth is, your project is too expensive and too...weird. Stuff that's strange like this always costs more than you expect and almost never works. But on another level, when I watch the videos of the creatures—I do feel, in all honesty, that these are people." She leaned back in her chair. "I do feel that, Greg."

"Me, too," Lipps said.

There was general agreement around the table.

"So you choose murder," Greg said softly. His heart was surging, making his temples pound.

"It is a sale, nothing more," Barrett replied. "And it will save this company."

"By sacrificing the Tanda!"

"Wait a minute," Cynthia said. "You not only accuse me of xenophobia, your attitude toward World is outrageous. *You're* xenophobic, damn you! Show me evidence that World Bio, one of the most respected firms of its kind there is, is going to harm them. In fact, Doctor Ma, who you will meet, wanted to see the whole 'humane clause' in the GSS contract. He wanted it incorporated in the contract of sale. *He* did, not us. As a safeguard for the Tanda. These people aren't monsters."

"We've had a relationship with World Biological since my father's time," Barrett added.

Greg knew that it was over. His mouth was no longer dry, he no longer had that awful, cloying sense of urgency to debate, to jump on their words, to force them to comply.

They would not comply. Worse, he had to admit the truth, that World Biological was indeed a reputable company. They were concerned about endangered species and had active programs in that area. It wasn't certain, and perhaps not even likely, that they would kill some of the Tanda in their experiments. No, they were perceptive scientists. Unlike Barrett, who had to face thorny human rights issues and was advised by an overly careful young lawyer, World was probably fixed on only one thing: intelligence was the most valuable commodity on earth, and who knew what a new, nonhuman form of it might bring in terms of innovation? Not seeing that made Robert Barrett historically short-sighted, just as certainly as it made the Tanda the most precious six creatures in the world.

"The future is slipping from our hands," Greg said. "Because the truth is, we are looking at a greater mind. We have it in our possession, and we are giving it away."

"If they're so brilliant, they are being entirely wasted on your idiotic assembly line idea," Lipps said harshly. "You should have told us this years ago."

"I didn't know years ago!"

"Well, now it's too late. We don't have enough cash to keep going."

Greg rose to his feet. "I'll begin preparing them for the transition," he said. "When will it occur? I mean, logistically."

"There will be a team down there from World Bio in two days," Cynthia said.

"That's awfully fast."

"A reflection of our concern," Barrett said, "and our need."

Greg stood. He prepared to leave.

Cynthia said, "We all love you, Greg. We have the utmost respect for you."

He just wanted to get out of here. He wanted to—he didn't know what. To walk. To walk for a long time.

"There's a future for you here," Barrett said. "Once they're gone, there's a paper to be published."

"A paper?"

"Certainly a paper. With all of your data, an entire book. At least that. My God, man, you made the discovery of the ages."

"But World—how will that look?"

"We can spin it. Let them play the human-level intelligence card.

That part of it, we edit out. Then, in a few years, they announce the incredible news."

"Whereupon I look like an idiot. We all do, for giving up something so valuable."

"We look like pioneers. But by then the Tanda will be the most watched creatures on earth. World Bio might possess them, but they will belong to the world."

He shook hands, he was embraced. Cynthia gave him a kiss, a sensation like having his cheek scraped by teeth.

He left, then, feeling a curious mixture of triumph and sick, dreadful sorrow.

For twenty minutes or so, he walked along 59th Street, but the thought of making his way into Central Park didn't last. He needed to get back to the Tanda, and now.

By the time he had reached the airport, his sorrow had become a stone in his soul. On the flight, he wept, concealing his tear-streaked face by staring down at the land far below, the broad and smiling fields of America.

13

THE PECULIAR INSTITUTION

He watched Beth's car disappear down the drive. Let her believe he was gonna wait. That was definitely best. He could get in that damn lab, he had no doubt about it. He hadn't seen it, true, but—well, he could get in.

Last night, they'd talked on the Barrett situation. Decided to wait a bit. See how things came together. For half the night they'd made love, and held one another for the other half. This morning, she'd looked him in the eye and said, "Promise." He'd looked back and said, "Promise."

It sounded like agreement, but it was just a word he was repeating, right?

"Beth's gone," he said into the morning cacophony.

He was looking at three possible outcomes. One, he failed and went to jail and she lost the apes. She'd come and cry over his misery and they'd both cry over the loss of the critters. Two, he got himself killed. She'd cry and bury him and wander for a while in her heart, then move on. That was Beth. Even if her life stopped, she would not stop. Three, he succeeded. She come at him with her fists, then dissolve into his arms on a wave of relief and happiness.

Well, hell, there was always the off chance that whatever cockamamie plan he came up with would work. Given Barrett's super security, any break-in plan was going to be cockamamie. But he was good at cockamamie. In fact, you could even say it was his forte.

For example, Iraq had been a cockamamie war and he'd had a cockamamie job, but he'd done it. He had a Heart and a couple of other medals to commemorate the pieces of himself he'd left in the desert sands. He hated it when it came into his mind, any of it. He could still smell the goddamn dust, still taste the oily smoke of death in the back of his throat. He could smell the blood, of fallen friends, of enemies.

When he dreamed about the close-in work he'd done, he'd get to shouting and scare Beth. He didn't want to scare Beth. He wanted to be a big, gentle bear to Beth. In fact, he was just a plain bear, dangerous as hell and too damn stubborn for his own good.

Saving animals was maybe compensation for killing people. When he'd joined up, he'd expected to be deployed to Club Army in Germany. But then came 911, his tour was extended and the next thing he knew, he was doing dangerous, ugly stuff for a living in a desert full of scared, confused people who did not want him there.

Some men learn they can kill and some that they can't, and most never find out. Certain sergeants can look at a guy and know how much of a killer he is, even if he doesn't. They can know the man who can do it with a rifle or a machine gun or a grenade, and they can know that other man, the one who can do it with his hands.

They make movies about snipers, clean work, somebody in the distance disappears, good visual. They make movies about grunts. But there are no movies about men like him. Sergeant Jim Clancy said, "You can go in there. You can do the job."

If someone comes at you with a knife and you can crush his windpipe before he cuts you, how old does he have to be for that to be okay? Someone with a caved in windpipe, they dance. Then they turn purple, then black.

You do a whole lot of that and the smell of your war is not explosives. It is piss and shit. Problem is, the skilled silent killer is so useful that he is in constant demand. Men, women, children—'remember,

Charlie, the target has made himself a target.' Even if she is thirteen. Even if she has the lashy eyes of a young deer. Even if she smells of gardenias.

The sort of war fought in the streets of Sadr City was a mixture of death and questions. The dead die, but the questions never leave you.

Back home and mustered out, at first he thought he was OK. But then the dreams came that were not dreams. His dead were with him, watching him, questioning him.

He sought some sort of deliverance. The VA delivered a guy with the blankest stare Charlie had ever seen. He was a listening machine sitting there on the other side of a steel desk. So he set out, first eastward toward enlightenment. He bicycled through Thailand, a Dharma Bum seeking peace and getting worms. Next, to darkest Africa to become a soldier of fortune, which is easy to do if you don't mind running drugs and risking jail in a lonely place. Then he found the mountains of Burundi, blue and dreaming in their ancient mists. He'd come across a young gorilla with a busted jaw, and the sighs coming out of that creature's mouth had changed his life. They were the most beautiful, helpless and tragic sounds he had ever known. Armed with his vet degree, he'd joined an NGO that treats gorillas.

They could tear him apart, but they didn't. In a gorilla forest, you know great suffering and great peace. They are dying, slipping into the cooking pots of the African diaspora, in Paris, in London, wherever men look back to the world they have lost, and lust after its wildness and its imagined largesse.

His childhood had been rough. Dad drank and beat. No brothers and sisters, so it was concentrated on him. Charlie had walked out of that house on his fifteenth birthday, lived on the streets until he could join up, and prepared to see the world. Afterward had come PTSD, vet school and a pilgrim's life, seeking for that one stream so sweet and so pure that it would wash him clean.

Now he spent his life tending to hurt apes and using his close-in skills with locks and tunnels and such to relieve suffering. He popped labs and took the monkeys, the chimps, whatever he could find. He'd once spent a night releasing something like twenty thousand mice.

Makeup mice. Don't want that lipstick to make m'lady's lips disintegrate.

Over the years, he had had become smarter and smarter about things like building plans, alarm systems and locks.

Most guys, they get in a war, they get desensitized. Others—the unlucky few—go down the opposite path. At this point in his life, Charlie couldn't even kill a bug without feeling regret. Not even a roach—which took his thoughts away from the Tanda and their prison to what he was doing right now, which was feeding the ribald gang who called the Center home. They needed to do something serious about the roach population in the storage area. Ape chow full of roaches, not good. The chimps didn't much care. In fact, they ate them. Moreland, though, had seen Beth and Charlie's disgust, so he was disgusted, too. It would mean yet more money to get somebody in here to figure out how to roach proof the bins without spraying.

As he worked, he also missed Beth. Caring for the apes was an extension of their marriage, really. They had each other and apes. There would be kids, too, and the kids would have mom and dad and each other and apes. That was how this family was gonna roll, and he and Beth planned a lot of kids. No could afford, only problem.

The capuchins would take food from their bin, but what they really enjoyed was snatching it from Charlie then racing triumphantly up their cage and eating it while shrieking at him. As always, he lingered long enough to make sure that everybody who was looking to steal got his chance.

The chimps were a different story. Henderson, the old alpha, had been getting beat up by Ron and Dooley, and had been sequestered in a space of his own. Now the three of them spent their time screaming at one another. One of the younger apes would soon be alpha. In the wild, Henderson might well get beaten so badly he would go off into the forest and die. Chimps were dark souls. In the wild, they fought wars. They committed murder. Never let it be said that man is the only animal that murders his own kind, or for that matter, that we are the only animal who laughs. Chimps laugh, and their smarter bonobo cousins even more. And monkeys laugh even more than apes do. If a capuchin gets your goat, he will be laughing like hell. Just sounds like he's screaming.

"Mornin', Moreland," he said when he reached their silverback escape artist.

Moreland watched him with his dark and concealing eyes.

"Still pissed off about the new lock? Or you want your lady to come feed you? You miss Beth?" Moreland might have reacted a little. "I miss Beth, too." He thought of the hell she was entering right about now. "A whole damn lot."

When he had completed the feeding, he made sure that the two staffers knew to hose down the chimps twice today. The summer flies were getting to them in the worst way, making them irritable and causing even more squabbling than usual.

Charlie worked methodically. At one point in his life, he had been the world's best-organized street person. Or maybe the world's only organized street person. He had done burglary, sure. Gotten into closed grocery stores after hours and eaten out of their takeout sections. No evidence of entry, no alarms triggered. That was where his skill with locks and shit really started, even more than in Iraq.

He wondered what kind of jerkoff had ever had the idea of enslaving the Tanda? What kind of shitkicker? Of course the Tanda were worth millions, so the greedy kind, for starters. Beth had said his name was Greg Keller. No Facebook presence, no Instagram or Linked In account, not even an entry in US Search. So, a ghost. Never good, that. People who hide generally don't do it for fun.

His grrrl was expected to use her brilliance to get the slaves to breeding. The hell. There would never be a baby until they were free to walk the streets.

Once he was finished on Murderer's Row, he went over to his two hundred thousand mile Ford F-3 Pickup, got in and started her up.

Here was his plan: he had no plan. Lie to Beth, say he was gonna wait on her say-so—yeah, that qualified as a plan. Just at the moment, he had a little means of getting into the place in his pocket. Get a quick looksee. He'd piss Beth off in the process for sure, but that would blow over.

He went clattering off listening to the radio, listening for the blues that he loved. As he banged along, he got a little excited about this thing. But no, that was a mistake. Ditch that. The eager soldier is a dying man.

His first step would be to look over the situation, then get in touch with some of his old gang of lab poppers. Mostly doctors and lawyers and Indian chiefs now, but you'd get 'em fired up over this baby. A little lawyering was going to come in real handy, too, and he was thinking about Larry Stein for that. He'd take the case *pro bono,* no question there.

He sang a little along with the radio. He liked the blues because life had made him sad. He was a generally sad man. Scared, too, now. Death did not appeal, but that might turn out to be part of this job.

In Iraq, he'd asked himself every morning, 'Am I willing to die today?' The answer was always the same: 'hell no.' But he went out anyway and did what he was told and came back and went to the latrine and tossed his cookies until he was crosseyed. Nobody gave a damn. Combat zone latrines are noisy places.

He hoped that he would live for the Tanda. Actually the second best choice was dying for them. If he was captured, the outcome was inevitable. Detectives would look for similar crimes. He'd go down for twenty years at least, and the apes would be gone. It sickened him to think of it, especially the stolen ones going back to those labs. Haysoos wept.

He drove along, turning it all over in his mind. Was it worth it to risk the critters in the Center for these guys?

Not even a question.

And then there it was, a black gleaming cube under the Texas sun. He didn't drive past and turn around. There would be cameras, and any kind of behavior that looked like a casing job was going to be noticed. Instead, he turned in the main entrance and stopped at the gate.

As Beth had reported, there was no intercom. Fine. He didn't care. If they let him I n, that would mean one type of plan. If they didn't, then another. He stared straight ahead. They'd be staring back, of course. What would they be thinking, though?

The gate swung open. As he approached the building, the glass walls momentarily blinded him, reflecting almost the full force of the sun directly onto his windshield. Closer yet, all he saw was glass, not a sign of life. The place looked like Darth Vader's country club.

A little to the south, he saw a plane turn slowly, silver in the bright sun. An airfield over there, private. So did it have twenty four hour radar coverage? That was important, because the airspace above the Barrett campus would be within the range of its approach control radar. Given the plan that was weaving in his mind, this could be a complication. He would be working out of Beyer Field, an airport which had absolutely no radar. In fact, it had little more than a tattered wind sock to guide the weary aviator. It was, in other words, it was perfect.

Barrett Scientific's Texas campus was set in the center of about fifteen acres of short cropped grass, not a bush or tree to be seen. He recognized the setting for what it was, a security measure. Isolate the facility, light up the perimeter with video surveillance and load it with sensors.

After he parked, he did a quick survey, examining the building methodically, starting at the top. There were some pretty good light fixtures up there. At night, this place would be able to make its own sunlight. Okay, that was noted.

He could not pick out any cameras, but they would be there. Every inch of the grounds would be covered, you could be sure of it. Except one place—the hole in the doughnut. He looked from light fixture to light fixture.

He'd return after dark to make certain, but his guess was that the roof would be a black shadow in the middle of a campus ablaze with light. There was no place nearby that you could get airborne with a hang glider and an ultralight would be too noisy. The result was that the roof itself would be the hole in the doughnut. Penetration theoretically impossible.

He did not like parachutes. First off, getting old Freddie Breyer to take him up at night for a jump over the city was liable to be a hassle. Second, he'd have to drop in from a long way off, because of that other airfield—Centex, it was called—and its radars.

But the roof was the way in, no question. One idea would be to rappel down the wall and pop in through the employee entrance using Her Nibs's key card. Hugging the wall, he'd be out of range of security cameras. Probably. Possibly.

He'd handled six chimps at once before. He'd pulled them out two by two, leaving the dominant male for last. They were too surprised and scared to put up much of a fight until they were in the truck, which they just about reduced to scrap.

How would the Tanda behave? He had to factor in the truth of it, which was that he had no idea.

As he walked toward the building, he noted that the parking lot was nearly empty in the middle of a workday. Interesting that there was way less staff than had been planned for. Eleven cars in a lot meant for a hundred. As he passed Beth's Volvo, he imagined her somewhere in that black glass hellhole, working right this minute with living miracles in a living hell. What a world.

Dropping on the roof would be dangerous but it was possible. Harder to know how a truck could be brought in. If it couldn't, the problems would multiply, because it was a half mile walk to the road from the facility. Doing that with a passel of scared whatsits in tow would be hard—in fact, probably too hard. But how could he take a second person in on penetration? He knew plenty of lunatics, but he was the only one who'd jump out of an airplane at night over a soup of powerlines, cellphone towers, church spires and other lethal obstacles.

Assuming he got the Tanda out, he would need a truck to be waiting. By that time, the alarms would be going crazy, so the move would need to be right quick. He'd have to get the Tanda to come through the halls of the structure, and they'd never been out of their containment, so they'd probably be pretty crazy.

Thinking about it, the only thing that didn't worry him was the exterior gates. They were garden-variety reinforced steel stuff. Once he got in, whoever was on the truck would blow their pneumatics at a signal. If the armature was busted properly, they'd open without triggering the alarm. It wouldn't be until the vehicle was moving up the driveway that the security center would get notified.

He got out of the truck. Taking his time as he crossed the parking lot, he drew closer to the building. Boy, was this place ever not Beth's style. She was a chintz curtain lady. Their bedroom was so fluffy that it bounced. However, if she detected the least bit of unconscious sexism in you, that soft-eyed baby doll became a mean momma real fast. He'd been there, done that. Beth had taught him what it meant to accept a woman as both feminine and equal, to get down deep inside yourself and root out those hidden assumptions that this smaller, weaker human being with her soft ways was in any way your inferior.

The employee entrance was a steel door with a keycard reader in the wall beside it under a lockable plastic cover. Probably locked at night. Big deal, crack it open with his trusty penknife. As he moved quickly toward the main entrance, he glanced again at the exterior lighting system. Full coverage, for sure, all grounds areas. The extraction would definitely have to be done under lights. Not nice. However, while he was on the roof he could set timed charges on the floods, so that they'd fail just as he was bringing the Tanda out. Yes, that would be on the list. There would still be plenty of lights in the grounds, but the sudden change in the level of illumination and the way shadows fell would be helpful.

He approached the main entrance. This was an important part of the ritual, and the part he liked the least. You had to see as much of the interior of a target structure as you could, get a look at the kind of security system that was in use, check out the locks and the strength of the door frames, determine the type of flooring, and see if you could estimate the depth of the security—was it a single level or was it layered? Were you looking at movement, laser, infrared, sonic, or even more? Above all, once he was inside, would Beth's keycard bypass anything, given that it would be after hours? If he was lucky, he'd get some idea by just looking around. He knew the kind of things to look for, such as keypads beside the card readers, which would allow for the use of bypass codes. And if he could manage to get to Beth's office, the trip back through the facility would tell him much of value.

He wouldn't have gotten through the gate if they hadn't made the truck's license plate. But now he had to have a reason for coming here, a good one. He had known that this would be the case, so he'd played a little game with Beth this morning, taking her reading glasses out of her briefcase just before she left.

He was rather surprised to find the lobby entrance locked. This was a fool's ploy. You gained nothing, and you broadcast that you were guarding something important. Better to let the world think you were at least somewhat open than to serve notice that you were afraid of intruders. He pressed the buzzer.

The door unlocked. A guard in US Security livery answered. Another mistake: don't broadcast the name of your security contractor to the world. The more you tell a potential intruder about yourself, the easier it is for him. There was that, but there was also the fact that the bright, tough man trying to slice him in half with his dark-eyed glare was part of the best security outfit in the country.

Without seeming to do more than gently bar his way, the guard moved to block his sight lines, which was a score point for Barrett Scientific. The man wasn't just preventing entry, he was minimizing what Charlie could see. That was serious skill.

"Good morning," he said, "I'm Charles Cooke, Beth's husband."

The guard looked at him. The face, not nice to begin with, hardened to sculpture.

"Her glasses," Charlie said, drawling a little and smiling a lot.

"I'll take them to her," the guard said.

"That's okay." He started to move past the guard. The guard, predictably, did not let that happen.

"You aren't allowed in."

"My wife works here. Is something wrong?"

"Look, I'll take them to her."

"Something's wrong."

"Nope."

"I want to see her. You go in and get her."

He started to close the door.

"Come on, man, you can't leave me standing out here in the sun. Let me wait in the lobby, for Chrissakes."

The guard's face revealed just the slightest flicker of suspicion. Charlie could read his thoughts, 'something funny here, so let him in and let control watch him while he's alone.'

At least, those were the thoughts that would have gone through Charlie's mind.His lips as tight as two strips of jerky, the guard opened the door wider. "Sit over there," he said.

Charlie found himself in a cold marble lobby. There were touches of tropical hardwood here and there, wood no doubt taken from old growth Sumatrans. Symbol of power: we consume what is rare.

He sat down on one of the benches. Like any jerk would, he stared around, eyebrows raised, eyes wide.

But as the old street kid gawked, the tightly wound professional calculated. There was a motion sensor in one corner of the ceiling, another in the opposite. He got up and strolled toward the back of the room, toward the door into the facility proper.

The door and jamb were steel, but the jamb wasn't steel backed. Even if it was locked both ways, you could crowbar it from either side.

The baseboards told him that there was a laser farm installed. A pain in the ass to negotiate, but you could bet it wasn't in two places: under six inches from the floor, and anywhere near the ceiling. So he could either grow wings or lose a hundred pounds.

Inside the facility, the corridors would be strung with lasers. Each office would probably have a couple, one across the window, one across the door.

As he returned to the couch, he had a look at the receptionist's security console. There was no actual receptionist, just the guard, which was also kind of interesting. It meant that the facility was not used to receiving visitors. It also meant that the people who came here were lower-level—suppliers, not customers or clients.

The door at the back of the lobby clicked.

"Charlie?"

"I got your glasses."

She stared at him. Hard. Very hard. "Charlie, no."

"You don't want 'em?"

She snatched them, then went up on tiptoe and kissed him on the forehead. "Thanks, honey, I can't *imagine* how I managed to forget them." She turned and hurried back to the door, her sneakers whispering. Then she swept her keycard and disappeared down a neon lit hallway.

He turned and left, ignoring the guard's following eyes. "Thank you," he said as he was buzzed out.

He went to his truck, got in, and sat there. He was shaking so hard he could barely manage the key. It was like Iraq after an operation, when you realized just how close you had come. Same thing happened to him after lab pops. One of these days, he was going to find that his courage was all used up. But not now, not yet. He could not fail here, he could not turn away.

Beth's warnings about the weapons and the security had been right. First, guards don't carry serious pistols unless they have shoot orders, and a Sig Sauer is a very serious pistol. It's an excellent defender, of course, but it is primarily a stopping weapon. It would blow up a man's chest. Instant death. Second, the security system was sophisticated and it was deep. A successful penetration would require not only extraordinary planning, but extraordinary luck.

How could he ask anybody else to play with him in a sandbox like this? They trusted him to the point of considering him a miracle worker. He would get them in, he would keep them safe, he would get them out. Except this time, maybe in a body bag.

No, this would need to be a solo run. He'd have to place the truck well off the campus and hope he could lead the Tanda to it, or have it attempt the run in only at the last possible moment.

Forcing himself to swallow the desert in his mouth, forcing the shaking to stop, he got the truck rolling and headed down the drive. Instinct made it feel like an escape, and it was all he could do not to jam on the gas. But it kept it normal, making himself drive like a man unconcerned.

On the chance that he was being followed, he didn't go directly home. This wasn't because he didn't want them to know where he'd come from. They already knew that. But any dick worth his ticket also knew that people clustered their chores. If you gotta take the glasses, then pick up the cleaning and mail the letters. If he went straight home, there would be suspicions. It was the kind of thing that a detective looking to justify his paycheck would put in a report. If he could surprise these people, he gave himself a thirty percent chance of getting in. But if they were waiting for trouble, that percentage went right to zero.

He'd brought actual letters to mail and a suit for the cleaners in the back seat. The fact that it hadn't been worn, let alone cleaned, in years was immaterial. You gotta walk the walk.

He headed out onto White Road, then back up I 35 and into his neck of the woods.

He'd get into that lab. Pop the sucker wide open. Those little critters in there— whatever they were—had just acquired a new best friend.

14

THE LOST

As she tried not to stomp off, Beth also tried to swallow her fury, but it was hard. Charlie had promised! They'd talked it over last night. He'd agreed that this was not something that could be fixed his way. She was taking it to a lawyer. Either the Tanda were people being held against their will or they were animals who had been smuggled in without the proper permits. Had to be, because no Tanda permit existed. She'd already texted Barney Rosen and told him she had an issue. Problem was, Barney had a tendency to disappear. He was a birder. They went into isolated places, did birders. But at least he was honest and well respected, unlike that idiotic reprobate Charlie favored, Larry Stein. The only reason that lunatic wasn't in jail was that the judges were all crooks, too.

She'd deal with Charlie tonight, and very sternly. She'd tell him that if he kept on, she was going to out him to Barrett's security chief.

But of course she wouldn't and he'd know that. But she had to stop him. These creeps were well capable of killing, she had no doubt of that. They might kill her man!

She had a busy day ahead, and the next thing was her first meeting with one of the females, the one code named Betty. She and Joe had fought, and the symmetry of the group had been compromised. It was her responsibility to find out why. Also, to find out whether or not Betty knew she was pregnant, and if so how she felt about it.

She'd set the meeting for eleven, during the Tandas' break time, telling Betty to come to her office at the appointed hour.

She'd done it this way very purposefully. She wanted to see whether or not Betty could keep an appointment based on clock watching. If she did, then Barrett had definitely incarcerated a human level intelligence here. Animals did not pass time, they waited. Their only sense of duration was the eternal now. The ability to perceive time and organize time was among the most fundamental indicators of higher intelligence.

But was a creature with human intelligence automatically a human being with human rights? Slave cases aside, no court had ever explored that question.

Well, if she had her way, that was about to change.

A moment later, Betty came in, still wearing her white head covering from the line. She was exhausted, her lips hanging slack from the effort she'd been making.

This was the first time Beth had seen one of the women at close range. She had big red eyes and a face that made you think of laughter.

Betty had kept the appointment at the designated time exactly. So, incredibly, what stood before Beth now, staring at her warily, was in her opinion definitely a fellow intelligent being, a human of another species.

"Thank you for coming," she said.

Betty signed 'yes.'

"You dance a lot on the line."

'Keller says.'

"He makes you dance?"

She nodded.

"Come on in, sit down. Let's talk some girl talk, you and me."

She came slowly closer to Beth, sidling along, averting her eyes.

"You can look at me."

She shook her head.

"Why not, Betty?"

She signed again, 'Hurts.'

"It hurts to look at me?"

Betty nodded, pointed to her eyes. Then she signed something so strange that Beth did not think at first that she had understood, and asked her to sign it again.

'The black hurts in our heads.'

"What black?"

'We have eyes. You have holes.'

What in the world could she mean?

"My eyes are green, Betty."

She shook her head, her hair streaming. Reaching her hands up so that she wouldn't have to look at Beth, she repeated, 'holes.'

"You see my eyes as holes? Do you see all of our eyes that way?'

A groan came out of her, rose into a thin, eerie wail, then slipped away into silence.

"But you watch TV."

She signed, 'Doesn't hurt in TV.'

Beth considered. "Did you ever see one of us who didn't look like that?"

Betty shook a finger.

"Look at me now."

Two shakes, emphatic.

"Do you know the word fear?"

She nodded.

"So you fear us? Is it the snickersnee? It's not here, you know."

Betty signed toward the door. She wanted to go.

Beth had an idea. Or no, an intuition. "Betty, if you can't look at me, can you touch me?"

For a moment, Betty remained motionless. She raised a tightly fisted hand, then lowered it.

"Open your fists. Relax." She held out her own hand.

Betty cringed.

Beth laughed a little, trying to put the Tanda at her ease. "Don't be afraid, really. No punishment planned."

Betty darted a glance at her. Another. Beth smiled.

'Pretty,' Betty signed.

"You're the one who's pretty."

'Red,' she signed, pointing at Beth's face.

Beth tried to understand. "What's red?"

A trembling finger, long and delicate, rose and touched Beth's lips. Then Betty snatched her hand back. She stared at the fingertip. Her eyes grew furtive. She made the sign for 'sorry'.

"Betty, that's lipstick. Here, I'll show you." She dug her lipstick out of her purse. "It makes your lips red. We women wear it. Would you like to wear it?"

Huge shaking of the head, backing toward the door.

"Oh, come on," Beth said. She opened the tube. "Don't you think it's pretty?"

Betty took it, sniffed it, got some on her nose.

Beth laughed again, and Betty sort of smiled. "Let me help you." There was a mirror on the wall above the examining table that stood against one wall of Beth's office. "Come on up here. We'll have a makeup lesson."

"Muggp. Mugg-upp!"

"That's right, Betty That's very good! Say it again. Two words. 'Make.' Say it."

"Ma*ggg*."

She had a soft voice and yet so deeply alien that it made Beth's skin crawl.

"Now say 'up.' Uhhhh-*puh*!"

"Uhhh-*puhhhh* Hp! Uh-*p*! Up! Up!"

"Betty, that's perfect! Do you know 'perfect'?

Betty nodded vigorously. "Mageup! Mageup!" She pointed to her lips.

"Okay, let's do it! Here, I'll guide your hand."

But Betty took the lipstick, handling it with startling grace and speed. She'd understood instantly, and spread it perfectly the first time. She peered into the mirror...and the sun rose in her face.

The smile made Beth want to clap her hands like a little girl. "Betty, you look absolutely fabulous!"

Betty signed so fast Beth couldn't even begin to follow her. She had to let it go. Then Betty stopped. As Beth returned her lipstick to her purse, she followed her movements with hungry eyes. Beth brought out her blusher. "Let's see how this looks." She demonstrated it to the fascinated Tanda. "It goes on your cheeks."

Betty's skin was a light tan, not a human color at all. But Beth's own skin had an olive glow from her Italian grandmother, so the blusher kind of worked as Betty brushed it on. She was just extraordinarily skillful with her hands. It was quite marvelous to watch. She also had an artist's eye, and applied it as expertly as she had the lipstick.

The next lesson was eyeliner, then mascara, and by the end of the process, Betty was smiling from ear to ear, her whole body trembling. She signed, 'I pretty, I pretty,' over and over again. Fluttering her eyes, she looked in the mirror. "Erren Cho," she said. She pointed to herself. "Erren!"

"What is Erren?"

"Keevee! Keevee!"

Maybe they were developing their own spoken language as well. "I only understand English."

"Unh!" She slapped herself in the side of the head. "Aye toopid!"

"You are very far from stupid."

"Erren an Kee vee."

"TV? Oh, *Ellen*! The Ellen show on TV!"

They laughed together again, and then, very suddenly and very gently—and very, very quickly, Betty took Beth's face in her hands and planted a little kiss on her cheek. "Pank oo, pank oo fo mah maggup—*mah* maggup!"

"Oh, you're welcome, baby. You're very welcome. Listen, we're gonna have a girl's club. You and me and Flutter and Jill, and we are gonna get ourselves made up and get our hair brushed out and just get to lookin' like a whole bunch of Ellens and whoever else we admire."

"Ya, ya!" But then she froze. Her face grew serious. Again, a hand came out. Fingers fluttered across Beth's chest, her blouse. Betty's other arm came up and crossed her own chest, concealing her long breasts.

Beth felt a cool breath of realization tickle her. In this moment, for only the second time in the whole stretching history of the world, a species on this old planet had made one of the greatest of all realizations.

"I can't give you my clothes," Beth said gently. "But I will bring you clothes. I will bring all of you clothes. You will not be naked anymore."

She pleaded with her big, carefully made up eyes. "Oooo. *Mmmm.*" She stroked the cloth. Her own breasts were now tightly hidden behind that arm. Beth recalled from Genesis, "And the eyes of them were opened, and they knew that they were naked. And then God said, 'Who told thee that thou wast naked? Hast thou eaten of the tree, whereof I commanded thee that thou shouldest not eat?'"

It came into Beth's mind that she was in a very strange place, here. It could easily be that this little moment of realization would echo in the ages of the Tanda, touching their memory and becoming part of their myth forever, mixed in with the story of Keller their awful god.

Betty had now retreated across the room, still covering her front as best she could with her hands. Her eyes darted here and there and she hunched. Her effort at concealment was painful to see.

What she wanted to do was to just put the poor woman in her car and head over to Wal-Mart and get her a starter outfit? And the others, too, why not take them? Then she thought of the armory she'd been shown, of the men in the gray uniforms, of the alarms and the guns and Keller's eyes, hard fanatical crystals.

"Betty, I'll bring you clothes tomorrow."

Betty looked up, glancing briefly at Beth's eyes, then looking away again, shaking her head as if she'd felt some secret pain.

"I will, Betty" She wondered how much the Tanda was actually understanding of this conversation. Did she possess the concept of tomorrow, or even know the word? "Sign 'tomorrow,' Betty Can you sign it?"

She brought her hand up to her cheek and twisted it, American sign for something happening in the future. But then she continued, drawing her right hand up her chest, middle finger extended. 'Feels.' 'Tomorrow feels.' She paused, as if waiting to be sure Beth was herself understanding.

"Tomorrow feels like what?"

Crouching, head bowed, Betty came to her. "Fa-veh. Fa-veh-veh."

"Oh, Betty" She went down to her, went down on her knees and put her arms around the lovely little Tanda woman. "Tomorrow feels like forever."

"*Rrrr*! Fe*rrr*-eh-veh!"

"You've got it—the 'r' sound. You're good, Betty. Very good!"

Betty shook her head. "No so gut. No-o-o."

"We'll practice! We'll all practice tomorrow, when I bring your clothes."

She signed, 'clothes, clothes, clothes.' Then, "Geen! G—*rrrr*—een! Peeze, meh *grrreeen*!"

"You like green?"

More nodding. Then an embrace. Beth felt the Tanda's lithe, muscular body tight against her, and smelled the faint sourness of her sweat. She stroked Betty's hair.

It came very suddenly, the sob that burst out of her. Tears flooded. "Maah," she said, 'maah...' She was clutching Beth's blouse in iron hands. "*Maah...maah*."

"Yes, your clothes, Betty. You will have clothes."

Betty had stiffened. She was breathing fast.

"Green is your favorite color?" Beth asked quickly.

"Faveo-o...oh!"

"Fave."

"Fave!"

"Oh."

"Oh!"

"Rit."

"*Rrrit* Fav-o-rit!"

"Green is your favorite color, and green you shall have to wear!"

Betty scampered over to the mirror again, looked at herself. Then she went to Beth's purse, muttering to herself, testing various word sounds. Gone was the simpering, bowing creature of a few minutes before. Her head was high, her shoulders were back. She'd forgotten her nakedness once again, in her eager zeal to get something from that purse.

"What do you—"

In a flash, the blue plastic hairbrush Beth carried with her was in Betty's hand. She held it high, glorying in its bristles and shaking her head as fast as she could, so that the wavy hair that cascaded down from the back of her head flashed about in the cold office light.

Beth took the brush and began brushing Betty's hair while Betty grinned and held her head back. As Beth brushed, intimacy and companionship grew between the two women, and Beth thought that this might be the moment she had been trying to reach from the beginning of the interview.

"Betty, do you know what pregnant means?" She made the hand shapes that represented a big belly. Betty stared. Was that wariness in her eyes? Anger? "Do you know what a baby is?"

Betty did the cradle gesture and smiled slightly.

"Why did Flutter and Jill kill her baby?"

There was a subtle stiffening of her muscles, but nothing to prepare Beth for what came next. For a few moments, Betty seemed to be choking. Then she jumped away from Beth. The wildness in those red eyes caused her to drop the brush. Instinct screamed at Beth to run, but then Betty threw back her head and howled and the grief there and the anger there caused Beth to go down to her level and throw open her arms to her.

She remained as still as a statue, her head thrown back, her fists clenched, howling and sobbing and choking.

"Betty! Betty!"

She stopped. Her lips twisted, her eyes squinted behind a

shimmer of tears. Her hands were made to curling claws and she came forward. Beth drew back. She thought she had the Tanda equivalent of a berserker chimp here, a creature who could not be reached, could not be deflected, and who was going to tear her limb from limb.

Just like that, the little, sweet, excited woman had disappeared into a raging animal, and it was between Beth and the door, which was also the only escape route. Right now, she was behind the charmed barrier of her own stare, which Betty could not meet. If she blinked, what might happen? She stared hard at Betty.

But then—literally before Beth's astonished eyes—she sucked the furious animal right back into the gentle surface that had been there before.

"Betty?"

Betty said, "eelos." She closed her tearing eyes, concentrated all her effort. "Eee los, Bef. *Eee lossss*, Bef!"

Ee loss? She started to ask her to sign it, but then she understood. "Oh my God." She had entirely misinterpreted the Tanda's signals. She wasn't expressing rage at all. It was sorrow: '*We are lost.*'

She had never before witnessed grief this awful, and in this depth, where emotions were this tremendous—for this was the grief of a whole species that was lost from its home and falling into the dark pits of the alien beings that had captured it.

They didn't fear us, but what we know. Something in them told them that our minds hid the secret of their own existence, and that was why, she felt sure, they saw our eyes as pits of darkness. That darkness was the mystery of their own truth.

"You know, don't you, what this place really is?"

Betty nodded, her face now filled with a new expression and a new meaning. Standing here, the little naked woman from the ruined forest displayed the dignity of a queen. And Beth went to her knees before the greatness of the tragedy that she had found, and the two women came at last into each other's arms, and held one another close.

15

THUNDER FROM THE EAST

The next morning, Beth arrived at the campus as the sun was just rising above the hills that dozed along the eastern horizon. She felt flat inside, drained from a night of fighting with Charlie and sleepless misery worrying about what he might be up to. His repeated denials had finally caused her to just explode, screaming herself hoarse and causing every ape and monkey in the Center to scream with her.

Charlie, poor Charlie, she should never, ever have told him a thing about what was happening at Barrett. Because that sweet guy who she loved to the depths of her soul was going to die here. He would come, she could not stop him and she knew it, and he would die here.

She'd called Barney ten times at least, leaving frantic messages that he had to explain things to Charlie, but the darned fool was off bird watching until Friday. Just like him. He was a big cheese in the annual hawk count that took place down on the Texas coast. There were still a few places in this country without cellphone coverage, and wherever he was down there, he was apparently in one of them. Or his phone was turned off. That would be pure Barney.

Beneath the golden clouds of dawn, she opened her car door to a riot of birdsong. Mockingbirds and cardinals and doves flitted about, big grackles bathed in the sprinklers that were hissing on the gleaming lawn. If the Tanda ever saw it, the green of it would elevate them to an ecstasy that she suspected would also be a torment.

She'd thought about that love of green. It was almost certainly an unformed memory of the forest they had been born in, something deep in their DNA.

The air was fragrant with the odor of the pink Oleanders that lined the property. Spiderwebs glowed in the dew that clung to the grass.

Toward morning, she'd had one of those awful waking dreams that seem, however briefly, to be true. For a moment, she'd been in a coffin. Buried alive. She'd cried out. Charlie had jumped out of bed, no doubt fearing that she was going to leap at him again, beat his chest and scream into his face.

The dream had gone shuddering off into her own darkness. They'd laid there until the gray of dawn, then gotten up and, saying little, then eaten their breakfast in silence.

She marched across the parking lot. She was laden with shopping bags, and there was no doubt that they were going to create a huge issue at some point during the day. She'd bought a selection of blouses and shirts, skirts and pants. She muttered, 'Love you, Charlie, love you.' Damn the tears that were blinding her, damn the emotional volcano inside that was making her as crazy as Betty had gotten yesterday.

If Keller got on her case about these clothes, she might just knock the man cold. She knew a few moves, she worked with apes. She could take that bastard right down. She'd like to just shoot him, and she hated herself for thinking a thing like that. Beth was about kindness and compassion and love and damn his soul for stirring up hate this intense in her.

On her way home last night, she'd stopped at the Wal-Mart on Vance-Jackson Road, and gotten some clothes that she thought would please the Tanda—bold prints, strong colors, simple design. Being a confirmed jeans and t-shirt person, she'd had some initial trouble getting things right. But the Tanda were going to do fine with what she was bringing them. Lots of green, to serve their inner hunger. Lots of bold design to excite their sense of fun.

She reached the employee entrance, put down her bags and paused. She'd been strictly cautioned against bringing anything in that wasn't authorized and logged. So, would the bags cause the alarm system to go off? If that happened, then she would have her confrontation earlier rather than later. But these clothes were going on the backs of the Tanda. That was definite.

She swiped her card. The door started buzzing. She hauled it open and went through. The stark hallway was silent but for the sound of the Coke machine rumbling in the company cafeteria. The same people who prepared food for the Tanda cooked for this cafeteria. No expense was spared. The food at Barrett Scientific was excellent. But the kitchen staff wasn't here yet. Now, the facility was still asleep. In fact, hers was one of just five cars in the lot: the night guards, the night manager and now her.

The Tanda had their breakfast at seven, and nobody else would be here before six thirty. Unless she stirred up the night staff, she had about forty minutes to put her plan in motion.

She went down to her office and spent some time taking the clothes out of the bags, carefully getting rid of any and all pins, which they obviously would not expect.

After she clothed the Tanda, her next step was going to be to educate them. She planned to start with speech and then reading. They would learn home economics and practical finance, how to drive—in short, everything they needed to live the most normal lives that they could. Then they were getting iPads and going on the internet. They would learn about the world, and then they were getting out of here. This was over. Barney would see to it, and when the public saw them, the public would explode with rage over what this company was up to.

When Keller objected to her plans, as he certainly would, she would argue that the Tanda would not have children because they sensed that they were in prison, even if they could not articulate it.

Burning in her mind, in her soul, was Betty's agony, and those slurred words rising up from the depth of need "ee *losss*"

"Once I was lost, but now I'm found," she muttered as she strode down the long, sterile corridor. She could never return them to their jungle, but she could help them find a place in ours.

Carrying folded clothes in her arms, she went to the control room. Harry Lerner was night manager. She didn't care for him, especially not the way he leered at her. Harry was an arrogant creep, not to put too fine a point on it.

"You need any help?" he asked.

"No help."

"Uh, can I ask what you're taking in there?"

"No." She glanced at the barrier camera to be sure that the Tanda were still in their rooms, then swiped her card through the reader. The barrier slid back.

Lerner followed her in. "Excuse me, but what is that stuff?"

"Stuff."

"Hey, baby, I'm not tryin' to make a scene, but there's rules. You can't introduce anything into the enclosure without prior authorization."

"Back off, Harry."

He came close to her. "I sure as hell had you pegged, I guess. I took one look at you, and I saw ball breaker written all over that pretty face. 'This one gets her way,' I thought. Now you come in here like this. Gimme crap like this. You could get me fired." As he spoke, he made a move to take the bundle out of her hands. She stepped back. He stank of sour beer. He'd probably been drinking all night as he watched over the Tanda, and now he was feeling a little mean and he'd like nothing better than to cause her trouble.

"Harry, I have two simple words for you: *back off*!" She turned and marched deeper into the enclosure.

"Goddamn you!"

She crossed the rec room, went down the two steps into the small common area. She was expecting Lerner to follow, but he stayed at his post. She knew, however, that he'd be watching her over the monitoring system. He would be on the phone to Keller, too, of course. Fine. Let it happen. Good old Greg was in New York and couldn't do a thing about it but scream.

"Hey, Betty," she called.

Betty appeared, looking bleary-eyed. Her makeup was a blurry memory, her lipstick gone except at the extreme edges of her long lips.

Betty looked at the bundle Beth was carrying. Her eyes flickered away, then returned. She looked harder. "Geen! Geen! Geen!" she shouted, almost leaping into Beth's arms. Her hands scrabbled frantically at the clothes. Laughing at her excitement, Beth helped her pull out a blouse—flowers against a green background.

Betty held it against herself, her grin wide. The others were gathering around now. They were grabbing at the clothes, holding them up.

"Let me help you," Beth said. The moment she tried to touch the blouse, Betty screamed and held it away. "Hey, don't worry, it's yours now and forever. Here, let's put it on you."

"Un *me*?"

Beth noticed that she was talking now rather than signing. She decided to respond in sign only if she had to. They could talk if they tried. If their vocal equipment limited them in some ways, she had no doubt that they'd find others. These people had perfectly good minds, and it is the job of the mind to find a way.

She got the blouse on Betty "Now, here's how you button it." She did the first button, and instantly Betty had the rest finished.

In moments, they all had clothes on—sort of. Jill was wearing shorts on her head and a green T, but backwards. Joe had on a blue-jeans skirt and a green blouse. Jack was dressed in a skirt, which would have looked a whole lot better on Jill. Flutter had tied jeans around her waist by the legs.

Patiently, Beth got blouses and shirts exchanged, and taught them how pants worked.

The skirts and shorts were too long on them, with the result that the Tanda presented a curiously old fashioned appearance as they paraded around, jumping up on their game table and dancing, then racing up and down between the far wall and the barrier at the other end of their rec room, the women's skirts and everybody's hair flying.

She watched them, taking what she realized was a mother's pleasure in their enjoyment, when it occurred to her that there were only five of them participating. She went into Crunch's room.

He was lying on his bed with his face against the wall.

"Crunch?" He did not move. She drew closer. "Crunch, you look like a man in need of pants."

He turned over, and when he did she was appalled at what she saw. The poor man was covered with contusions and burns. He'd been struck with the cattle prod easily a couple of dozen times. She leaned closer. No effort had been made to dress his wounds.

She reached out, touched his hand.

He sat up, hung his head.

"Crunch?"

He signed, 'Me bad.'

For a moment her mind was blank. Then she took out her phone and snapped some pictures, holding it so that—she hoped—the action wouldn't be picked up on the surveillance cameras.

The truth here was plain. This man had been tortured. There was no other way to describe it. "Who did this?"

His hands flickered. She could not follow the frantic motions.

"Slow down, Crunch."

'I go to up top. He punish me.'

"Up top? What do you mean, 'up top?'"

'I go to line. Not hole. But Joe, he is not bottom again. I am bottom forever.' He slapped himself on the forehead. "Evah!"

It wasn't exactly gibberish. But she could hardly believe that Joe had gotten hold of the prod, or that he would use it on another of the Tanda.

"Joe," she called.

He came prancing in. When Crunch saw his shorts and brown golf shirt, his eyes widened. Then he looked even more miserable.

"You can have clothes, too, Crunch," Beth said. "I got some especially for you. Big for a big guy."

The gratitude in Crunch's face as she helped him into his own clothes almost melted her. She spent half her time in here fighting tears.

"Joe," she asked, "what happened to him?"

Joe looked away, his eyelids fluttering. The expression wasn't a human one, but it communicated an emotion very clearly: Joe felt guilty about this.

So he was somehow responsible. But how could the Tanda get at that prod through a door that was not only locked but required a keycard? Or was that a stupid question, given that Moreland could pick padlocks with twigs? The Tanda had great dexterity and far more intelligence.

"Did you stick him?"

Both Tanda shook their heads.

"Who was it, then?"

"Gerner," Joe said.

"Harry Lerner? When?"

They looked blank. Perhaps their concept of time was not yet complex enough to enable them to understand a question about a past event. Tomorrow, they understood. Appointments, they could make. But yesterday for them had no duration. The past was just that--past.

They were a step beyond the edge of Eden, the Tanda, just starting eastward into the land of time that the bible calls the valley of bones, because it is where you come to understand death. She was the serpent in their tree of knowledge, and she was also the angel with the sword who would forever banish them into the desert of longing and memory, and that thing that distinguishes us and terrorizes us, that we call the self. Their green dreams were destined to become their Eden.

"Why was he stuck, Joe?"

To her great surprise, his face fell apart. It happened in stages. First, the lips drooped. Then tears swam into the eyes. Then the head sank down. If there was on this Earth a more poignant or intense expression of guilt, she had not seen it.

Joe began signing. 'He thought Crunch went in the tunnel. But it was me.' He drew a long, choking breath. "Ah soee. Ah soee."

"You aren't to blame, Joe, no matter what you did. Harry should never have punished any of you like this."

The Big Voice said, "Breakfast Cheerios, boys and girls!"

The two Tanda shot off like rockets, their new shirttails flapping behind them. Well, that was the end of this conversation, but not of this situation. That bastard has reason to worry about being fired now, because it was either him or her, Greg Keller could take his choice, and if it was her, he could forget getting any breeding going. Harry Lerner would never spend another night in this facility. If she could, she was going to get him charged with animal abuse. If the company wouldn't allow that, then they were going to have to hit him with a nasty fine in addition to firing him, or they would see that brutalized Tanda on the internet.

Keller said, "You've been a busy girl."

She whirled around. "Where did you come from?"

"I took the redeye. I want to know what in the name of God you're up to."

"They won't breed because instinct tells them they're confined. You want them to breed, you've got to get them out of this hole. Clothes are the first step."

He gave her a hollow look. She didn't find it comfortable, obviously, but also she didn't understand it. She'd expected yelling and screaming.

"There's somebody I want you to meet," he said.

"You realize that Lerner abused one of the animals."

He nodded. "There was an escape attempt. He was overzealous in his response."

She could not have been more surprised. In fact, floored. "An escape attempt? Are you sure?"

"One of them—or maybe more, maybe even all of them—got into

the air conditioning system. They were heard by the night guard in the lobby."

"As I said, they know that they're in prison."

"This is their world."

"It's not a world, it's a goddamn supermax."

She'd expected push back, but all she got was an ironic little laugh, bitter.

He turned and began moving toward the barrier. As they went through the rec room, he commented, "Clothes are dangerous. They'll get themselves caught in the machinery."

"They far too dexterous. When was this escape attempt?"

"Night before last."

"And they weren't seen? With all the surveillance—"

"It's on the tapes. Somebody hadn't been doing their job."

Lerner, she hoped. "You knew this yesterday and I wasn't told?"

"Need to know. You had none."

"I most assuredly did have a need to know. In fact, it's essential that I know anything to do with their behavior. Immediately."

"Is it?" he asked.

"Of course! For God's sake!"

"The question was rhetorical."

"What's that supposed to mean?"

Again the bitter little chuckle.

They went into his office. A man was sitting before the TV watching Keller's collection of Tanda videotapes. "Doctor Ma," Keller said.

The man stood up and turned around. Smiling, he came forward. He was trim, his face pleasantly soft, his brown eyes gentle. He wore what Beth recognized as a finely tailored blue suit.

"Doctor Ma, may I introduce our staff primatologist, Doctor Elizabeth Cooke? Doctor Cooke was our behavioral specialist."

Was? Had he said *was*?

"I will be looking forward to learning all you have discovered," Dr. Ma said.

"It's not much. Not in a few days."

"I am sure it is a great deal. One with such an illustrious reputation must see very quickly what it takes those like me, who are nothing but mere technicians, a great deal of time to learn."

She smiled and nodded, and wondered if his statement had been intended as an insult or a compliment. "Are you joining us, Doctor? I'm sorry, but I'm confused. Greg, help me here."

Greg smiled tightly. "Your severance package vested as soon as you signed the contract," he said. "You'll get twenty-five percent of a year's salary, and your medical coverage will continue for twenty-four months or until you get another job."

This was a damn exit interview. She was being fired.

"I've been here four days!"

"Doctor, I am afraid that we are responsible for the dismissal of the staff. I would like to offer you to continue your studies with us, but, in my country, you know, it is not so easy."

She glared at Keller. "Will you tell me what in hell is going on here?"

"Sit down," Keller said. He gestured toward the chairs in front of his fireplace.

Beth sat on the edge of one of them, Keller on the edge of another. Only Dr. Ma relaxed, and he did so formally, crossing his legs and folding his hands in his lap, leaning forward with a rigid smile on his face.

"Barrett Scientific has concluded a sale to World Biological. They have purchased the Tanda," Keller said.

As he spoke, he seemed to gaze into some inner world, as if he was traveling to a distant island of the mind.

"We will transport them on Monday," Dr. Ma said. "In the interim, we wish you to prepare them for the journey. They must understand enough so that they will not be afraid." He gazed at her, holding it so long that it became unsettling. "We would not want to lose any of our investment."

She couldn't talk. Her throat wouldn't work. It must be like this when you're told you have terminal cancer. The news silences you. The doctor waits.

First, she wanted sympathy. Then she got mad.

"I know World Bio," she said. They were working with CRISPR, among other things, creating new forms of animal—humans, too, it was rumored.

Dr Ma smiled again. "Do you have a metric on their intelligence," he asked.

"There's no standard."

"Of course."

She thought that the Tanda were headed from one awful situation into another. What happened to them at World Bio nobody would ever know, nobody except them, and they would know every terrible second of it.

"I think that they are lovely beings," Dr. Ma said. "Do you know, when I was a young student, I used to compose music for the Guzheng. They thought I would be a musician. Illustrious composer, even. I am afraid not! But the lovely Tanda, they inspire thoughts in music." He leaned forward. "I know, I can see it in your eyes, the shock of this. Please do not assume that we will do some primitive thing to them. We are interested in this wonderful new mind. They will be treated as honored guests."

False or true? She could not know. "How will you keep them?"

He shrugged, not meeting her eyes. "As you do. In a pleasant and comfortable atmosphere."

"You should free them."

Again, the smile came, and this time the truth came with it. "In Thai, that word does not have the same meaning. Do you know, I am not even sure what you are saying, when you say 'freedom' in this country. Do you mean that they should be free to wander the streets, perhaps to starve and die there? Free to be murdered, perhaps, by some superstitious fool? What freedom do you mean?"

"Doctor Ma, you don't have to sell her on anything. She's an employee."

"I have watched you work with them, Doctor Cooke. You are very skilled and empathetic." He smile gently. "Is it Revlon, that lipstick?"

All the time that she had been working with them, he had been her silent witness. His silent presence felt like a violation of her life somehow.

"Revlon, yes," she said. She didn't go into the animal testing issue, not now, but Revlon hadn't done it in 30 years.

"Clothing them is corrupting," Keller said harshly, and for the first time his anger showed through the carefully maintained shell. "And the lipstick."

"They need space—inner space, a sense of self and place and belonging. If they cannot go outside, then at least let them have some possessions that enable them to express themselves."

Keller gazed at her with eyes like stones. "Lipstick and shirts hardly qualify."

"Of course they qualify. These people are naked!"

"That is a very optimistic characterization!"

"They're people and you know it, both of you. But you don't want them to have anything that might empower them in any way whatsoever, do you?"

Keller scoffed. Ma said nothing.

"You have no insight, Greg. You're completely unaware of what you've done here. You've imprisoned these people."

"I have protected these animals."

"I concur, and very effectively, too, Doctor Keller," Ma said.

"You know what this is? This is self-deluded garbage. They're people being treated like zoo animals, shut up in prison for the crime of existing."

"They don't even know what a zoo is," Keller snapped.

"Their hearts know that they're imprisoned." She went to her feet. "You want to send them to Thailand, you do it on your own. You get that monster Harry Lerner who beat Crunch up with the goddamn cattle prod to help you."

"You used it."

"Not twenty times! And I didn't know at the time what I was actually dealing with, because you didn't tell me. I thought I had an extremely bright animal on my hands, that might need physical correction to help it understand. It took me a few more meetings to see that they possessed our level of intelligence, but had been deprived of information. Intentionally. By you! It's not a crime in any law book, but that doesn't mean that there isn't crime in this facility, Doctor. Your crime. Your company's crime."

"There's no crime here."

She went face to face with him. "A crime against humanity--*theirs*!"

With that, she turned around and walked out of the office. She was acutely aware of her sneakers snapping on the floor. She threw open the big doors and strode past Dr. Keller's secretarial pool, populated only by a silent, expressionless Rebecca

She didn't know where she should go, so she went to her own office. She closed the door—not that closed doors mattered in this labyrinth of cameras. She dropped down into her desk chair. For a time, she stared at her view and tried various ways of not exploding. Deep breaths. Thinking about something else. Shutting her eyes real tight.

She wanted to let the Tanda out right this second—which would fail, of course.

The Tanda were being moved on Monday. Today was Thursday.

Damn you and your birds, Barney, come back!

She understood her situation very clearly: she was helpless.

16

NIGHT WORK

Charlie crossed the cracked tarmac and entered the enormous old hangar. In it were seven planes, all small, all elderly. In fact, one of them was a Cessna 170, which put it back to well before he or Freddie Breyer were even motes in God's eye. "Hey, Fred," he yelled. "Wake up, you old sonofabitch."

Fred came out from under the cowling of a something that looked real tired. "She's got a godforsaken engine mount," he said affably. "Tear herself apart, you spank her fanny even a little bit."

"When'd you last fly her?"

He glanced at his watch. "'Bout noon. Flag job." An advertising banner lay alongside the plane.

In country, Fred had crashed fourteen times that he'd talk about. He would come in lower and slower than any other fixed wing pilot in the army. And the man could see. He could see a sniper painted desert tan and hiding in a sliver of shadow. From the air.

"Question is, Fred, why are you still alive?"

"Question is, what's a shitfaced old druggie like you doin' in a clean and sober shithole like this?"

"I got a job only a crazy man would do and you are a crazy man."

"You wanna buy a 1967 Bellanca Viking full of roaches I can't get rid of?"

"Yeah, why not?" He pulled out his wallet, produced a five dollar bill. "Can you make change?"

"Lotta planes got roaches. People toss their cookies, and—"

"No, Fred, close that door, please."

"What in hell do you want, if I may be so bold?"

"I'm going to be doing a little skydiving, and I need a fellow-adventurer to take me up."

Fred took a deep breath, let it out with a long sigh. "You go to one of them frou-frou skydiving places, buddy-boy. Get the girlie men to help you."

"I need a racing chute, black on black. A Spectra 170, say."

Fred looked him up and down. "Go with a 190."

"I'll blow away." It was a chute for a heavysider.

"The hell you will, Santa Claus."

"Another thing, the job happens at two o in the morning."

Fred thought a moment, during which his normal frown turned into a deeply fissured scowl. "There's so much stupidity in that idea, I don't know where to start shitting on it."

"There's more. You go in low."

"How low?"

"Three hundred, say."

"What are you doin', stealing the goddamn beacons off cell towers?"

Charlie threw his hat on the floor and stomped. "How in hell ever did you guess? Love those beacons. Got 'em all over the house."

"Corporal Charlie, what kind of cash up front are we looking at?"

Charlie was going to be limited here. He couldn't let Beth know this was going down, and she watched the accounts like a beady-eyed Sister of Mercy. So what he had done was to max out the cash advance on his one credit card. He had seven hundred and twenty dollars in his pocket, and Fred wasn't his only stop. "Three hundred bucks, which has to cover thirty minutes airtime and rental on the chute."

"Oh, so I have to buy a fifteen hundred dollar chute and rent it to you for squat. Nothing doing, ole buddy ole pal. And why the fuck are you using a racer? You gotta learn that chute. It will not forgive."

"I know the goddamn chute."

"When's the last time you jumped outa a airplane, pops?"

"Not all that long ago."

"I think Cheney and company were still trying to kill us, last time you did a dump. And racers weren't army issue. So you ain't never so much as tried one on."

He'd expected this, so he pulled out his ticket.

"Well, I'll be damned. What a boy you are."

Cleverish, maybe. He'd forged it himself on Beth's Dell. A little Photoshop, a few JPEGs pulled off certain dark internet 'ID hobbyist' websites, and hey presto, here was a skydiver with thirty dumps behind him, the last ten with a racing chute on his fanny.

"It's gonna be five hundred bucks, my man, and you go rent your own damn chute."

"Screw you."

"Screw me? I think not. I'll go three hundred and fifty bucks and not a penny less. I gotta put gas in the airplane, wear it and tear it—"

"Very damn little."

"And maybe I got a dead man on the ground to explain, which could cost me my own damn ticket, without which I am living out of a grocery basket."

There was truth in that. "You gotta get the chute for me. I'll give you the cash."

Fred nodded slowly. That was Freddie, thinking took him time.

"When does this happen?"

"Dunno. Week or two. Three, outside. You get the equipment ready, I call you and I say, 'Where's my pizza?' At that point, you know I'll be here in an hour.

"You call here in the middle of the night and ask for a pizza? And what if I'm not here?"

"You'll be here."

"Ten bucks a day to hang out, man. I got a life."

"You have no life. You ain't even got beer money, let alone woman money."

"I got a date tonight."

"There is no date. Plus you live right here in this hangar." He pointed to the office hut on the back wall. Inside, there was a desk, a chair, a hotplate, an ancient computer and a pile of yellow sheets. And a cot. "Your date tonight's the same as every night. With a bunch of old airplanes."

"They got souls, man. Airplanes get souls, you fly 'em high enough and wild enough. And these babies, they may look like shit, but they all been way up there where the furies wail."

"Does every goddamn poet land in a hole?"

"Every poet of the sky, boy. God, I remember you, fuckin' covered with lampblack, droppin' into the middle of nowhere in the middle of the night, fuckin' *alone*. Christ, you were some kind of unbelievable nut, Charlie. Thing is, what're you up to now, dumping over the fuckin' city in the middle of the night? There's no place around here you can do a survivable dump, night or day, man."

Charlie gave him as careful and as intense a look as he could give somebody. He used all the power that was in him, the power of his spirit and the past they had shared, and he kept on until every gram of curiosity was leached out of Fred's weathered puss. By slow degrees, it became like it did when he was concentrating on a mission, almost childlike, as if he had turned into an exceptionally serious little boy. He was as still as a leaf before a storm.

"Okay," he said, "that's it, then. I know everything I need to know. Want to. I'll be on call."

Charlie went out and got in his truck. There was still more to do, and more people to meet. He had to be at Dickie Pharr's house at one, which meant clattering halfway across the metro area in an hour, not a small feat in an F3 that relied strictly on the grace of the almighty to go over forty.

He rattled along, getting honked at by the endless succession of Lexuses and Beamers and Mercedeses that defined traffic on the north side.

Her nibs was from two wealthy north side families, no less. The

Fricks and the Fracks, he called 'em, rich but no cigar when it came to an ape farm and a husband they thought belonged in one of the cages.

As he drove, he sang, "When the saints, when the saints go marchin' in, I want to be in that number, when the fuckin' saints go marchin' in!" Then he yelled at the Lexuses and the Beamers, "My babies will be free, they will be, will be, will be free you fuck-doggie-dogs." Nobody heard that, so it was okay. Then he yelled, "I'm gonna get you outa that fuckin' hole, you baby *thangs*!"

There was something way down deep in him that was about dead Iraqi kids, and making that right was part of this, and making it right for all the monkeys he'd shot for fun when he was zoo collecting in Brazil, and paying man and animal back for once having been somebody who just simply enjoyed killing. His life was giveback, and vet school had been what he wanted to somehow get through. Maybe could've been a chiropractor or a dentist, but that didn't feel helpful enough. He'd wanted the full goddamn Monty, medical school. His undergrad work was not on their wavelength, though. Advanced Alcohol Metabolism, Womanizing 101 to 303, Cannabis Cultavia.

Texas A&M had overlooked those particular courses, and the rest of his transcript, truth to tell, looked pretty good. It is not easy to become a duck and horse doctor, though. In fact, the challenge of it easily rivaled medical school. He had worked harder getting his sheepskin than he ever had at anything else. He worked hard. He wanted to be the best thing that happened to any animal he repaired.

Each one he helped, he felt that some part of his soul got free. In his mind, the dirty, scared, mean kids he had killed had become his saints, and it was up to his saints if he would ever walk free. They would have killed him—would have cut his balls off, in fact, and made him eat them before he died—but he'd decided to overlook their little indiscretions. No, for Charlie Cooke, God had seventy-two human faces, and too many animal faces to count.

He came to the little trailer park where another of his old buddies resided. Dickie actually owned the park. He'd always said, 'Be a landlord or sell a big ticket item, that's the road to ride.' So, the guy comes home, he works his ass off selling goddamn big rigs for ten years, and he makes some money. He buys a little place, sixteen acres of trailers and pecan trees name of Big Oaks, and so he's done both, sold a big ticket item and been a landlord.

Charlie guided his truck carefully through the puddles and reefs of little kids, past the burned out communal grills and the fleabag dogs, to the old Airstream way back in the back that was so corroded it looked like it had been pissed on by the Jolly Green Giant. A truly awful dog showed him its teeth as he walked up, but instead of growling, it banged its tail on the ground.

He went in. "You need some trailer polish, bro', plus there's some kinda crockodog or gatorpooch or somethin' on your stoop."

"Jesus God. My boy has come home."

They had fucked in time to the tune of "Made in the U.S.A." while the whores under them belted out the lyrics in Arabic. You got whores with razor blades in their cunts in country. You had to have a care.

"I got a lab to pop."

"Well, shit, you see my old dog out there? I kicked a guy's head in, he was fuckin' wit her wit a goddamn .22 pistol. Shot off one of her dewlaps."

"Which tells me you still care about creatures."

"I'd still put leeches back, we had leeches in this hole. Wanna meet my bedbugs? Polite, but not too polite."

"Okay, so you're still on the side of the angels, is what you're sayin'."

"What's the mission?"

The reason that this man had a Silver Star was that he did not hesitate, and once he was going, did not stop.

"We gotta get us a good truck. Few tons, enough to bust through a fairly upstanding gate. You take it in on my signal."

"Okay. Where you gonna be?"

"Oh, I'll drop in a little early, get things put together right. We're takin' out six apes."

"Just six? Gorillas?"

"Something like that. They're real precious and the bulls are gonna want them back real bad. We carry them to the Center."

"Where they mix in with the crowd you already got there."

No sense in telling him anything extra. He wouldn't want to hear it, anyway. "You got it, bro. How's it goin' wit you?"

"I play pinochle at night, watch the news. Driftin' an dreamin,' bro."

"Well, hell. That sounds real good."

"'Cept I ain't fucked anything under two hundred and fifty pounds in years. Remember the way they smelled, man? How their hair went ever which way?"

"Shit yes."

"That sweet smell. What the fuck was that?"

"Death, man."

"Oh, yeah, I guess it was. Hoors smelled a death in country, that's right. Good beer, though. What in fuck was that stuff?"

"Head to Head."

"Yeah. Shit, Head to Head! Get sentimental about the goddamndest things, bro. I got me a pot a pretty brave chili brewin'. You want a bunch a chili and a Shiner? I got a whole lotta Texas Special in here."

To refuse or to spit in his face would have amounted to the same thing in Dickie's eyes, so they sat down at the little formica table across from the kitchenette and ate chili that was so good you had believe it had been sent down from a firestorm in heaven, and chased it with beer that was made to chase chili like that. "Well, that was good enough to kill," Charlie said. "You learned yourself a little cookin'."

"Hell, I didn't cook that. A Mexican woman comes around here and cooks and fucks most evenings. Cooks and fucks. Her old man ever sobers up, he'll probably kill me."

"You mean the other way around."

Fred held up his hands. "Hey, I did my killin' for Uncle. That *chicano* wants to come in here and put a knife in me, all he gotta do is open the door. Hell, I deserve it, I been fuckin' his wife for eight years." He smiled like a big old tomcat. "She not only don't charge rent, she provides the food!" If lung cancer could laugh, it would sound like Dickie sounded right now.

"You okay, bro?"

"Hell no! You put my goddamn medals in my coffin, man. You remember that, or I'll come and haunt ya!"

"You gonna need some cash for the rig? Would fifty be enough?"

"Shit on your money. You're my damn brother. Closer than a brother. I'm rich anyways." He leaned forward, whispered. "Don't tell nobody, but this fuckin' trailer park's worth a couple mil. The locals find out, they'll be standin' in line to cut ole Dickie while he sleeps."

Charlie realized a very profound thing about this old friend of his. This man could not be killed by the irate *chicano,* because this man was already dead. Charlie bowed his head in awe, because he had understood that he was sitting at a formica table in heaven.

"One night I'll call you. Could be two weeks, three weeks. I dunno. You'll hear me say, 'Where's my fuckin' pizza?' Then I will be gone. At that point, you get the rig, which needs to be ready at all times, and you proceed to 10715 White Road. You know where it is, north of the loop, out there toward Helotes."

"Yeah, there's a lot of fancy corporate shit over that way."

"Well, this one is fancy as they come. There is security. They will know you are intruding. On my signal, you crash the gate, go up the drive which curves to compel you to maintain a low speed, then you stop on the front of the building. You back up to the lobby doors, close as you can get. Open the bay. You will have to help me get these critters in. They will be very scared, and they will be the strangest goddamn things you have ever laid eyes on. Do not be surprised if they talk."

"Holy shit, man."

"You don't want to do it?"

"The fuck! I want to. Oh, man. Take me to 'em." He leaned back, took a pull on his beer. "You know, I always knew we'd be fuckin' around with some kinda alien life form one of these days. Remember that time—where the hell were we, somewheres in the marshes—we were lyin' out under the stars in that little firebase, waitin' for the

Sunni Saints to cornhole us? We musta been tokin' pretty heavy. Anyways, that goddamn big meteor comes down. A fuckin' spaceship."

"We were toking heavy. There was no spaceship."

"But these are aliens. You're telling me we're popping aliens outa some kind of CIA detention complex."

That was so far from where Charlie wanted to be, he didn't even know how to get back. "No CIA," he said. "No spacemen. Just some suffering critters. Big time."

"Well, I'll be sure and introduce myself. You remember that little boy I took out? That little sentry I shot the heart out of, turned out to be about twelve? Sometimes I dream he's watching me. Just watching. Like, 'you took my future.' Like, 'why, man?' He was so fuckin' beautiful, that child. He hadn't happened yet. Do you get where I'm comin' from?" He was silent for a moment. "Not a mark a life on him."

"This ain't aliens and it ain't kids. Only know this. It is a holy thing we will do that night. A holy thing."

"All lab popping is holy."

"All the bad shit you ever done, this makes up for it. This is the heart of the holy. God is gonna be there, man. Right there in the truck beside you. God is."

Dickie got up, almost filling the space in his modest trailer. "I worry about tornadoes," he said, "floods, explosions. Trailer parks attract disaster, so if God's involved, will you please tell him to lay off?" He pulled a bottle of tequila out of the freezer. "Cuervo," he said, "but not the shit they sell here. Fuckin' soft as a sister's tit, you gotta buy this in Mex." He poured himself a shot, poured another for Charlie. "Now this, *this* is holy."

They drank the tequila together, and then Charlie got up and took his leave. You fight beside a guy like they had, you fall in love. You can never say exactly what it is or how it works, but it is there in you, and it never ends. "Buddy," he said, "thanks."

"Fuck you, don't thank me now. Thank me if we live."

"Well, yeah, maybe not, then. It's gonna be shitty, I have to tell you."

"'Course it is. If it wasn't you wouldn't a come here and et up all my damn chili. You got the appetite of some kinda goddamn monster."

"I am a goddamn monster."

They hugged and Charlie pulled out. As he went down the walkway, the crockodog snarled a long, dreamy snarl but did not open its eyes. He needed to be home and have the apes tended before Her Nibs showed up. There must be not the least suspicion of what he was doing. She had been pretty fiery last night. If he wasn't careful she was gonna get out that little shotgun of hers and march him into a cage and keep him in there with Moreland or somebody. The capuchins, speaking of tornadoes. Before he returned, though, he had to pay a visit to another and very different comrade, Lawyer Stein. He was unlike that goody two-shoes Beth favored, cross the ts, dot the i's Bernie or whatever his name was. Lawyer Stein used the law like a damn submachine gun. He was also a working man, not off counting pterodactyls or whatever kept Bernie out in the *brasada* most of the time.

Whoever heard of a lawyer obsessed with birds? Guy was nuts. You need your lawyer, you need your lawyer.

Lawyer Stein had his office in the Transit Tower, the world's only octagonal skyscraper. Built in 1929, it looked like a gothic cathedral that some wildass had remodeled into a big brick rocket. Damndest thing.

When he entered, he had to say that the air conditioning felt awful good on this sticky-hot afternoon. He enjoyed the breeze that came down on his considerable bald spot as the elevator whisked him up to twenty-six.

Ginny was not sitting in her usual place, enthroned in the lobby of Roberts, Williams, Stein and Herbert. He looked down into the rapidly congealing face of what appeared to be about a twenty year old tartlet. "I'd like to see Mr. Stein, please."

"And you are?"

"Mr. Fuckall. Tell him Mr. Fuckall wants to see him."

She did not blink, more power to her. "I'm sorry, sir, but do you have an appointment?" She consulted what looked like a copy of Vanity Fair. "Because there's no Mr. Fuckall on his list." She pronounced it sort of off-kilter, 'Fookall,' so she wouldn't have to buy into the Anglo-Saxonism too profoundly.

He reached over and picked up her telephone. "Excuse me," she said. He punched in Larry's private line, which was 1398, after the number of rounds he'd fired in Falluja.

"Hey, it's me."

"Charlie! Jesus, you here?"

"Indeedy dee.'"

"We got work to do?"

"Nah, I'm here for the view."

As soon as he put the phone down, Larry came striding out. He looked as cowboy as ever, Larry did, in contrast with his fancy office and his fancy receptionist. His boots were pretty fancy, though. "We gonna kick ass?" He brayed the question.

They headed back toward his office.

"What happened to Ginny?"

"She got in trouble with one of the wives."

"Which one?"

"Mine."

Charlie took a quiet pleasure in knowing that the tight little receptionist behind them was gathering her jaw up off the floor. What was a dirty old bum doing in here, and friendly with Mr. Big, too?

You could hardly notice the slight sway in Larry's gait. You would never imagine that it was due to an artificial foot. There had been a day, a pretty damn long time ago now, when he had been a scared kid bleeding from a stump in the desert, and the gentlemen of death were coming to get him with a piece of canvas to drag him along in. They were gonna take him downtown and have some fun with him.

You went with them, you died, but not for a bit.

Uncle Army had reached him faster than the berobed gentlemen, and carried him into the sky and away. Just.

The only reason that Charlie and Larry knew each other is that

Charlie had gotten a hole blasted in his butt and ended up in the same medical unit. Larry was a rich kid out of Andover and Harvard and big oil. Now he was a rich lawyer with a house that had more windows in it than a fleet of Greyhounds.

"I'm gonna have a peck of trouble," Charlie said.

"Fuckin' Moreland! You oughta sell that ape to a weenie factory."

"This is nothin' to do with Moreland. I got a big project, my man, which if it doesn't land me at least in county stir, I will be very damn surprised. I'm gonna need your services, plus a little cash."

"You have grant problems already, my boy. I can't keep feedin' you quarters forever."

"Sure you can. Now listen up, because you are about to hear the most amazing damn thing you have ever heard."

"Okay, amaze me."

"My fem goes and finds herself a job at Barrett Scientific."

"The—uh—what do they do?"

"Scientific shit! Sheesh! So she goes in there, and what the job is about, is she has to work on behavioral issues with a group of six hominids."

He waited for Larry to explode. Did not happen.

"You know what a hominid is?"

Larry remained blank.

"Damn you, I don't like rich people very much, but I have to tell you, I find rich morons exceptionally disappointing. A hominid is a species of nonhuman, but somewhere in our line. Not a ape."

"The Abominable Snowman, like?"

"No, that's an ape, if it exists. I'm talking about something entirely and totally incredible."

"The Abominable Snowman would be pretty incredible."

"These are intelligent beings. Five feet or so tall. Hair sort of like us, hands and feet like us. Can't breed with us, though, so not human beings."

Larry seemed to click over once or twice. Then he blinked real fast, like he did when he got a good hand in poker. "God for fucking damned," he said.

"There are six of them. Maybe the last six on earth. Probably. And these suits have them living naked and in total captivity. They've never even seen a fucking tree. And what's this about, you ask? Why fuck with them like this?"

"It does seem a little harsh."

"The theory of the corporate running dogs is that, since they ain't human, they got no rights. They're breeding them as work animals to do really smart shit like build computers."

"Slavery, then."

"Nope. Animals. Less than slaves."

"Oh my, that is ugly."

"'Cept they won't breed, not being stupid. My wife is supposed to tickle their toes until they do."

That shut him up, even made him turn around in his chair and regard his big, flat view halfway across the state. This was highly unusual behavior. Larry was not a quiet man. In fact, he was real loud man. Big, too, and so dyed-in-the-wool Texas that he still wore string ties and an old Stetson so ripe with sweat that you didn't want to be downwind of it on a hot day. Ever watch a lawyer cut and rope in a rodeo? 'I ride in rodeos 'cause I like the taste of cow shit,' was how he explained it. The crowd would get kind of talkative when the foot flew off, which it generally did. When he and Rachel square danced, keeping the thing on made him look like he was prancing through a fire. Charlie, who fiddled on the world's cheapest, sweetest violin, would go so fast that old Larry, he'd threaten to sue.

"Shitola," he said at last. "Hay-soos wept."

Charlie entertained a foolish hope. "Tell me that holding them prisoner is illegal and you can get 'em out with some kinda writ." A nice clean court case would beat all hell out of dumping in a racing chute the likes of which he'd never even been near, let alone had packed on his dumb ass.

"I need more facts. Not human, that's certain?"

"There's DNA. Not human."

"Then they do own 'em. They surely do." He thought about it. "Animal cruelty?"

"They're not being starved or anything. Kept in a sealed facility."

"A cage? Small, hopefully."

"Nah, Beth says it's a facility. They're healthy, she says. Just—you know—imprisoned."

Larry sighed. "Well, fuck a duck," he said at last. "It's perfect. Slaves are back 'cause they ain't slaves."

"I'm gonna take 'em out."

"Ah, yes, you live in another world with another set of laws. So you're going to burgle the place, and if you get your ass caught at last, which you eminently deserve, you want to be able to pick up the phone and grouse about pizza and I come down and habeas your corpus outa there."

"Right."

"Sure. No problem. But long term, there could be jail. You know that."

"I've always known that, every time."

"And so far your corpus has never had to be habeased."

"I won't lie, Larry. This one is gonna be hard."

"Hearin' you say that scares me."

"Well, I have a feeling that these company men want their slaves a whole lot more than Triad wanted a bunch of chimps with light sockets in their heads. These things are real valuable, be my guess."

"To get em out legal, we'd have to make new law, and that's always a problem."

"What is going to go down is this. I am going to pop this lab. I am going to get the creatures. I am then going to transport them to the Center."

"And the big boys are gonna follow you right to your doorstep with a sheriff and some paperwork, and they are going to take their critters back."

"Which is the actual, real reason I am here. Remember, these are people. They are held in prison right now. People! You have to make the case that God wants you to make, which is that any of his creatures who are as intelligent as we are count as much as us. Make them count, Larry."

That shut Larry up. But not for long. "As intelli-fuckin'-gent as *we are*? Jesus Christ!"

"Beth thinks maybe even more."

"Oot toot toot," he said, one of the odd little turns of phrase that meant he was thinking. "I'll get on it."

"Is there a case?"

"Mm. Could be we have an argument. Not sure what it is, though. But I'll tell you, my brother, what some judge says or doesn't say isn't gonna be what's ultimately important. What's ultimately important is, do they get citizenship?"

"I hadn't thought about that."

"No, because that's my job—thinking, I mean. Point is, if they can apply for and be granted citizenship, then the company's got no more case. There's nothing in the citizenship laws says you have to be human. 'Of sound mind' is what it says. 'Could be any kind of mind. Alligator, Martian—just gotta be sound, which means the person is able to pass the citizenship test. Could they pass it?"

"Be my guess. Sooner or later."

"So whatcha call these buggers?"

"Tanda, Orang Tanda. Means shadow man. They lived in a forest that got turned into dashboards and coffins."

Larry got up, the polite signal that came just before he threw your ass out of his office, which had happened to Charlie more than a few times. Charlie stood with him.

"You've given me a hell of a case, my man," he said. "I'm gonna be a famous do-gooder."

"Sorry for the hassle."

"I must set the people free."

They hugged, and Charlie took off. It turned out he was moving faster than he'd expected, so he stopped and got himself an Orange sno-cone at a stand, and ate it awash in nostalgia. He was on the middle west side now, deep San Antonio, run according to ancient Latino codes, a place of honor and danger, but also an affable place with space for kids to cut up a little. He'd smoked his first joint here, humped his first chick and boosted his first car here. Some kind of a lemon. Engine fell out. The guy he'd boosted it from got all pissed off when the cops found it.

As he drove the old highways, the same thing started to happen that used to come down on him in country, which was that the demon fear began to possess him. Death, this time, like in battle. Death. It scared him, no way to get past that. Leaving Beth behind to weep and mourn, that not only scared him, it made him sad. That was just mean. One thing about a good marriage, the last one to die has the worst karma. Beth did not need to suffer the pain of loss that would follow his demise.

By the time he was turning down their shady drive, he had decided to find himself a skydiving school and take a few dumps in racing chutes to get the feel of the things. That'd be priority for next week. Meanwhile, he'd worm more info out of Her Nibs about the interior layout of the facility, do it by subtle inches. Hopefully subtle. Sometimes that did not work with her. She saw through shit. So maybe just not go there at all.

By the time he could safely run the chute at night, he'd also have a complete plan of the campus in his cranium...and Beth wouldn't even know what was going down. Hopefully.

He reached home. And a damn thing happened. He glanced at his watch. For pushing against his thirty years, he'd kept careful time on this old Ebel, won in a poker game, and not a crooked one, either. It just kept on keepin' on. So why the hell was it saying that it was three sixteen, given that Beth's car was sitting in the carport big as life?

Maybe they got out early on Friday. But no, this was Thursday. 'Not real good,' he thought as he moved toward the awfully silent house, 'not real good at all.'

He went in. "Hello?"

No answer.

"Sweetie? Dear heart?" He went across the dining room with her priceless family antiques and bluebonnet landscape on the wall, and down the hall that led to the bedrooms. He waded into the fluff of their girl-blue sanctum.

She was buried in the canopied bed that he had neglected to make up. She lay on her tummy, her face pushed into in a pillow. He grew careful. You didn't approach her tragedies with a frontal assault. He was burning to know what the hell had happened, but if he just asked, he was liable to get waved away. Then he'd have to go into the living room and sit there rubbing his big, clumsy hands together and waiting, maybe for hours.

Carefully, he sat down. No reaction. He laid a hand on her hair and stroked. A little stirring. She was so delicate, this pale flower of a woman who was far and away the most impactful human being he had ever known. She marched through life on her long, willowy legs, her huge eyes flashing with sheer human strength. Nothing kept her down, not a woman who could stand up to an enraged mountain gorilla and win with ease.

Whatever this was, though, it was different. She was down. Way down.

He leaned over and kissed her tapering neck.

"Miss Nibs? Excuse me for being a nosy parker, but hey..."

She flounced over onto her back. "You guessed it. I got fired."

He sure as hell hadn't guessed anything of the kind. In fact, he was so surprised that his mouth actually dropped open.

She laughed—a harsh bark. "So they've been sold. Problem solved."

Now he was really bowled over. Sold to who? What was going on, here?

As she explained, a molten river of dread flowed through him, and the more he heard, the faster it flowed. He knew about World Biological. It had taken on a lot of the animal testing work that U.S. labs had been offloading. It was cosmetic testing heaven.

But these were intelligent beings. A bio lab wouldn't be interested in them as testbeds for mascara and foot cream. A bio lab would be interested in how they ticked. Take some apart, for sure, get a looky-loo.

"What's the story?"

"I haven't pieced it all together yet, but they're being moved in a few days."Charlie could barely hear her. The world was falling down around him. He had the same sense of disorientation he'd had during the earthquake that had hit while he was on R&R that time, an inner and outer landslide.

"When," he asked in what turned out to be a cracking whisper.

"Monday."

His heart started chugging. What had been a fun, satisfying and very worthy project had just turned into a dire and immediate emergency. He had to somehow put the whole thing together, like, now.

Okay, this was no different than unexpected incoming. You handled it. He inventoried the situation. The truck would be okay. Larry was ready any damn time to wave a writ in some cop's face. Dickie could go up on a half hour's notice.

The problem was him. The damn chute. The sky tends not to forgive mistakes, and even if he did manage to stay in control all the way down, that roof was gonna be an awfully small target. Hell, he wouldn't even be able to see it until he almost on it, not at night. And what if there was wind, or a thunderstorm, or any number of a dozen other problems?

It occurred to him not to go, but that was out of the question. Completely. The Tanda might damn well end up on slides.

He had two choices: either succeed or die trying in such a way that it would bring the kind of publicity that would draw the world's attention to the poor buggers.

He wanted to just throw back his head and yell "fuck" so loud the ceiling fixture would implode. But he had to be all gentle and commiserating, keep her as calm as he could. She wasn't stupid, she'd know damn well if he went, like, tomorrow night, that it was basically a kamikaze operation. She'd hide that damn keycard of hers for sure, hide it well.

He said, "Never you mind. You had a hell of an adventure. But World Bio—I know about those guys."

"You do?"

"And this I can tell you, and it is from the heart. Everything's gonna be fine, love. It's gonna be just fine."

17

THE WIZARD

Crunch had his shorts on his head. He looked so stupid Joe could hardly bear it. He hated the idea of the shatterfaces seeing it. Everybody else had mixed up all the clothes except him and Betty, and they wore theirs the way Beth said, just like in TV. The thing was, Betty thought she had a spider in her and that was scaring him. How did she get a spider in her? It hurt an awful lot to get them out, because you had to *hit* and *rip* and *pull* and then it came out but it was all wet and red and you had to get rid of it 'cause it might get in somebody else.

Joe had this dream: their little doll that Keller called "Gorilla" is lying on the floor and Gorilla begins to move. Gorilla moves slowly across the room. He is coming toward their bed. Joe is scared. Gorilla should not be moving, Gorilla is a toy. As if Joe's fears somehow inspire Gorilla, Gorilla comes to his feet. He's all floppy and his arms are dangling and his big blank eyes are staring. They are staring straight at Betty. Joe tries to protect Betty, but he is frozen. He can't put himself between Betty and Gorilla. So he yells, he yells to wake up Betty and warn her, but all that comes out of his mouth is a whisper. As Gorilla comes closer, Betty begins to smile in her sleep, as if she knows that Gorilla is there and she likes it, she likes what Gorilla is going to do.

Now Gorilla is standing over their bed. Huge hands Joe cannot see are holding him down. He tries to lift an arm, tries to lift his head, tries but can't. His chest is mashed worse than if Crunch was sitting on him.

Gorilla goes between Betty's legs, and now Joe so scared that he has tears on his face, he can feel them. Gorilla goes in Betty, deeper and deeper until all you can see are his legs, then just his feet. All the time Betty wiggles just like it was feeling good, just like when Joe does her.

With a great big yell Joe gets free. He leaps up out of bed, he grabs Betty, he hugs her, he just wants to be twined up together with her forever. Then he remembers. He remembers Gorilla. For a second, he is about to yell and tear at his own hair, he is so scared. Then he sees Gorilla on the floor. He sees Gorilla! He goes and grabs Gorilla and takes him and puts him under Crunch and Flutter's bed. Let Gorilla live there.

So it was not Gorilla that Joe had seen. It was a spider, and that was how he knew a spider had gotten into Betty.

Things were very wrong and confused now. There was a spider in Betty and Crunch was all beat up, and how could it be that the Big Voice didn't tell them to go on the line? They had to, it was after breakfast. Everybody hung around in rec. It was awful quiet around here. Why was it so quiet? Sam Beach had closed the kitchen. Joe said to Crunch, "Get pans off top."

Crunch signed 'No. This is my hat.'

"Tak, stoop."

"Ah nah...nah..."

Crunch was the worst talker. Everybody else was getting better. Betty tried to sound like like Ellen DeGeneris and Joe like Stephen Colbert. Flutter practiced Oprah. Jill wanted to sound like Melissa Rauch. Crunch didn't try anybody. Dumb Crunch.

Greg Keller stood staring out his office window, seeing nothing.

When he had opened his eyes this morning, he had briefly experienced the rush of excitement that had characterized his every awakening for the years since he had acquired the Tanda. But by the time he had shaved, he was miserable. He had cancelled the line today. Why run it? They hated it anyway. He sat in his office watching the Tanda milling about in their recreational area, zooming in on first one of them and then another. Look at Joe, that inquisitive creature, once again their subtle and persistent leader. He was teaching them to talk by making it a fad and a game. Greg had forbidden talk, but he didn't care now. He had spent hours gazing at their private sign, watching its incredible intricacy in slow motion. Nobody could ever hope to understand all that finger movement. His ability to know their thoughts had been disappearing down the speeding path of their sign, so he was actually rather glad that they were beginning to speak.

Then he caught himself. Why did he care? They were gone. No longer part of his life. He watched Joe hug Betty. And look at her, closing her eyes, rubbing her cheek against his. They loved, yes, as he had known for a long time. He had known that they were the equal to the human. He had known this, also, for a long time.

He touched them with his eyes and his longing. They were the love of his life. He was their protector, their servant, also—and this, to him, was the most meaningful part of it—he was their mentor and leader. Greg had never considered marriage. He'd spent the first twelve years of his career collecting plants in impossible places, then had gone Sumatra and the accidental discovery of the Tanda, and his world had changed. The extreme secrecy of his work with them made social life awkward. He had to lie about what he did. He had to remember the lies. He was a scientist, not an espionage agent. After a few dates, he'd decided that his life was here. His condo, still barely furnished, was just a place to park.

The future that now confronted him was an abyss. He might not kill himself, but that was as yet undecided. He'd see if he could put anything of interest together. Give it a year. If not, then he would take out the little pistol he kept in a strongbox in his bedroom closet and eat it for dinner.

He kept watching, compulsively zooming in on first one and then another, trying to understand how he could bear what was coming.

Look at Crunch, with that pair of paisley underwear on his head. He was a card, a joker, less verbal than Joe but more appealing in many ways. Joe was darkly self-contained. Crunch was outgoing and cheerful, except for the period when he had been boss. After his brief accession to the crown, Joe had dominated him even more firmly. Joe was usually the gentlest of creatures, sweet and quick to weep, and yet also a dictator capable of a dictator's rage.

If World broke the group up, they would suffer terribly. They might die of grief. If that happened Joe would be the first. Then they all would. He knew the titanic power of their emotions, and he knew that what was coming would for them be a descent into hell.

He zoomed in on Joe, whose proud glasses were askew on his face. When he'd found him, he'd been not much bigger than a human hand, his skin so pale it was almost transparent, his emerald eyes huge, his face radiating grief and fear. He'd clung to Greg, largely because he had nothing else to cling to. He'd cried the soft, persistent cries of the Tanda baby, cries that a mother would hear, but not a predator.

It was because their jungle had never died that the Tanda had taken a different evolutionary path from us. But now that it had—or rather, been clear cut—this other intelligent species, almost gone but not quite, was following in the ancient footsteps of man, forced out of the protective arms of its own jungle.

Joe looked up at the clock. Greg had realized some weeks ago that he could tell time. Joe took off his glasses, obviously reflecting on why they weren't on the line.

Would World Bio let him keep the glasses? Given that they were just frames, would they know that they were more to him than a toy? He needed to tell Ma about them. And the way they loved each other, and how important it was to keep the couples together.

He realized that he was crying. He ignored it.

They were milling now, growing more and more nervous. That idiot woman had given them clothes, and look what he would now have to show Dr. Ma. Males in skirts, Crunch's creative use of his shorts, females strutting about in the tightest possible shirts, males slouching in the loosest blouses. Some matters of taste were species-universal, apparently. The females had managed to use the shirts as a means of cleavage display, and they sashayed around pushing their breasts out and grinning at each other over the new attention they were getting from the males.

Grief swept him, ice cold. They would soon be suffering and they would beg him for deliverance, but he would not be there to help them. They would call out to their god, pray to him, scream for him, beg for him to come. But his time had ended. Greg Keller was still breathing, sure, but his life was over.

"Dr. Keller, Dr. Ma is here."

Rebecca's smoothly professional voice now bore a note of quiet sadness. In fact, the whole campus was quiet. Harry Lerner had been let go the moment Greg saw Crunch's condition, fired with a note of prejudice in his record, damn the pig. Today would be the last day for Jim Thomas. He'd told Beth Cooke to surrender her security key and identification on Monday afternoon. As for the support staff, they had two weeks to clean up the facility, then they were terminated, too.

Dr. Ma came in. "Hey, Greg," he said. Gone was the suit, and with it the formality of their first meetings. He was wearing jeans and a plaid cowboy shirt. "I'm ready to be introduced to the Tanda," he said. He gazed at the monitor, watching them at their listless rec room play. "Is that a game?"

"It's Clue. They like Clue."

"And what is this?"

"A logic game disguised as a mystery story that takes place in a mansion where a houseguest has been murdered. You must assemble clues to identify the murderer, whose name is on a hidden card."

"A logic game," he said absently, almost to himself. "Why do they play a logic game?"

"I've shut down their assembly line, so they're rather at a loss," Greg explained.

"No, I mean not why. That's the wrong word. It is 'how?' How can they do this?"

"You're buying them in part because of their intelligence. They are very intelligent. Their lack of information and experience makes them seem a little simple, but it's an illusion, believe me."

He was silent, watching. Then he said, "How are they, emotionally? Will we have trouble from the change of environment? Will we get into difficulty?"

"Honestly, I don't know. I think not, but I can't be sure. My belief is that a better facility will really excite them. If you have more space, perhaps, or access to the outdoors, they might get over their upset pretty quickly. I never gave them that because I didn't want them to lose their enthusiasm for the assembly line project. What we've done is given them access to television, which they love, but not to programs that feature outdoor views, except fleetingly. We wanted them to see a controlled vision of the world."

Ma sat watching them. "They are going to be in a setting that's designed for scientific research. I am afraid that they will live in cages." He chuckled. "I doubt that my directors will agree to provide television for research animals."

Keller fought back a rise of acid in his stomach. "If you cage them and abandon their minds," he said, striving to control the tremor that had come into his voice, "you will have trouble."

Again, Ma smiled. It was a rather strange reaction, Greg thought, to what was liable to be a serious problem for him. He looked as if a distant memory of some joke had come back to amuse him once again. "What are those absurd clothes? What are they wearing?"

"Dr. Cooke was experimenting with various means of making them more comfortable in their surroundings. You know of the breeding problem. She thought that offering them more cultural artifacts might induce a better response to their environment, and thus more enthusiasm about babies."

"We will inseminate and isolate. The babies will be brought to term."

"And if the mothers reject them after birth?"

"One way or another, they will be raised." He went to his feet. "Now, let's go down. I'm eager to meet my new charges."

Joe was the first to hear the buzz that signaled the opening of the barrier. He rushed forward, as he always did. Keller came through with another new shatterface. Joe had been wanting this to happen ever since he had succeeded, if only briefly, in looking into Beth's eyes. Could he do it again? He immediately raised his head. By forcing himself, he had managed to glance at Keller from time to time. But what of this new shatterface, how would it feel to dare his shatter?

His whole self wanted not to look into those dark pits. But he had looked and he must look again. So he raised his eyes—and once again it was like being set on fire inside his head. This shatterface was actually the worst he'd ever seen. It had glowing eyes, not dark eyes, and they burned even hotter than the dark fire of the others.

Behind him he heard the others stirring nervously and moving away. The new shatterface was smaller than Keller and Beth and Harry Lerner. He was also wearing colored clothes, blue and white with a very colorful neck rope.

If Joe could not look, he could at least talk. He said, "G'marnin, Kerrer."

The new shatterface burst into laughter. "Hoh, hoh," he went, "oh, hoh hoh hoh!" Then he said, "Listen to him, he can't pronounce the 'L!' They belong to Asia, Dr. Keller. It is the certain mark!" Then he went, "hoh hoh hoh" some more. Joe knew it wasn't laughter. That was only what it was supposed to sound like.

"Hello, Joe," Keller said. He extended his hand, and Joe shook. The others gathered closer, curious about the new shatterface.

"This is Doctor Ma, kids. Can everybody say 'Doctor Ma?'"

"Dakoma," Flutter said.

"Very good, Flutter. How about you, Crunch?"

"Dama."

Joe said, "G'marnin, Dokorma." Then he repeated it: "Doctor Mmma."

"Good morning."

Joe forced himself to raise his eyes again, to look straight at the shatterface that was saying so many strange things, first at its tiny mouth, then its narrow nose that looked like who could possibly get any air through that thing, then up a little higher.

Again, fire. In the center of each blazing horror was a terrifying hole into the unknown. But Joe was still looking. For the first time in his life, he was looking into the eyes of a strange shatterface without feeling so much terror and pain that it was unbearable. His eyes actually burned, but he was *looking*, he was doing it!

"Dokorma," he said, forcing his mouth to work, "shake!" He put out his hand.

"This one is very good," Doctor Ma said.

"That's Joe. Shake his hand."

"Is it safe?"

"They're fairly clean."

Joe took the hand. It was narrow and small like his own. Solemnly, he shook it the same way they did in TV.

Doctor Ma withdrew it. He spoke low and quickly. "Do they know?"

Joe saw Keller shake his head once sharply. He did not like that shake, did not like the tone of the question.

Betty noticed, too, and came close to Joe. His hand grasped hers. Something was happening that was different. But what? Betty signed, 'It's not good.'

Joe signed back, 'No.'

Jack signed, 'That shatterface stinks.'

Then they were all signing. 'It's scary, it's mean, it's weird.' And finally, from Crunch: 'It's from Oz.'

"What's going on?" the new shatterface asked.

"They're talking about you."

"And saying what?"

"We don't know."

"You don't know their sign?"

Keller shook his head and motioned to the new shatterface to be silent.

A fist twisted around in Joe's stomach and tightening came in his throat, and his breakfast came shooting out of him. It splashed all over the new shatterface, which jumped away making a noise like, 'meewlllew!'

The stink of the vomit mixed with a new odor, one that was as sweet as it was poop-stinky. The smell was fear. It was coming off the new shatterface.

Flutter threw back her head and screamed at the very top of her lungs, bellowing so loud the ceiling almost came down. Crunch ripped the shorts off his head and did his stations, tearing back and forth, slamming his hand down at each one, then repeating the process. Jill and Jack threw their arms around one another and started crying.

Joe didn't understand what had come over everybody any more than he understood what had made his stomach go crazy. Waves of feeling went through him like when they yelled in TV, and he yelled, too, he yelled and yelled right at the new shatterface, right in its face but no longer looking at its eyes.

Betty and Flutter started following Crunch. Jill ripped her skirt off and began jumping from table to table. Jack rolled around on the floor shaking his head back and forth and making his hair go all crazy.

Joe felt hate. He knew it was hate. He knew from Oz what hate was. He hated the new shatterface. He hated its smell and its looks and above all, he hated its super shatter eyes. His whole body pulsated with so much hate that he was actually shaking, shaking and hating, and making his hair fly in front of his face like Jack's was, but he was not lying down, he was right in front of the shatterface, who said, "Is this somekindaritual" real fast.

"I don't know!"

"You don't know? You had better know. I expect you to tell me why it soiled my shoes!"

Keller took the shatterface by the arm and went out through the barrier.

Gradually, the people got better. Jack lay exhausted. The ones doing Crunch's stations with him started dancing instead. Betty and Joe held each other, running their hands up each other's backs and kissing for a long time, and that made Joe feel warm inside. The hate disappeared, and he was so very glad yet again that Betty had not stayed with Crunch.

Everybody gathered close to Joe. They were back on his side, all of them. He was way away from being bottomsider, especially now that they were scared.

Joe thought, trying to sort matters out. The line was down. The Big Voice called them no more. Keller had this new Dokorma from Oz who was ugly and scary and mean.

Had they done wrong? He decided to pray to the Blessed Version. He knelt down, so they all did. He folded his hands like Mother Angelica used to, and they all did, too. He bowed his head. They did not. They were watching him. He started saying the Holy Version prayer. "Hey maree muddagad, horee maree muddagad, hey maree muddagad" but it didn't help like it was supposed to, and he once again became angry at the Holy Version, who was just another shatterface after all. Sister Angelica was no good either.

Ma strode down the corridor, Keller following.

"Perhaps you shouldn't take them," Greg said.

"Don't even think about embarrassing me with my institute. You will prepare them and I will take them. That's an end to it. The schedule will be adhered to strictly. They will arrive on the grounds of the institute on Wednesday next, as I have promised my directors. There will be no delay."

Greg followed him as he strode along, passing quickly through the control room and down the corridor. "Where's that primatologist, Dr. Keller?"

"She's been given notice."

"I need her!"

Greg was not too surprised to find her in her office. She was packing boxes. Slowly.

"Doctor," Ma asked, striding in, "how long do you think they can safely be tranquilized?"

Red, hollow eyes stared at them. She looked like a trapped tigress, dangerous if touched, and immensely sad. "I'm not a vet," she said.

"Your husband Charles is a vet. Haven't you asked him such a question?"

Greg was confused. "Her husband isn't secured. He knows nothing about the Tanda."

"That's a lovely fantasy," Ma commented, taking a framed photo from her hand. "Do you fly?"

In the picture, Beth and her husband stood beside a red airplane. Charles Cooke was a rough looking man, very different from the delicate beauty beside him. The man's good looks, Greg thought, had a savage quality to them. By contrast, she was pale and smooth and poetic. Greg thought that their sex must be fierce and wonderful, and he envied Charles Cooke.

Beth took the picture back from Ma without answering.

"Do you know that there exist files on your husband in my country, going back some years?"

Greg saw Beth's surprise, inexpertly concealed by a glance away, revealed by unconscious crossing of the legs into a defensive posture.

"Why would that be?" he asked Ma. He kept his eyes on Beth.

"He was identified many times, and even photographed. Even so, he was really an expert."

"His war experience distresses him," Beth said.

"But not his experience since."

"We know him as the manager of Beth's primate shelter."

"I refer to his experience with the laboratories," Ma continued smoothly.

"Beth," Greg asked, "what laboratories?"

Ma continued. "We at World have to thank him. He was the reason that Trident shifted its business eastward. That is a big contract. But, Doctors, obviously there is a problem. I mean, a security problem."

"What's he talking about, Beth?"

She shook her head.

"I am talking about the fact that Charles Cooke has a history of breaking into laboratories and freeing animals. Their primate center was originally founded to house animals freed in this way from Trident's facility."

"That's not true."

"Certainly it is. We have friends in the animal rights movement who keep us abreast of happenings. That's why we moved when we did on the Tanda." He smiled. "The moment you hired this charming and dedicated worker, we knew that they would soon be gone."

Greg sucked breath between his teeth. Could this be true? They had done a damned thorough check. "Was he ever charged?" he asked quickly, fearing for an awful moment that something had been missed in the extensive criminal records search done on both of them.

"He has never been caught. He is very stealthy. He uses skills he learned in the military."

"What did he do in Iraq, Beth?"

"I don't know. It's classified."

Greg studied her. In hiring her, he'd hoped to save his project. But what he'd actually done was opened the door to a wolf who would have stolen his treasure, and by so doing lost it to other, even smarter predators.

"And lab busting?"

"I have no knowledge of him being involved in any lab busting."

"We generate a hundred million dollar a year with our testing program," Ma said. "We are most interested in protecting it."

Beth said, "So you fund radical animal rights groups in this country, to make sure that they can afford to raise hell here. That way, more lab work goes to you."

Ma said nothing.

"Tell me this," Beth continued, "are you going to kill all the Tanda or just some? Because if you only kill a few, I'd recommend you do them in couples. Grief factor."

"What we do is none of your concern. What is of your concern is keeping your husband far away from this campus for the next few days."

"My husband has no plans to enter Barrett Scientific."

"If he does, he can expect a very strong greeting. There will be many more armed guards surrounding this place, starting tonight. They will take whatever legal steps they feel are necessary to protect our property. That includes shooting on sight any intruder they see."

"Breaking the law?"

"If the intruder is armed, we have a right."

"Charlie hasn't touched a gun since he left the military."

Ma smiled softly. "In such situations, who can know what may appear to be in a man's hand? Perhaps only a screwdriver or a lock pick. But it's dark, the guard must make an instant decision and the man is a trespasser. Under Texas law, as you know, the risk is his." The smiled faded. He shook his head, as if contemplating a tragic mistake.

"In other words, all intruders will be shot."

"In other words, if your husband comes here, that would be unwise."

Greg was appalled. This woman was a damned Trojan Horse. World Bio or no World Bio, the lab was due to be invaded and the Tanda taken. He held out his hand. "Give me your keycard and your identification tag."

She handed them to him with a smile. "It doesn't matter," she said. "I was a good choice, Greg, incidentally. He'd never try this place, it's shut too tight. If he got caught in a lab action, we'd lose the Center." She turned toward Ma. The smile remained, in it something approaching pity. Contempt. Well, why not? He'd won. "Your suspicions are quite groundless."

Ma stood. He bowed formally. "You have lost, my dear. Dr. Keller may be naïve, but I am not naïve. Do not try anything reckless. This building will be quite secure over the weekend, and your husband will be a very specific target."

Her eyes flickered to Greg's, then met them. "My husband never intended to steal the Tanda. He doesn't even know they exist."

"Doctor Keller, we are also well aware of your feelings. I am personally aware of them. If our roles were reversed, I would be in a very bad state of mind. In fact, I might even be tempted to assist Charlie."

"I'm an employee of Barrett Scientific. I would never do anything to betray their trust."

"Ah, but your wishes live in your eyes. And wishes do find ways."

As he had come to his feet, Greg stood, also. "Are we done here, Dr. Ma?"

"There will be a great deal of emotion among the animals, and I am sure they will want to appeal to you." He gazed at Greg, seeking his eyes like an exploring, urgent lover.

"I will sedate them before you move them. After that, I assure you, they will feel no fear."

"Until they wake up," Beth said.

Greg heard a sound, then realized that it had come out of him, a choked, stifled moan.

Beth threw her remaining belongings into a box.

It would take Greg a lot longer to pack, at least the whole of next week. A man cannot disassemble his whole world in an hour. A man cannot be thrown away, and with him his whole life, so easily as that.

18

THE MAN FROM THE SKY

The tiny plane hopped and shuddered and roared through the night. Below, the city lights seemed awfully close. "Jesus, man, are we still on the ground or what?"

"Might as well be!"

"I gotta have more alty if I'm gonna jump outa this thing!"

"You said three! *Three*!

"Fucakroo, that's a flasher—pull up!

"Funny, ain't it, the longer you live, the longer you want to." They cleared a cell tower by about ten feet.

"God help me!"

"I fly around like this all the time. Whaddaya think I do for a living, work for normal people?"

"Holy God, that tower! We're at two!"

"This altimeter is paranoid. In fact, the whole plane is, you ask me. Need me a damn plane whisperer is what I need."

"I don't wanta be killed by a chimney! I got work on me tonight, Bro!"

"You told me to come in under any approach control paint. I'll pop up just before I dump you."

Charlie thought, 'It's been nice knowin' you, pal.' He said, "Great!"

There were all kinds of reasons to feel bad about this situation, and over the course of the past two days, their number had only multiplied. The net of it was that he was poorly equipped, badly prepared and just plain not ready at all, and this plane wasn't on the ground because the ground was twenty feet below its wheels. Maybe.

He had dropped into the desert at night under a round chute without such niceties as the altimeter and GPS that were now strapped to his chest. In Iraq, you often had to work out the location of the drop after impact. That wasn't the official story, of course, but you combine bad intelligence with bad planning, missing equipment and a whole hell of a lot of toke, and that was where you ended up.

Fred hit the throttle and the engine noise rose from a frantic scream to a panic-stricken shriek. What was amazing here was that Fred didn't also have a chute.

Time passed, the same kind of eternity of minutes he'd known in his youth, with the difference that now he had tasted of the wine and knew the secret of why war always involves old men sending the young to die. The old bastards had tasted of the wine and so preferred to spend their wars on the near side of the river. Let the boys go. Let the boys float down into the dark.

He punched Fred in the shoulder. "How fuckin' long?"

"Three fuckin' minutes," he yelled back.

"Do the burst, my boy."

"Oh, yeah." He wound his radio to the agreed frequency and opened the mike three times in succession. They listened to the static, but nothing came back. So what in fuck-all had happened to Dickie and the rig?

The hot steel bands that had been compressing Charlie's chest snapped as something like relief flooded through him. No Dickie, no go.

The responding bursts came, one, two, three.

"That's a go," Fred yelled.

"Yeah." Somewhere down there, Dickie was waiting with the truck, prepared on the next signal to crash the Barrett gates.

The GPS told him that they were three miles from the campus.

Fred had pulled up, and their altitude was now six hundred feet. Charlie threw the lever on the drop door. With a blasting roar, the floor fell open. No more talking was possible. Charlie was alone now, alone with mother night. He thought of Beth sleeping back there in the dark somewhere. O Beth, you beloved of my heart, will I ever see you again?

"On five! Two miles!"

He inventoried—crowbar, HEET ANFOs, pistol, armored gloves in case the animals were in a biting mood, screwdriver set, hammers, power drill and cord. He did not have a tranquilizer gun. If you used such a thing on a creature as smart as these were supposed to be, when you knocked the first one out, the others would go bananas.

He'd have loved to have some plastique to do the lights, but the HEET had been a damn lucky break and he'd been glad to get it. Whatever happened on the ground, it was going to go down under full illumination.

Given that Her Nibs's keycard had been confiscated, he was also going to need to go in off the roof, not down its side. He was gonna need HEET to blow a door, so it was gonna be noisy. So he would also have to be fast.

There hadn't been any time to go down to the buildings department and look at the structural plans, so he would hit the roof blind. Google Earth had revealed ductwork and pipe exhausts. Nothing unusual, but a lot that could deball anyone fool enough to dump into it in the dark. He was wearing heavy boots and a leather brace between his legs. Call it vanity, but he did not care to leave his junk behind on a damn sewer exhaust.

"Go, go, go!"

As Charlie launched himself into the night, the wind noise rose about fifty decibels. His face stretched to breaking, he yelled hell to murder. The world went crazy, lights in flight, his brain banging around in his head, his mouth wide open, screams you felt rather than heard.

His hand went up, grasped at nothing. Oh, okay, no rip, time to die.

Then his training kicked in. It was long ago, and he was dropping into the deadly night, the sweet scent of the night desert filling his nostrils once again.

He got himself stabilized, the lights stopped whirling around, and he managed to pull his rip within about five seconds of the optimal time. When the canopy spread, he still had altitude, not a lot, but some.

Oh, my, it was lovely here in the night, in the sensual summer air, above the ocean of lights. You were not going to find that roof visually, not amid this glorious confusion. That was where his sweet little GPS came in, telling him where he was within a few feet. He had the sense of being part of a wonderful machinery, the satellites above, the electronics glowing on his chest, the math of chute and wind.

There was also a little chest pain, and that had to be acknowledged. Yeah, that was there. Hadn't been in his youth, no way.

Well, it was time. He had about ten seconds left for his ritual. As he had above the whispering dunes, he pulled out his dick and ritually pissed. To be able to do this, to literally piss into the wind, you had to achieve a certain inner calm. Who knew, maybe some poor soul down there would feel some raindrops on a clear night, and think that a miracle was in progress.

"When the saints, when the saints go marching in!"

Okay, cut that. Focus. He was within half a mile of the target and his altitude was five hundred feet. He scooped canopy. This was going to be a needful little maneuver, this was. His whole body hungered for altitude. But he couldn't worry about that now. Now, it was time to find the drop zone. He scanned ahead and to the right. No joy. Then to the left. Lights glowing amid big shade trees. Four hundred feet. Christ, oh, Christ, he was gonna end up going down some asshole's chimney.

"I'm gonna be in that number, when the saints—!"

Lord love me, that four-sided geometry of darkness over there, that was it! Oh, yes, precision now, precision and care. Coming in, dropping—lose some scoop, get a little to the right, oh, she was a dream. Not like the mean silk of yesteryear that took you where it damn well felt like going, even if it was down into some hole full of cutthroats with complicated imaginations.

Concentrate, boy! Two hundred, get ready to flare. Relax, you dumb fuck!

Shit, the grounds were alive with guards! Would you look at that. One, two, three, four—eight of the fuckers he could spot and he could only see one strip of lawn. Armed, too. Boy, they were ready for somethin', those gentlemen. He didn't carry a gun, couldn't stand the smell of 'em.

He sailed in over their heads, so close he could smell their cigarette smoke. The edge of the roof blotted out the light from below and he flared the chute with all his might and main, grunting and fighting...but not too hard. You flare more than you want to flare, and you were gonna get a whole lot of roof gravel up your wazoo, and that would not be nearly as funny as it sounded.

He went limp. *Wham*, pain in the right leg, real bad. Then he was sliding. A damn gust had grabbed the chute. Fuck, oh, fuck, he was gonna show the fucking thing for sure—oh, fuckaroo!

But it pulled down. Damn, this was a sweet baby doll of a parachute. It sank obediently to the rooftop with hardly a snap of the damn wrist. He unhitched his harness, then gathered the chute up, hobbling on one leg while the other screamed every fuck-forsaken curse in the book and some that would never be in the damn thing!

When the saints go marching in, my love, when the saints...

O Beth, o mistress mine...I am off in the night and fog, I am dying.

He lay on his side with his teeth clenched tight on his tongue. A hand that was trembling like the wing of a gut-shot duck flitted along his thigh. No telltale bulge, not that he could feel. So it was a spiral break or some damn thing.

"Hail Mary, mother a God, pray for us assholes..."

And then, and then—yes! Yes, the pain was less! Mary you are a bee-you-ti-ful lady and please please forgive me my foul tongue. Compassion a God, oh, it's getting better. It. Is. Getting. Better.

A bruise, a damn *bruise* and the old man thinks he's been amputated. In the old days, he ate pain like candy. No more. He lay looking up at the dim stars. Beetlejuice, Orion, whatever. Used to be he could navigate by the damn things, by eye. Not enough of 'em visible in the metro light-stink.

Beth my love, I will bring them to you, the miracles in the hole. Whisper: "When the saints go marchin' in, I'm gonna be in that number...Lawdy lawd." He found himself able to rise to a sitting position. What had happened was that he'd bounced against the roof of the stairwell as he came down, hit it with his thigh. Panic had made him think he'd broken the leg.

He could feel her hands on his pain, the cool healing fingers. Beth, I miss you so, I left with no word of goodbye.

He had dumped in the middle of the night and ended up just exactly where he'd been intending to go. The proverbial money shot.

So what did it get him? A whole lot closer to death, you wanna know the truth. All those guards were there for a reason, which was that a visitor was expected.

He looked at his watch. One seven.

The whole eternity of the jump had unfolded in just four minutes, two of them under an open canopy.

He would have liked to have laughed, in fact, to have bellowed with laughter. Instead, he pulled out his crowbar. His original plan of rappelling down the side of the building and going through employee entrance with Beth's keycard wouldn't have worked anyway, not with all those goons crawling around down there. Lucky thing, actually. If he had brought the keycard, he would never have also brought the HEET, which was now essential.

He lightened up his kit, shedding the altimeter and putting the GPS in a side pocket. He had to lose the chute, all fifteen hundred bucks of it. When the check to pay for it hit their account, momma was gonna spank his butt. Of course, maybe by then they would have the Tanda lounging in the parlor, so all would be forgiven.

He moved over to the door. Was it alarmed? No telltales visible in the faint glow that illuminated the roof. Breakable with the bar, looked like it. So okay, let's do this.

He positioned the bar beside the lock, drove it between the door and the jamb. *Cra-a-a-k*! Oops, that was loud. Any of you goons hear that? He waited. He could see two of them, could see the radios on the belts, the nighties and pistols on their hips. But they did not appear alerted in any way.

So...do it again. *CR-A-A-Wham!*

Aieee! Might as well have used the HEET.

A guard's face shone up in the light that flooded down on the campus. Charlie waited, but the guy didn't lift his radio to his face, or even finger it. Then he looked down again, toward the driveway.

The door came swinging open, revealing a neon-lit stairwell.

Sail away ladies.

No alarm so far, at least, none that he could hear. He examined the area, looking for switches, wires, anything.

And there it was, a magnetic switch set flush with the door. Somewhere deep inside the building, at some control console, a red light was now flashing.

Okay, time to run like hell and he did—into the structure. If he was going to be stopped now, they would have to do it by force. As he vaulted down the stairs, he wobbled slightly because of the still-throbbing leg.

He paused at a door. 2nd Floor, it said. Beth had described the situation enough so that he knew that the animals were on the ground floor, the executive suites above. There was a control room, he knew that, and the Tanda were behind a door that she had described as being like a vault. That would be where he put the HEET to use... assuming he lived long enough.

He went down another two landings. 1st Floor. The best approach wouldn't be frontal, not if there was a control room and the animals were behind a vault door. He proceeded to the basement.

Now, this was more like it—storage space, a large walk-in refrigerator, the building's support systems. It was a forced air system, which was good. Ducts were tunnels, and tunnels were his forte. Thing was, the system would narrow every time it branched off to another area. There would be ducts he couldn't manage. Still, it was a big system, and he might be able to at least get closer to the Tanda through it.

Also, once he was inside, he was going to be hard to trace. Given the lack of security on the roof, he could be reasonably sure that the ductwork wasn't alarmed, either. It was a good system, but not DoD level security, thank you God.

He reached up and opened the inspection hatch on the main feeder duct to the first floor. It started sucking air, creating a draft across the back of his neck.

He transferred his trusty sap to his hand. He'd had since it had been made for him in Falluja for twenty cents. It was a very fine sap, the best camel hide filled with lead B-Bs. He knew it was good, because the same family made them for the other side. With this sap, he could do anything he wanted, from knocking a man unconscious for a couple of minutes to killing him, with everything from a bad night's sleep to a full-bore coma in between.

He opened what he called his night kit, and withdrew from it a small hook tied to a couple of feet of line. The hook he attached to the inside lip of the latch that held the access hatch closed. He'd been around the block too many times to leave anything open behind him. Rule one: you are a ghost, and ghosts don't leave the door open.

With his penlight in his mouth, he lifted himself into the duct. It was going to be a steep climb, this one.

He drew the hatch closed and, bracing himself so he wouldn't go crashing through the filter into the huge fan that moaned just below, he latched it firmly with a thumb and started climbing. He knew that it would seem longer than it was, and this turned out to be the case. Braced against the sides like this, inching along, a foot felt like a thousand feet. Up he went, another inch, another inch, until his legs were starting to shake and he had to recognize that his thigh had indeed taken a pretty serious hit. He was wounded. That was the fact. As time passed, he would have more and more trouble with the leg. Any moment now, it could become useless.

He reached the T of the duct. He assumed that each secondary would be exactly half the size of the main feeder, but here he got a break: the duct that led to the first floor was wider, the opposite of what was usually the case. But of course it would be. The Tanda were in a sealed space. Without windows, they needed a more powerful air flow.

He got himself into it and lay flat for a while, getting his strength back, working the trembling out, building a wall around the pain radiatin g from the leg.

Okay, not gonna work. He opened his kit and took out some pills, two Hydrocodone and a Benny to counteract any wooziness that they might cause. This would hopefully give him a little more time on the leg. He began moving along the duct, face down, pushing with his toes and pulling with the flats of his hands, exactly as he had done in the tunnels under the Euphrates. When guys heard he did dumps, they would get these haunted, scared expressions on their faces. When they heard he also worked tunnels, they would close down, not wanting to befriend a man who was certain to die, not wanting to risk being asked to volunteer.

Hell, he liked night dumps and he liked tunnels. Look at it this way, you were far less exposed to enemy fire in a tunnel. He moved along, sliding at once through his past and through this slick aluminum duct. Ahead, there was another branching. Here, the duct was going to definitely get tight. If he'd had any sort of spare tire at all, this would have been it. But he didn't have a spare tire. He might be going toward fifty, but he was as hard a steel, was Charlie Cooke. His woman enjoyed muscles.

'Beth,' he thought as he pushed himself along, 'Beth, I will come back to you, Beth I will come back.' He would bring the Tanda to her, these creatures who had found a place in her heart, which was the finest and biggest heart that he knew.

He was real tight now, so tight that he could never return the way he had come. Then he heard a sound. He stopped moving. He held his breath. It came again, a crackling, urgent voice saying something that sounded almost like English. A moment later another, higher voice repeated the same phrase.

It was them. He knew it by the cold in his blood and the thunder of his heart. He had just heard, for the first time in his life, the sound of another intelligent species expressing itself. The crackling urgency, the edge of song in the tone, none of this was human.

Boy, she had not said how they sounded, but this was—oh, my, it was *way* eerie. Not human at all, *wow*.

He was so glad that he had done this insane thing to come here that he would have whooped and thrown his hat down if he'd been able.

He moved along, pushing himself, keeping up his pace to a fast six inches or so a minute.

Then he came to a grate. He peered out...and found himself looking down at the famous control room. The eighteen inch register was pretty standard for a large room full of electronic equipment. When he got the grate off, he would be just able to squeeze through. No question, though, that he would be as vulnerable as hell on the way down.

There was something worse. Much worse. The control room was empty of people, but not of things. Lying on the floor in a sad, crumpled mass was his parachute.

Christ o God, they'd found the damn thing and had *not* put on the alarm. Did that mean they were onto him, watching him? Or had they simply been unable to find him yet? That would explain the empty control room: everybody was out looking. But it could also be a trap. If they did him now, they would get one guy. If they waited until he made his move, they'd get the whole whatever it was.

Yeah, him and Dickie. Big fuckin' deal and a half. Boy, a moment like this called for toke. You did wonderful war work while high. Something about toke made death seem funny. Lotta guys died laughing over there, all sides.

All he had now was a Benny buzz and an opiate slump that left him essentially evened out, just damned tetchy.

So, he went on. Why stop at the control room? Why not just see if he could get a little closer to those alien voices?

He went along until he found a grate that had been recently reinforced. Yeah, somebody had worked on this baby. Steel plates bolted it to the wall. You were not going to open it from the other side. From here, though, it was just a matter of having the right tools.

Below him was a room full of square Formica tables and plastic-backed chairs. Things were a shambles.

He began unscrewing the reinforcing plates. It was while he was doing this that he noticed that his watch said that it was closing in on two. The trip down had been real fast, the rest of the penetration real slow. He sped up his work. The screws were well-seated, but he got them done soon enough. Now he took out his hook and line again, and hooked the grate. He then pushed it out. It scraped, then swung free, dangling amid a cloud of dust into the nearly dark room.

He worked himself well into the opening before it became clear that he could not make this, not as things stood. He'd have to thin down by lightening up, but what could he risk leaving behind?

The GPS unit went, then he redistributed his pockets, making himself as narrow as he could. He turned his head, raised his left arm, and got his head and a shoulder out. Pressing against the far edge of the grate with his underarm, he maneuvered to pull his right arm out. Now he became overweighted, and was in danger of sliding out and dropping head first to the floor. He reached back with both hands and grabbed the edges of the grate, then pulled his legs out. Pain killer or no pain killer, *that hurt.*

Amid waves of pain, he dropped the six feet to the floor, landed hard and rolled amid a clatter of equipment. He went still, waiting for any and all reaction to the noise.

There was one: it was silence. It was greater than normal, inattentive silence, though. It was the listening silence of a nervous sniper in the dark of an alley in Mosul, the sigh of somebody breathing quiet in a hell-black tunnel. Then he smelled a smell. It was sharp, the smell of sweat. It was a little flowery, ripe fruit in it. It was...different. Cinnamon, the salty breath of an animal...and the smell of—what the hell—Beth's perfume.

The Tanda. He was smelling them in this their place. Against all odds, he had achieved penetration.

19

CHARLIE'S DEVILS

They were in the common area practicing how to talk when Betty heard something that she had never heard before, a sort of a *boompf* that came from out in rec. She went closer to Joe, who had been trying to teach them the "L" sound. He shook her off, he was busy right now. He had ideas that they could have their own talk just like they had their own sign. He would make up their words and change around shatterface words and they could talk without the dumbheads—

It came again, and this time he did stop. He sniffed the air.

A shatterface was out in rec, and it did not smell good. It had the salty smell they got when they were scared like that one Keller had brought earlier. Joe was not liking shatterfaces even a little bit anymore. They had not given much food today. The Big Voice was gone away. He even missed the line and sort of missed being in the hole. The worst part was, the window into TV was gone. He did not like the world without the way things had always been and especially without being able to see out into TV. He wanted Stephen Colbert and he wanted to dance and he wanted to have fun like they always did, and to dream about getting into TV. Was TV gone forever with the Big Voice? If so, then what happened to Keller and the others?

Something was wrong among the shatterfaces. It made him feel all grunched up in his stomach to think about. What was going on? Was TV gone and just the world left? If so, where was it? Where was Keller? And the Holy Version hadn't helped again. She was a load of baloney.

A sound came from rec, a clank of metal. Joe went to his feet. Betty held close to him. Everybody bunched up behind him. He looked along the dark hall. There was a shatterface out there in the middle of the night, no question.

Shatterfaces did not come in here when it was dark. They never did, so what was going on? Joe could call to it. He could talk now. He took a deep scent. And this was—

Another new shatterface. It was really funny smelling. Was it *scared*? Yes. Was it *mad*? Yes. But *what was that other smell*? It clung to the back of your mouth, that smell. But it also had another quality to it—the same feeling came from it that came from the air that came in from TV.

The shatterface came toward them, shining ahead of it a tiny, bright light. Joe could feel the people behind him. He wanted to be behind them.

New shatterfaces always came with Keller first. Always. So where was he? "Kerrer," Joe said. Silence. He could see nothing behind the new shatterface and his light. In fact, the new shatterface was nothing but smell and shadows. "Kerrer!"

Greg sat in his office watching his monitors. At his feet, Ma lay with his arms taped behind him and his legs taped to each other, and more tape closing his mouth. They had been here since this afternoon, and Ma's nose was dripping mucus. From time to time he would moan. His pants were soaking with urine, his shirt with sweat. His head was caked with drying blood, a result of getting kicked after Greg came back from the roof and found him halfway to the phone. He'd gone up after he heard a scraping sound somewhere deep in the building. He'd found a parachute. Charles Cooke, he had no doubt.

He regretted hurting Ma. He had never before injured another human being, never in his life, not even as a child. And yet that kick had been one of the most enjoyable things he had ever done.

He had showed Ma his little gun, which he had brought in from home. Maybe later, he would use it. It was a compact, extremely deadly pistol, an AMG Backup, a .38 that was the size of a .22. For twenty years, it had stayed in his bedside table giving him what was probably a false sense of security. It was now as warm as a kitten from all the handling it had been getting.

As gently as if it was a woman's sweet cheek, Greg brushed his fingers across the button that triggered the lockdown system and secured the building. But he did not press it. Not that the fact that the doors were all locked down would stop Charlie Cooke. He was really terribly good, moving like a shadow, coming on like a ghost. He would have made an impressive cat, that man.

He watched Charlie approach the Tanda.

Charlie saw them first as a group of dark shapes backlit by what appeared to be a low-power night light. They were big-shouldered and long of arm. You could believe they were apes, and for a moment he was afraid that Beth had thrown his life away on an overblown enthusiasm.

When they began moving toward him, he shone his flashlight at them. The face of the nearest one became dimly visible in the beam. He sucked in breath, held it. His first instinct was to turn and run. Beth hadn't mentioned being afraid. But this was not the middle of the day and he wasn't being introduced to this experience with the backup of somebody like Greg Keller, who was familiar with them.

The thing that was so unsettling was not that the face of the leader appeared brutal or even ugly, but that it was so intent. The eyes had nothing of an ape's inlooking glaze. Their emerald green made them shine like menacing little lanterns. The lips were thin and human but still all wrong somehow. Too thin, too complex in the way they were held.

The creature, wearing shorts and a slightly ripped Polo shirt, took another step forward. Behind it, he saw the five others, all in varying states of confused dress.

Simultaneously fighting the shakes and smiling, he went down on one knee. "Hey," he said. He pointed the light at his own face, hoping they'd see past the black grease. "My name's Charlie. I'm Beth's husband. You know Beth?"

Silence.

"Want to go out? Want to go out with me?"

More silence.

Could a human being possibly feel more alone? He was trapped here in hostile territory with a bunch of alien beings, and they looked strong and more than a little harsh, and real, real smart. Beth was right about that. You could see it instantly. The Tanda were bright.

"Want to take a ride? You guys like to ride in a car?"

There was a stirring. "Gride," a voice said.

"It's *rrr*ide," another corrected.

"We ride?"

"Yeah, you go out, get in the car, get a hamburger. You like hamburgers?"

The one in front stepped forward. He glared straight at Charlie's face, to the point that it looked like a dominance ritual and Charlie was tempted to stare right back just like he would with Moreland or one of the chimps. But the others all seemed to be having trouble, as if looking at him was physically painful.

Boy, was this ever a high-level strangeness situation.

"Steben Corberr," the leader said.

What the hell did *that* mean?

Another one said, "Erren? Erren in TV?"

"Ellen?"

It's face, which was slathered in lipstick, lit up "Erren!"

"Ellen DeGeneris?"

"Go Erren in TV. Me go Erren!"

"Pepsikora?" a big one toward the back said.

That he could understand. “Yeah,” he said, “Pepsi Cola. Damn swimming pools full of Pepsi Cola!”

Thing was, he had to use the HEET now, blow that fuckin’ door the dipshits had put between the Tanda and the rest of the damn world, and how did he explain HEET to these critters? “Gonna be a big bang,” he said. “Real big!”

He trotted over to the barrier, which was just where Beth had said it was. It was a normal metal door, a slider. He went to work setting the explosives.

HEET was a good design, capable of producing a powerful but compact blast. Now he pulled out his cellphone. Until this moment, it hadn’t occurred to him that he might not get a signal.

Thankfully, one appeared, a single dot on the strength meter. He made the call. Dickie answered on ring three, as agreed. “Pizza,” Charlie said. The reply was a hangup, but that was exactly what Charlie wanted to hear. It meant that everything was okay, and the truck would be outside in minutes.

Now came the tricky bit. Charlie was too knowledgeable to think his chances were even remotely good. The brutal fact was that the guards were not going to miss a tonner truck blasting through their gate. And what about those guns of theirs? What the hell did he do about the guns?

So, okay, he got some HEET set and fused. Behind him, the Tanda had come closer. They were full of curiosity, God knew. Beth had not mentioned to him how damn strange they looked. He found red eyes and emerald eyes and yellow eyes just plain creepy, and those broad, complicated faces weren’t cute, not like she’d implied. Cut isn’t real and they were real and they were scared and confused and desperate. So did the stares he was getting mean they were about to go into attack mode? In an ape, that’s exactly what it would mean.

Maybe it was just him, but their eyes, when you looked directly into the damn things, seemed to just go on forever. They had what he saw as faintly demonic smiles on their wide mouths. Plus, when they stopped moving, they just went dead still. Lots of jungle critters possessed that survival mechanism, but to see it in action in something as weird as this and as creepy human as this was just real disturbing.

Beth had probably not seen that they had violence in them, but any soldier would tell you immediately that the Tanda were a force to be reckoned with if they got mad or scared. No wonder they were kept in confinement. It wasn't only because they were so incredible. You let them out, and you just could not know what might happen.

He got ready to blow the HEET. "Okay, kids, this is gonna be just horrible." He thought they understood him, because they moved back. It was eerie, being understood this well by critters. "Gonna go bang real loud. You know what loud means?"

Emerald eyes nodded slowly.

"OK, *loud*, get ready for it!"

The fuse went down fast and the HEET sure as hell went bang. The bang made the Tanda real chatty. In fact, they erupted into screaming and leaping and rolling and grimacing. They looked like they had gotten roman candles blasted up their asses.

Light poured in from the control room outside. And the Tanda noticed this light. Emerald Eyes came forward a step, then another. Another pointed its awful, glittering red eyes at Charlie. A wicked-looking grin twisted across its face. It said, "Tee vee! Tee vee!"

TV again? Why the hell were they so hipped on TV? You'd think Ellen DeGeneris was a fertility goddess.

"Come," Charlie said, motioning with his hands. "TV!"

At first, they all shrank away. But then Emerald Eyes seemed to get the right idea. He pulled at them and yelled and spat sign so fast Charlie could only see blurs where his hands should be.

Jesus, Mary and Jehosophat, Beth did not mention that they were this damn conversational. They were having a damn meeting and he now had maybe five minutes. Very maybe. Unless this whole shebang got into something like perfect co-ordination, it was headed south.

Beth had certainly been right about one thing: they had never been out of this enclosure because the open door was scaring them one whole hell of a lot more than the blast.

Now they started running stations, half of them, just like upset apes. The other three were—well, recoiling was the only word.

"We gotta go now, boys and girls." More running, more clinging to each other, lotta yelling. "Hey! Go! Go now!" He added in an undertone, "You're fuckin' free, you jerks."

"Tee vee," Emerald Eyes shouted. Then he really belted it out: "*TEE VEEEEEE*!"

That stopped them.

The leader yelled, "Go in Tee Vee! Go in Stephen Cobber, go in Erren, go in Seinferd! C'mon, go!" He took his nearest compadre by the hips and stood it facing the door. "Betty in Erren! *Erren*, Betty!" Then he grabbed the big one. "Go in Iruvrucy, Cwunch!" He pushed Cwunch until he was packed up behind Betty like a sardine.

Calling, cajoling, yelling the names of television programs in his rattling, eager voice, he got them lined up like a little train, boxcar to boxcar. Then he got in front.

Charlie looked at them. "Toot toot?"

"Go in Tee Vee now peeze! O peeze! Eee go in TEE *VEE*!"

Go *in* TV? What kinda screwy worldview had been fed to these critters, anyway? "Follow me."

Instantly, the little leader grabbed his hips. So he marched off, followed by a centipede of Tanda*s* walking in lockstep behind him. This sandwich deal was apparently important to them, so he kept his steps small enough to make it work.

They sped down the hall in a double-quick shuffle.

Maybe Moses and the Israelites entered Cana like this, who the hell knew? Scuttling along as fast as he could, he took a right down a long hall and hoped that was the door that opened onto the lobby. Best guess, he now had three minutes before the truck was there.

No less. And he had no idea how to get to the lobby.

This wasn't going south anymore. That had already happened. He shuffled his Tanda choo-choo down one hall after another, and now his damn leg was biting him again.

Greg watched the lanky thief. He wasn't taking a very straight route, but he was certainly heading for the main entrance. Every cell in his body screamed at him to stop them. But this was what had to be. His beautiful babies were leaving him. Before now, it had been an abstraction, something that would happen soon, but not now.

He said to himself, 'Don't go down there, Gregory, because you will kill that man and he's their only hope.

He looked over toward Ma. Still out? Hard to tell.

He repeated to himself again, 'don't go down there,' but then he saw them appear in the lobby, heading for the main entrance, moving fast. He clutched his gun which was in his pocket. Go now! Stop them!

No, no don't.

His mind turned to the awful morass of immorality and drugs and murder and cruelty that was out there. The arrogant fool at the head of their line was leading innocents to the slaughter.

He couldn't let it happen, no, it was beyond his strength.

He burst out of his office and sprinted down the hallway, the pistol heavy in his hand. One turn, another, a corridor, the stairs taken three at a time and he yelled—

"*Stop!*"

Frozen moment: Dear old Charlie looked as if he'd turned to stone, six Tanda locked up behind him. The Tanda fell into each other, and then the rigid line collapsed as everybody turned around and came rushing back toward him.

"Kerrer, Kerrer," they called, their lips turning upward, their eyes disappearing into masses of crinkles as those super-nova smiles spread across their faces. They swarmed around him and he threw open his arms and went down on one knee. Joe grabbed his face and yelled, "Ee takin' us in tee vee! In tee vee!"

He was there then, standing behind them. Greg looked up at him. "Welcome, Mr. Cooke. I've been expecting you."

"I've been expecting you, too."

"These are my children."

Automobile lights, dimmed by the heavily smoked glass, shone in from the front.

He pointed the gun at Charlie's lean face.

Charlie didn't even blink. "You're too close," he said. There was a calm in his voice that was almost supernatural. Greg had never heard anything quite like it.

"Too close not to."

"I'm gonna give you a chance to put it down."

Sensing the tension, the Tanda clustered close around Greg. Flutter held his waist, her head against his thigh. Only Crunch and Joe were hanging back. They kept looking around, their mouths gaping. Greg felt his finger tightening on the trigger. As many a man has been, he was horrified at the way the act of murder takes on a life of its own. There was so much hate in him for this man, burning in his soul and stinging in his sweat.

And yet it was entirely irrational. He knew that. The Tanda would be better off with Beth and Charles than with Dr. Ma. Of course they would, and that was why he was letting this happen.

He seethed inside. This was the best thing but he didn't want it. He did *not*!

Charlie closed his eyes. This made Greg even more angry—at who, at what he no longer knew. His anger was about being servant to a hard master, about all the compromises he had made to keep his beloved children to himself, about all the life and the joys of life that he had given up for them, all that he had let pass him by.

Charlie's calm in the face of death was truly unsettling. Somebody shouted "Scumbag!" the dumb, brainless word vibrating through the silence. Greg could hardly believe that it was his own voice, harsh and hoarse and so ugly that it seemed unclean. But it had felt good to utter that cry, deeply, deeply good.

He raised the gun, squeezed the trigger. There was a blow. A bolt of purest pain shot up his arm. He cried out and flipped backward, dumping Flutter, who scrambled to her feet, mewling and holding her hands over her head.

Then he was looking up into the bright green eyes of Joe. "We go in tee vee," he said from between bared teeth. His wet, sour breath washed Keller's face.

Incredibly, it was Joe who had hit him. Of all the unexpected, impossible things, Joe had actually struck a blow against his god.

"It's hell out there—do you know hell, do you have that concept? It's got murder and starvation and death and filth. You know nothing of these things, Joe."

"We go in tee vee!"

"Joe, it's a terrible place. All of you, it's—" He caught himself short, his conflicted mind returning to the thought of what awaited them if they did not go. "—it's—" For one of the very few times in his life, he could not find words.

Joe had his hands on Greg's, and thus also on his gun. He wasn't pulling at it, but it was clear that he could. Greg's finger was still curled around the trigger, but it no longer had a killing life of its own. Of course Joe knew what a gun was. He watched TV.

Joe's face was now inches away from Greg's. His eyes were swimming with tears. And the gun, incredibly, was slowly turning...toward Greg.

Greg understood for the first time how very badly Joe wanted the outside world. If the gun would give it to him, he would use it.

Deep within Greg's inner self, a huge old door began creaking open. "TV," he repeated, "is a terrible place."

"It's freedom for them," Charlie said. "And they need it and you know that. Look, your goons gotta be all over my driver by now, man. We were looking at a five minute turnaround, tops, before they controlled the situation. It's controlled by now and they're gonna beat the shit out of him, or worse."

Greg came to his feet. Joe was still tugging on the gun. He looked at Charlie and said, "Karlee." He was trying to get some sort of instruction.

"Talk to him, Charlie. He's asking you what they should do."

"Get in the truck," Charlie said.

The Tanda bunched up, confused. Greg knew that their knowledge would be spotty. They rarely saw cars and trucks. Their TV was confined to indoor shows.

"He means go through that door over there and get in the big room that's on the other side."

Joe looked up at him. His eyes now were hard little berries from some dangerous jungle plant. "No room! We go in tee vee!"

Greg took him by the hand, the irony of the thing drawing a bitter laugh out of him. "This is the way to TV." He led him to the door and opened it. Joe threw back his head and took huge gulps of air and howled out the purest, most intense, most explosive cry of joy that Greg had ever heard or imagined possible. And he understood, for the first time, how very great their need had been. The others came behind, tentative, eyes as big as plates, looking around, lips slack on their astonished faces.

"Not tee vee," Jack whispered.

"S'here," Joe snapped.

"Go in the truck," Charlie said.

Three guards appeared from around the front of the vehicle, moving slowly, their pistols out. They were watching Greg for some signal.

"They're going tonight," he said smoothly.

"Mr. Ma said—"

"They're moving tonight! Right now!"

"Dr. Keller, you can't—"

"Right now! For security reasons!"

"In a Ryder truck?"

He motioned to the fourth guard, who had the driver at gunpoint. "Put it away."

There was no change.

"Put it away! Now!"

Slowly, the guard holstered his gun.

The Tanda got in the truck, and Charlie and his driver closed the bay. From within, there came a burst of frightened muttering. Greg's heart broke for them yet again, in yet another new way. They would not understand this confinement, coming just moments after they had first felt freedom.

The truck began to move off.

There was movement in the doorway. Greg turned and was stunned to see Dr. Ma, his clothes ripped, duct tape dangling from one wrist and an angry mass of black blood on his left temple. "Stop them," he cried, his voice hoarse.

As if caught in the flash of an explosion, the guards froze.

Ma lurched through the door. "Stop them!"

A gun roared, another. The truck's gears ground. It began to increase speed, its tires screaming as it swung perilously through the driveway's curves.

Greg picked up his own pistol, which Joe had dropped as he entered the truck, and thrust it against Ma's back. "Call them off," he said quietly.

"You'll die for this," Ma snarled. "In the end."

He jabbed the pistol hard. "Do it!"

"Let them go," Ma barked.

Hector Quarry, the security chief, turned around in surprise.

"He said let them go!" Greg shouted. "He didn't know about the change in plan. He hadn't gotten the call."

They were gone now, though, well and completely gone, the lights of the truck disappearing off down the road.

Greg took Ma inside with him. He marched him across the lobby and into the first office he could find. Then he hit him in the side of the head with the gun, the way he'd seen it done in the movies. Ma went "nuh" and sank to the floor. The earlier wound began to flow blood again.

Leaving Ma in a heap, Greg went along the silent corridor, through the barrier door and down into the Tandas' space. As he moved through the rooms, he turned on lights, tapping the gray squares that located the concealed switches. He righted a couple of chairs in rec, straightened some tables. Then he went down into the sleeping quarters. There lay Gorilla, and their games.

He reached down and picked up Gorilla—then threw it with all his bitter might against the wall of Joe's room. That one, he had been the problem, that dissatisfied little prick.

When the altars grow dust and the temples slide into ruin, there remains only the god, alone with his memories.

He went over to the heavy door that opened onto the line. It stood silent also, looking now, with its complex workstations. He laughed a little. We humans, we lost our jungle, too. Once we were the Tanda, thrust out onto the unknown plain, naked and afraid.

He wandered into Jack and Jill's space and sat on the bed. He took out his gun. Hitler had put his pistol in his mouth. He would have been advised by men who knew the ways of the gun, so Greg did the same.

He sat like that, tasting the nasty steel of it, the bitterness of the gun oil. In a perfect world, the cruel and foolish gods die...in a perfect world.

The shot was a tiny incident, an afterthought in a great journey. There was a jolt, a curious light spreading, and the sense that he had soiled himself.

The body pitched forward rather than back, for the hard-point bullet made such a clean hole that the impact was not enough to send him on one of those sprawling, operatic trajectories of death.

Consciousness didn't end at once. It took time for the hemorrhage to flood the shattered brain. So he was aware of feeling suddenly disembodied. Then he saw a light. It buoyed his spirit, that light, and drew him to his feet. He began to follow it.

But the light was fast, it dimmed and receded, and soon was enveloped in a darkness of a kind he had never known before. This darkness worried him, for it contained no hopeful stars. Where did one go from here?

"Where" he asked, "where?" And then was gone.

The room the Tanda were in lurched and shook and Joe ran round and round in it. He ran and he screamed and he fought, hammering at the walls, trying to pry up the floor, banging on the rattling doors.

He had to get out of here, this was even littler than the world, and it was *not*—definitely *not*—TV. They had tricked him, they had lied. Keller had lied and Charlie had lied and all shatterfaces lied all the time.

He could hear the others crying and screaming, and Crunch blundering around trying to run stations. He couldn't, though. There was no rec in this awful place, no chairs, no nothing!

Joe found that he could get his fingers outside. He could slide them up and reach a bar, and push the bar...and then the door swung down. It made a great big bang.

"TV!"

It was in the form of a flat thing that went off below and behind them into the dark, and big green shadows on the sides. It wasn't any program he'd ever seen, but it was TV okay, he was sure.

TV stopped moving. He heard a screech, then quick voices. Charlie and the other shatterface were talking.

Joe got out. His feet hit the warm, flat stuff. Behind him, the others came...but they stopped.

'TV,' he signed, 'come on!'

Nobody moved. Joe heard the shatterfaces approaching. He signed again, signed hard.

Crunch came down.

At that moment, the shatterfaces appeared around the side of the thing. It was a giant car, Joe saw the wheels. So they'd been going on a road and that meant that this was definitely TV. They were deep in TV. He grabbed Crunch's hand and pulled him off into the green fluff. The shatterfaces did not see.

He wanted to call Betty, to get her down too, but he dared not speak, not with the two shatterfaces right there. Crunch tried to break away from him, to go back. But then the door was shut with a huge *bang-clang*. Next thing he knew, the big car was going off.

Joe ran on the flat stuff, chasing the truck car, Crunch right with him. "Betty," Joe called, "Betty, Betty!" And Crunch called, "Futter, Futter, *Futter*!"

The thing was awful fast. It was the fastest thing ever there was.

So they had to stop. They stopped in the middle of the dark. The truck went away, taking its noise—and all the people—with it.

In the quiet that was left behind, Crunch came close to Joe. They were not friends, but they were also very alone right now. They couldn't even see to sign, not in dark this deep.

All around them, there were voices, funny little voices that went *eek eek* and *choot choot* and *bazzzeeeiiiiaaass....* There were smells, too, so many new smell! The air was so sweet that it made Joe cry to smell the life in it.

His sex swung to life and he threw his head back in a great passion of raw desire, the very essence of the fertile night, and he let forth a huge, happy, terrified and lonely howl. Crunch joined him, and they stood with their hands grasping their organs as if they were talismans in the rage of storm. Again they howled, and again, and then both at the same moment saw the firmament above, as a million living eyes in a great, black creature, magnificent and strange.

This huge creature overspread all of TV. It awed them completely, causing their jaws to gape and their hands to drop as they stood looking up, two small beings in the mystery, and as we became men by the light and wonder of the stars, so did they, feeling tiny beneath the flooding heavens. Just as our ancestors had, they huddled close one to the other, their souls seeking some help beneath the firmament—and that, as it had with us all those millennia ago ago, was what made them see the smallness of other beside them and want his safety and cherish his life, and know that he, also, was lost.

20

A NEW LAND

It was the hour before dawn, when the hard south Texas fields may sometimes be improbably kissed by dew. It is an illusion that the sun will soon drive back into the few corners of shade that may survive its rising.

Beth's eyes opened. She heard a clattering sound, a grinding of gears. She listened. The sound grew, resolving into the groan of a big, tired engine under stress.

"Charlie?"

He wasn't in bed. She felt the sheets. Hadn't been for some time. Was there some kind of an early delivery? Nothing was scheduled, and since this was Saturday, it was highly unlikely that anybody would just turn up.

Her mind went back to the arrival of the chimps, of the capuchins.

She threw off the covers and surged out of bed, thrusting her feet into the stout leather slippers she'd made by cutting down an old pair of boots. She didn't want to get bitten by a scorpion again, not soon or ever. She still had a tender knot in her left insole.

She went out onto the kitchen porch. The sound of the truck had stopped, and now all you could hear was the occasional, intimate rustle of an errant leaf falling from one of the live oaks that surrounded the house. Being evergreens, they shed a bit all the time.

"Charlie?"

Still no response.

She went down the path a short distance. Then she saw it, a huge grill in the predawn shadows. She could hear a hot radiator clanking softly as it cooled.

"Charlie?"

She went closer to the truck, then around to the back.

"I think they're real scared," Charlie said. He was standing in the truck body with Dickie. There was a pile of animals on the floor of the bay, all pressed up against the front wall.

She got up into the bay. She thought: *'Orang-utans.'* Terrified. "Where'd you get 'em?" she asked.

"Now, if that ain't the funniest question of the day! Hay-*soos*!"

"Maybe I shouldn't ask. I—" She stopped, looked again. What was that she saw? "Give me your light."

"Now, try to stay calm—"

"You told me she knew all about it," Dickie said petulantly.

Her light shone on a wide-eyed face. "What in the..." Then she saw that they were dressed, sort of—and the clothes were instantly familiar. "Charlie!"

"Sh! Take it easy!"

She rushed to them—it was Jack and Betty and Jill, and under the pile so just her nose stuck out, Flutter. "Oh babies, babies, it's me., it's Beth, you remember Beth." She looked back at Charlie. "That place was a fortress!"

He said, "They're in shock. A bit."

They were indeed, their faces grimacing with fright. Apes sometimes arrived in a state something like this.

She took Betty's hands and held them between her own. They were icy. The poor Tandas, they were as cold as death. But breathing, yes, everybody was breathing.

"Where's Joe and Crunch?"

Charlie peered in. "Aw, *shit*!"

"You left them behind?"

"No way!"

"They got off the truck, man," Dickie said. "Musta happened when the door jumped on us."

"Charlie—" She stood up from the Tandas. "You have to find them. Right away."

"We gotta go back, Dickie," he said. "We got two of 'em on the loose."

"Fuckin-A, man! It's fuckin' dangerous back there!"

"Take my car, Dick. You do it, you do it now. You find them."

"How? You tell me and I will."

"The place the door fell open," Charlie said. "You're right about that. Go back there."

"Dick, go, please!" The thought of those two poor fellas out there, struggling to cope with an enormous, complicated and lethal world of which they knew nothing made her want to crawl out of her skin. "Now! Right now!"

"Okay! But it's been half an hour already. They're bound to be back in the brush somewheres. I'm not gonna find 'em, not one guy alone."

Beth took Charlie by the shoulders. "For God's sakes, don't let's screw this up any more!"

"Just hold on. Lives were risked, here. You respect that, girl."

"Dickie, *go*!" She tossed him her keys and he finally left, muttering to himself.

"Okay, we gotta get them inside."

"Yeah, this ain't healthy, here."

She tried to get Betty to her feet. The Tanda did not come. "Hey, guys, it's me, Beth. You remember Beth, don't you? It's me."

A single eye was opened, one of Jack's yellow eyes with the red flecks. He said, "Uhhoowwrr."

"I can't understand you."

He did not try again.

"Look, Charlie, go to a 24 hour McDonald's. Load up with hamburgers—plain ones. Then get Pepsi, even if you have to go somewhere else to find it. And Mounds bars. Find a whole bunch of Mounds and Snickers."

"How about rice and apples, man?" he asked. "Be better for them."

"It's what they're used to." Again, she tugged at Betty, who seemed the most conscious. "They're not doped?"

"Not by me."

She went to him and threw her arms around him and kissed him hard.

He kissed back. "Oh, Jesus, Babes," he whispered. "I almost bought it on the way down."

"Down? Down from where?"

"I went in by chute."

"By parachute? At night?"

"There wasn't a lotta wind."

She threw herself against him again, stroking his hair, his face. Then she lay against his chest. "Never die, baby. Never, never die."

"I'll give it a shot."

She broke away and returned to the Tanda. "You're magnificent, Charles Cooke, to do this."

"Christ, Babes, they were worth the risk."

She touched Jack, got her arms around him, drew him close to her. He cuddled into her arms like a child. As she got to her feet, she struggled not to fall. He lay limp, gazing up at her as if entranced. "We'll put them in the spare room," she said.

"There's a good cage. I got the guys to clean it up real nice."

"No."

"We can't have apes in the house."

"They're not apes!"

"Man, yeah. Yeah. What was I thinking?" He shook his head. "Okay, that's cool. It's weird but it's cool."

"My damn foot, I can't carry him." She gave him Jack, whom he took into the house. A moment later, he reappeared. She waited as he hurried back and forth, carrying one and then another. When only

Betty was left, she came and latched onto Beth, and Beth staggered off with her as best she could.

"Cho," she moaned, "Cho..."

"We gotta get that truck under cover," Charlie said as she brought the last Tanda in. "Dickie was supposed to get it out of here before first light."

"What does it matter? They're gonna know where the Tanda are."

"Maybe we'll get lucky."

"Go for the food, Charlie. They're gonna be coming out of this... state. They're gonna be ravenous. And thirsty."

He took off, leaving her to cope with the reviving Tanda.

She noted that Jack had been watching her for some time, his quick eyes following every move. He and Jill sat against back the wall of the room with their arms thrown over one another's shoulders. Betty and Flutter were huddled up together in a ball. Beth thought they must be devastated by the disappearance of their mates, and she was going to need all of her empathy and skills to help them. And if Crunch and Joe were never located—well, that would be a long, hard bridge to cross.

Jill stirred herself and went to Beth's dressing table. "Chikshick," she said. "Chickshick!" Triumphantly, she held up a lipstick.

"Lipstick," Beth said, "LLLL".

Jill was struggling to get it opened. Beth held out her hand. "I can do it," she said. For a moment, Jill regarded her through narrow eyes. She held the lipstick tight. Beth smiled. "You're pretty," she said.

"P.t! P.t!"

"Yes, very pretty, Jill. Let me help you." She got Jill's lips well covered. Jack watched. Over in the corner, Flutter and Betty remained motionless.

"Me," Jack said, moving quickly to Beth's side and presenting his lips.

Beth put lipstick on him, too, and he and Jill began to parade around the room.

Then Betty stirred, groaned, rose up and ran from one side of the room to the other and back again. She stopped before the closet door, peered in and screeched. Finally, she squatted in the middle of the floor and urinated, the liquid rushing out with a great splash and spreading across the rug. She groaned and buried her face in her hands.

"It's all right, love," Beth said, going to her. The Tanda had bathrooms. They were not given to soiling their space. "This is where you go," Beth told them, opening the door to the downstairs bathroom. They crowded in. At once, Jack started using the toilet. When he was finished, Jill followed, squatting with a relieved grin on her face. "After you're done, you push this lever," Beth explained, pointing to the flush. Their toilets had automatic flushes.

Betty and Flutter huddled together in a corner of the spare room while Jack and Jill explored, signing back and forth so fast their hands were a blur. They found the hall closet and busied themselves in it, sorting through Beth's old prom gowns and Chanel suits of her days as a social girl. For their own sakes, Beth supposed, they would have to be taught the difference between male and female dress. But not now, not today when they were at once in anguish and filled with wonder.

She looked down at poor Betty. Big, disconsolate eyes peered back. "Betty," she said, "let me clean that up for you—" She stopped. She examined the puddle more closely. There was no urine odor, and it had come out with a splash, not in a stream.

But—no! Oh, God, NO!

Of course, it was pee, it had to be.

She touched it and sniffed her fingers.

"Charlie," she shouted. "Charlie!" But of course he'd just left, and damnit he was not a cellphone person, of course. "Those things are like standing under a streetlight," he would say. "I need that like a pair of cuffs on my wrists."

"CHARLIE!"

Only the night wind answered, and Betty, whimpering softly, her hands clutching toward Beth's.

Betty had just broken her waters.

She was going to have a baby right here, right now, a preemie.

Beth had no idea if four months was too premature for a Tanda infant to develop normally outside of the womb. If it was, Betty's baby was going to die. Nobody would be able to save such a child, not without any experience of the medical needs of this species. Barrett Scientific had done little to really study them, beyond doing the DNA testing and analysis needed to prove they weren't human.

She hadn't even had time to give the Tanda physicals, or use the services of a vet. Or, why a vet? They needed medical, not veterinary attention. They were as human as us, just different.

"It's okay, Betty," she said, going down to her. Close, she reeked of sweat and the faint musk of the waters. Her eyes shut tight, the poor, trembling creature clung to Beth. As she got her onto the narrow, unmade spare room bed, her legs remained pulled up almost to her chest. Betty was in pain. In a human woman that would not be a good sign, not this early in the process.

"Does anybody know 'sick?' Betty is sick. We have to help Betty"

Jill and Flutter came over. Flutter said gravely, "Pider."

Beth remembered the horror of the way they aborted each other. If they started to do that to Betty this late in term, there was little question but that both mother and infant would die.

Betty looked at Flutter, eyes wide. She shook her head. "No pider."

Beth laid a hand on Betty's cheek. "Do you want your baby?"

Betty's eyes radiated her puzzlement.

Flutter repeated more forcefully, "Pider!"

"It's not a spider in her," Beth said. "It's somebody just like you, only very little and very much in need of love. Do you know the word 'love.'"

Jill and Jack came up, wiggling their hips and pushing their bright red lips out. Betty reached out a hand. "Mee," she said, "mee" and pursed her lips, too.

Baby or no baby, Beth had to make sure that everybody had lipstick.

In the middle of the application, though, Betty groaned and doubled up, then began making high mewing sounds and gasping.

This frightened the others, and they started rushing around the room beating their heads with their fists. When the cries went on, they clapped their hands over their trim little ears.

"It's a contraction," Beth shouted. "Don't be afraid."

Betty cried out and they all did the same.

"Breathe, Betty, breathe deep!"

She didn't understand. Her face was twisted, her teeth clenched, tears popping out of her tightly-closed eyes. Beth could see that she was already well-dilated.

God, Charlie, I need you!

The contraction finally released and Betty relaxed, gasping and choking. She said, "oh," then again, "oh!"

"It's okay that it hurts, it's good! When it hurts, you *push*, Betty. Like this, from your stomach." Beth demonstrated. "*Puuuush*! Do you understand, honey?"

Betty grunted and pushed, and said, "*Buuush*!"

And breathe, pant—do you know *pant*—like this." Beth panted. Betty panted, and so did everybody else.

"That's right, Betty Just exactly right! You *push* and you *pant* when it hurts. Oh, Betty, don't be scared. This is wonderful! This is happy!" She clapped her hands, a hollow sound in the sunken end of the night. Plastering a grin on her face to conceal her terror, she added, "We're gonna have a baby! A baby is a miracle!"

Where was he? Why was he so very slow?

Betty began panting. Her face grew pale. The absurd application of lipstick became smeared as she shook her head back and forth.

"Push, Betty, *push*!"

They all pushed and Betty did, too. "*Buuusshhh!*" She grabbed the edges of the bed and grunted deep, and everybody else grunted with her. They caught on fast, these guys. Beth saw a little blue bulge appear in her vagina. The baby was crowning!

God, God, what should she do? She'd never delivered a baby before, and she didn't know anything more than what was in old movies. Anyway, nobody in the world had ever delivered a Tanda baby.

They were all staring at Betty with exactly the same expression on their faces—slack-jawed amazement.

"Yes," Beth said, "it's a baby, not a spider at all. A little bitty one just like you, who will grow up and—"

"*Huuuunnnhhhhhooooooo*!" Betty thrust her pelvis forward, grabbing at herself, her fingers scrabbling across the slowly emerging head. The Tanda had wide hips, and Betty's were especially accommodating, so it was happening fast. But it hurt, obviously, it hurt terribly and Betty's eyes were swimming with tears.

Beth bent to her and kissed her cheeks and her tears and held her. "Cho," Betty said in a tiny, exhausted voice, "'M'Cho..."

"Joe is coming soon, darling.' He's coming." She hoped to God that was true. Dick had been in the desert with Charlie, so maybe it was. Whatever, Dick was going to be a whole lot better than a confused Tanda outdoors for the first time. "He's coming very soon."

Somebody hit her shoulder, one of the other Tandas trying to get her attention. She leaned away Betty, looked down—and there between the woman's trembling legs, blue behind a caul of afterbirth, was a small face. The mouth, infinitely delicate, was open just slightly, as if it was a tiny angel about to sing.

She feared that the child was dead in the caul. But then the lips quivered. In fact, the whole little body was in subtle motion.

God, Charlie, where are you? When he came back, she was going to beat the goof up.

No she wasn't. He had done this, he had brought them out. This was Charlie's miracle.

She lifted the baby and pulled at the caul. Was this normal for the Tanda? There was no way to know. The little creature came out of its sheltering afterbirth gleaming wet and the color of a rose in the dew. It was still attached to Betty by a knotty umbilical. Beth had no idea how to cut an umbilical. With scissors? A knife? *Charrrrllllieee*!

The baby—it wasn't breathing. No, no definitely not. She had to cut the umbilical. Then it would start, that would do it.

Betty saw her baby. She lifted herself to look more closely and Beth backed away to get the scissors and they all saw it. Betty took it in her arms, she gazed down at it. "Ahhhoooo," she cooed, "aaah-hhhoooo..."

Jack began rushing up and down the room, banging on the window sill and the door jamb. Flutter and Jill came near, their fingers reaching out to touch the tiny thing. Then Jack came and kissed the only part of Betty he could get close to, which was the top of her head.

Beth watched the little group reforming itself around mother and child. She was seeing instinct take over, causing everyone to rally around the baby.

If this had happened even a few hours ago, this infant would have died or been killed as a "spider."

Damn miracle.

As if protecting this sacred space, Jack now hovered near the door, rushing over from time to time to take another look. Flutter and Jill held Betty and Betty held her baby.

Beth, with the scissors, had to somehow get in there and cut that umbilical. She did it quickly, but when they saw what had happened, there was an immediate uproar. Jill grew furious and yelled at her, an impossible salad of unformed words. Flutter ran away and hid in the closet under the old party dresses that Jack and Jill had pulled down. Jack came roaring toward her, screaming and waving his arms, his teeth bared. The primate was rising from his depths. Beyond that display, Beth knew, was the same mayhem that drove chimps to tear one another apart and men to go to war.

The baby's color went from pink to blue and its lips began to twitch. It was struggling for air now. Oh, Jesus, what had she done? She should have waited for Charlie, he would have known if this was right or not.

"I have to," she said, taking the tiny body from Betty, who growled low, a mother's warning. Beth held the little thing by its feet. It was so very small, not even nine inches long. Using a single fingers, she spanked its tiny buttocks.

Nothing. The baby was turning a darker blue. She could feel it twisting and struggling.

Again she spanked, this time a little harder. There was a sort of gurgle, then some material came out of the mouth, dark red and thick.

From off in the distance she heard a familiar voice, "Come an git it!"

"*Charlie*!"

"Get 'em while they're hot!"

"Charlie, help me!"

"Beth?"

"Charlie, I'm delivering a baby in here!"

He came in, moving fast, as silent as smoke. "Shit, 's blue as Satan's balls."

"I know it's blue!"

The Tanda were gathered around, seething. They were about to lay into her, she knew it.

"That ain't workin.'"

"I know it."

"Try CPR."

"You did it in Iraq." She gave him the little thing, eliciting a more menacing growl from Betty. Jack bared his teeth.

"Nobody this small." Charlie took it in one of his huge hands and began using the thumb and forefinger of the other to press the tiny chest, press and release, press and release. "Why didn't you say she was pregnant?"

"I didn't know she was *this* pregnant!"

He pressed and released, pressed and released, and gradually the baby's skin went from dark blue to light blue, then to pink. The tiny lips quivered.

"It's awful preemie, Beth."

The baby squealed, a pitiful little creaking sound. Charlie stopped pumping its chest. The squeal died away.

"Shit, we need—" He stopped. Nothing happened. He started again. "Look, as a vet, I'm telling you, we need a hospital."

"I know, but how can we?"

"We gotta just do it."

Any healthcare pro would know instantly that the Tanda weren't human, but these people needed and deserved the full support of the medical establishment, just like anybody else.

"Okay. I'll take Betty and the baby," she said. "You stay here with the rest of them."

She took Betty's hand, but they all came. Charlie followed with the baby in the crook of one arm, pumping its chest with the other.

The Tanda got into a tight line behind Betty, then tightened up on Charlie.

"Looks like we're all going," Charlie said.

The next thing Beth knew, the whole gang was piled into her Volvo, heading for the medical complex ten miles east of the Center. She drove as fast as she dared.

Charlie was beside her and all of the Tanda were crowded into the back except Betty, who crouched at his feet with her head in his lap, her hand on her baby. He kept up steady CPR. From time to time, the little mouth puckered and there was a squall no louder than the crinkle of a hummingbird.

Beth watched the back seat in the rearview mirror for signs of panic, but the Tanda were too amazed to do that. They were like tourists, grinning and staring, signing furiously to each other. Occasionally she'd hear somebody exclaim "tee vee" or "Iruvrucy!" or the name of some other program as they attempted to fit the real world into their imaginary universe of television programs.

"How's the baby?"

"Still not breathing on his own."

"Christ, Charlie, how're we gonna spin this at the hospital?"

"I have no idea."

Possibilities rushed at her, one worse than the last. First problem, the admitting nurse. She'd see an animal. But then the mother, also apparently some sort of animal, would talk—sort of. Then what would happen?

The Tanda weren't being introduced to the outside world so much as being dropped into it like some kind of a bomb. The memory of the media circus that had erupted around Moreland was still painful. This would be more than a circus. It would be a wild free-for-all, an eruption of hysterical media madness. And in it—somewhere in all the confusion and frenzy—she very much feared that Barrett Scientific would get their property back, and the Tanda would at once be transferred to their new owners, and that would be that. As for this little, tiny guy struggling to live, he would be swept away at some point in the storm.

She pulled out her cellphone and called Dr. Chris on his private number. She'd known him all her life. He was one of her father's closest friends. If anybody could get the baby past University Hospital admissions, it was him.

"It's Beth."

"Beth? Are you okay?"

"I'm on my way to University with a preemie that's not breathing and I need help."

"A preemie? What preemie?"

"It's not mine, Chris! You'd've known if I was pregnant."

"A...uh...ape?"

"No! No they're from—they're people, Chris! They're from Sumatra. The baby's come prematurely and it's an emergency!"

"I'll have the preemie unit waiting."

She hung up. "We say they're from Sumatra."

"They look like—"

"We just say it!"

"It won't work. Call him back. Warn him."

"How? What do I say?"

"The truth! It's all we have."

She hammered in his number. "Chris, it's me again. Listen. Listen to me carefully. They are not human, strictly speaking."

"Beth, they aren't going to treat an animal."

"They aren't animals! They have human intelligence. Maybe more. They were kept hidden by a company that was going to sell them as slaves. We got them out and now we've got this baby Chris, and he's dying, he's just dying here in the car and—"

"Hold it! Slow down! Beth, I can't figure out what you're talking about. What do you want me to do?"

"Help us! They are another species of intelligent primate, no different from us. Maybe even smarter."

"Well, maybe—what do they look like? Can they pass?"

"Listen to me! This baby is dying. He needs airway assistance. He needs—God only knows what he needs. But he's gotta be at least—"

"Watch out," Charlie yelled.

"Sorry!" She'd almost driven up the tailpipe of a semi that loomed ahead of them in the misty predawn.

"If they look okay—"

"Chris, they don't look even one little bit human, but they talk and they wear clothes and they're—oh, God, what am I going to do?"

"A vet—"

"I've got one sitting right beside me and he's saying we need a hospital."

"Okay. I'll manage it somehow, Beth. Does your dad know about this?"

"God, not him." She wheeled the car into the curving drive that led to the emergency room, and glory be, a team in medical greens was assembling in the doorway. They had an isolette and oxygen.

"Chris, where are you?" she yelled into her phone.

Then she saw him coming out onto the receiving dock, just throwing on his own greens. He must have been in the hospital. 'You don't want to go into medicine,' Dad used to say. 'Look at Chris, he never slows down.' Yes, look at him, and thank the stars that guide him.

With him were two nurses and an orderly.

The Tanda were dressed in some of her frilly old gowns, red pumps, underpants and all that crazy makeup...sweet Jesus.

As they pulled up, Charlie threw open the door. "I've got life," he shouted as he and Betty exited the car. "*ER*," Betty shouted.

"Stay in the car," Beth bellowed as the rest of the Tanda tumbled out, all crying "ER, ER" and rushing around hugging the personnel and yelling garbled versions of the names of various characters in the old TV series.

"They're from Sumatra," Charlie yelled as Chris took the baby and ran with him, followed by the emergency team. The Tanda raced into the admitting area shouting and waving their arms, grinning at the staff with their huge grins.

"They're from Sumatra," Charlie kept shouting.

The reaction was electrifying. People leaped up from behind desks. Some ran screaming, closed themselves in offices, went racing off down halls. Two security guards appeared, nightsticks in hand.

"It's okay," Chris said, "they're my patients."

"*Patients*?" one of the guards yelled.

People were backing away. The atmosphere of terror was thick. A guard's nervous hand drew his pistol.

"We in ER tee vee," Jill shrilled.

"I need her insurance card," a nurse yammered as Chris, Betty, the baby and the rest of them disappeared into the depths of the hospital.

Dropping her own card on the surprised woman's desk, Beth ran to catch up with the others. The nurse came after her. "Name, please!"

"Betty" she said.

"Last name?"

"Mrs. Betty Joe. Mrs. Joe. Husband Mr. Joe.

Jack announced, "ER shair!" and dropped into a wheelchair. He began rolling himself backward with his feet.

Flutter came up and held out her hand to Beth. "Riptick! Riptick!"

Chris herded the whole crowd into an empty room. "DO NOT let them out, Beth," he said, and dashed off to help the baby.

A nurse came in. The Tanda were making the hospital bed do the jitterbug, the girls racing the controls, which they had figured out instantly, while Jack pretended to be the patient.

"Don't fool with that," the nurse said, casually slapping Flutter's hand. "How old are these children?"

"Nine to eleven," Beth said briskly, thankful for the tiny favor of this woman's remarkable inattention to detail.

But then the nurse glanced around, blinked. Her face froze. She backed toward the door.

"Please," Beth said, "give the baby a chance."

"They're—what are they?"

"They're people!"

"No—no—they—" Her eyes pleaded. Beth saw the fear there, blood-deep and primitive. Even in these familiar human eyes, she could see the sick sheen of animal terror.

"They're hominids. People, but of another species."

Jill went toward the nurse, smiling. "Eeeawrrr," she said, "Ah wuvve yew!"

The nurse backed away. "Get it away from me!"

"Please, they're just like us. They're not dangerous."

Jill reached out her hand. The nurse's eyes were tearing, she was now pressed flat against the door. "POLICE," she screamed.

"No! No, please!"

The Tanda recoiled for a moment at her cry. But then something happened that Beth later saw as a miracle of insight. First Flutter said, "'E keerd. 'E so *keerd*!"

Then Jack and Jill held out their hands. Their faces melted. "Hep ah bebe," Jill said, "we *wuve* ew!"

"We wuve ew," the others said, moving toward the nurse. She was in tears, but her hands came trembling out, and fingers began touching fingers.

"My God, my dear God," she kept saying.

There came a hammering on the door. "Kristin!"

"I'm—I'm okay. It's okay!"

Beth heard a small sound, a tiny "oh!" coming from the next room. Then she heard Betty's much louder "OH!"

A minute passed, another. Agony. Then, from through the door, another of those tiny sounds, still hardly worthy of being called a cry.

The door swung open and Betty appeared. She had an olive drab hospital sheet in her arms. Peering out from deep within was a tiny face, looking more like a frog than a Tanda. It was pink again, and wriggling, its red eyes open.

"There was an airway obstruction," Chris said. "Not uncommon in babies born a little early."

Beth ran into his arms.

"He's about two months out," Chris added.

"I had no idea she was this close," Beth said.

"Ma beebee. *Ma* beebee!"

"Yeah, Betty, *your* baby!" Beth went to her.

Betty looked up at her, met her eyes. "Pank oo, Bef."

Beth almost collapsed against Betty But instead she put her hand on the tiny head of the infant, whose big eyes gazed deeply into hers with the timeless curiosity and incomprehension of the newborn.

"We need to move this crowd outa here right quick," Chris said.

"Is he safe?" Beth asked.

"This infant is a medical unknown. You're going to have to be alert for any reddening or swelling anywhere on his body, or any sign of fever or rash, any respiratory infection." He glanced at Charlie. "You've treated preemie apes?"

"They rarely survive."

"Then we have to be extremely vigilant."

"Admit him," Beth said.

"It won't work," the nurse said.

"No, it won't," Chris agreed.

"Admit him!"

"Bethie, the hospital will not take him and there's nothing we can do about it. Not even your dad. He looks like—"

"Something from Neptune," the nurse said emphatically.

Beth faced it. They were right. "Then what do we do?"

Chris went down to Betty, spoke with excessive care. "Do you understand me?"

Betty nodded.

"She understands English perfectly well," Beth snapped. Charlie elbowed her. He was right. Betty was perfectly capable of speaking for herself.

"You have a beautiful boy."

"Cho? Wan mah guy."

Chris glanced up.

"That's the name of her husband. Joe."

"Joe," Chris said. "Are you going to call him after his dad?"

Betty began to weep a little, her head sinking onto her chest.

"We lost track of Joe," Charlie said.

"How long have you been in America, Betty?"

She looked at him, a question in her eyes. "Merker is uvthee," she sang in a high, haunting voice, "tweet rand...tweet rand...

"Now, listen to me, Betty. If your baby has any rash, or if he coughs, or has a red area on his body, you tell Charlie and Beth right away. Right away."

"Grash?"

"She doesn't know what a rash is?"

"I doubt it. We'll be caring for the baby with her."

"I'll come by to examine him every day. And you know who to call. At the least sign, Beth. The least sign."

They moved off, Charlie and Chris and Beth shepherding the Tanda along. As they passed through the waiting room, a little boy with both of his hands swathed in bandages shouted, "Aliens, Mom, they got *aliens* here!"

"It's okay, they're from Sumatra," Charlie said.

A man began moving in a curiously slow manner, coming toward them. Two swift steps and Charlie was between him and the Tanda. They continued on, oblivious to what looked to Beth like serious menace.

Then Jack ran up to the child. "ER beebee," he said.

The woman screamed. "It touched him! It touched my son!"

The man took something out of his pocket that looked like a small knife. Charlie went close to him, facing him down. The knife disappeared.

A security guard ushered the Tanda through the door.

"Awa cah!" Flutter said, dashing toward the Volvo.

But the others stopped. They looked up at the dawn sky, which was lowering and cloudy. They bunched together. Beth began to herd them along. "Come on," she said, "it's time to go."

"This is outside," Charlie explained to them, coming up from behind. "Outside world."

"What da ding-dong issa *dat ting*?"

"It's the clouds," Beth said to Charlie, "they've never seen clouds."

"They're just nothin'. Just smoke. You know smoke?"

They were blank, their eyes reflecting their uneasiness.

The baby mewled, hardly even a cry. "We have to get him on her teat," Beth said.

"Let's go home, everything's fine at home."

"Ome, ome, ome," Jill said. In the back, she cuddled up to Jack. "'E godda bebbie."

"Ayah!" Betty said. Then, "aeeeeeeaaaahhh!" as the baby began to nurse.

Beth said, "It's okay, Betty, that's how he eats! You give him his food out of your breasts."

"Bussds...buss-ts. Rr rr—brrusts," Jack said. He laid his head against Flutter's chest. She had a more prominent bust than Jill.

"Ain't they great, Jack?" Charlie said.

"I fink so, Sharie. Uh-huh."

'Their language,' Beth thought, 'is improving faster than I would have believed.' Given what they'd been through in the past few hours, it had to be said that they possessed a fine capacity to recover from shock. Their openness was childlike, but there was nothing childish about the speed with which they were grasping the meanings of the world that confronted them. And yet the ways of the Tanda mind was not human, not quite. They'd come out of their enclosure thinking that the rest of the world consisted of television shows, and now were integrating that misconception into their new understanding of reality without entirely abandoning it as a human might have. The Tanda mind did its groundwork differently, but it was also very sharp. Once it understood the actual way things worked, it was going to be an innovative new presence in the world, Beth felt certain.

The car mounted a low hill. Before them spread a view of the city.

The clouds were breaking, and the distant towers rose into a cathedral of sunbeams.

From the back seat, there was silence. When Beth glanced back, she saw the faces lined up, all staring, all eyes gleaming with the purest excitement she had ever seen, all smiles wide and innocent and yet at the same time deep with the mystery of this new mind.

Beth reached across and took Charlie's hand. Betty, curled up at his feet, nursed and muttered and cooed.

"Thank you, Charlie," Beth said to her crazy hero or whatever the hell he was. "Thank you for getting them out. Thank you for saving the baby."

"Thank you, lady mine. For finding them."

Then Jill's face was in hers, the deep green eyes full of sparkle. "Ew wuve 'im" she sang. "Ew wuve 'im!"

Beth struggled to keep the road in sight around the Tanda's witchy grin. The last thing they needed was to attract the attention of some traffic cop. "I love him, Jill," she said, "that I certainly do."

"E came got us! Ay!"

"He sure did!"

"Wha! 'S booty! Awl booty!"

Booty. She meant 'beauty.' She found it beautiful, the world. She came up, getting involved with the shifter, scrunching between the two front seats, her blue dress all askew, her early morning lipstick now covering half of her face. "Dat uh—in tee vee?"

"No, TV's just little, and way far away. TV is stories. You know stories?"

"Rack Rundun!"

"Keller read you Jack London?"

"Roarin' Camp," Jack yelled.

Keller was a very strange man. What bizarre logic had gotten him to read Jack London to them? But of course she knew. They had recently been children. His kids. In fact, they were really just adolescents. She could imagine what it must have been like three or four years ago, before the assembly line and the pressure from above, when they were children and Greg Keller was their father, reading them stories, tucking them in, teaching them what little he wanted them to know of the world.

Now the rest of them were edging their way up to the front. Soon the front seat of this car was going to be real packed, if she wasn't firm with them.

"Okay, folks, everybody to the back. Chop chop! You too, Jack!"

They swept into the back seat, instantly obedient. Of course they were, the poor things would remember that cattle prod very clearly.

"TV is a story in pictures. It's not a real place." She gestured. "This is a real place. This is the big, real world."

There was now a Tanda face at each window. They were silent, absorbing what they saw as best they were able.

"Ohhh gowden rarches," Flutter howled. She beat her hands on the glass as the others pressed to see. Even Betty craned her neck and said, "gowden narches, *narches*!"

"Wouldn't you know," Charlie said.

The first thing that the Tanda had recognized of the whole wide and wonderful world around them was a McDonalds'. No doubt they'd identified them from the bags brought into their commissary, or maybe from TV commercials.

"You guys hungry?"

"Mee mee," Betty yelled, accidentally separating her baby from its nipple. It went, "eeuhh!" and returned at once to its task. "Ah so hungee, Ah *sooo* hungeee!"

Charlie patted her cheek. "I bet you are, darlin.'"

"Reawl reawl hungee!"

"We have McDonalds' at home, as much as you can eat."

Betty kissed his fingers, and sat with her head against his knees. How she could possibly be so folded up Beth could hardly imagine. The Tanda were as flexible as monkeys, another jungle adaptation.

When they got home, the first thing she saw was that Dick was back, and she hoped to God that there was going to be a joyous reunion with Joe and Crunch.

But the place was quiet, and he was quiet at the kitchen table. He came to his feet as they entered. Nothing needed to be said.

"We had a baby," Beth announced. No sense in mentioning the lost ones. Their names would only bring renewed grief to Flutter and Betty. Poor Betty, to gain a child, lose a husband and discover a new world all in the same few hours.

"Goddamn," Dick said. He went to Betty and peeked in the blanket she was carrying. "What a beaut!"

Betty flushed almost as red as her smear of lipstick, and absolutely purred with pride.

21

SHATTERFACE HELL

Joe opened his eyes. He hadn't slept very deeply in this eerie dark world of TV, so when the lights went on again and things started making noises, he was ready.

Beside him, Crunch snored. Still asleep, the dummy.

Joe sat up, and beheld before him the strangest and most wonderful vision he had ever seen. "Oh," he said. He held out his hands, trying to feel ahead but of course when you were in the show, there wouldn't be any glass. So could they look out now, and see the world from inside TV?

There was green everywhere, and dancing little blue and Orange things on the floor. They were dotted with drops of water that gleamed in long streams of light coming from way off. It smelled like air conditioning, but stronger and richer than he had ever smelled before.

He was ready for the Big Voice to call them to breakfast, but there seemed to be no Big Voice inside TV. Also, there was no breakfast. But it was so pretty. So very, very pretty.

Crunch moaned and hid his head in some of the green stuff.

Then a brightness appeared low against the world. It was so shiny you couldn't look at it.

Crunch forced himself to squint in the same direction that Joe was squinting. He signed, 'is that fire?'

"Dunno."

Keller said fire was bad, hurt you. Crunch whimpered and returned to keeping his head down.

But Joe shook him again. He signed, 'go.'

'In *fire*?'

"Skakkerface here," Joe whispered.

'Sign!'

"No, yew tak. We tak!"

The softest shatterface voice either of them had ever heard said, "Who the heck are you?"

Standing before them with his hands on his hips was a little bitty shatterface with its face glowing like gold in the light of the big fire that was going slowly up toward the ceiling. Instead of dark shatterface eyes, this one had big brown ones that you could look right at. He'd seen shatterface kids in TV, but they weren't there much, so he'd thought they'd be rare. Now, here was one right in front of them.

It was so sweet looking, the little shatterface, that Joe wanted to hug it. But when he moved toward it, it took a step back. "My daddy's got a gun," it said, it's voice now a screech.

"Wanna gun," Joe said. He smiled, attempting to ingratiate himself. "Give Joe gun."

The little shatterface shook its head hard from side to side.

Then it turned and ran toward a big box. It stopped and put its hands on its hips again. It called toward the building. "Momma, there's two Chewbaccas in the vacant lot behind the house, and one of 'em's durn near naked!"

'Naked' meant Crunch, with his darned pants on his head. Why couldn't he dress properly? Joe wanted to make a good impression in TV, and you didn't do that by acting stupid. Joe signed to him, 'You are naked. You can't be naked in TV.' Then he returned his attention to the little shatterface. He'd never seen any people in TV, just shatterfaces, so he had to assume that this was going to stay true. It meant that they had to get the shatterfaces to like them, and he was getting two different messages from this one. The first was that it had never seen a person before. The second was more ominous: it was scared.

It turned around again, once again facing toward the big box. "Mom-MA, the back yard has naked Chewbaccas in it and it's very embarrassing back here!" Then it turned back to them. "You better go inside if you don't want the cops after you." It marched off toward the box. It called back, "I have Honey Nut Cheerios in limited quantities and some milk. Are you from an empire planet, or are you rebels?"

Joe did not know what to say. Where *were* they from? In fact, where were they now? This wasn't any TV show he'd ever seen.

Joe took Crunch's hand. He was responsible for Crunch, both for getting him to leave the world and to leave the truck. Gently, he removed the pants from Crunch's head. 'Put them on your bottom,' he signed.

Crunch did as he was asked.

The little shatterface had walked across the green to the big box. He opened a door. "Come on," he said.

What was this box, anyway?

"Come on, we have a bunch of Cheerios."

Cheerios were good food, and Joe was hungry. So Joe entered the box, bringing an unwilling and uneasy Crunch along. Inside, it was sort of like the world, but there was stuff everywhere. He saw blurs of color and strange glowing openings that let you look out at the bigness, and a long narrow table that had the kitchen behind it.

On this table was a good ole box of Cheerios, okaaaay! Plus there was a bowl with the biggest, most beautiful fruit in it Joe had ever seen. He was so hungry and so glad to see fruit and cereal, he grabbed an apple and bit into it.

"Mom, Mom! The Chewbaccas are eating the wax fruit!"

Joe had never eaten anything he didn't like, but this apple he did not like. It was hard and it hurt his teeth and it was real dry. He threw it down, spitting the stones it had turned into onto the ground.

Next he poured himself a bowl of cereal and covered it with milk. Crunch took the box and poured it straight down his throat, then drank milk out of the carton to wet it. As they ate, Joe observed the little shatterface. He picked it up and kissed it on its face. It laughed and he liked that, so he kissed it again. It got in his lap and pulled on his hair. "Chewbaccas got a lotta hair," it said. "You ain't got much."

"No," Joe said. "Pepul."

"Who Kewkaka?" Crunch asked.

The little shatterface went into Crunch's lap. "*You*! You're a Chewbacca! Only you're supposed to go, 'eeennnnnnhhh,' not talk."

It was good that the little shatterface had gone in Crunch's lap. It meant that it wasn't so scared anymore. Joe went close to them and gave it a big smile. "Name," he asked.

"Game? What game?"

Joe knew his pronunciation was dumb. He pointed at the shatterface. "Yo' *name*."

"Jerry."

"Gerrarr..."

"Jerry. I'm Jerry!"

"Jerry, I Joe. E's Cunch."

"Lunch? That's hours from now."

Joe was silenced by that reply. Crunch was right here.

Then Joe saw an even smaller shatterface on the floor. It was hard. He picked it up.

The little shatterface went out of Crunch's lap and came back in Joe's. "That's my G.I. Joe," it chirped. "He is very important to me."

"Okeh, Jerry," Joe said.

When Keller said the word 'important' you better listen or you got the snickersnee. But how could somebody who shrunk and then got as hard as a chair leg and didn't say anything be important to anybody? Crunch decided that G.I. Joe was like Gorilla, except even worse off. Gorilla was floppy but at least he could move. Gorilla had been scary. He had gone under their beds.

Gently, Joe put the little doll on the table. He needed to ask Jerry some questions. "Weh is 'is pace," was the first one.

"Pace?"

"Prraace? Weh prrace?"

"Stone Oak."

"Weh Tone oke?"

"*Stone* Oak."

He'd never heard of that show, and it made him realize how lost he and Crunch actually were. Betty could be anywhere, in any program, anywhere in TV

"What channel Tone Oke?"

"What?"

"TV channel."

"TV channel?"

"Wha one we on?"

The little shatterface sighed. "You are one crazy Chewbacca."

"My wife in another program."

"Mah too! Mah!" Crunch pointed at himself and nodded hard.

There were all kinds of doors around here. Joe opened one. He recognized a pantry like the one back in rec only full of all sorts of wonderful new stuff.

Smelling it all, Crunch came over and got a box and tore into it. The stuff inside was brown like cereal, but in thin wafers. Joe started eating them too.

"Hey! You're making huge graham cracker crumbs. Mom, I am NOT making these awful crumbs!" The little shatterface stomped around on the floor.

"Jerry, you better not make a mess!"

Joe stopped eating the wafers. Crunch followed suit. That voice had been another shatterface, a big one. Joe wanted to talk to it. He wanted to find out if it knew Keller or Charlie or Beth or what programs their wives were in.

"Mom, we have to be nice to these Chewbaccas. They're our friends in the federation! I think they're refugees from a rebel planet and everything!"

At that moment, the big shatterface came in. It had round things all over its head. Its body was wrapped in yellow cloth. In its mouth was a cigarette like Roberts used to have.

Crunch liked to smoke, so he got a huge grin on his face. "Siggert," he said. He pursed his lips at her and wiggled all over with anticipation. "'Moke! Me 'moke!"

Joe went toward the shatterface, putting out his hand and saying, "Hi, ahm Joe. Hiya!"

The shatterface's head went down. The cigarette fell to the floor.

Joe looked at the cigarette, then back up at the shatterface. It was shaking. He smiled his biggest smile and said again, "Hiya!"

The little one said, "Mom?" in a voice that made Joe feel shivers along his neck.

Then the big shatterface's head came back up and its mouth opened and it bawled out a terrific scream. The scream went right through Joe, right down to his toes, a tremendous, heart-bursting shriek.

It was even more scared than the little one had been at first. Joe realized that these shatterfaces had never, ever seen people. How could that be, though? Was the world that far away? The shatterfaces in TV didn't seem to know about anything but their own programs, it was true. So maybe no shatterface knew anything except its own program, and people weren't in them.

"*Jereee*," the big shatterface yelled.

The little one started screaming, too, a sound high and sharp in your ears, mixing with the bellows of the big one.

The big one grabbed a knife, then its eyes filled with real dark and very scary shadows. Both shatterfaces were shrieking now, and the big one was swinging the knife so fast it hissed.

Then Crunch made a *yowtch*.

White stuff came out of the big shatterface's mouth, spattering all over the floor and the walls and everywhere. It got to a phone and gabbled wildly. Pee came out of it and spattered on the floor. The little shatterface screamed and screamed and threw things, the Cheerios box, the tiny hard shatterface, a bunch of spoons. The big one kept swooping the knife and yammering at the phone.

Tears came in Crunch's eyes because he hurt. Joe went to the door to the outside and opened it. He gestured to Crunch, and they both ran out.

This was not the door they'd come in. Here was a path with cars on it, and a whole bunch of boxes like the one they'd just come out of. Bright yellow and gold and pink leaves danced amid the green, and something going 'click click click' spewed water around in a gleaming circle.

"Booful," Joe said, but he did not hesitate here long, not with the shatterfaces in the box still howling like that.

'Where are we going?' Crunch signed.

A car came along. The shatterfaces in it looked out at them. It slowed down, and Joe trotted up to it.

"We need Kerrer," he shouted, "get Kerrer!"

The car roared, then it hopped along the path making screeching noises. Then the shatterfaces inside started jerking back and forth and barking. Their eyes got full of shadows and you couldn't look at them anymore.

All of these shatterfaces were crazy and he did not want to be in this program any more. Maybe if they stopped being crazy for a second, they would take them back to the world. He went toward the car, holding out his hands. The car lurched along, then stopped and started growling. Were cars alive? He peered in the window. "Hiya," he said again.

The three shatterfaces inside burst out the doors on the far side. They ran off, except one ended up lying on the ground on its back, and it used its heels to push itself along in the green fuzz. Its hands were fists, and the fists socked the air. All the screaming brought others out the doors of boxes, and they all started screaming, everybody in the whole place.

Far away but getting nearer, Crunch heard a long and terrible wail.

'We gotta get outa this show,' Crunch signed frantically.

Joe didn't bother to answer. He had no idea how. Where was good ole Seinfeld? Where was Stephen Colbert?

Finally he did the only thing he could think of, which was to run. He ran as fast as he could. As he followed along, Crunch was crying and mewling and rubbing at a place where red stuff was coming out of his chest.

They ran farther and farther away, down between two of the boxes and behind them onto a big floor covered with green stick stuff. Surrounded though Joe was by more beauty than he had ever seen or imagined possible, his nose filled with wonderful smells and his eyes with richly colorful sights, he was also consumed by terror and confusion.

Because they had to, they stopped and rested for a while, breathing hard. The fire in the ceiling made a lot of heat. They had not felt much heat before, and it made them gasp and sweat. "I tirty," Crunch said.

"Tirsty," Joe corrected him. He had to figure this out. How to get the shatterfaces to stop acting crazy? But why were they? That was what was so hard to understand.

Overhead, something began going *pop pop pop*. Joe looked up to see a huge bug crawling along the immense blue ceiling. The bug talked. It said, "STAY WHERE YOU ARE!" Then it crawled closer, until it was directly overhead. "STAY WHERE YOU ARE." It started getting bigger.

The noise got really loud. It began making wind, hot, mean wind that was full of stinging dust.

They did not stay where they were. They ran as fast as they possibly could. "STOP," the voice shouted. It was a mean, hard voice. There was something awful about that bug. For one thing, it was awful big for a bug. But that's definitely what it was. It flew, it had big shiney eyes and feet. It was a giant bug.

Once in a while in TV, Joe had seen things that flew, but never something like this.

When they were some distance away, they looked back at the giant bug. It was way up again, going toward the blue ceiling.

Then there was a whistle and a tree beside them went *rrrinnggg*. Joe could see shatterfaces back in a group near the buildings. There was another sound, *ssst*! Hot air splashed his face.

They were being shot at, just like on Oz. That meant if it hit you,

you fell down forever. Joe did not want to fall down forever, he wanted to be home with Betty and he wanted some Pepsi and some more Cheerios and to play Clue and have a nice time and everything.

Zzzzzeeeoooowww!

That burned his neck! He ran. The bug swooped down again. It said, "DO NOT MOVE! RAISE YOUR HANDS IN THE AIR!"

There were trees nearby and it was dark in there, so that was where Joe went. He ran past the shatterface boxes, down through the short green fuzz and into the tall fuzz beyond. His feet splashed in water, then he went up the other side.

Overhead, the *pop pop pop* continued. That giant bug never stopped its awful talk. Joe went in among the poles and Crunch came, too. They were lost in TV and getting shot at and screamed at and chased. He'd never thought it would be like this.

This was like Oz, but the green everywhere and the big blue ceiling, and the talking bug up there—it was not Oz, no way.

Flap in the grass, then an echoing *cra-ack* far away.

"C'mon," Joe yelled. He dove into the tall poles where it was darker. The *pop pop* of the bug got softer.

He went along, moving quickly, staying as much in the green stuff as he could. Behind him, he could hear Crunch panting and making little, scared sounds. Poor Crunch was leaking where he'd been cut by that screaming shatterface.

Joe was tired, but he did not plan to stop. Instead, he changed his gait, finding a long, loping stride that felt right, somehow. Crunch lagged behind.

"C'mon!"

"Gukkgann..."

Crunch's dumb talk made no sense. Too bad. Joe just kept going. Probably, Crunch was signing. Signing wasn't for TV. Couldn't see it in the dark, couldn't see it if you were running like now. Signing was for the place they had called the world, which he had realized was actually just a few little rooms somewhere.

Now the *pop popping* of the bug came and went, getting steadily more faint. Good. Joe guessed that the bug couldn't see them through the green, and so wasn't able to follow them. He began to twist and turn and swerve, in order to stay under the thickest green all the time.

Soon, though, there was a change. Now the tall poles were gone and there was nothing but more green fuzz on the floor. Pretty far way away, there was a low wall. Behind it was another of the shatter-face places with boxes set in rows. Inside them, there would be more shatterfaces, of course. All crazy? He hoped not.

Then he heard a new sound, *wow wow wow*, and saw a low slung animal with a face as long as your foot. It was near a shatterface box on this side of the wall.

This animal was obviously crazy just like the shatterfaces. It couldn't go anywhere, though. It was clawing and running but staying in exactly the same place, glaring at them and doing its *wow wow wowing* like all getout. Joe saw that it had a ring around its neck that was strung to a little hut of its own. With no hands to take that off, what was it gonna do?

But no, it was coming anyway, dragging its hut along behind it. Boy, was that thing going crazy! Even worse than the shatterfaces. Joe did not think it would be good to let it get close. Fortunately, the hut it had to drag was slowing it down.

What was it about people that made all these shatterfaces and other things go crazy? The thought that they were out here in deep TV surrounded by crazy everything made his throat get all shriveled inside. He thought maybe there was no escape for them. Maybe they were lost in this program forever.

What about Betty and the others. Were they in trouble, too? Were any of them still moving around? In his mind's eye, he saw a picture of Betty's face with her lips smiling and the look in her eyes making him so happy.

Crunch started doing something really stupid. He started putting the shorts back on his head. As he did it, he glared at Joe. He was being defiant, showing him who was boss.

Joe swung his arm as fast and as hard as he ever had in his life, giving Crunch the biggest punch he'd ever given anybody. It connected with his cheek and made him stagger along. His face went almost purple. His eyes grew big.

Joe pointed at the pants and Crunch put them on right.

The animal was closer now, dragging its hut, and Joe could hear the bug crawling across the ceiling and off in the distance the moan of some other kind of monster, also getting louder.

They could not go back, so they had to go forward, which meant crossing the green fuzz and going in among the shatterface boxes.

WOW WOW WOW! The animal was right here, it's eyes wild, its teeth bared. It was going to eat them up for sure.

The two of them ran off. Now, though, the bug came down an invisible thread, and all the tall green fuzz bent away from it as it landed on the floor. Other bugs with shiny black faces came out of it. They started shooting guns, and Joe and Crunch headed for the wall, to try to jump it and hide among the shatterface boxes.

When they scrambled up over its rough skin, they found a place that they hadn't been able to see before. No shatterface boxes, no green. Instead, there were lots of cars here. Crunch followed along behind. There had to be more cars than in all of the rest of TV put together and they darted among them as far behind them, the littler bugs that the big bug had let out of its stomach came running.

Crunch started to slow down.

'The bugs have guns, they will kill us,' Joe signed back at him. It was too complicated to say.

When he saw that sign, Crunch started running harder again.

Joe had to concentrate, because this program was real confusing and real dangerous. No wonder Keller had never shown it.

In this program, all the shatterfaces hated the people. It also had an awful lot of cars that just sat there not going anywhere. Or no, there was one moving. It had a shatterface in it.

"Gasses!" Crunch said. He grinned. Crunch was crazy about glasses, and that shatterface was wearing some. Joe had long since lost his, and he wanted some, too.

But most of all, he wanted to find Betty. He was missing her so bad. He'd never missed anybody before and it hurt terribly. In fact, since they'd been out in TV, it seemed like everything hurt or scared you or made you sad. Joe had wanted so much to go in it. He remembered begging Bef, and how mad he'd been when she said no.

Even looking at the ceiling hurt, now that the fire had crawled halfway up it. That fire was the hardest thing to look at there ever was. Plus, it made you hotter than you ever got on the line, it made you *real* hot, and being out here on this floor with all the cars was a whole lot hotter than in the green fuzz.

A car with a woman shatterface in it went away to a place where there were even more cars going here and there. Then another car moved along nearby. In it was a male shatterface.

'We go in a car,' he signed to Crunch.

Crunch nodded, then signed, 'where?'

'Somewhere not here.'

Crunch went up to a sleeping car and said, "Hiya!"

A couple of little shatterfaces came up. They were on small boards with wheels. Joe hid. He did not want more shatterface craziness. Crunch did not hide.

When he went out from between the cars, the two small shatterfaces whispered together. Their faces went as gray as a wall. Spit-up came out of one of their mouths. Then they ran away, leaving the wheelie things to clatter on the floor.

Joe ignored them, concentrating instead on the car. You could not go in. It just sat there in the heat, not willing to open. He hated things that wouldn't open, and he kicked it.

Then he saw a big shatterface coming. This shatterface was moving fast. It had keys, which Joe understood all too well. Cars were shatterfaces-only, just like the barrier.

The shatterface got to a car, which went *boo-leep* when he did a little bounce with his hand. Didn't even touch it. He opened the back and put bags of stuff inside. But he dropped a big yellow thing which rolled off. He said "shit," and went after it.

Immediately, Joe ran over and got in. Crunch, worried and slapping him nervously on the shoulder, followed. It smelled *wonderful* in here! But it was hot, it was real hot. The smell though—they were both so hungry that their mouths started watering. Joe had never smelled anything so sweet, so delicious. He reached into a bag and brought out a big golden thing with spikes on the top. He and Crunch just forgot everything else in the world and tore into it.

It was gold inside and juicy and sweet and it made Joe howl with pleasure, throw back his head and just sing it out. And the next second there was a tremendous crash and Crunch was dragged out of the car and was on the ground under the shatterface that had opened it. It held Crunch down and started hitting him.

"No," Joe said. When he got the snickersnee he always smiled and tried to make up, so he went down and tried to look in the red, bulging shatterface and smile. But the shatterface went all wild. It hammered Crunch real hard. He screamed and cried and jerked his head from side to side to avoid the blows. Joe decided that this was Oz after all, and the shatterface was making Crunch go still forever.

The whole scene slowed down and turned into flashes. Flash, the shatterface's white teeth. Flash, Crunch's desperate eyes. Flash, blood of Crunch on the floor.

Never, ever had Joe laid a violent hand on a shatterface. They had the right to punish people, not the other way around. But he had to. He had to punish the shatterface. Otherwise, Crunch would not get up anymore.

He went behind him and straddled his back. The shatterface's muscles were rippling with strength. In its hand was the yellow fruit that had rolled away. It was hitting Crunch with it, and the fruit was breaking up and flying all over the place.

Joe laced his fingers together and made a double big fist. He brought it down powerfully and neatly, on the back of the shatterface's head.

The shatterface turned into a big bag and flumped down onto Crunch. It took Joe pulling and Crunch pushing to get it off. Then Crunch came rushing up and grabbed Joe and hugged him. The shatterface breathed grumbling, broken breaths.

"Getta cah," Joe said. He and Crunch went in the car. But how to make it go? It had a round wheel. That would turn it, Joe understood that instantly. There were gauges like on some of the lines. All of them pointed at zero. Down under, there were pedals. If he sat in the seat, he could touch one pedal but not the other one with his toes.

"Go," he told it. "Go!"

There were levers. He pushed and pulled. Nothing happened. Buttons. They didn't do anything, either.

Behind the car, the shatterface went, "goaashit...aoggaah..." He spit, you could hear it, like Jack would when he was mad.

Crunch was shaking so badly that he could barely control himself. He huddled up against the back seat and closed his eyes. Then the shatterface rose up behind the car. Its eyes were horrible and black, it's mouth was showing teeth. But then it stopped, frozen to the spot. It stared into the car. Joe stared back. He bared his teeth, too.

"SWEET JESUS!" it yelled. Then it rushed away.

Joe went into the back seat. He held Crunch tight, trying to get him to quit shaking. "Keerd," Crunch said.

"Me kaird, too. Me kaird."

He knew that they had to get out of here. Just like in Oz, you gotta get out of the lockup, get into the big prison, or you're gonna get cut by Vern or gunned by somebody. As they left the car, Crunch grabbed for another big fruit. "Groun gas," Joe said, pulling it out of his hand and throwing it down. Growling, Crunch went for it again. "Groun gas!" Joe said.

Crunch finally understood. People got ground glass in their food in Oz. It hurt you bad and made you go on the floor going "uaan-nugg," and red spit coming out.

They found the roller things the little shatterfaces had left behind and picked them them up. When you went on them you didn't have to run, but just push along with your foot.

They were both crying but they couldn't stop and they knew it. They got on the things and soon were gliding along on them, pushing with their feet and crying as they swept along.

They glided away, but where? No way to tell. Away from here, that was all.

22

MURDER

Charles Mulk was brought into the Prue Substation by Patrolman Williams, who'd been sent to pick him up from the zoo. Assistant Chief Herman Ballard greeted him.

"We've got this video from the chopper," he said. "We don't know where they are right now, but do know that one of them is showing blood."

"I thought you were firing rubber bullets," the zoo official said tersely.

"We aren't firing anything. There have been numerous civilian attacks. We've disarmed about ten civilian shooters so far."

"We'll use rubber bullets as a last resort," Chief Ballard affirmed. "But we need to know how to control these animals."

At a nod from Ballard, a patrolman ran the video. The two creatures were hustling across an open field toward some live oak and cedar brush. Mulk was instantly riveted by their appearance. They did not move like apes, they had a human gait. He couldn't see their faces, but the hair was not consistent with any primate. It was strangely cut, true, but that was human hair, he felt sure, flowing down their backs like that.

That decided him. "Okay," he said, "I've seen enough. What you have here are two human beings wearing clumsy costumes. These are not apes." He chuckled. "Unless, of course, bigfoot is five feet tall."

There was a ripple of laughter.

"The woman whose house they invaded claimed that they attempted to talk."

"They would, since they're people. Look, my guess is that it's pledge week at some fraternity. Call the colleges. You'll soon have this thing narrowed down."

"The guy in the parking lot said they were aliens. One had red eyes."

"You'll have worse reports than that, believe me. But my expectation is that you're looking at pranksters."

"No you are not!"

They all turned. Chief Ballard said, "This is Rosa Korlite, Doctor Mulk. She had a face-to-face encounter in her home."

"One had red eyes, the other emerald green."

"Contact lenses," Mulk said. "They've worked on their disguises."

"Call costume shops," Ballard said to one of the cops. "I want a list of everybody they've rented ape suits to. And try the costume departments at the colleges. Has anybody made any costumes that fit the description?"

"These weren't suits! These were creatures! They weren't in masks, they were—one of them was even naked down below. It had...male parts."

"Frontal anatomy?"

"You could see it, if that's what you mean."

"No ape has an anatomy like ours," Mulk said, his voice calm with authority. "You were looking at two made-up humans."

"No. No way. No way at all."

A telephone rang. One of the patrolmen answered it. He talked for a couple of minutes, then hung up. "Report on the assault victim. Severe contusions about the chest. Concussion. Dislocated jaw. Broken teeth. Badly cut eye."

"That clears up one thing," Ballard said.

"Which is?" Williams asked.

"Whatever this is, it sure as hell ain't no prank. I'm declaring an all-points city emergency right now. Let 'em know downtown. I want these boys closed down before they do murder, and I want this kept as quiet as we can. Plead with the press. We need some time here, otherwise half of the city's gonna be out there packin' heat.'

Joe watched a gleaming silver tube slowly cross the blue ceiling. There were no bugs crawling up there now, at least. Very faintly, a voice was coming down, grumbling low. This creature growled like the bug, except its growl was one real long *grrroooarrrrr...*

"'S not a seelin," Joe said. "'S somepin' else..." He gazed up.

Both of them were hungry and thirsty and their feet hurt from the hot streets and the stones and all the unaccustomed running. They'd been rolling the scooters for what seemed like a long time.

"Na in Oz," Crunch said.

"'Knowit, ding-dong," Joe snapped.

"Wanna kiwl us," Crunch said. He was breathing hard from pushing along on the little roller.

"Knowit." What Joe did not know was why. They were lost in a program where shatterfaces killed people.

Crunch stopped. He pointed. "Monald," he said. "Monald!"

Joe saw golden arches familiar from food bags and TV. *They* were nice, they fed you! There were good shatterfaces in McDonalds, had to be, or they wouldn't have always been giving the people food. But it was far away, out where there were all kinds of cars and shatterfaces around.

Joe's mouth quivered. Crunch moaned. Knowing how dangerous it was, they nevertheless struggled closer.

It was a sort of hutch made of glass. The shatterfaces inside were eating and that looked good.

Off in the sky, but getting louder, came the *pop pop pop* of a prowling bug.

A few miles away and shortly before noon, Dr. Robert Barrett and his attorney had marched into the San Antonio campus. They were met by Dr. Ma, two officials from World Biological, a uniformed general, a tall man in a blue polo shirt who looked as if he belonged on a golf course, and World's three lead attorneys. There were brief handshakes, no introductions. Nobody smiled.

"Dr. Ma," Barrett began, "let me apologize on behalf of my company for the discomfort you have personally suffered." Ma's head was extensively bandaged. His right eye was swollen shut.

He bowed, but not very deep, Bob Barrett noticed, not very deep at all. Of course not. Why would he, look at him and at the failure he had overseen. No matter if World recovered the Tanda or not, the catastrophe had dramatically set back Dr. Ma's career.

It had been worse for Greg, of course. That tragic genius left behind a disgraced career ended by suicide. When the story of the Tanda story eventually surfaced in the media—as it would, and sooner rather than later, Bob had no doubt—Greg was going to come off as cruel, greedy and heartless. The brilliant and compassionate sides of the man would be lost. Gone would be his extraordinary accomplishments, of not only discovering the planet's only other truly intelligent species, but also saving it from extinction.

They moved into the second floor conference room. "Rebecca," Bob said to Greg's sorrowing, bleary-eyed secretary, "let's get this opened up."

She flung open the drapes, letting thin sunlight in through the heavily tinted windows. The two groups took their places on opposite sides of the table.

"Gentlemen," Bob began, "let me first state that we do not expect to take an adversarial position, here. This is not adversarial."

"No," Ma said, "not for you, given that you have our thirty million dollars."

Bob replied, "We need to solve our mutual problem."

"Dr. Barrett, it's our problem, not yours, but it is you who must solve it. You. Not us." Dr. Ma's voice was crisp. "We know where the

Tanda are. It's no secret. They are not ten miles from here. Get them back, Dr. Barrett."

Michael Helmond spoke in Bob's defense. "We're planning to take action immediately." He opened a file. "A civil complaint has been filed alleging wrongful conversion of the property. We're asking for an order that will allow us to recover it. The order will be good for ten days. We'll be able to execute it immediately."

As Mike spoke, he turned his bright, uneasy eyes on Bob. He would remove his pen from his pocket, only to glance down at it and tuck it away again. When Mike stopped, the only sound in the room was the whisper of his movement.

At last Ma said, "You know that the primate center will oppose."

"We're in Judge Barton's court, Doctor. He'll let us get the animals first, then talk."

"They'll ask that we be restrained from moving them out of the state," Sam Hister, World's attorney, replied. "They will be granted that much relief until the matter is adjudicated." x

The general, who had not been introduced, now spoke. "We do not want to become entangled in American legal system."

Attempting to create the appearance of a smile, the man in the Polo shirt revealed his teeth. "What is needed here is decisive action." His voice was not loud, but it filled the room.

"Thank you, Mr. Atitarn," Ma said.

Mr. Atitarn was the real boss, Bob knew. He had been introduced in the most perfunctory manner. But he was the actual center of this meeting. "In this country, the use of force can be difficult," Bob said, addressing him directly.

"It is difficult anywhere," Atitarn replied smoothly. "But your orders and injunctions will only lead to delay, which will increase the danger of press coverage. If that happens, we're going to be painted as monsters. Slavers, even."

"And yet we have created a beautiful facility for them," Ma said. "It has trees and grass. An excellent facility. Much better, if you will excuse me, than here." He gestured vaguely toward the back of the building. “That kind of confinement—it’s no good. Cruel. Even in cages, the Tanda will be better off with us.”

“Can you perhaps send in troops,” the general asked, “given that there is a diplomatic matter involved? The theft of state property? World can be considered a state enterprise.”

“There is no provision for that sort of action,” Mike Helmond replied.

Bob knew perfectly well that World was a private company, and so would any judge asked to rule on the matter. Even if for some bizarre reason it was judged a diplomatic dispute, the military would never be involved.

“You must hire a team to recover our property,” Atitarn said. “Do it, and without delay.”

“Use force,” Bob asked. “Is that what you’re asking?”

Atitarn bowed his head slightly.

Bob knew who would be held responsible if this didn’t work—he would, him and his company. World Biological would remain safely in the shadows. But what choice did he have? They were right, the legal route was going to be full of problems. “If we attempt to penetrate the primate center and fail, two things happen. Our people go to jail and the Tanda are moved to a more secure location.”

The general said, “No matter what we do or don’t do, that could happen at any moment. We must act, and quickly. This is our hope.”

“It’ll be breaking and entering,” Mike said. “A felony.”

The general smiled. “We are taking what belongs to us.”

“Taking the animals isn’t a crime. Entering the Cookes’ property to do so is. Property rights are very important in this country.”

Atitarn leaned toward Bob. “Dr. Barrett, you are going to do this. You lost the Tanda. You must recover them.”

“Not by force. I don’t have the resources.”

“You will do it.”

“Not by force. It’s absurd!”

“What is absurd is that you let Greg Keller manage the transfer of animals he loved to people he despised, with the result that there was a failure he probably orchestrated.”

"There's no evidence of that."

"He ordered the security guards to remain on their stations when it was known that an intruder had entered the building."

"You don't know that."

Ma reached into his pocket and drew out his phone. He touched an app, and in a moment, Greg's voice began to speak. 'I know there's an entry. That's why I want you guys outside. When he tries to leave with the Tanda, you'll be there.'"

The moment Bob heard Greg's words, he knew that this would be a lawsuit that Barrett Scientific would not be able to win.

"You see, he let them go, Dr. Barrett."

"No, he tried to place the guards where they would intercept them."

"You were probably hoping that the Tanda would be stolen, too. You're as much in love with them as he was."

"Absolute balderdash, Doctor Ma."

"We'll review the matter in detail later. More immediately, you must make it right. If you don't know how to assemble the proper forces, we will advise you."

"I can't think what sort of advice would help. You're asking me to violate the law and I won't."

"We can compel you, Doctor."

"Are you threatening my client?" Mike asked.

"Yes, Mr. Helmond, I am doing exactly that. I am demanding that he get our property back to us by any effective means."

"We'll file for our order first thing in the morning. The sheriff will be there with a truck by noon."

"We cannot prevent you from seeking remedy in the comic-opera American judicial system, but you must also agree to first go in and get the animals by force."

"If they *are* animals, of course,' Barrett said. "If they're human beings, then we have violated antislavery laws and everybody in this room is in terrible trouble." He gestured across the table. "Including you."

"So, we are agreed," Atitarn said. "You will take your American legal action, but you will also put more effective methods in action at once."

Bob looked at Mike, who would not meet his eyes. Mike knew that there would be a suit. Mike knew that it would devastate Barrett Scientific.

In that moment, he knew what he had to do to save the situation. It was something he had never dreamed he would actually do. The idea was loathsome. It was dangerous. But it would save his company, and him. He cleared his throat. Was he a good liar? He didn't really know. But their reaction to his next few words would tell him.

"Yes," he said, "we are agreed."

Mike's eyebrows went up, but he remained silent.

"Very well," Ma said. "Which leads to the next issue." He drew an iPad out of his briefcase. The photos on it had been taken at long range. They clearly showed the Tanda outdoors at the primate center, moving from a car toward the Cookes' house. "There are only four," he said. "As you see."

"The other two must be inside."

"They are not inside. Two of the Tanda are at large."

Bob was too stunned to speak.

"Perhaps you have not understood," the general snapped. "Two of the animals are gone."

Recovering himself as best he could, Bob said, "Let's mount a search."

Atitarn responded, "A search is already mounted. We have been listening to the police scanner. We picked up a report of a woman terrorized by a fraternity prank—boys in costume invaded her home."

"This was the Tanda? You know that?"

"There has been quite a police operation mounted to catch these pranksters, since they have now also mauled a man in a parking lot. The descriptions of them are exact. Without knowing it, the police are chasing two escaped Tanda."

"Do you have any idea of where they are now?"

"I am advising the search using my knowledge of them," Dr. Ma said. "It is inadequate, of course, but perhaps it is more than the police have."

Atitarn leaned back and stared at the ceiling. "I must return to this matter of the legal approach. I cannot say no, but I can say that it is unwise."

"We shouldn't even try the legal route. Is that what you're saying?"

Atitarn nodded. "You risk press."

"I can control that."

"This is the United States. You can't control anything."

"Then you don't want us to try the legal route at all?"

"You may engage in these useless activities, but be absolutely certain that the media doesn't become involved."

"The media must already be involved if the two escapees are causing such an uproar."

"This is why you must take the necessary steps to recover them, and quickly. We need speed, here. We need them all in our plane and out of the country as soon as possible."

"I understand."

"You understand nothing! You're a fool!"

"Now, wait a minute."

"You will obtain the ones the Cookes have in their possession by whatever means necessary. We will find the two that are at large."

"Our four will be delivered to you without delay," Bob said, standing up and smiling his most confident smile. He felt like he was going to lose his breakfast.

"Charlie Cooke has significant personal resources," Ma said. "Don't forget that, not for a moment."

"Sometimes the river is safest where the rocks are sharpest, because it is there that the water rises most infrequently," Atitarn said.

"Excellent advice," Mike said as Atitarn, Ma and the general filed out.

"What did he mean"" Bob asked when they were gone.

"Hell if I know. Let's get down to business. We've got a lot of work to do."

23

MAYHEM

Betty's baby—pitifully thin and bearing a strong, if ironic, resemblance to a spindly little spider—struggled. Hour after hour, the tiny voice was raised in pain. The tormented burr became a background to life in a house full of Tanda. When the baby's breathing started to labor, he brought a specialist in premature infants with him, Doctor Robert Hewett.

At first Hewett was appalled by the Tanda, but his scientific curiosity soon overcame his reticence. His program of care brought little Charlie some comfort and sleep. His mother had named him after their savior, which was how the Tanda regarded Charlie Cooke.

"The big danger here is exhaustion," Hewett explained. "A baby this small can expire in minutes just from trying too hard to stay alive."

Baby Charlie's tiny face, peering up out of the sheet in which his mother cradled him, had become a part of every heart in the primate center. At first, seeing him was a shock. All Tanda, it seemed, are born with bright red eyes in the same way that many humans are born with blue. But the little guy started smiling early, and his huge Tanda grin would win over the most fearful observer. A finger, lowered into his world, would be greeted by two eager little hands. Charlie was fighting for his life, clinging to it, as if on some deep level he knew—or his soul did—that he represented the hope of his kind.

Even the apes began to soften toward the Tanda, who had initially terrified them so badly that Charlie and Beth were concerned that some of the older ones might suffer heart attacks.

Betty was in an uneasy heaven, parading around with Charlie in his green hospital sheet, showing him again and again, first to the capuchins, then to the chimps, then to Moreland who would rush back and forth in apparent deep cogitation whenever the baby was visible to him. He moved, at these moments, like an enormous Groucho Marx, taking long, low strides, his head down and one hand on his chin.

Dr. Hewett believed that activity and stimulation would be good for the baby. "But you have to understand," he told Beth and Charlie privately, "I'm operating on guesswork, here. Observation and educated guesses. Or, I hope they're educated. The simple fact is that this baby could die without warning, and we might never know why."

Beth and Charlie lived with that, but they told Betty only that he was getting stronger every day, which was also true. She lavished love on her baby. In fact, the tenderness and the devotion—the beauty of it, the awesome power—awakened the mother in Beth, and she began to dream of a pregnancy of her own.

Evenings, Betty and Flutter began a ritual that, for some time, Beth and Charlie did not quite understand. They would go out into the disused side pasture and make long calls, their voices echoing softly in the rising shadows. These were not the calls of animals. Rather, they had an almost operatic complexity to them, rising to a trembling pitch that hung on the air, then descending into sighs and silence.

Nothing was said about what they were doing, but it soon became clear to Beth that they were calling their lost men, and grieving for them.

So much was packed into each day that it seemed hard to believe by the Wednesday after their coming, that the Tanda had not been here forever.

On that afternoon, Chris appeared at about three. As his car came up the drive, curious, excited Tanda ran out into the road yelling "Cah! Cah!" and waving their hands. Betty heard and came running, too, cradling baby Charlie.

Beth emerged from the kitchen drying her hands on her apron, looking to her husband very damn wonderful, her fair skin flushed and curls stuck to her forehead.

She had been cooking the Tanda spaghetti. Charlie thought she was right to figure that it was time to start introducing them to a more complex diet than the unvarying five meals Greg Keller had allowed them. Charlie also had plans for them. School, for one thing. Reading, writing, the whole magilla. He'd probably be a lousy teacher, but Her Nibs would help him and get it done, for sure. The Tanda would get an education.

Chris came up to the porch, surrounded by wall-eyed Tanda. He was still wearing his greens and stethoscope. "Afternoon," he said. He went down to Jill. "Tell me your name."

"Kill."

"Do this." He bared his teeth. Now put your tongue against the roof of your mouth and make a noise."

"Ssshill. Shill!"

"Better!"

"Ah Shill! *Ah Shill*!"

"Better. Where are you from?"

"Umakra."

"Sort of understandable."

"They're getting better fast," Beth said.

"Where did you get them?"

The question was slipped in, she knew, very carefully. She thought, 'He's talked to Daddy. I need to be very careful, here.'

"They're people," she said.

"Pepul," Jack agreed.

"Ma bee bee," Betty said, holding her child up for Chris to see. Chris took the baby, which made Betty grin.

"Ew dewiber 'im," Flutter said.

"Good God, you're right. I delivered him."

"In ER! On tee-vee!"

"Guys, how did you get them? May I know?"

Charlie coughed. "Turned up on the doorstep."

"They belong to somebody, don't they?"

"Daddy sent you, didn't he?"

"Your parents asked me to find out what's going on."

Charlie said, "They won't ask us themselves, Chris, let alone come out here to this wonderful, special place that by some kind of a miracle their daughter has created. That's what's going on. It's what's been going on ever since we started the Center. They have to accept her, because she is going to be doing this."

"Are they stolen?"

"Chris, that woman understands that you delivered Betty's baby. She just told you that. Do you really believe for one moment that she could be stolen property? Or have we rolled back the law here in Texas?"

"Kidnapped, then?"

"They were released from unlawful imprisonment. They came of their own free will." Charlie's tone was quietly electric.

"What're you gonna tell Daddy, Chris?"

Chris was involved with Betty and the baby. "That he doesn't need a go-between."

Beth could have kissed him.

"Take monkey chow?" Jill asked. She and Jack enjoyed feeding the capuchins.

"At three," Beth said. "That's in about thirty minutes. You go in the kitchen, look at the clock. Tell me what it says."

The two Tanda went in together, joining forces for this new project.

"They've been learning more about time. It's actually two, not two thirty, so I'm half an hour off. Let's see how they handle it."

They came out. Flutter said, "Firty more minutes dan firty!" She made some gestures, attempting to communicate the situation.

"Where was the small hand?"

"Two."

"The big hand?"

She made another motion, indicating that it was a little past the twelve.

"Say it."

"Affa d'tweve."

"So you're right, Flutter. Thirty more than thirty minutes."

"This is just beyond belief," Chris said.

"Cah! Cah!" Again, the Tanda raced for the driveway. At first, Beth thought it was Dickie, but she didn't recognize the small van.

Betty was at the head of the little band, holding out her baby, grinning from ear to ear. "Joe," she cried, "ooo *Joe*!"

The van stopped. It was white, very clean, a Chrysler. The windows were tinted. Inside, only shapes were visible. A man got out on the driver's side. He raised the rear deck, and came around to the Tanda. He was wearing a uniform.

Charlie started running first. Then Beth was following him.

As they went closer, another uniformed man got out. He was wearing a gun and a straw Stetson. He positioned himself between the running Cookes and the vehicle. The Tanda were getting right on in, full of eager excitement, happily obeying the officer's gestures.

"This is illegal," Beth screamed. "Illegal," she shrieked.

"Hey, Lady, back off!"

From inside, she could hear the Tanda responding to her fear by yelling and pounding on the windows. There was the clang of an interior cage being shut, then the *chuff* of the van's rear access door being closed.

Beth tried to push past the sheriff's deputy.

"Look, I'm gonna have to cuff you."

Charlie said, "Guys, we gotta talk, here."

The other officer appeared. He had Betty's baby. "I only got a recovery order for four of 'em. You get to keep this one." He held him out. The baby was crying, his tiny voice like that of a large bee. From inside the van, Betty was screaming and hammering on the sides of a cage that was fitted in the back.

The two sheriffs got in the van. At that moment, Chris came up. "What's going on here?"

"They got some kind of an order be my guess. They're kidnapping these people."

Charlie asked Chris for his phone.

Chris gave it to him. Charlie pumped in numbers. "Larry. Charlie. Yeah, the rubber and the road, they just met. They got a court order." Beth saw papers in his hand. "Yeah, he gave it to me. Deputy Phil Ford. Got Deputy Roger Carter in tow." He listened. "Okay. Okay! Hold on, don't hang up." He ran over to the driver's window. "Guys, where are you taking them?"

The window did not budge. Instead, the van started up, began turning around. It was all happening with dizzying speed.

"Come on! Hey!" Charlie ran alongside the van. "Give me this, hey!"

The van accelerated, leaving him in a cloud of dust. He listened to the cellphone for a second more. Then he started racing back toward the house. "Chris," he shouted, "gotta follow!"

As he leaped into Chris's Beamer, Charlie said "I'll drive."

"Oh, God, Charlie, it's only two weeks old."

"Gonna live easily two more in the next ten minutes, Brother!"

Charlie handed the cellphone to Beth. "It's my lawyer," he said. "He's going over to the courthouse with a temporary restraining order, get 'em back for ten days while we fight out the slavery issue. But we gotta know where they are if it's gonna be served."

When the Beamer reached the end of the drive, the van was nowhere in sight. Without hesitation, Charlie took a right toward town. "Freshest dust," he said. He floored it.

Beth was trying to comfort the baby, which was wriggling and crying.

"Keep him warm," Chris said. "We're gonna have to get him to his mother soon. No formula for an unknown infant, and a preemie. He's gotta have her or he doesn't make it."

"How long?"

"No idea."

Beth held the struggling little creature over her shoulder, listening to his tiny, agonized wail.

"You know anybody in the media," Charlie asked Chris. "Real well? Golfing buddy type well?"

"Bill Knowlton at KOMI TV. News director."

"Call him. Tell him it's the story—" The van became visible, cresting a hill about a mile ahead. "—story of the millennium!" The Beamer leaped ahead as he smashed the accelerator to the floor.

"Hundred and thirty," Chris said.

"Hundred and forty," Charlie replied.

Beth held the baby. The van grew slowly larger in view ahead.

"Oh, Christ," Charlie said. He hit the brakes.

"What is it?" Beth asked.

"Prowl car pulled in behind us. Too far back to get a radar fix, but he's comin' fast."

"Jesus how did you see that?"

"Lookin' for it."

They drove on, carefully maintaining legal speed.

"Charlie, I can't see them!"

"Hold on."

"We can't lose them!"

"Ah, there they go, up on 35."

He swung onto the interstate a few car lengths behind them. They accelerated.

"Speed up!"

"I still got that cop."

"Are they losing us?"

"Looks like it."

Beth slammed her foot against the firewall.

"Take it easy, Hon."

"I can't take it easy." She stared ahead. The van was nowhere to be seen.

Joe had forced Crunch to stay away from the McDonalds, hungry and thirsty as they were. Instead, they went into an area of big grass and stayed in there while Joe thought. He'd thought long and hard, and come to certain conclusions.

One: nothing was like he had believed.

Two: shatterfaces were scared of people and wanted to kill them.

Three: he had no idea how to get back to their old world or how to find their wives.

Those were the facts. He looked up, trying to find the top of the ceiling or whatever it was, to somehow establish a border in that biggest of all places, as if doing that might begin to give this impossible world some sort of definition. But the blue overhead remained open and endless. It was just itself, there.

As they waited, the light began to slowly go dim. It became golden again, like it was when they first woke up. Then it slowly went away. Joe thought that it must be all air up there. It was just air that went on forever, blue air that turned slowly black and filled with tiny glowing eyes.

The trees began to whisper, and the grass to murmur in a language that Joe felt he could answer in his heart, that had meaning deeper than any words.

He had decided to call the blue 'upoo' and the bright light that crept across it 'sparkaa.'

Once darkness came sleep called them, drawing their eyes closed and making them cuddle up against each other. So they rode, the two Tanda, deep into a second dark and friendless night.

Crunch jumped to his feet. "Hoooo-ooooo! Ohhoooooo!"

He was standing in front of the hugest, most incredible thing that had ever been. For a moment, Joe thought he was going to walk over and get on it, but then he realized that it was actually far away.

"Bootiful," he said, looking at the bright roundness of it. It came up past the tops of the trees as they watched, riding clear in the lower reaches of upoo.

The two of them stood together, instinctively joining hands, awed far beyond their few words at their first vision of the moon. They had no idea what it was or why it was there, only that it was incredible and wonderful and that it stirred within them a deep rhythm that made them want to move but not in any way they could fathom, and a longing that made them also want to sing. So they danced beneath the moon, two small men in its concealing light, dancing slowly round and round, raising their heads and making their long hair sway in the moonlight. The Song of the Tanda was released from where it hid deep in their souls. The long notes that issued from their throats had in past ages crossed jungle miles, eerie and wild, at once as intimate as the voices of owls and as far-ranging as the song of the wolf.

Now, though, in this place, the sounds did not reach the souls of other Tanda, but rather made customers and clerks in a nearby 7-11 gaze in uneasy wonder toward the night beyond the neon.

Later, they lay in the moon's light and gazed up at it. Joe thought maybe it was the Holy Version. He said to it, "Oo bootiful ina upoo, gimme a drink."

"I firsty," Crunch said.

"So firsty, yeh."

They slept then, because they were more exhausted even than they were parched. Toward morning, an opossum came and sniffed Joe's ankles, then humped off into the shadows. Later still, the dawn chorus began, and it was to the song of birds that the two Tanda awoke.

"I hongee," Crunch moaned. "I *soo firsty*!"

When they stood up, they could see the McDonalds. Too much in need now to resist, they went toward it.

Closer to it, the air around was scented with their favorite food. Had they not been dehydrated, and dangerously so, they would have been drooling like starving dogs.

Crunch signed, 'We go in?'

Joe still didn't know exactly what happened inside. "We watch."

He soon understood that you went up to the counter and talked. But what did you say? Plus, the shatterfaces got all different stuff, so they had to be talking about one thing and another. What were the right words, though? You couldn't hear anything on this side of the glass.

Joe signed, 'We go. We listen to McDonald words.'

Sometimes sign came in handy. They could communicate as much as they needed to without being overheard.

A little shatterface peered down a long tube. It was in a place full of other such things, tubes and slides and things. This place was outdoors, but attached to the McDonalds.

Joe jumped back, but not in time. "I see you," it squealed.

There was a door from here into the McDonalds rec room and he and Crunch went through it immediately.

Oh, it was so cool in here! And it smelled—oh, it smelled like rec at suppertime, only better and stronger than rec ever had. Joe felt the hollow woe of homesickness, not knowing what it was, only that it made him ache in a way he had never known before.

Crunch felt it, too and expressed his loneliness by saying softly, "Miss Fugger."

"Miss Betty."

TV was a big, lonely place. And to think he'd believed it to be small. He had actually believed once that you had to shrink to get in it, even worried that you'd be flat.

A shatterface at the xxcounter said, "Eggmakfuffin beffas."

Joe mouthed the words to himself. "Egmafuffin beffas. Bef*tas*."

No, not quite. "Egmakmuffin." That was better. "Egmakmuffin beftas." Sounded just right.

He went out from behind some chairs where they had been keeping low. As he moved toward the counter, he felt Crunch get into lockstep. He didn't want that. The shatterfaces never went in line. But how could he explain that to Crunch now?

So they approached the counter like that, the one in tattered shorts sandwiched behind the one in tattered pants. Joe put on his biggest grin, smiling so hard his face felt like it was going to break.

There was a woman shatterface at the counter. It turned its head and said something. Then another one that was sitting and eating started to slowly get up. A noise sounded, a squeal. The female that had made it rushed out to where the little shatterfaces were.

"Eggak muffin beffas," Joe said.

Crunch tried it. "Eggafuffin..." Shamed by the ridiculous sound of the attempt, he covered his face with his hands.

The shatterface behind the counter stepped backward. It pushed into a bunch of machines, one of which swayed and tipped. Brown liquid spilled everywhere and the shatterface screamed. It was a short, sharp sound, like an explosion.

Other shatterfaces back there started shrieking and gabbling so fast you couldn't follow.

"Eggakmuffin befas!" Joe pleaded. Inwardly, he withered. He'd done a poor job of talking, a really poor job. "Bekfas," he muttered.

The one he was talking to seemed to fold up. She disappeared below the counter. Then others went outside, all yelling. A big one came out from where there was cooking going on. It was huge and covered from head to foot with dark brown dye. In its hand was the biggest knife that Joe had ever seen. This terrible knife could cut you right in half. Behind him, he heard Crunch taken in a sharp breath, then felt him break away.

Clutching the hole in his chest, Crunch ran out to where the little shatterfaces were shrieking like birds. Joe ran behind him. There was a vibrating whine and the knife shattered the glass of a big window. He caught up with Joe and they climbed a wall and jumped down, then ran out into the middle of a car path—and a car came screaming toward them. Then another one joined it, this one coming from the other way. Then more of them were coming, their silver grills gleaming in fierce light from the great sparka that was rising into the upoo. More and cars came, all screaming, all gleaming in the morning light.

Crunch put his hands on his head and sat down. He went still.

Joe knew that this was a mistake, and he struggled and fought to get him to move. It was in that moment, in that terrible place, with cars coming at them from every direction and all the heat and the screaming and the fire overhead, that he realized how much he wanted Crunch to be alive, and wanted him to be happy in his life, and loved his friend.

"Crush," he said, "*Crush*," and dragged at him with all his might. Slowly, Crunch raised his head—and they both looked into the bellowing face of the longest car in the world. Looking down at them out of its huge front window was a shatterface with a cap on its head. You could see its teeth.

There was only one thing to do, and that was lie flat. Joe did it and there was a shaking, banging, blasting roar and a great shadow passing overhead, and then the thing had gone over them.

Pulling as hard as he could, dragging him, Joe finally got him off to the side of the car river. Here, there was a low place. Here, some bushes that they could go in. The bushes made a little shade, and Joe was grateful for it.

Finally, Crunch came out and was no longer still. "I keerd," he moaned.

"We keerd."

They had not been in the shade long when they once again heard the *pop pop pop.* Here came the bug again, way low, its enormous awful eyes gleaming and seeming to penetrate directly into Joe's own depths. It swung overhead, sending down a wind so strong that it hurt them and made them hold their heads.

It was going to get on the ground. And now they saw also that all the cars had stopped. This was because there were other cars with flashing lights all over them that formed walls up and down, that the rest of the cars could not go through.

"Crush, go," Joe cried. He ran. Far ahead, he saw a place that went down. In it there was mud. He went in there. Behind him, Crunch came and he was glad.

Soon they were surrounded by high green stuff that hid them better than any of it had so far. Crunch let out a grunt of such total amazement that Joe stopped. He was looking up. Joe followed his gaze.

Hanging above them on long green sticks of tall plants were huge yellow things with big black eyes in the middle. "Purdee," Crunch said, his voice cracking from thirst. "Soo-oo purdee."

"So big," Joe said. "Big fawers."

"Faaras."

"Real big yarra fawers!"

"Yarra fawers, hey!"

"Hey! Hey!"

They went round and round, looking up at all the yellow flowers dancing in the light. The shatterface world was a terrible place, but there were things in it beautiful beyond the best dream of the night, things made of pure happiness.

Then came voices, shatterfaces nearby. Joe and Crunch crouched down.

"Went inna culvert," one said. There was a crackle and a hiss and a more distant one said some numbers.

Before his face, Joe was seeing the most awful thing he had ever seen. It was all he could do not to cry out as he watched the thing slither along in the damp and shadows.

"They gonna git inna sewer, they gone down there."

"Good, that'll be the fire department's problem."

They made slow laughter together. It reminded him of home after work and after rec, when Keller came in and they talked over the day. Sometimes he would laugh softly like that. Joe longed, in one part of his mind, to sit in Keller's lap again and be rocked, while in the other part he watched the thing slither and spikkle out its forked tongue, and look around with its black empty eyes like Gorilla had.

They could hear its movement, *ssssss*, as it came along the damp, uneven floor. *Ssss,* it came closer...*ssssss*. Now it was pointing its head this way, that way...the forked tongue tasting the air. It had a nasty musk smell, like when they forgot the sheets on the beds too long. As they watched it, the head stopped swaying. The forked tongue went in and out. It was pointing right at them.

The eyes were black with a yellow rim. It was not an arm's length away. Crunch made a small sound, a kind of swallowed cry.

Instantly, a shatterface voice from nearby said, "hear that?"

Just as fast, the thing went *chuck* and it was a coiled up ball. And then a long piece of corn on the end of it started going *Brrrdt! Brrrdt! Brrrdt!*

Joe thought it was the most frightening sound he had ever heard. He could see, in the thing's mouth, the tips of big, big teeth.

A shatterface voice said, "Don' look now, but we got a rattler down here."

Brrrdt it went, then *brrrrdddttt thuthuthuht!* And it flashed out, its mouth wide, its head lunging through the green stalks.

"Fuck! Oh, fuck me! Jesus H. I got—aw, *shit*! Call goddamn EMS! Officer down, I got bit by a damn *snake*!"

Joe and Crunch crept away just as quickly and quietly as did the snake, but in an altogether different direction. They wriggled deep into thick brush and hid there. Even so, Joe thought that they might soon get found, but he didn't sign this to Crunch. Crunch would panic and run, and then they would be caught for sure.

The sheriff's van raced along the highway, the Tanda in the back huddled together in terror, all except Betty.

She shook the bars and shook them, but they would not give way. She felt as if her chest was itself a cage, and something in it was it pounding to get out. The combination of being trapped and having her baby taken from her stripped away the patina of orderly behavior that had characterized her life at the Cookes' house. The most powerful instinct in nature took over—a mother's desire to protect her child. So she screamed and howled and ran back and forth grabbing the mesh walls of the cage and shaking them with preternatural fury. Flutter and Jack and Jill recoiled from her, huddling together in the farthest corner that they could, watching her with wide, terrified eyes.

She threw herself to the floor and rolled and bellowed. She raced to the front and tried to communicate with the two shatterfaces who were driving, but no language came out, nothing but incoherent shrieks of pure anguish and pure rage.

The others tried to help her, but she threw them off like so many rags, leaping away from them, slashing at them with her open hands, with her fists.

Flutter called, "Bef! Bef!" between Betty's howls. But Bef was not in this car. Jack yelled for Keller. Then all three of them yelled for Charlie. Betty did not stop trying to break the cage, to get away. Her energy was boundless, she was like a creature made of iron and fire. She hammered on the thick black mesh. Wild-eyed, she gnawed at the lock. Then she went to the front again and hollered at the shatter-faces, sticking her fingers through the mesh in an effort to somehow reach them.

The Tanda had been soaking up experience and processing it at high speed. Their knowledge of reality had doubled, tripled, quadrupled by the hour. They had realized that the shatterfaces in the van were enemies, and that they had been foolish to get in it in the first place.

This made them canny, all except Betty, who was far too upset to think at all, and they began to try to figure out some means of rescuing themselves. They had tasted of freedom, walking the paths at the Center, watching over Betty and the baby, being able to run to greet visitors or not as they pleased, and go and come while the caged animals remained where they were. They had understood that Keller's world had been a cage, and now they were caged again, and they wanted *out*. But they also understood that if were to have any chance at all, they had to get Betty calmed down. They knew that this cage would be opened to get them out, and that moment would be a chance to escape.

Betty gave up shaking the back of the cage and rushed again to the front. "Peeze," she screamed, grappling through the mesh with her fingers, "Ma bebe, ma bebe, *peeeze*!" The last 'please' extended into a long howl of agony that evolved into a bellow of rage. Then she stopped, gasping, her chest heaving. She tore at her own hair, ripping it out in clumps.

Jack approached her. He was not a leader. He was a worker, and that was how he saw himself. He worked the line with excellence, but he wasn't interested in who led. Let it be Joe or Crunch. So he did not make demands of Betty. He just went close to her and stayed there, rushing back and forth beside her, putting his hands on her when he could, and signing 'be okay, be okay,' over and over again.

From time to time she would shriek at him, then run and grab the mesh again, shaking it, trying to shake the whole car to pieces. Blood ran from her hands from tearing at the bars, and sprayed from her mouth from biting the wire and the lock.

Flutter and Jill, who had been staying out of the way and signing and talking to each other, now took action. They surrounded Betty and held her between them. She shrieked and tore at them, covering them with her own blood and adding some of theirs to the mix.

Finally, though, she slumped. As if her bones had turned to water, the whole of her body sagged into their arms. Her screams became long, trembling sobs. They lowered her to the floor, then when she just lay there, took her between them. She lay cradled in the love of her friends.

Jack signed to her, 'love, love,' crossing his fists over his heart and bowing toward her again and again and again. And finally a hand came, a trembling hand, and reached for him, for his face, and the fingers slid along his cheek, leaving a trail of rose-pink blood.

"Ma bebe," she said miserably, her jaw working, tears pouring from her eyes. "Ma bebe, Kak! Ohhh Kak get ma bebe!"

Jack's own throat choked with helpless rage. In his mind, he could hear the baby crying, and in hers he knew the cries would be much louder. He knew that they'd been stupid to trust shatterfaces they didn't know. But so much had changed so fast. Their faces didn't shatter you anymore. Their eyes were no longer full of shadows. Jack could not have said it, none of them could, but they understood enough now to know that the shatterfaces' knowledge of the real world had been the source of the darkness in their eyes.

Though he was inarticulate, Jack was clever and he was the most practical of all the Tanda. He was well aware that there would soon come a time when the shatterfaces would want them to get out of the van. That would be their chance.

He signed 'quiet down,' moving his hands decisively at Betty. She looked at him, but through vague, uncomprehending eyes. He then did about the most violent thing he had ever done in his life, which was to grab her shoulder and force her to look into his eyes. "Beddy," he said, "wisen to me. Beddy, *wis-ten*!"

Slowly, her tear-filled eyes became more focused. Flutter and Jill gathered round. He signed, 'they will open the cage. We be very quiet. Then all outside, we run.'

"Where?" Betty asked.

He signed, 'away from here.'

"Mah bebe..."

"Find. We find," Flutter said.

They laid their hands together, the group of them. "We find." The van continued on. They waited—for what they did not know. A chance, any chance. But they did not, any of them, believe in their hearts that one would come their way.

Joe and Crunch struggled on, getting hungrier, thirstier and more tired as the sun-scorched hours wore on. They climbed a bank out of the brushy area—only to confront yet another mass of cars sweeping back and forth, a crazy river of metal and whining tires.

Across from the lines of cars was a huge building. On it, Joe read the word "HEB."

"Heeb," he said. He did not realize that he had begun to read. But the pressure of this struggle, grasping from moment to moment for life and freedom, was expanding his mind at great speed.

The building was huge. Maybe there was a world in it where they could live like they used to live. Joe now thought of their old place as a refuge. In his love and kindness, Keller had been hiding them from the other shatterfaces because he'd known how much they would be hated.

If only he could understand why Keller *didn't* hate them, or Beth or Charlie. If he knew, then maybe he could use that to make all the shatterfaces be nicer.

"Go in Heeb?" Crunch asked. His voice was a raw whisper.

"Go in Heeb."

Carefully, they crossed the road, timing their quick movements to avoid the cars.

Neither said it, but they both wanted to go back to the world. TV was horrible. TV was crazy. Where was Seinfeld? Where was Ellen? Above all, where were Flutter and Betty?

Where were they supposed to be going, anyway? This program was too big. It was awful in here. They both wanted back on the line, and as far as Crunch was concerned, being bottomsider was fine as long as he could get all the food he could eat and all the Pepsi he could drink, and to be loved by everybody and most of all, by Flutter. But he didn't have anything except two tormented feet, a leak in his chest and being scared, scared, scared.

Joe chose a door at the near end of a long bank of doors, and went through it. Crunch knew that he had no idea what this was either or why to go in here, but what could he do except follow? Joe was looking for Betty the same way he was for Flutter. He just went along, pretty much without hope.

Inside, Joe turned to him. His smile was wide. Then Crunch's smile was just as wide.

What they saw before them was the most wonderful thing ever. There were long rows of things and so much color and so many good smells and such wonderful looking stuff that they were almost ready to fall over.

"Pessi," Crunch said. He ran a few steps. He could not imagine what he was seeing, could not believe that there could be this much Pepsi. This must be where every single shatterface there was came to get it.

Then he saw more. He saw millions and piles of cans of other stuff, too. He went along the aisle, looking at the beautiful cans. "Gape," Joe said, reading one. Then, "Coke." Then "Mmmann doo. Muntan Doo!" He took a can. He knew how to open these.

The Mountain Dew can cracked and he smelled inside. He smiled, nodded to Crunch.

Crunch smelled in one with different writing on it. "Big Red."

Should they drink? They were now agonizingly thirsty. But these were new smells.

Joe took a taste...and it was pretty good. Crunch sipped his. It was funny tasting, not like Pepsi at all.

There were more cans, many more, too many more to count. Joe was starting to drink and Crunch was getting another can when shatterfaces appeared. But then they moved quickly away. Good, gone. At the end of the hard, slick path, they found a long row of big open bins full of cold and packages with pictures of food on them.

Crunch got in one of the bins and lay down because it was so deliciously cool. When he pushed his feet against the wall, that felt really good where they had been burning.

Joe saw meat and veggies and potatoes on the packages in the bins. He tore off the paper, but inside it was all hard and cold and you had to lick it to get any and it was no good. So he threw that away.

A shatterface said, "A man has collapsed over here." It had come up from behind.

Joe got Crunch and they went off. Here, around the next corner, were stacks of Oranges and apples. Joe loved apples. He got one and ate it and it was so crisp and juicy and sweet and he was so hungry that big noises came out of him, groaning and sobbing and gobbling that he could not stop.

Crunch was wary. Were the other apples made of stone like the one in the shatterface box? Carefully, he bit into one. No, they were good, they were *so good*!

Joe got about four bites and Crunch got two when they were found again. "Excuse me," said a shatterface in a white apron. It was coming fast. They got out of that part of the Heeb and went around a corner. Here there were tall glass doors, and inside were boxes with pictures of all kinds of different food, and other little cardboard cartons with more food pictures. Joe opened one of the doors and went in.

He smelled ice cream in here. It was inside round boxes. Behind the rows of it there was a dark, bigger room. Joe and Crunch pushed the food aside to get into this room. They wanted to hide and eat ice cream undisturbed.

Before they could do it, a shatterface peered in at them. Crunch smiled. The shatterface ran off yelling that they were in the freezer.

So they went out the door again and this time they saw bacon. Bacon you only got every once in a while but bacon was just the best there was! They went after the bacon, opening the plastic with their teeth.

The bacon was all limp and cold and dead. What had happened to it? Crunch ate some, but he shook his head. It was no good.

Then Joe saw something that amazed him, and gave him the first little touch of hope that he'd had since the car ran away with everybody else in it. This was a beautiful eye up near the ceiling. It was just like the eyes in the ceilings at home.

"Keller," he said, pointing.

Crunch's face lit up. "Kerrer, come git us," he shouted.

They set up a cry, "Kerrer, Kerrer," waving at Keller's TV eye. But Keller did not come through any doors. Then the Big Voice said, "Will all customers please leave the store. Please leave your purchases behind. All customers, please leave the store quickly and calmly. There is a police emergency taking place inside the building."

The Big Voice! Rec must be somewhere here! Joe looked around, his mind seeking for some sight of the control room and the barrier. Oh, how he'd like to be back behind that barrier!

Another voice, even bigger than the Big Voice said, "DO NOT MOVE. YOU WILL NOT BE HARMED." It was the meanest, hardest, most frightening voice yet.

They both ran, racing straight back toward and through a swinging door into a place full of huge boxes. This ended in a sun-drenched area where there were giant cars like the one Charlie had used to take the people into TV.

"Gonna kiwl us," Crunch gasped, "*kiwl* us!"

"Ah know it."

They jumped off the big platform they were on and ran out into the sun. And then without warning, they were standing in front of a new shatterface. He said, "Joe."

They took out running as fast as they could. Behind them, a whole new pack of shatterfaces followed. There seemed no escape, no place to go this time. The shatterfaces got closer.

"Get ready to deploy," one of them bawled. "They are in the box!"

Then Joe saw something ahead of them. Legs. Shatterfaces standing in a line.

It was hopeless. They were trapped. Except that Crunch ran up a pole a little ways. He went so quickly and so easily that for a moment Joe was too surprised to follow. But when he tried, he discovered that it was easy for him, too. Below them, an orange net clattered against the pole and fell to the ground.

A shatterface pointed a gun. "Okay, come down," it said.

"They're animals, you fool. Just shoot!"

"We got orders get 'em alive, Asshole."

"Yeah, we're gonna have the cops on us inside of a minute. We can't get 'em, we shoot 'em, and *those* are our orders."

"Joe! Crunch!"

"For God's sake, give me that gun!"

A fight broke out among the shatterfaces. Crunch took a deep breath and made a long jump. He dropped, rolling along in dust.

"Aw, *shit*! Crunch, Joe. Hey—*hoo-hoo*—nice apes!"

Joe followed Crunch. He sailed out into the air, his arms windmilling. Then his feet were in dirt.

"Les' go," Crunch said.

They took advantage of all the motionless cars around them to provide hiding places.

"Go fas'," Joe said, but he didn't need to say it. They'd both heard their names and seen the guns and understood enough of the talk to know that their lives were in the balance.

They reached the end of the mass of cars. Beyond it was a little building under some big trees. Smoke was coming out of the building, and the smoke smelled real good. A sign on the front said BBQ. Joe had no idea what that meant, or how it was said. But the best smell he had ever smelled in his life was coming out of there. Licking the hard food in the Heeb had made his mouth water. The one drink and the few bites of apple had made him even hungrier and thirstier than before.

They had to go in there, no matter what had happened at the McDonalds. They had to eat and drink more, and they had to do that now.

It was darker inside. The smell was so wonderful that it made Joe want to show Betty and be happy here with her.

Somehow, he had to make these shatterfaces be good to him and Crunch. He looked up at their faces. Summoning up all of his inner strength, he gave them his biggest, best smile. "*Peeeeze,*" he said. "*Oh peeeeze.*"

The shatterfaces looked down at him, one a man and one a woman.

Joe thought maybe if he mentioned Keller it would help. "I fend a Kerrer," he said. "Yew no Kerrer?" He smiled again. Then he inhaled. "Mmmm!" he said. "We rike food! We hongee!"

Crunch came behind him. "We rike eat." He touched Joe's shoulder. If they got thrown out again, and had to keep running, their end had come. They were too tired.

Joe reached back and put his hand on Crunch's hand. He felt Crunch's grip, weak but there. It made him less scared, and he said more boldly, "Peeze, food for us. Peeze be good. Kerrer! Kerrer!"

One of them came from behind the counter. It had a big piece of wood it was holding up. It said, "Dewyew rekkanize Jeezus Krise as yer lawd an saver?"

Joe said, "Huh?"

It said, "'R yew creatures uva dark?"

It was talking to them, not screaming. They begged with their hands, holding them out and pleading . "Food, peeze, food," Joe said.

Crunch said, "Prrreeeze!"

"Bert," the woman shatterface said, "these people are just deformed. At's all it is."

Bert lowered the baseball bat.

"Meewul," Crunch said, pointing into his open mouth.

"One—no two—two meals coming up," the female said. "Rib special."

"'At's got a price on it," the male said.

"You dumb cracker, and I thought you were such a Christian."

"Which I am."

"Then you give them this food. Look at 'em, dressed in rags. They ain't got nothin.'" She leaned over the counter. "Sorry, fellas, he's not real bright." She showed her teeth in one of those little tight little shatterface smiles that could so easily turn mean.

She said, "Here y'are."

"Here y'are," Crunch repeated.

She slid two funny plates. Paper. Each one had hard bread in it and sticks that smelled so good Joe started crying. He took one in his mouth. It had hard insides but the outside was thick and full of juice and tasted so good that Joe could not stop eating it, not for one second.

Far too soon, the sticks were stripped clean. There were other things there, brown and swimming in gravy. Were they bugs? He tasted them, then ate them all by lifting the plate and pouring them in his mouth.

"They're hungry all right, Bert," the female said. "Real hungry. Lookit them beans goin' down."

Smiling from ear to ear, tears at the edges of his eyes, Crunch said, "Hongee! Hongee! Firsty! Firsty!"

"Ice tea," she said. She gave them tall, icy glasses of brown stuff that tasted real, real good.

Then there were two men there. They came in and spread a net across the whole place so you could not get around it.

Joe and Crunch vaulted the counter and dove out through the back, then ran off as fast as they possibly could, still clutching chunks of food. Instinct took them away from the open spaces and back into the weeds that choked the trench behind the row of structures.

There came a loud *wham*, then another one. Joe sped up. The shatterfaces were shooting at them, he knew. "Huwwy, Cunch," he shouted. Another *whammm* and Crunch tripped and fell, his body skidding along the black flat behind the store.

"Getim!" a shatterface yelled. It started running up, its teeth showing.

Crunch got to his feet and came on. They went into the tall grass and continued, slipping and sliding in the toilet-smelling goo that covered the floor. The the shatterfaces behind them shouted and occasionally fired their guns, and came ever closer.

24

A BABY IS DYING

Larry's PI, David Baxter, had called to say that there was a foreign registered plane of some sort at Centex Air, a private field north of San Antonio, not far from Barrett Scientific.

Hoping to find the van there and the Tanda not yet departed on that plane, Charlie and Beth and Chris raced toward it. The baby, cuddled in Beth's lap, was still screaming, but his little voice was getting weaker by the minute. His squirming was growing less, too. Baby Charlie was fading like a mayfly in the afternoon.

"How far," Beth asked. She'd never been there.

Charlie didn't answer, meaning that it was farther than he'd like.

"Oh, God, what if they're taking off right now?"

"Then we're in even worse trouble," Chris said. "This baby is about gone."

"Charlie, if I have to, I'll try to get them to take him."

Charlie didn't answer. He was both driving the car and now back on the cellphone with Larry. "He's on his way, he's got the restraining order," he said as he hung up.

"Gonna be a near thing," Chris responded.

They nearly passed a glistening sign, "Centex Aviation." As he hit the brakes and turned into the drive, he almost lost control of the car.

"Take it easy," Chris said.

"No."

They pulled into the parking lot and got out. Beth held the baby close, keeping him as warm as she possibly could. In just the past few minutes, his voice had declined to a low mumble, not even a burr. Even if he got food, would it save him now? Would anything save him? They ran toward the flight line.

"Charlie," a voice called, loud and full of Texas. Beth recognized Bill Knowlton, who'd come out to the Center a few times on stories... especially the Moreland story. Chris was a persuasive man, God love him.

Bill had obviously been waiting in his car. He now ran to catch up with them. "What are we doing?" he called.

"Saving some people from kidnapping and death," Charlie shouted back at him.

"Uh—yeah. Will you slow down?"

They did not slow down. "They're putting them on a plane right now. Kidnapping them to somewhere in Asia."

The group blasted through the doors into the plush private lounge.

"Asia?"

"We assume."

"You say kidnapping them?"

"Yep." Beth didn't show him the baby, not yet. Out on the concrete apron stood a white private jet, elegant and gleaming, and the ugliest thing that she had ever seen.

"It's a Gulfstream 5," Charlie said. "Got a 6,500 mile range. They can get anywhere in south Asia in two hops." He turned and looked at Beth. His expression had a hardness, a determination, that scared her a little bit. "Once that plane is in the air, they're gone."

Then she saw the van. It was out on the apron, sitting there in the pounding heat of the sun. "Are they already on the plane?" Chris asked. The passenger door was opened, a set of stairs standing in readiness.

"Bill, get out there," Charlie said.

"You got it." As Bill ran, his camera crew appeared from around the side of the building. They stormed out onto the apron. Charlie joined them, quickly slinging some of their equipment over his shoulder. By the time they reached the van, he was carrying a battery pack and a camera. He'd put on his dark glasses. He looked like a member of the crew.

"Chris, he's gonna try to take them!"

"Where's that lawyer?"

At the approach of the TV crew, the two sheriff's deputies got out of the van. At the same time, more men came down out of the plane. Beth recognized Doctor Ma, but none of the others.

When they saw the TV crew, they stopped. Then Ma strode to the van, where the deputies were unlocking the back.

"Are you in charge here?" Bill asked him.

"Please," he said, "this is government business. You have no right to be here."

"Don't tell me my rights. I know my rights."

"Get them on the plane," Ma said.

Beth came up to him. She opened the sheet and held out the baby. "You're killing him," she said.

He looked at little Charlie, then immediately stepped back. "Where did this come from?"

"Betty had him yesterday."

"It's sick," he said.

"He's starving. He needs his mother."

He regarded Beth. "This one may go." He gestured toward the TV crew. "But if you take pictures, then not. I am sorry."

There erupted from the rear of the van a great shrieking. The whole vehicle shook. Instinct drew Bill Knowlton and his crew closer to the sound and the story. "Christ almighty," he said, as they got around behind the van far enough to see inside.

Betty hurled herself against the cage door again and again.

Jack tried to stop her but she kicked him away, causing him to go hurtling across the cage. He hit the front wall and slumped.

Jill and Flutter made the sign for quiet again and again. Betty finally stopped shaking the bars, but her whole body continued to heave and tremble. When the faint sound of the baby once again reached her ears, she leaped up again, pressing herself so hard to the mesh that her skin bulged through in big squares.

Jack crawled over, brushing himself off, shaking his head to recover his balance. He signed, 'Be quiet, when the door opens we run to Beth and Charlie."

"Bef?" She threw back her head and screamed, "*BEF BEF BEF!*"

She saw men with cameras, and she saw Big Charlie. "Charlie! Charlie! Peeze! Peeze, ma bebe!" Again she threw herself against the bars. "Bebe, Charlie! Peeze!" She was trying to smile, to beg in what she imagined might be an appealing manner. Her face was tear-soaked and her hands bloody.

As Charlie approached, everybody stuck their fingers out between the bars of the cage.

"These are the Tanda," Charlie said into Bill's camera. "They're refugees from the destruction of their jungle habitat in Sumatra. They have human-equivalent intelligence, but they're being treated as animals. They've been sold to a foreign company for millions of dollars by Barrett Scientific. At least one of them is going to be dismembered for analysis."

"Not true," Ma said, pushing in front of him. "These animals have been held in close confinement here in the states for years. We want to give them a better life."

"These *people* have been cruelly and irresponsibly confined. But there's no reason to go on treating them as slaves. They need—"

Beth came up with the baby, and whatever plan the Tanda had hatched to appear docile until they could run away now failed completely. All four of them burst into crying and screaming, their fingers twiddling eagerly through the bars. The baby's tired voice was barely audible, just a miserable whisper.

Beth held the baby up for the cameras, and for the world, to see. "Are we live?" she asked.

"Live," Bill replied.

"This is the baby World Bio proposes to leave behind to die."

"I did not say this!" Ma shouted.

"Please, let the mother feed her baby."

There fell then a silence before the waiting cameras. "Open it," Ma said at last. Then, to the Tanda. "You will get the baby. You will then walk to the airplane. You—"

"Just do it," Chris said. "For God's sake, hurry!"

The deputies unlocked the cage. Instantly, the door slammed open and Betty was out, roaring with joy and fear.

She presented an extraordinary and heartbreaking appearance to the cameras—a small, shaggy haired woman with a smear of lipstick on her mouth, her dress askew, her blouse thrown open to expose engorged breasts, her hands ripped and bloody, her body covered with swellings and bruises.

She clutched up toward Beth. "Bef, peeze! Peeze, peeze!"

Beth knelt and gave her the baby, dropping the sheet as she did so. The Tanda might play to the camera just by the nature of their suffering, but Beth knew television, and she knew the effect this baby was having and would continue to have.

It took the teat immediately, and Betty threw back her head, her eyes screwed shut, the most powerful expression on her face of bliss and relief that Beth had ever seen in this life.

"We go," Ma said. He held out his hand to Jack. "Come, Jack."

The Tanda set up an immediate howl of protest. "Go home wif Bef! Go home wif Sharlee!"

"We go now," Ma said. "To a better home. Better!" He began to lead them, and they began to go, straggling and slow, but obedient. Betty had forgotten everything except her baby. You could have led her off a cliff now that she had him back.

They were being taken right to the plane.

"Stop him," Beth screamed, "Charlie! Stop him!"

"I can't stop him, he's got the law!"

Just then a car appeared. It was coming fast, and Beth knew who it must be.

"Go up the steps," Ma ordered the Tanda.

Larry Stein's black Porsche Carrera came slurrying to a stop. He leaped out.

"World Bio knows nothing about this," he yelled. "These people don't have any legitimate order of recovery from any judge." He pointed to the two deputies, who were already jumping into their van. "Those men are impersonating officers." And then he pointed to the plane. "Its flight plan takes it to Colombia."

The door of the plane closed. The engines began to rev. The van roared away.

Larry ran across the tarmac. "I have a restraining order! They're to return the animals pending judicial inquiry. Not to mention the D.A. and probably the F.B.I."

Charlie hardly heard him. A moment of truth had come. Legal niceties didn't matter anymore. This was now between a couple of tons of airplane and a guy. He ran up under the body, through the hot blast from the right engine.

"Charlie!" Beth ran after him.

"Jesus Christ," Chris shouted, following.

"Get this!" Bill yelled at his crew.

Charlie attached himself to the right landing gear, wrapping his legs around it.

Beth uttered a cry, which was swept away in the roar of the engines.

The plane began picking up speed. Charlie examined the strut, then looked up into the wheel bay. He took out his pocketknife and opened it between his hand and his teeth. Wind began blowing against his back, buffeting him and pressing him against the strut. An inch below his toes, the tire was whining. Every bump threatened to knock him off. He knew that, at some point, he would be blown off, or the plane would successfully take off and retract its gear. If he hadn't accomplished his task by then, he would have to let go. Otherwise, the gear would be damaged as it crushed his body, and the plane would crash. He could not risk the Tanda.

He saw a hydraulic line deep in the wheel bay. It was above his head, clamped to the wing bracing. This would be the line to the gear. He climbed, felt himself slip, grabbed for purchase, raised himself again. The pitch of the engines increased. The tire below him began to snap as it hit bumps. Wind tore at him. They were heading for the runway, a quick taxi. If they got this thing airborne, he was a dead man.

Reaching as far as he could, he contacted the hose with the blade. He stretched until his shoulder threatened to pop right out of its socket—but he could just manage a nick. No good. He had to get closer.

They were on the runway now. He could feel the pause as the plane lined up to take off. He used the moment to climb higher, until his head was well up into the wheel well. He sliced into the hard, steel reinforced material. Never let it be said that the Gulfstream is lightly built.

They began their takeoff roll. 'What a hell of a dumb way to die,' he thought. He'd never been afraid of death. Never. But now, God damn it, he was too scared to shit.

He cut and cut and cut, sawing with all the strength he possessed. The engines roared, the wind screamed—and bright green hydraulic fluid poured down over him, a glorious gusher of deliverance. He whooped, he hollered...and he also cut three or four electric wires. He didn't know what kind of backup this aircraft had, but there would be some sort of redundancy.

The ground shot away fast. This baby could move. He latched his arms and legs around the strut, drawing himself up into the wheel well as far as possible—maybe twelve inches. The wind tore at him, screaming around his legs, plunging him into a hell of noise. Even though he was facing the ground, he could see nothing more than a blur. He let out one of those yells of his. He heard the gear motors start...and the gear he was on began to move.

God help me. It's either be crushed to death or drop off.

When Beth saw the plane rise from the runway she screamed again, her agony every bit as terrible as Betty's. "*Charlie*," she bellowed, running wildly. She could see the black lump on that landing gear. "*Charlie*!"

Chris grabbed her from behind. She half turned toward him—and saw beside him her dad and mother. She was crying, feeling the most bitter and terrible sorrow she had ever known, and in an instant they were her parents again and she threw herself into their arms, a little girl who had fought and been beaten and needed the arms of home.

She didn't want to listen to the jet, above all she didn't want to see her Charlie fall. "Please no," she whispered into her father's chest, "please no."

Charlie was now in the situation that he had assumed would take his life. As the plane picked up speed, it felt as if his back was being blowtorched. He was pressed too hard against the strut to move, but if he slipped to one side or the other, he would be blown off instantly.

He could sense, sort of, that the plane was banking, but he couldn't tell much else. He forced his eyes to a squint. Far below, he saw a row of houses with swimming pools. That'd be the Gardens. Maybe he'd fall into the same pool Moreland had so enjoyed. Ironies of life, right?

Beth saw that Larry had alerted the police, who now arrived on the apron in six carloads, light bars flashing and sirens screaming. Bill Townsend, God love him, was having the time of his life. His expression was somber, though. He knew as well as the others what must be happening—probably had already happened—in the sky.

A city fire truck also appeared. Overhead, there was no sign of the jet.

A cop leaned out of one of the cars."They just declared an emergency," he said.

Beth was between her parents. She felt her mother's arm come around her. In just these few minutes everything in this family had changed. Everything.

"Where's the plane?" she asked. Nobody answered. The police cars were now lined up on both sides of the runway.

For a moment, she wondered how her parents had known to come, then realized that it was, of course, the TV. This drama was being enacted across the whole city.

Ambulances now appeared, also deploying along the runway. The fire truck began spreading foam.

"There they are!"

The jet was coming in low. When Beth didn't see Charlie she cried out again. Then—then, yes! She did see him—and a different kind of terror made her scream in a new way, choked and awful with hope.

Chris came close. "Light headed? Feel faint?"

"Just scared!"

"I hear you."

"God be with us," her father said.

On the strut, Charlie was fighting a relentless drift toward unconsciousness. At least he knew that he had cut the right line. This landing gear wasn't going anywhere. From the flow of hydraulic fluid still streaming out above him, he thought that the maneuvers he felt must mean that they were returning to Centex.

Inside the plane, Ma and Barrett were like cobras cornered against a wall.

"Divert to another airport, at least," Barrett bawled into the backs of the two pilots.

"We've got a major hydraulic emergency. This plane isn't going anywhere but down."

"We oughta shoot 'em," Atitarn grumbled.

"We've played in your little theatrical event long enough," Ma said to Barrett. He sat back in one of the luxurious seats. "I'm going to deny everything."

Atitarn looked at the Tanda, crowded against the bars that confined them to the back of the cabin. "Scum," he said, "stupid scum."

"Go Bef," Jack said.

"'Go Bef' indeed. You are stupid, aren't you? Too stupid to speak more than a little pidgin"

"Not toopid! You toopid!"

The plane lurched.

"You'll kill us all!" Barrett yelled to the pilot.

"This baby is landing where ever it happens to be, Doctor. We'll be lucky to make it down alive, any of us."

Shuddering, it returned to the straight and level. But it was descending now, no question about that at all.

"You're gonna be an accessory," Barrett said to Ma. "It's going to mean jail time."

"We ought to cut his throat," Atitarn said.

"Don't even think about it," Ma said. "Right now we're accessories to his crime. I don't want to be charged with murder."

"I might not even have committed a crime. I'm not sure."

"Barrett Scientific defrauded World Bio."

"It failed to deliver on a contract, the reason being that a party to the operation died unexpectedly. That's not going to be called fraud."

"We're on our way to Colombia with the animals. We're stealing!"

"Calm down! Barrett is a closely held company. I'm the major shareholder. Last time I looked, you can't steal from yourself. We've got twelve million dollars of World's money."

"You have it."

"Hold on, you're getting your cut."

"I am," Ma said. He nodded toward Atitarn. "Him too. And the general?"

"The general went home. If you want to lubricate him, that's your business."

The plane yawed to the right, then almost onto its side, then shuddered back to level flight.

"You've killed us all," Ma snarled.

"Nonsense. If we get to Colombia, we'll sell these creatures for far more than we got from your employer. Former employer." He hesitated. Tell Ma the good news or not?

Ma glared at him in silence. Atitarn stared out the window. The Tanda cowered. A year ago, Bob had received a text from a Russian biological group offering fifty million dollars for the Tanda if they could be delivered in Colombia. Given that the group planned to dissect at least one of the animals, he hadn't even considered answering, not until last night. The response was immediate. The deal was still on the table.

"If we bring this off, we return World's money, my company is not only saved but well paid, I go back to New York and you gentlemen by yachts and condos in Monte Carlo."

The plane shuddered. "What in *hell* is wrong," Bob shouted toward the cockpit.

"Shut up and fasten your seatbelt!"

The engine note changed. Houses were passing just below.

"It's crashing," Ma snarled.

Bob looked back at the restless, squirming Tanda, the one with her baby in her arms, the others pressing against the cage. He laughed. At them. Jeered. And it felt wonderful.

A moment later, something began beeping in the cockpit. Atitarn braced for impact against the seat in front of him. Bob found himself washed by rage. To be so close to the fortune of a lifetime and safety for his company, and then this!

The plane heaved.

Atitarn vomited.

"Life is not so precious, my friend," Ma said gently.

Atitarn coughed and huddled against a window, staring hungrily at the ground.

The jet shuddered and yawed.

Bob glared at the Tanda, who looked back at him, their expressions gently pleading. He thought, 'If I die, so do you, you little bastards,' and took pleasure in it.

Down in the wheel well, Charlie found his mind working with the same precision that had characterized his thought processes in battle. He knew that the plane was landing, had known it since the flaps had been lowered. He hadn't been able to hear the servos, of course, but could feel the difference in the way she flew. For one thing, the wind against his tormented back was a little less. He was being sanded rather than blowtorched. For another, the plane kept wallowing, a result of the pilots having control problems due to reduced hydraulic pressure.

Long before he thought it would happen, there came a tremendous blow from beneath his feet, a blow that almost knocked him off the strut, that left him clinging by his knees and his fingers.

The tire started spinning again, then there was another blow the equal of the first, and this time he heard the squeal and smelled the searing rubber. He looked down at the racing runway, a wild pattern of skid marks speeding past like crazed snakes.

The plane slowed, then slowed more. Then something cold and stinking came up around him, splashing against his back and running down his face, soaking him.

They'd foamed the runway. The coolness of it felt kind of good, but the odor was wicked.

The airplane stopped. He put his feet down. Yes, there was ground there. He backed away from the strut. The engines behind him wound down. Until they were completely silent, he waited, ready to jump back on again if he had to. He had no way of knowing what was going on in the cabin. Any damn thing could still happen.

Checking himself, he decided that he felt sort of okay. His back was going to require a hospital stay, for sure, but he thought he'd live.

A pair of eyes was staring at him through a plastic face shield. He stared back. "Rough flight," he managed to croak. Then the lights went out. He knew he was falling, and that was the last thing he knew.

When Beth saw him coming out from under the plane on a stretcher, lying on his belly with his red, raw back exposed to the air, it was all she could do not to buckle and gag. She'd always laughed at the idea of fainting at the sight of blood, but the look of him—like a slab of runny hamburger—made her dizzy, and it made the world around her seem small and distant and unimportant.

Chris ran over to him, hurried along beside the stretcher, then came back. "It's probably mostly on the surface, hon," Chris said. "Windburn from hell." Then he went with Charlie into one of the ambulances. "University," he shouted as they closed the doors. "We'll be in trauma," he called to Beth.

Siren wailing, the ambulance moved off.

Police officers stationed themselves at the door of the airplane. After a moment, it opened with a clank. Two men came carefully down the lightweight stair the firemen had provided. They were in uniform. Pilots.

Larry went up the steps, Beth behind him. The fire safety officer shouted at them to stop, but they'd moved too quickly for him.

"Nobody else board this plane," the safety officer commanded, when Beth's dad tried to follow.

Larry found Barrett slumped in a seat. "I have this service," he said. "It's a restraining order. Do you understand this?"

Barrett snatched it out of his hand. "Get 'em," he said, "before they shit all over themselves."

"Hi," Beth said.

Four faces peered out at her, eyes narrow, uncomprehending and suspicious.

"Go home?" Betty said. "*Peeze* go home, Bef!"

Beth opened the cage and they came out, moving quickly, and followed her down.

"Yuck," Flutter said when they became involved in the foam.

Betty held her baby high. "No good for bebe." Instantly, he began to cry. Cooing, she brought him back down. "So hongeee, sooo hooongee," she said as he latched on and began sucking.

"We need to get them back to the center," she told her parents. They could have all fitted into Chris's Beamer, but either he or Charlie had the keys.

"Is there a truck?"

"No, mother, there is no truck. No more trucks."

"But—in a car—surely not."

"They do very well in cars."

Beth and her mom rode in front with her dad, the two of them jammed into the passenger seat of his Lexus. The back was piled with Tanda. Police cars escorted them, and Bill's crew, now along with crews from every other station in town, followed.

Chris called on the cellphone to report on Charlie. He was

suffering from exposure, contusions, a severe windburn to his back and an inability to believe that he was still alive.

Her father reached over and put his hand on hers. In the back seat, the Tanda huddled together, occasionally signing to one another.

Beth asked her father, "You're the one behind the restraining order, aren't you?"

He nodded.

"But how—how did you get involved, Dad?"

"Larry Stein called yesterday. Wanted me to put in the good word if Charlie ended up in the slammer. That's where it started. Then, when this thing showed up on TV, I ran over to the courthouse and convinced Judge Alaniz to sign on the dotted line."

"Thank you, Daddy."

Her mother choked back a sob. "I'm proud of you, Daughter." She touched Beth's hand. Their fingers entwined. "Just like the old days, right? Like we were."

"Momma, yeah." Beth said no more, fearing that the least wrong word could still re-ignite the anger and the rejection that had poisoned this family.

"I was on your property a few days back," her dad said. "I wanted to come up to the house."

"You should've."

"What would have happened?"

"Oh, Daddy, I don't know. But you're welcome now. You're both very welcome."

They drove on.

Back at Centex, Dr. Robert Barrett, to his great astonishment, had been cuffed and had his rights read to him. He was under arrest for falsification of customs forms and animal cruelty. Ma and Atitarn had been left on the tarmac by the departing mob of police, presumably free to return to wherever they had come from, but without what they had come for, of course. As for World Bio's money, the Barrett board would certainly return it to them.

Evening was falling when the car arrived at the Center. Luis was on the row, just starting the evening feeding. Mooreland whooped gently when he realized that Beth was back, and the chimps and the capuchins set up an eager ruckus. Then, when they smelled the Tanda, the level of excitement increased dramatically. After their initial horror, the apes and monkeys had been bonding with the Tanda, helped along by Beth's including them in feeding time.

As the Tanda got out, Beth said, "Jack, can you guys go down and say hello to the row? I want to get Betty and the baby comfortable."

The three Tanda hurried down to the cages. "Her-ro," Flutter yelled.

"It's he*llo*," Jill instructed, "got an *l. Llll...*" Then they were out of sight. The voices of the apes rose in greeting.

"They're absolutely amazing," her mother said.

"A new world, Mom. New ways of thinking, new eyes and new ideas."

Betty sucked in breath and just howled, her eyes bulging, her mouth wide. Beth's mother screamed, Beth screamed, her dad clapped his hands over his ears. The TV crew, who was just descending from their truck, fumbled and yelled.

Beth thought, 'oh, God, the baby's dead. "Betty, what's the matter, Betty?" But then little Charlie began to fret. The baby was anything but dead.

Betty seemed not to notice. Her furiously nursing infant in her arms, she stood frozen and staring off into the deepening evening. Across the rolling Texas fields, just above the edge of the horizon, rose the moon, full but for a sliver.

Beth put her arm around the Tanda's shoulders. "Beautiful, isn't it?"

"Bootiful," Betty said. "*Bootiful*, ooooh!"

"We call it the moon. Can you say 'moon?'"

"Moon, grabig! Grabig *mooooooon*!"

"The great big moon." She looked to her parents, to the TV crewmen and their cameras, to the cops who had escorted them. "The whole world is new for them," she said. "It's all completely new."

"And so for us, my daughter," her dad said. "For all of us, the world is also that—just a little bit new."

From down amid the cages there came howls. Then three wide-eyed Tanda came racing up the path, hurrying into Beth's open arms. They'd seen the moon, too. Beth reflected that, perhaps for only the second time in the sea of ages, it was being observed by a new intelligence.

"At the moon," Betty explained to the others, "the grabig *moooooon*!"

Betty came close to Beth, looked up at her. "I want Joe," she said softly. "Flutter wants Crunch." They were the clearest, best pronounced sentences Beth had ever heard from her lips. "Where dey?"

"Somewhere, Betty. They've gotta be somewhere."

Unless, of course, they were dead.

25

CHILDREN OF THE WORLD

A blow to Joe's back woke him up gasping, but before he could turn to see what was happening, another one struck him in the head so hard he saw a flash and heard a terrible crack. He pressed himself against the back of the steel box they'd been sleeping in, but the shatterfaces peering in all had sticks and more blows struck him, hitting his head, his back, his legs, hitting him so hard his teeth banged.

Next to him, Crunch was howling in pain. Warding off the blows as best he could, Joe fought his way to his knees.

They had hidden in this alley because it seemed safe, and the big steel boxes were full of food bits. Some of it had been stinky, but not all. Then it had been dark but now it was light, so they weren't hidden anymore. There had been light times and dark times, four of them now, maybe more.

"Top," Joe cried, "peez top!" He tried to shelter Crunch, who was taking the worst of the blows. "Ee do nutin', do nutin! Top!"

The shatterfaces were laughing and shouting so much that they didn't even seem to hear. Another blow hit Joe's head, and for a second the world went away. Then he saw a big, thick wooden bat being wielded to hit Crunch and threw himself on top of him.

The screaming was loud now, hoarse and excited. "Get the fuck outa our ally, you bums," a little one shouted, and dealt him a punishing blow to the shoulder. Another one yelled "you pissed on my wall," and a stinging slap landed across his butt.

Joe used a moment when they were concentrating on Crunch to jump up onto the top of the box. He balanced on the rim and screamed his loudest scream at the vicious little shatterfaces.

They stared up at him. One of them said, "It's the damn *aliens*!"

"Holy shit!"

"Get away!" Joe shouted. He shook his fists, "stop hittin' 'im! Stop it!"

They didn't need to be told. They were backing away already. Then they all screamed at once and ran off up the alley.

Silence fell. "I hurt, I hurt," Crunch moaned.

Joe looked Crunch over. He had a bleeding wound above one eye and dark, caked blood on his chest from the knife wound. "Big Oz," Joe said. That was what this program was. Had to be. Since Oz was a prison, it also meant that they would never get out, but he didn't say that to Crunch. "You get up, okay?"

He came to his feet, swaying. "Why, Joe? *Why*?"

Joe shrugged. Telling him would only make him more sad.

Crunch said, "I so tirsty," he said, "soo *th*irsty."

"Yeh me too. Get pepicola right now down my throat."

"Me too."

They went out of the alley and into the morning light. There were cars here and there, and real good smells were coming out of a store. Shatterfaces hurried in, then came out with white bags. They put on the dark glasses and caps they had stolen from a store, and drew the bills of the caps down low.

"Ga' money?" Crunch asked.

"Gasum yeh."

"Okey gemme coffee bagel, dey gat dat. Or donut, two're okay."

Joe had realized money was needed yesterday afternoon. He had gone up to one shatterface after another asking, "peez, peeze money fer us." Mostly, they didn't even look at you, but sometimes they did, and once a lady, she said, "I saw you on TV!" She gave them a bunch of money, putting it in Joe's hand. Then she got on her cellphone. When they saw that, they ran.

Joe reflected that he had gotten what he wished for. They sure were in TV—in blotchy clothes and getting beat up all the time in this crazy mean Oz spinoff.

"Hey, car," Joe said, pointing to one that had pulled up to the curb. It had just let a shatterface out of its stomach, so he knew it was awake. "Lemme in! Lemme in, car!" But the car ignored him. He hated being ignored by cars because it reminded him of struggling at the barrier for all those years. But they all ignored him, always. They even carried dogs with their big noses sticking out. Anybody but people.

In the old world, he was never thirsty or hungry and all the punishment he took was an occasional *yowtch* with the snickersnee. In Big Oz, you were always hungry and thirsty and every day brought a whole new crop of *yowtches*. He'd gotten used to being beaten by shatterfaces, screamed at by shatterfaces, run away from by shatterfaces, shot at by shatterfaces.

He had started wondering about something. If this was the shatterface world, where was the people world? Surely it couldn't have been in just those few little rooms, and just the six of them. He worried that maybe there were no other people anywhere, so then what were they? What were people that there would be so few?

As he went into the food store, the bell over the door tinkled. He smelled hot bread and meat and coffee. Going on experience, he did not raise his head except to just glance at the menu. He'd figured out reading pretty well. You made the sounds of the letters real fast together, and that made the word come out.

This one didn't have donuts or bagels like that other one yesterday. This one had meat food.

"Befas tasso," he said, holding up two fingers.

"Excuse me?"

Oh, he'd have to run out. They didn't understand. He was way off.

"Tasso," he said again, glancing up at the menu. 'Breakfast taco," it said, .98.

T was the *tuh* sound. A was the *aa* sound. C was the *ss* sound. Then O. So what was wrong? Why didn't they get it? He tried again, speaking as carefully and clearly as he could. "Bek-fas tasso." He held up two fingers.

"Oh *taco*! Yeah! Two breakfast tacos."

C made the *k* sound, too? Okay. "Two bekfas takos!"

"Beef, bean, or chorizo?"

"Beef." That was meat. Meat was good, it lasted longer than other stuff. "Coffee brak, two."

"Two beef breakfast tacos, two black coffees, you got it, amigo. Where you boys from?"

Joe kept his head down.

The man looked closer. "I think I saw your friends on TV. Hell yes, you're the Tanda! Hey, just a minute." He turned around. "Dad! Dad, you gotta come out here, meet somebody!"

Joe got ready to run.

"Hey, hey relax! We ain't gonna hurt you here. Take it easy, fellas. You—" He pointed to the window where Crunch was lingering, glancing in from under his cap. "—come on in!"

Joe backed away. Crunch started to break for it.

The man came around the counter. "We ain't gonna hurt you fellas! This is a nice place, here, we don't hurt nobody." He came down, pointed to a little symbol on the door. "The Mazuza. We're Sephardics, see. We've been persecuted, Mr. Tanda, all the way from Spain to Mexico to Texas, and we aren't going to hurt you."

Joe still backed away.

He put a hand out and touched Joe's shoulder. "You're hungry and you're dirty and you're all beat all up. You need a shower, some clean clothes."

A big fat one with gray hair came out. "Oh my gosh," it said. "We have special guests here today!" Then, to Joe: "Habla usted espanol?"

"Dad, they barely speak English."

"No speak Spanish? Okay. I thought it would be easier for them maybe."

"Because it's easier for you. What opportunity would they have had to learn Spanish?"

"Well, they're here on the west side of San Antonio where there are just a *few* of us Mexicans. But no matter, welcome! Welcome!"

When he smiled, Joe smiled back...sort of.

A female in a black dress came out. She had plates of food. "This will make them at their ease, yes," she said. "Do you like Mexican food?"

Crunch, drawn in by the tortillas, the wonderful smelling insides, the pretty red tomato and green lettuce, came closer. "Mekin food," he said. He took a deep sniff. "Mmmmm! Mmmmm!" He smiled his biggest smile.

"Oh, they're sweet, look at that face!"

"Got a lotta teeth," the old one muttered.

"He has a very big smile," the woman said. "That's by the grace of God, it's what he has been given to charm his way in life."

There were tables like the tables in rec, but just two of them in the tiny storefront. She put the food down on one.

Joe dug into his pocket where he kept his money and pulled out the wet, green wad. Carefully, he unfolded it. There were three bills each with different numbers on it. Two had "5" one had "1" and the third had "20." Joe was not yet completely certain how this worked, only that it did. When you gave a 20, you might get back a whole bunch of others. When you 'bought' something, the shatterfaces shuffled around with the money. Sometimes they did not give the thing to you. Sometimes they said, "not enuff." Then you had to go away, because that meant you could not take it.

"Not enuff?"

"This we do for God. You keep your money," the young shatterface male said.

Crunch picked up his taco and bit into it. "Ah'm eatin'," he said. His lower lip had a beard of lettuce, which he sucked in. Then he savored his coffee. "Mmm," he said as he slurped it. "Goot goot goot!"

Joe ate quietly and quickly. He was waiting for this to fall apart. Crunch was more confident, smiling and trying to get them to smile back. He and Crunch were different people with different natures. Joe had understood that, and it was okay by him. Crunch could make his fool mistakes on his own.

For Joe's part, he was just glad to have this food and, while it lasted, the good will of the shatterfaces. They could change in an instant. That was their nature as he had observed it. Right now, they were smiling at Crunch nicely enough and he was smiling back. In another moment, they could be coming at them with sticks, just like the ones in the alley. Crunch never expected surprises, but Joe tried always to be ready for anything.

"They're the two got lost," the old shatterface male said.

"I know it. Is this a 9-1-1 call, or what?"

"Hell yes, it's a 9-1-1 call. And we gotta get 'em outa the front, here."

"Why? They're famous!"

"You gonna want to eat in here with that stink? They smell like they been in a sewer."

"Orlando, keep your voice down."

"Sorry. But they stink, Rosa. This is not good for business."

"Pictures first." Joe watched the woman use her cellphone, pointing it at them as they ate. People couldn't have those. They had to be good to have, though because the shatterfaces could push their voices through them.

"Come on now, fellas," the female said, "let's go now." She whispered, "This is the biggest news in the history of this family. We're gonna be famous!" She straightened up. "We're representatives of the whole west side now, so let's make it proud."

The young male used his phone. Early on, Joe had tried to use a different kind of one he'd found sticking up in a box on a street corner. He'd talked into it like the shatterfaces did. He said, "Betty," but all it said back was *bzeeee*. He'd shouted into it, "Bef, Charlie, Bef! Joe and Crunch are somewhere. We somewhere!" It had replied "mrnt, mrnt, mrnt!" on and on and wouldn't say another ding-dong thing.

The phone was just another of the wonderful things like cars and the barrier door, that only worked for the shatterface.

When all of a sudden men in uniforms came in the door, Joe was not surprised at all. Without a word, without even thinking about it, he took off, leaping the counter and going out through the back. As usual, Crunch came along behind, howling and raging with surprise.

"*Madre de Dios*," the old shatterface yelled after them, "those suckers are *fast*!"

That was the end of that. Uniforms and yellow nets went together. Above all things, and no matter how hard the shatterface world was on them, they did not want ever again to be confined in anything.

Down this way was a wide street lined by shatterface houses. They said, "house" for where they went at night, "store" for where they went at day. Day was when the 'sun' crossed upoo. 'Night' was for when the black curtain with all the lights on it came down. The black curtain of the night. They would lie on the velvet grass and stare back at the night eyes. If the moon came, it would call them to dance. They would clap to keep time, Crunch fast, Joe slow, in ascending and descending waves, dancing the moon to the top of the sky.

Somewhere deep in himself, Joe remembered the moon. He had lived in another word, now a dream, where the moon was called *oonuu*. *Onuu* flew in the dark.

They ran until they were under a lot of shade, then they went up the trunk of a tree. It was easy for them to climb, way easier than it was for shatterfaces. Plus, they could jump from limb to limb, do that pretty good.

They had also discovered that they could get real still, so you felt like you were melted into the tree and part of the tree. Then the shatterface might look right at you and not see you. If the shatterface still came closer, there would be a dark that would come. What was in this dark they didn't know. You could see, though, even though you couldn't move. This would happen when the shatterface was very close but hadn't seen you yet. Then the shatterface would go right past.

They heard the sorrowful wail of a chaser car. Cars did not like anything, it seemed. They growled constantly when they had a shatterface in their stomach. Then they would go, "yeet yeet!" to another car, and the shatterface inside would go, "fugya moron!" or something like that. Then the cars would yeet and yeet as the shatterfaces sat inside.

Joe could understand why cars would be pissed off. They did all the work while the shatterface just sat there. No wonder they were sour creatures.

A moaning started now ahead of them. Typical. When the shatterfaces chased you, they made all kinds of noise, for whatever reason. At least it let you know they were coming.

Joe scampered into the top of the tree, Crunch right behind him. They jumped off onto the roof of one of the homes, treading lightly so the shatterfaces inside wouldn't hear them. If you weren't careful, you'd think you were safe when the truth was that they had heard you. Then they'd come out of the home and fire guns at you.

"Keep low," Joe said. "Guns."

"Ah wanna gun," Crunch moaned.

"Never gonna shoot fer us. Never gonna." Joe was bitter about the way everything did what shatterfaces wanted, but not them.

"They're on that roof," a voice shouted from below. Then their Big Voice said, "STAY WHERE YOU ARE. WE WILL NOT HURT YOU."

Crunch pressed close to Joe. "Hurt, Joe, it go *hurt*!"

"Yeh." Joe looked back toward the tree. No use going back there. Too far to the next house to jump. And this whole place was surrounded by shatterfaces, plus more and more of the cars were groaning up and stopping. Then there came the *pop pop pop* of what Joe and Crunch now understood was a thing like a car that took shatterfaces in the sky. It was not a big bug.

"Upcar," Crunch said.

The upcar would chase them when they ran, but they'd gotten away from it before.

They looked one way and another, seeking a way out. In every direction, there were more shatterfaces.

Crunch gave Joe a long, searching look.

Joe stared back at him. "Purty now," he said.

"Yeh."

"I want Betty now."

"I want Futter now."

Joe thought on Betty. "I close mah eyes," he said.

"Yeh," Crunch said.

Crunch laid his arm around Joe's shoulders. Joe leaned his head over, and Crunch leaned his too, so they were touching. He heard Crunch breathing in and out, in and out.

"I love you, I sayin' to Betty."

"I wuve yew, I sayin' to Futter."

Joe had understood more about death. It was a big, dark something that was in the middle of everybody, the shatterface and person alike.

He knew this because they had seen a fluffy animal get bashed by a car, and gone and looked at it and seen that it had no life. Crunch had said, "dat is dead?"

Joe had seen the change in it, the way it's eyes had gone empty. He said, "yeh, dat is." And the word became part of them. "Dead." "Def." And after they had understood death, no shatterface had black shatter eyes anymore.

The wind had whispered in the green leaves then, when they had stood over the dead animal. It had fluttered the hair of the puffy big tail. Joe had felt the hair, and Crunch had, too.

"Purty," Crunch had said.

"Sooo soffff," Joe had said.

They had decided that the wind was saying goodbye to the pretty thing and the wind whispered now, just the same way. Joe looked up. White blumps glided in the sky. They were so wonderful pretty that every time he looked up and saw them, tears came in his eyes. At night, he imagined that he walked in the hills of the clouds.

"WE WILL NOT HURT YOU."

Crunch said, "We go in def now."

"Yeh." All those shatterfaces and cars and guns meant only one thing: they were here to kill. "We go in def."

Crunch tapped his own chest. "Futter," he said.

Joe knew what he meant. Betty was in his chest, too, he could feel her there. He tapped it. "Betty."

The voices of the shatterfaces grew ever louder, the swarms of them ever closer. Joe and Crunch waited to die.

At the primate center, Betty absorbed the beautyt of the dawn chorus. She had been learning about birds and animals from Beth, and she told little Charlie, "That's the cardinal singing, and the mockingbird standing on the fence over there, and the bluebird will be along soon."

She had taken him to the place on the hill that she had claimed as her special spot. Here she came to meditate, which Beth had explained was to look into yourself. Even though it hurt, because that was where Joe lived, she loved to do it—because that was where Joe lived. She talked to Joe inside her. Each morning, she told him about the baby, his progress, how strong he was getting, all of it. She told Joe inside her everything.

Also, this was her church where she came to pray. She had come to think that there might be somebody living in the song of the mockingbird and the drift of the clouds, in the blue of the day sky and the jewels of the night sky, in the running of the little water that curled around the base of her hill, and also inside her, deep inside where her heart moved the blood of life and her husband lived.

It was to this nameless presence that she directed her whispered prayer, "Send Joe here, make Joe come to our place. And Crunch." She held Charlie up to the sky, to the blue and the white clouds. "My baby asks it, too."

She drew Charlie close to herself again, and nestled him in her breast. She went near the hummingbird bush, where they buzzed and whizzed, and sat in her place there. Tanda were not like human beings. They weren't strangers in the Earth, not yet. They still belonged to the forests, and thus also to the balance of the natural world. This meant that the wild creatures weren't afraid of them like they were of humans. So the hummingbirds came as they always did, buzzing so close around Betty and Charlie that their speeding wings tickled her face, and their curious hovering made Charlie stare and move his arms.

The mockingbird came and stood on her arm and gazed at her face, first with one eye and then the other. She had brought a little bread and some seeds, and the whitewing doves and the finches came to eat, and then the blazing red cardinal and his soft brown wife, who had a nest in the old tree just below this hill.

Soon, Flutter joined her. At first, all the birds flew away, but then they came back. "Bekfas," Flutter said. "Plus Beeb before schooltime."

Because the first news crew to interview them had been from the BBC, "Beeb" had become their nickname for all TV crews. They now understood that the world outside their prison was not a collection of television shows, and found watching themselves on the evening news excruciating and hilarious.

There had been all kinds of crews, each one with a different name. Enbeesee noos, Seebes noos, C-en-en, Nip on TV—she couldn't even remember them all. And Beeb, of course. They had been invited to the Houses of Parliament. She had asked Beth, "How many houses does he have?" Beth had said, "later."

Flutter sat down beside her. She peered at Charlie, then kissed his forehead. Betty knew that she wanted a baby. She also knew that Flutter did not like quiet time like this, when you had to think of who you had lost.

When the night was old and dark, Flutter would lie weeping softly into her pillow. Flutter leaned against Betty and sighed. Betty said, "They gonna come. Today, tomorrow, they gonna come."

"Lemme hold Charlie."

Betty gave her the baby. Beth had explained the way the pleasure of sex turned into the joy of a baby. So Jack and Jill were trying to have a baby. Flutter wanted one, too, but loving between man and woman felt so close, it seemed too sweet to share. Jill and Jack did not want to share.

"Hell, you guys'll manage somehow," Big Charlie had said. "It always works out in the end."

Big Charlie was healing, but he still walked like he had a board strapped to his back. He had gotten them out of the bad airplane. Although what he had done had been explained, Betty was not too clear on it. When she saw airplanes overhead, she wondered, 'Were we in the sky?' And also, 'How could anything bad happen in the beautiful sky?'

They sat for a while, until they heard voices down at the house. The humans never stopped talking. But they had to. With those little, frozen faces, they had no other way to communicate but to talk. Tanda could have a whole conversation in glances, looks, frowns and smiles, clarified with an occasional word or bit of sign.

"Beebs comin'," Flutter said.

"Approach carefully," Betty heard Beth tell the beebs as they approached. They stopped a little way off. "If we go closer, they'll fly away."

"The Tanda can fly?" It was a woman with black hair and what Betty would once have thought of as an almost unbearably painful shatterface. But the shadows had lifted.

"The birds," Beth said sharply. "The birds aren't afraid of them."

"Lucky them" the woman replied. Her voice cut the silence. Betty had divided humans by their voice tones, into goodvoices and nastyvoices. This was a nastyvoice.

Two of the other beebs began pointing cameras at Betty and Flutter.

"Do the birds always do this?" the nastyvoice asked.

"Yeh," Betty said. As she watched them all fly away, she thought how sad the humans must be, never to have an animal touch them just because it enjoyed them.

"She's my thinker," Beth said to the beebs. "She comes out here every day at dawn with her baby, and lifts him up like you saw. Can you tell them why you do that, Betty?"

"My baby pretty." It was not her habit to say much of what was inside her to the humans. It wasn't that she didn't like them. But there was a reason that the birds would not land on them, and the opossum and the coyote would run from them. It was this—this difference, call it—that kept her from giving any more of her inner self to them than she had to.

"You offer your baby to the sky? Like a sacrifice? Would you sacrifice it to your god?"

The beeb nastyvoice woman was thin and vibrating with something that Betty perceived as cruelty. She did not reply to the crazy jumble of questions. She signed to Flutter, 'She's ugly.'

Flutter said, "uh-huh."

'I am waiting for her to go.'

After a moment, Beth said, "Um, I'm sorry, but their sign language means that they would like you to leave now. Perhaps you can pick it up again after breakfast."

"Do they do blood sacrifice? Is that why it was getting ready to throw the baby?"

"Listen, Monica, you're drawing a lot of conclusions that aren't there."

"The only reason she stopped was she saw us."

"Monica, she lifts him up like that every morning. I don't know why. It's her business. But obviously it has nothing to do with sacrifice or he'd already be dead."

"Look, I'm just trying to do my job. We need to find a level of interest for our viewers."

"'Mother Tanda offers infant in blood rite.' That the sort of thing you mean?"

Betty had heard every word, and understood enough to think that Monica must lead a life that had no tenderness in it. She took Charlie to her. "Hode Charlie?"

"Excuse me?'

She lifted the baby closer to her. "Get this," Monica snapped and she took him. Then her voice died away. Betty knew what was happening, the same thing that happened to anybody who looked in Charlie's eyes. "Oh my God," Monica said.

"Yes," Beth agreed.

Monica barely whispered, "I'm—oh. Oh!" She thrust the baby back into Betty's arms, then hurried away, her head down, hunched in on herself.

"Come on, Betty," Beth said. "You need your breakfast."

Betty signed to Flutter, 'Beeb is scared of herself.'

Flutter nodded. It was something that happened to some of the humans. It was sad.

They went down to the kitchen, and Betty ate an orange and a banana and a bowl of Cheerios. Then she had cottage cheese. During this time, Charlie lay on his floor blanket and squirmed and grunted and batted at his ball and his stuffed gorilla, which was the first toy Betty had chosen for him at the Kaybee. She had not told Beth the story of Gorilla, who had been the doll of all of them when they were children. Gorilla reminded her of Keller and the old world, which had been wrong and bad, but also comfortable and familiar. As she had come to understand more about what had happened, she found herself both angry at Keller and loving Keller at the same time. She had been looking inside herself to see how that worked. By doing this, she had learned, among other things, that she could be nice to somebody like Monica, while at the same time protecting her heart from her.

She loved Keller and Sam Beach and Jim Thomas, and she missed them all. She would have missed Harry Lerner, but she would never forget what he did to Crunch. That was the thing about the human: it was an unpredictable creature. You might love them and be grateful to them, but you must never forget that for every Beth there was a Monica, for every Charlie a Keller.

"Bath time," Beth said. She picked Charlie up.

They bathed the baby in the kitchen sink. He was too young to flop around much, but his face lit up with pleasure when he felt the warm water.

"He wikes it so much," Betty said.

Beth moved aside, letting Betty control the situation. She was always polite to a fault, was Betty, but she definitely preferred to be responsible for everything concerning her baby.

Beth was glad to see that the abrasive Monica and her crew were packing up outside.

Baby Charlie grinned his wide Tanda grin and kicked and splashed. Betty clapped her hands and peered close at him.

They loved water, the Tanda. Beth thought that this was because of their evolutionary heritage in the jungle. Their skin needed lots of lotion or they got very dry, another legacy of having evolved in a perpetually humid environment.

The National Geographic and the Smithsonian were sending a joint expedition to Sumatra. With the full co-operation of the Indonesian government, a search was on for any remaining Orang Tanda. In recent years, Indonesia had made a tremendous effort to preserve the great forests of the *Kerinci Seblat* as a national park, and it was hoped that more of the shadow men of the forest might yet be found there.

Already, bloggers were saying that the Tanda should be repatriated to the jungle. "Put them on a plane and send them back where they came from. It's only right."

They would die there, of course, as they were. But people didn't think about that. Compassion is too often lost to the symmetry of an idea. The Tanda were here. For better or worse, this was now their world.

If more were found, though, there would come a time of meeting between the American and Indonesian Tanda, Beth felt sure. What would it mean, she wondered, what would come of it?

Charlie came in, moving stiffly, his now ever-present clipboard in his hand. "The agent says that NBC won the auction on the two hour special."

"Oh?"

"Two mil," he said casually.

There was the book deal, the feature film, now the documentary special, plus all the news organizations and the photo services, the magazines, and Google, which had bought the right to create and maintain the Tanda's web presence. "That gets us to six million," she said. The moment she had realized that there was going to be enough money to keep the primate center safe, she had lost interest in the whole financial thing. Fortunately, Charlie and Mom, both of whom had good heads for figures, had not. Mom was now the Center's treasurer and Charlie its chief financial officer. Dad was the Center's assistant director and Larry Stein its legal counsel.

Baby Charlie was doing more splashing today than ever, which made him very happy indeed. He squealed and Betty squealed with him, then leaned down and rubbed noses with him.

"I think Jill's preggers," Charlie said.

Betty stopped. She turned around. Her yellow eyes went wide. Watching the smile that broke out across her face, Beth reflected on the capacity of the spirit for healing. Just a short while ago, Betty would have looked askance and muttered, "'pider."

Did they even remember?

Yes, of course they did. In the night, one after another of them would thrash and cry out, then come into the safety of Beth and Charlie's bed. Most mornings, in fact, they woke up under a pile of Tanda.

Lessons started promptly at nine, and Beth had made it a rule that anybody who wasn't finished with breakfast had to come anyway. The Tanda were still children, after all—the oldest was barely fifteen. They were physically as mature at ten as human children were at about thirteen, and Chris thought that their natural lifespan in the jungle about had been like ours had been during the stone age—twenty-five to thirty years. Here, especially with their powerful immune systems, they could be expected to live much longer.

They were indeed children, though, and all they knew of discipline was that crazy assembly line of Greg Keller's. The social organization that they had formed among themselves was purely instinctive, devoid of any of the subtleties of relationship that were potentially available to creatures of their native intellect and emotional depth.

You changed that with focus and discipline, by providing clear and definite borders that they could push against and test, and in so doing, discover who they really were. And you changed it with teaching. They drank knowledge in huge gulps. Every day after basics, they took a long walk around the property, naming birds and plants and stones, learning about the way springs worked, and why the little stream sometimes roared and sometimes stopped completely, and what thunder and lightning were, and what the journey of the seasons meant.

When it rained, they went outside and danced and held their faces up to it and lolled their tongues. When the wind blew, they gathered close to Beth and Charlie and cooed softly among themselves. At night, they sang. Their wordless tunes would drift through the night air, haunting the heart. Because they seemed to be discovering a music of their own within themselves, Beth had held off introducing them to human music.

When the moon rose, they would make a humming chorus out on Betty's hill, their voices trembling across the night as ours must have back in deep time. They would dance then, too, slow shadows at first, then faster and faster, until the pure soul emerged from within and they clapped complex rhythms and chanted with such intensity that it invaded your own blood with a hunger you could never satisfy, to dance as they danced, surrendered to the mystery and power of nature itself.

Charlie startled her by laying a hand on her shoulder. "How can anyone be so quiet!"

"Beth," he said, "could you come in the office a minute?"

She turned to him in surprise, reacting to something in his voice that she had not heard in a while—the excessively calm undertone that emerged when he was afraid.

He closed the door behind them. "Beth, I'm sorry to say that the police are bringing in Joe and Crunch."

His eyes told her the rest. "Oh, no," she said.

"They were found dead on a roof about half an hour ago."

"On a roof? Were they shot? What happened?"

"It's not clear."

"Call Chris! I want—" She sobbed, and as quickly stopped herself. She was a mother now, of four sensitive, vulnerable teenagers, one with a fatherless child. She sucked in her breath and her gut. "How do we do this?"

"Tell them."

"No! Don't tell them anything. They'll have a lot of working through to do. We need to be sure they have plenty of time. Days. We need to clear the calendar."

"This is gonna happen today, Darlin'. The bodies will be here in half an hour. Less."

They went out together into the kitchen. Betty was drying the baby. The others were lingering over coffee and juice, idly listening to Morning Edition on the radio. How they had laughed when the program had reported on them and they'd heard themselves talking on the radio. It had started a massive 'better pronunciation' campaign among them. "We tound rike *dopes*," was how Jack had put it.

Beth looked from one of them to the other. They had not understood death yet, not fully. She'd been working toward it, using history lessons to lead them toward an understanding of why the people of the past were no more.

"Guys," she began. The faces all turned to her, the eyes expectant, merry. They loved lessons. In fact, they loved all their days. They loved life. Now she must reveal to them, the shadow. "Guys, Joe and Crunch are coming home."

Silence. Then Flutter gasped, put her hands to her cheeks. They all erupted into laughter, chatter, station running all through the house. Only Betty hung back. She was watching Beth's face. Betty was a sensitive soul, and she could read Beth like a book.

"Bef?" She held out her hand. Beth took it. "Bad?"

Beth nodded.

"Okeh." Her voice was choked. Her long lips trembled. Then she got a chair. She put it in the middle of the room. She gave Beth her baby and got up on it. Then she took little Charlie and raised him high.

"Betty?"

She did not reply. What was she doing? Was she going to drop him because his father was dead?

"Betty?"

"Show him to my Joe."

Beth felt instantly ashamed, to have even considered that. But that part of the human spirit is very deep within us, a legacy of our own long, hard history.

All eyes were on Betty. She came down, went to Flutter and embraced her with the baby between them. "You know when they don't move anymore?" She looked into Flutter's eyes. "Remember the possum Charlie got outa the chimp's place?"

Flutter nodded. "It didn't move, but then it did."

Betty looked steadily into her eyes.

"Crunch moves! Crunch talks!"

"No."

"He talk! He walk!"

Betty shook her head

Beth's heart was just ripping itself to shreds. She drank in the face of the baby, his happy, ever-wondering eyes, now the soft pink of a young rose. Her husband beside her made a thick, coarse sound. She did not try to comfort him. She knew that when he cried, he needed it to be ignored.

Flutter and Betty were sobbing in each other's arms, the other two Tandas close to them, each in a different state of grief. Jill's head was bowed, Jack's was high, his expression resolute.

"Crunch gonna move," Flutter said. She nodded hard, her hair flying "He is, he is!"

They all heard the police cars approaching with their sirens wailing. Each one remembered the last time this had happened, when the governor had come to welcome the Tandas to the State of Texas. Always, over all the happy times, there had been the pall of loss. Now it would be permanent.

"Let's go," Beth said. She marched across the kitchen. But Betty stopped her. Gently, Betty took her place at the head to the line. "We go first." And carrying her baby, she went out to show him, Beth knew, to her husband.

There was a police car emerging from a cloud of dust on the road. Everything was still, very still. Betty walked resolutely forward. "Come on, Flutter," she said. She held little Charlie close and held Flutter's hand. The two women walked side by side.

A policeman came out of the car, his face covered with dust, his clothes torn. His eyes were hollow with grief. Silently, he opened the rear door.

Betty said to herself, 'it's alright to cry. But you have to cry strong.'

Inside the back seat, she saw only a pile of stuff. Ratty clothes. And there was a smell—rotting garbage. But she knew what was in that garbage.—Joe, dead. Crunch, dead.

She laid baby Charlie on the edge of the seat, then went in and touched Joe's closed eyes. She didn't know if the dead could see, so she lifted his head a little and drew them open with her fingers.

She got Charlie and held him up. "He's us," she said. "I call him Charlie 'cause it such a purty name."

"Purty name."

At first, nobody else heard except Betty.

Joe's eyes opened. He stretched himself. "You ded, Betty?"

"You alive?"

"Dunno."

Crunch clambered up and got out of the car. Howling, Flutter threw her arms around him. She hooked onto him with her arms and her legs and they swung round and round.

Betty and Joe stood absolutely still. Joe was looking at the baby, his eyes narrow and careful.

"What the hell," one of the cops yelled.

Emotions were exploding in Beth with such power that she could not speak. Charlie's tears became frank and open, his whole body shaking with sobs.

"They were stone dead," the cop said, his voice trembling.

Charlie said, "My guess is that it's a possum response. It must be instinctive."

"Well, hell, they sure looked dead," the cop said. "But this is great!"

Joe was unsteady on his feet, standing there in his dumpy, dirty clothes. He gazed long at Betty, then back at the baby. A frown flickered across his face. He backed away. "'Pider."

"Not a spider," she said, "We make him. Our baby."

He continued to back away.

"Our baby is good!"

He shook his head, then held out his hands as if to push the baby away.

Betty marched right up to him and held little Charlie before him. "This is us!"

Joe's eyes narrowed. The moment trembled. He looked down into the blanket. His hands moved toward his child. His fists closed and he withdrew.

She held him out.

He looked down for a long time. "Bebe?"

"Yeh."

He took the child, who squirmed a little, trying to get back to his mother's warmth.

The two of them enclosed the baby in their embrace.

Flutter said to Crunch, "You get me one or I hit you in the head."

"I get you one," Crunch said.

"You're a father, now, Joe," Beth said.

"Hey," Big Charlie said, "it happens."

"I gotta bebe."

"Say hi," Betty said in the shadow of their embrace.

"Hi, bebe."

"Come on, Joe. Come see our home. We have our own bed and I can cook."

"What that?"

"I'll show you.

Beth watched them as they returned to the house, hanging back by herself, her own husband beside her. The feelings she was experiencing now were nameless--too beautiful, she thought, to be named.

"Charlie?"

His hand took hers. "You want one?"

"Oh, yes."

"There'll be a lot of them around here soon, Wife."

That felt good to hear, and it felt exactly right. "A lot of them, Husband."

As the excited crowd of Tanda moved toward the house, Betty slowed and hung back. She stopped under the big old live oak that shaded it.

She thought to herself, 'am I sure about him?' She had assumed that Joe would have matured, too, but the real Joe was a smelly, floppy-dressed creature with an innocent grin and big, empty eyes. He still talked like the children they all so recently had been.

As she watched him moving along with the others, he also stopped. He turned around and stood waiting for her. He stood proud, and as she came to him he seemed to grow in size. He lifted one of his long, sensitive hands and smiled a little. The hand came to her chin, lifted it.

"Your eyes're mah eyes," he said. "Ee see us? Us?"

In that moment, looking into his soft, rose-red eyes, she knew that it was true. "We see us, Joe. You and me and our baby."

"Wife of me. Husband of you. Our bebe?.

Charlie began to fret, and she put him on her teat.

Joe's stared, his lips slack, his eyes wide.

"Way he eats," she explained. "His food is in me."

For a moment more, Joe watched. Then, all in awe, he took her free hand and held it against his cheek. "Wuve yew."

"Love you, Joe."

Slowly, and together now in just the way she had hoped, man and wife went home, their child, and a new world, cradled between them.

The End

Printed in Great Britain
by Amazon